Praise for #1 *New York Times* bestselling author

NORA ROBERTS

"You can't bottle wish fulfillment, but Nora Roberts
certainly knows how to put it on the page."
—*New York Times*

"Romance will never die as long as the megaselling Roberts
keeps writing it."
—*Kirkus Reviews*

"Roberts is indeed a word artist, painting her story and her
characters with vitality and verve."
—*Los Angeles Daily News*

"A superb author…Ms. Roberts is an enormously gifted
writer whose incredible range and intensity
guarantee the very best of reading."
—*Rave Reviews*

"A consistently entertaining writer."
—*USA TODAY*

"The publishing world might be
hard-pressed to find an author with a more diverse style
or fertile imagination than Roberts."
—*Publishers Weekly*

Dear Reader,

When we give our heart to someone, we are making a promise, whether we say it aloud or not. These two riveting classics by bestselling author Nora Roberts explore how this unspoken vow between lovers is tested when secrets get in the way.

In *The Art of Deception,* after being thrown together by circumstance, Kirby Fairchild and Adam Haines find themselves falling hard for each other. Only thing is they both suspect the other is hiding something. As the nights and days wear on, and well-kept secrets are revealed, love isn't the only thing hanging in the balance….

In *Storm Warning,* Autumn Gallagher comes face-to-face with ex-lover Lucas MacLean. As much as she'd like to, Autumn can't ignore the love still blazing inside her—or the evidence suggesting Lucas could be guilty of murder. Lucas may still be a mystery to her, but there is nothing mysterious about her feelings for him, or the yearning she reads in his eyes.

These stories prove that the road to love is rarely smooth, but if we open our hearts and take a chance on the journey, we will discover that when we reach our destination it was all worth it…and so much more.

Enjoy!

The Editors

Silhouette Books

NORA ROBERTS

WHISPERED PROMISES

Published by Silhouette Books
America's Publisher of Contemporary Romance

SILHOUETTE BOOKS

Recycling programs for this product may not exist in your area.

WHISPERED PROMISES

ISBN-13: 978-0-373-28172-5

Copyright © 2013 by Harlequin Books S.A.

The publisher acknowledges the copyright holder of the individual works as follows:

THE ART OF DECEPTION
Copyright © 1986 by Nora Roberts

STORM WARNING
Copyright © 1984 by Nora Roberts

Visit Silhouette Books at www.Harlequin.com

Printed in U.S.A.

CONTENTS

THE ART OF DECEPTION

For the Romance Writers of America,
in gratitude for the friends I've made
and the friends still to come.

Chapter 1

It was more like a castle than a house. The stone was gray, but beveled at the edges, Herodian-style, so that it shimmered with underlying colors. Towers and turrets jutted toward the sky, joined together by a crenellated roof. Windows were mullioned, long and narrow with diamond-shaped panes.

The structure—Adam would never think of it as anything so ordinary as a house—loomed over the Hudson, audacious and eccentric and, if such things were possible, pleased with itself. If the stories were true, it suited its owner perfectly.

All it required, Adam decided as he crossed the flagstone courtyard, was a dragon and a moat.

Two grinning gargoyles sat on either side of the wide stone steps. He passed by them with a reservation natural to a practical man. Gargoyles and turrets could be accepted in their proper place—but not in rural New York, a few hours' drive out of Manhattan.

Deciding to reserve judgment, he lifted the heavy brass knocker and let it fall against a door of thick Honduras mahogany. After a third pounding, the door creaked open. With strained patience, Adam looked down at a small woman with huge gray eyes, black braids and a soot-streaked face. She wore a rumpled sweatshirt and jeans that had seen better days. Lazily, she rubbed her nose with the back of her hand and stared back.

"Hullo."

He bit back a sigh, thinking that if the staff ran to half-witted maids, the next few weeks were going to be very tedious. "I'm Adam Haines. Mr. Fairchild is expecting me," he enunciated.

Her eyes narrowed with curiosity or suspicion, he couldn't be sure. "Expecting you?" Her accent was broad New England. After another moment of staring, she frowned, shrugged, then moved aside to let him in.

The hall was wide and seemingly endless. The paneling gleamed a dull deep brown in the diffused light. Streaks of sun poured out of a high angled window and fell over the small woman, but he barely noticed. Paintings. For the moment, Adam forgot the fatigue of the journey and his annoyance. He forgot everything else but the paintings.

Van Gogh, Renoir, Monet. A museum could claim no finer exhibition. The power pulled at him. The hues, the tints, the brush strokes, and the overall magnificence they combined to create, tugged at his senses. Perhaps, in some strange way, Fairchild had been right to house them in something like a fortress. Turning, Adam saw the maid with her hands loosely folded, her huge gray eyes on his face. Impatience sprang back.

"Run along, will you? Tell Mr. Fairchild I'm here."

"And who might you be?" Obviously impatience didn't affect her.

"Adam Haines," he repeated. He was a man accustomed to servants—and one who expected efficiency.

"Ayah, so you said."

How could her eyes be smoky and clear at the same time? he wondered fleetingly. He gave a moment's thought to the fact that they reflected a maturity and intelligence at odds with her braids and smeared face. "Young lady…" He paced the words, slowly and distinctly. "Mr. Fairchild is expecting me. Just tell him I'm here. Can you handle that?"

A sudden dazzling smile lit her face. "Ayah."

The smile threw him off. He noticed for the first time that she had an exquisite mouth, full and sculpted. And there was something…something under the soot. Without thinking, he lifted a hand, intending to brush some off. The tempest hit.

"I can't do it! I tell you it's impossible. A travesty!" A man barreled down the long, curved stairs at an alarming rate. His face was shrouded in tragedy, his voice croaked with doom. "This is all your fault." Coming to a breathless stop, he pointed a long, thin finger at the little maid. "It's on your head, make no mistake."

Robin Goodfellow, Adam thought instantly. The man was the picture of Puck, short with a spritely build, a face molded on cherubic lines. The spare thatch of light hair nearly stood on end. He seemed to dance. His thin legs lifted and fell on the landing as he waved the long finger at the dark-haired woman. She remained serenely undisturbed.

"Your blood pressure's rising every second, Mr. Fairchild. You'd better take a deep breath or two before you have a spell."

"Spell!" Insulted, he danced faster. His face glowed pink with the effort. "I don't have spells, girl. I've never had a spell in my life."

"There's always a first time." She nodded, keeping her fingers lightly linked. "Mr. Adam Haines is here to see you."

"Haines? What the devil does Haines have to do with it? It's the end, I tell you. The climax." He placed a hand dramatically over his heart. The pale blue eyes watered so that for one awful moment, Adam thought he'd weep. "Haines?" he repeated. Abruptly he focused on Adam with a brilliant smile. "I'm expecting you, aren't I?"

Cautiously Adam offered his hand. "Yes."

"Glad you could come, I've been looking forward to it." Still showing his teeth, he pumped Adam's hand. "Into the parlor," he said, moving his grip from Adam's hand to his arm. "We'll have a drink." He walked with the quick bouncing stride of a man who hadn't a worry in the world.

In the parlor Adam had a quick impression of antiques and old magazines. At a wave of Fairchild's hand he sat on a horsehair sofa that was remarkably uncomfortable. The maid went to an enormous stone fireplace and began to scrub out the hearth with quick, tuneful little whistles.

"I'm having Scotch," Fairchild decided, and reached for a decanter of Chivas Regal.

"That'll be fine."

"I admire your work, Adam Haines." Fairchild offered the Scotch with a steady hand. His face was calm, his voice moderate. Adam wondered if he'd imagined the scene on the stairs.

"Thank you." Sipping Scotch, Adam studied the little genius across from him.

Small networks of lines crept out from Fairchild's eyes and mouth. Without them and the thinning hair, he might have been taken for a very young man. His aura of youth seemed to spring from an inner vitality, a feverish energy. The eyes were pure, unfaded blue. Adam knew they could see beyond what others saw.

Philip Fairchild was, indisputably, one of the greatest living artists of the twentieth century. His style ranged from the flamboyant to the elegant, with a touch of everything in between. For more than thirty years, he'd enjoyed a position of fame, wealth and respect in artistic and popular circles, something very few people in his profession achieved during their lifetime.

Enjoy it he did, with a temperament that ranged from pompous to irascible to generous. From time to time he invited other artists to his house on the Hudson, to spend weeks or months working, absorbing or simply relaxing. At other times, he barred everyone from the door and went into total seclusion.

"I appreciate the opportunity to work here for a few weeks, Mr. Fairchild."

"My pleasure." The artist sipped Scotch and sat, gesturing with a regal wave of his hand—the king granting benediction.

Adam successfully hid a smirk. "I'm looking forward to studying some of your paintings up close. There's such incredible variety in your work."

"I live for variety," Fairchild said with a giggle. From the hearth came a distinct snort. "Disrespectful brat," Fairchild muttered into his drink. When he scowled at her, the maid tossed a braid over her shoulder and plopped her rag noisily into the bucket. "Cards!" Fairchild bellowed, so suddenly Adam nearly dumped the Scotch in his lap.

"I beg your pardon?"

"No need for that," Fairchild said graciously and shouted again. At the second bellow the epitome of butlers walked into the parlor.

"Yes, Mr. Fairchild." His voice was grave, lightly British. The dark suit he wore was a discreet contrast to the white hair and pale skin. He held himself like a soldier.

"See to Mr. Haines's car, Cards, and his luggage. The Wedgwood guest room."

"Very good, sir," the butler agreed after a slight nod from the woman at the hearth.

"And put his equipment in Kirby's studio," Fairchild added, grinning as the hearth scrubber choked. "Plenty of room for both of you," he told Adam before he scowled. "My daughter, you know. She's doing sculpture, up to her elbows in clay or chipping at wood and marble. I can't cope with it." Gripping his glass in both hands, Fairchild bowed his head. "God knows I try. I've put my soul into it. And for what?" he demanded, jerking his head up again. "For what?"

"I'm afraid I—"

"Failure!" Fairchild moaned, interrupting him. "To have to deal with failure at my age. It's on your head," he told the little brunette again. "You have to live with it—if you can."

Turning, she sat on the hearth, folded her legs under her and rubbed more soot on her nose. "You can hardly blame me if you have four thumbs and your soul's lost." The accent was gone. Her voice was low and smooth, hinting of European finishing schools. Adam's eyes narrowed. "You're determined to be better than I," she went on. "Therefore, you were doomed to fail before you began."

"Doomed to fail! Doomed to fail, am I?" He was up and dancing again, Scotch sloshing around in his glass. "Philip Fairchild will overcome, you heartless brat. He shall triumph! You'll eat your words."

"Nonsense." Deliberately, she yawned. "You have your medium, Papa, and I have mine. Learn to live with it."

"Never." He slammed a hand against his heart again. "Defeat is a four-letter word."

"Six," she corrected, and, rising, commandeered the rest of his Scotch.

He scowled at her, then at his empty glass. "I was speaking metaphorically."

"How clever." She kissed his cheek, transferring soot.

"Your face is filthy," Fairchild grumbled.

Lifting a brow, she ran a finger down his cheek. "So's yours."

They grinned at each other. For a flash, the resemblance was so striking, Adam wondered how he'd missed it. Kirby Fairchild, Philip's only child, a well-respected artist and eccentric in her own right. Just what, Adam wondered, was the darling of the jet set doing scrubbing out hearths?

"Come along, Adam." Kirby turned to him with a

casual smile. "I'll show you to your room. You look tired. Oh, Papa," she added as she moved to the door, "this week's issue of *People* came. It's on the server. That'll keep him entertained," she said to Adam as she led him up the stairs.

He followed her slowly, noting that she walked with the faultless grace of a woman who'd been taught how to move. The pigtails swung at her back. Jeans, worn white at the stress points, had no designer label on the back pocket. Her canvas Nikes had broken shoelaces.

Kirby glided along the second floor, passing half a dozen doors before she stopped. She glanced at her hands, then at Adam. "You'd better open it. I'll get the knob filthy."

He pushed open the door and felt like he was stepping back in time. Wedgwood blue dominated the color scheme. The furniture was all Middle Georgian— carved armchairs, ornately worked tables. Again there were paintings, but this time, it was the woman behind him who held his attention.

"Why did you do that?"

"Do what?"

"Put on that act at the door." He walked back to where she stood at the threshold. Looking down, he calculated that she barely topped five feet. For the second time he had the urge to brush the soot from her face to discover what lay beneath.

"You looked so polished, and you positively glowered." She leaned a shoulder against the doorjamb. There was an elegance about him that intrigued her, because his eyes were sharp and arrogant. Though she didn't smile, the amusement in her expression was soft and ripe. "You were expecting a dimwitted parlor maid, so I made it easy for you. Cocktails at seven. Can you find your way back, or shall I come for you?"

He'd make do with that for now. "I'll find it."

"All right. *Ciao*, Adam."

Unwillingly fascinated, he watched her until she'd turned the corner at the end of the hall. Perhaps Kirby Fairchild would be as interesting a nut to crack as her father. But that was for later.

Adam closed the door and locked it. His bags were already set neatly beside the rosewood wardrobe. Taking the briefcase, Adam spun the combination lock and drew up the lid. He pulled out a small transmitter and flicked a switch.

"I'm in."

"Password," came the reply.

He swore, softly and distinctly. "Seagull. And that is, without a doubt, the most ridiculous password on record."

"Routine, Adam. We've got to follow routine."

"Sure." There'd been nothing routine since he'd stopped his car at the end of the winding uphill drive. "I'm in, McIntyre, and I want you to know how much I appreciate your dumping me in this madhouse." With a flick of his thumb, he cut McIntyre off.

Without stopping to wash, Kirby jogged up the steps to her father's studio. She opened the door, then slammed it so that jars and tubes of paint shuddered on their shelves.

"What have you done this time?" she demanded.

"I'm starting over." Wispy brows knit, he huddled over a moist lump of clay. "Fresh start. Rebirth."

"I'm not talking about your futile attempts with clay.

Adam Haines," she said before he could retort. Like a small tank, she advanced on him. Years before, Kirby had learned size was of no consequence if you had a knack for intimidation. She'd developed it meticulously. Slamming her palms down on his worktable, she stood nose to nose with him. "What the hell do you mean by asking him here and not even telling me?"

"Now, now, Kirby." Fairchild hadn't lived six decades without knowing when to dodge and weave. "It simply slipped my mind."

Better than anyone else, Kirby knew nothing slipped his mind. "What're you up to now, Papa?"

"Up to?" He smiled guilelessly.

"Why did you ask him here now, of all times?"

"I've admired his work. So've you," he pointed out when her mouth thinned. "He wrote such a nice letter about *Scarlet Moon* when it was exhibited at the Metropolitan last month."

Her brow lifted, an elegant movement under a layer of soot. "You don't invite everyone who compliments your work."

"Of course not, my sweet. That would be impossible. One must be…selective. Now I must get back to my work while the mood's flowing."

"Something's going to flow," she promised. "Papa, if you've a new scheme after you promised—"

"Kirby!" His round, smooth face quivered with emotion. His lips trembled. It was only one of his talents. "You'd doubt the word of your own father? The seed that spawned you?"

"That makes me sound like a gardenia, and it won't work." She crossed her arms over her chest. Frowning, Fairchild poked at the unformed clay.

"My motives are completely altruistic."

"Hah."

"Adam Haines is a brilliant young artist. You've said so yourself."

"Yes, he is, and I'm sure he'd be delightful company under different circumstances." She leaned forward, grabbing her father's chin in her hand. "Not now."

"Ungracious," Fairchild said with disapproval. "Your mother, rest her soul, would be very disappointed in you."

Kirby ground her teeth. "Papa, the Van Gogh!"

"Coming along nicely," he assured her. "Just a few more days."

Knowing she was in danger of tearing out her hair, she stalked to the tower window. "Oh, bloody murder."

Senility, she decided. It had to be senility. How could he consider having that man here now? Next week, next month, but now? That man, Kirby thought ruthlessly, was nobody's fool.

At first glance she'd decided he wasn't just attractive—very attractive—but sharp. Those big camel's eyes gleamed with intelligence. The long, thin mouth equaled determination. Perhaps he was a bit pompous in his bearing and manner, but he wasn't soft. No, she was certain instinctively that Adam Haines would be hard as nails.

She'd like to do him in bronze, she mused. The straight nose, the sharp angles and planes in his face. His hair was nearly the color of deep, polished bronze, and just a tad too long for convention. She'd want to capture his air of arrogance and authority. But not now!

Sighing, she moved her shoulders. Behind her back, Fairchild grinned. When she turned back to him, he was studiously intent on his clay.

"He'll want to come up here, you know." Despite the soot, she dipped her hands in her pockets. They had a problem; now it had to be dealt with. For the better part of her life, Kirby had sorted through the confusion her father gleefully created. The truth was, she'd have had it no other way. "It would seem odd if we didn't show him your studio."

"We'll show him tomorrow."

"He mustn't see the Van Gogh." Kirby planted her feet, prepared to do battle on this one point, if not the others. "You're not going to make this more complicated than you already have."

"He won't see it. Why should he?" Fairchild glanced up briefly, eyes wide. "It has nothing to do with him."

Though she realized it was foolish, Kirby was reassured. No, he wouldn't see it, she thought. Her father might be a little…unique, she decided, but he wasn't careless. Neither was she. "Thank God it's nearly finished."

"Another few days and off it goes, high into the mountains of South America." He made a vague, sweeping gesture with his hands.

Moving over, Kirby uncovered the canvas that stood on an easel in the far corner. She studied it as an artist, as a lover of art and as a daughter.

The pastoral scene was not peaceful but vibrant. The brush strokes were jagged, almost fierce, so that the simple setting had a frenzied kind of motion. No, it didn't sit still waiting for admiration. It reached out and grabbed by the throat. It spoke of pain, of triumph, of agonies and joys. Her lips tilted because she had no choice. Van Gogh, she knew, could have done no better.

"Papa." When she turned her head, their eyes met in perfect understanding. "You are incomparable."

* * *

By seven, Kirby had not only resigned herself to their house guest, but was prepared to enjoy him. It was a basic trait of her character to enjoy what she had to put up with. As she poured vermouth into a glass, she realized she was looking forward to seeing him again, and to getting beneath the surface gloss. She had a feeling there might be some fascinating layers in Adam Haines.

She dropped into a high-backed chair, crossed her legs and tuned back in to her father's rantings.

"It hates me, fails me at every turn. Why, Kirby?" He spread his hands in an impassioned plea. "I'm a good man, loving father, faithful friend."

"It's your attitude, Papa." She shrugged a shoulder as she drank. "Your emotional plane's faulty."

"There's nothing wrong with my emotional plane." Sniffing, Fairchild lifted his glass. "Not a damn thing wrong with it. It's the clay that's the problem, not me."

"You're cocky," she said simply. Fairchild made a sound like a train straining up a long hill.

"Cocky? *Cocky?* What the devil kind of word is that?"

"Adjective. Two syllables, five letters."

Adam heard the byplay as he walked toward the parlor. After a peaceful afternoon, he wondered if he was ready to cope with another bout of madness. Fairchild's voice was rising steadily, and as Adam paused in the doorway, he saw that the artist was up and shuffling again.

McIntyre was going to pay for this, Adam decided. He'd see to it that revenge was slow and thorough. When Fairchild pointed an accusing finger, Adam followed its direction. For an instant he was totally and uncharacteristically stunned.

The woman in the chair was so completely removed from the grimy, pigtailed chimney sweep, he found it nearly impossible to associate the two. She wore a thin silk dress as dark as her hair, draped at the bodice and slit up the side to show off one smooth thigh. He studied her profile as she watched her father rant. It was gently molded, classically oval with a very subtle sweep of cheekbones. Her lips were full, curved now in just a hint of a smile. Without the soot, her skin was somewhere between gold and honey with a look of luxurious softness. Only the eyes reminded him this was the same woman—gray and large and amused. Lifting one hand, she tossed back the dark hair that covered her shoulders.

There was something more than beauty here. Adam knew he'd seen women with more beauty than Kirby Fairchild. But there was something… He groped for the word, but it eluded him.

As if sensing him, she turned—just her head. Again she stared at him, openly and with curiosity, as her father continued his ravings. Slowly, very slowly, she smiled. Adam felt the power slam into him.

Sex, he realized abruptly. Kirby Fairchild exuded sex the way other women exuded perfume. Raw, unapologetic sex.

With a quick assessment typical of him, Adam decided she wouldn't be easy to deceive. However he handled Fairchild, he'd have to tread carefully with Fairchild's daughter. He decided as well that he already wanted to make love to her. He'd have to tread *very* carefully.

"Adam." She spoke in a soft voice that nonetheless

carried over her father's shouting. "You seem to have found us. Come in, Papa's nearly done."

"Done? I'm undone. And by my own child." Fairchild moved toward Adam as he entered the room. "Cocky, she says. I ask you, is that a word for a daughter to use?"

"An aperitif?" Kirby asked. She rose with a fluid motion that Adam had always associated with tall, willowy women.

"Yes, thank you."

"Your room's agreeable?" His face wreathed in smiles again, Fairchild plopped down on the sofa.

"Very agreeable." The best way to handle it, Adam decided, was to pretend everything was normal. Pretenses were, after all, part of the game. "You have an... exceptional house."

"I'm fond of it." Content, Fairchild leaned back. "It was built near the turn of the century by a wealthy and insane English lord. You'll take Adam on a tour tomorrow, won't you, Kirby?"

"Of course." As she handed Adam a glass, she smiled into his eyes. Diamonds, cold as ice, glittered at her ears. He could feel the heat rise.

"I'm looking forward to it." Style, he concluded. Whether natural or developed, Miss Fairchild had style.

She smiled over the rim of her own glass, thinking precisely the same thing about Adam. "We aim to please."

A cautious man, Adam turned to Fairchild again. "Your art collection rivals a museum's. The Titian in my room is fabulous."

The Titian, Kirby thought in quick panic. How could she have forgotten it? What in God's name could she do about it? No difference. It made no difference, she reassured herself. It couldn't, because there was nothing to be done.

"The Hudson scene on the west wall—" Adam turned to her just as Kirby was telling herself to relax "—is that your work?"

"My... Oh, yes." She smiled as she remembered. She'd deal with the Titian at the first opportunity. "I'd forgotten that. It's sentimental, I'm afraid. I was home from school and had a crush on the chauffeur's son. We used to neck down there."

"He had buck teeth," Fairchild reminded her with a snort.

"Love conquers all," Kirby decided.

"The Hudson River bank is a hell of a place to lose your virginity," her father stated, suddenly severe. He swirled his drink, then downed it.

Enjoying the abrupt paternal disapproval, she decided to poke at it. "I didn't lose my virginity on the Hudson River bank." Amusement glimmered in her eyes. "I lost it in a Renault in Paris."

Love conquers all, Adam repeated silently.

"Dinner is served," Cards announced with dignity from the doorway.

"And about time, too." Fairchild leaped up. "A man could starve in his own home."

With a smile at her father's retreating back, Kirby offered Adam her hand. "Shall we go in?"

In the dining room, Fairchild's paintings dominated. An enormous Waterford chandelier showered light over mahogany and crystal. A massive stone fireplace thundered with flame and light. There were scents of burning wood, candles and roasted meat. There was Breton lace and silver. Still, his paintings dominated.

It appeared he had no distinct style. Art was his style, whether he depicted a sprawling, light-filled landscape or a gentle, shadowy portrait. Bold brush strokes or delicate ones, oils streaked on with a pallet knife or misty watercolors, he'd done them all. Magnificently.

As varied as his paintings were his opinions on other artists. While they sat at the long, laden table, Fairchild spoke of each artist personally, as if he'd been transported back in time and had developed relationships with Raphael, Goya, Manet.

His theories were intriguing, his knowledge was impressive. The artist in Adam responded to him. The practical part, the part that had come to do a job, remained cautious. The opposing forces made him uncomfortable. His attraction to the woman across from him made him itchy.

He cursed McIntyre.

Adam decided the weeks with the Fairchilds might be interesting despite their eccentricities. He didn't care for the complications, but he'd allowed himself to be pulled in. For now, he'd sit back and observe, waiting for the time to act.

The information he had on them was sketchy. Fairchild was just past sixty, a widower of nearly twenty years. His art and his talent were no secrets, but his personal life was veiled. Perhaps due to temperament. Perhaps, Adam mused, due to necessity.

About Kirby, he knew almost nothing. Professionally, she'd kept a low profile until her first showing the year before. Though it had been an unprecedented success, both she and her father rarely sought publicity for their work. Personally, she was often written up in the glossies and tabloids as she jetted to Saint

Moritz with this year's tennis champion or to Marti-
nique with the current Hollywood golden boy. He knew
she was twenty-seven and unmarried. Not for lack of
opportunity, he concluded. She was the type of woman
men would constantly pursue. In another century, duels
would have been fought over her. Adam thought she'd
have enjoyed the melodrama.

From their viewpoint, the Fairchilds knew of Adam
only what was public knowledge. He'd been born under
comfortable circumstances, giving him both the time
and means to develop his talent. At the age of twenty,
his reputation as an artist had begun to take root. A
dozen years later, he was well established. He'd lived
in Paris, then in Switzerland, before settling back in
the States.

Still, during his twenties, he'd traveled often while
painting. With Adam, his art had always come first.
However, under the poised exterior, under the practical-
ity and sophistication, there was a taste for adventure
and a streak of cunning. So there had been McIntyre.

He'd just have to learn control, Adam told himself
as he thought of McIntyre. He'd just have to learn how
to say no, absolutely no. The next time Mac had an inspiration, he could go to hell with it.

When they settled back in the parlor with coffee
and brandy, Adam calculated that he could finish the
job in a couple of weeks. True, the place was immense,
but there were only a handful of people in it. After his
tour he'd know his way around well enough. Then it
would be routine.

Satisfied, he concentrated on Kirby. At the moment
she was the perfect hostess—charming, personable. All
class and sophistication. She was, momentarily, pre-

cisely the type of woman who'd always appealed to him—well-groomed, well-mannered, intelligent, lovely. The room smelled of hothouse roses, wood smoke and her own tenuous scent, which seemed to blend the two. Adam began to relax with it.

"Why don't you play, Kirby?" Fairchild poured a second brandy for himself and Adam. "It helps clear my mind."

"All right." With a quick smile for Adam, Kirby moved to the far end of the room, running a finger over a wing-shaped instrument he'd taken for a small piano.

It took only a few notes for him to realize he'd been wrong. A harpsichord, he thought, astonished. The tinny music floated up. Bach. Adam recognized the composer and wondered if he'd fallen down the rabbit hole. No one—no one normal—played Bach on a harpsichord in a castle in the twentieth century.

Fairchild sat, his eyes half closed, one thin finger tapping, while Kirby continued to play. Her eyes were grave, her mouth was faintly moist and sober. Suddenly, without missing a note or moving another muscle, she sent Adam a slow wink. The notes flowed into Brahms. In that instant, Adam knew he was not only going to take her to bed. He was going to paint her.

"I've got it!" Fairchild leaped up and scrambled around the room. "I've got it. Inspiration. The golden light!"

"Amen," Kirby murmured.

"I'll show you, you wicked child." Grinning like one of his gargoyles, Fairchild leaned over the harpsichord. "By the end of the week, I'll have a piece that'll make anything you've ever done look like a doorstop."

Kirby raised her brows and kissed him on the mouth. "Goat droppings."

"You'll eat your words," he warned as he dashed out of the room.

"I sincerely hope not." Rising, she picked up her drink. "Papa has a nasty competitive streak." Which constantly pleased her. "More brandy?"

"Your father has a...unique personality." An emerald flashed on her hand as she filled her glass again. He saw her hands were narrow, delicate against the hard glitter of the stone. But there'd be strength in them, he reminded himself as he moved to the bar to join her. Strength was indispensable to an artist.

"You're diplomatic." She turned and looked up at him. There was the faintest hint of rose on her lips. "You're a very diplomatic person, aren't you, Adam?"

He'd already learned not to trust the nunlike expression. "Under some circumstances."

"Under most circumstances. Too bad."

"Is it?"

Because she enjoyed personal contact during any kind of confrontation, she kept her eyes on his while she drank. Her irises were the purest gray he'd ever seen, with no hint of other colors. "I think you'd be a very interesting man if you didn't bind yourself up. I believe you think everything through very carefully."

"You see that as a problem?" His voice had cooled. "It's a remarkable observation after such a short time."

No, he wouldn't be a bore, she decided, pleased with his annoyance. It was lack of emotion Kirby found tedious. "I could've come by it easily enough after an hour, but I'd already seen your work. Besides talent, you have self-control, dignity and a strong sense of the conventional."

"Why do I feel as though I've been insulted?"

"Perceptive, too." She smiled, that slow curving of lips that was fascinating to watch. When he answered it, she made up her mind quickly. She'd always found it the best way. Still watching him, she set down her brandy. "I'm impulsive," she explained. "I want to see what it feels like."

Her arms were around him, her lips on his, in a move that caught him completely off balance. He had a very brief impression of wood smoke and roses, of incredible softness and strength, before she drew back. The hint of a smile remained as she picked up her brandy and finished it off. She'd enjoyed the brief kiss, but she'd enjoyed shocking him a great deal more.

"Very nice," she said with borderline approval. "Breakfast is from seven on. Just ring for Cards if you need anything. Good night."

She turned to leave, but he took her arm. Kirby found herself whirled around. When their bodies collided, the surprise was hers.

"You caught me off guard," he said softly. "I can do much better than nice."

He took her mouth swiftly, molding her to him. Soft to hard, thin silk to crisp linen. There was something primitive in her taste, something…ageless. She brought to his mind the woods on an autumn evening—dark, pungent and full of small mysteries.

The kiss lengthened, deepened without plan on either side. Her response was instant, as her responses often were. It was boundless as they often were. She moved her hands from his shoulders, to his neck, to his face, as if she were already sculpting. Something vibrated between them.

For the moment, blood ruled. She was accustomed to it; he wasn't. He was accustomed to reason, but he found none here. Here was heat and passion, needs and desires without questions or answers.

Ultimately, reluctantly, he drew back. Caution, because he was used to winning, was his way.

She could still taste him. Kirby wondered, as she felt his breath feather over her lips, how she'd misjudged him. Her head was spinning, something new for her. She understood heated blood, a fast pulse, but not the clouding of her mind.

Not certain how long he'd have the advantage, Adam smiled at her. "Better?"

"Yes." She waited until the floor became solid under her feet again. "That was quite an improvement." Like her father, she knew when to dodge and weave. She eased herself away and moved to the doorway. She'd have to do some thinking, and some reevaluating. "How long are you here, Adam?"

"Four weeks," he told her, finding it odd she didn't know.

"Do you intend to sleep with me before you go?"

Torn between amusement and admiration, he stared at her. He respected candor, but he wasn't used to it in quite so blunt a form. In this case, he decided to follow suit. "Yes."

She nodded, ignoring the little thrill that raced up her spine. Games—she liked to play them. To win them. Kirby sensed one was just beginning between her and Adam. "I'll have to think about that, won't I? Good night."

Chapter 2

Shafts of morning light streamed in the long windows of the dining room and tossed their diamond pattern on the floor. Outside the trees were touched with September. Leaves blushed from salmon to crimson, the colors mixed with golds and rusts and the last stubborn greens. The lawn was alive with fall flowers and shrubs that seemed caught on fire. Adam had his back to the view as he studied Fairchild's paintings.

Again, Adam was struck with the incredible variety of styles Fairchild cultivated. There was a still life with the light and shadows of a Goya, a landscape with the frantic colors of a Van Gogh, a portrait with the sensitivity and grace of a Raphael. Because of its subject, it was the portrait that drew him.

A frail, dark-haired woman looked out from the canvas. There was an air of serenity, of patience, about

her. The eyes were the same pure gray as Kirby's, but
the features were gentler, more even. Kirby's mother
had been a rare beauty, a rare woman who looked like
she'd had both strength and understanding. While she
wouldn't have scrubbed at a hearth, she would have understood the daughter who did. That Adam could see
this, be certain of it, without ever having met Rachel
Fairchild, was only proof of Fairchild's genius. He created life with oil and brush.

The next painting, executed in the style of Gainsbor-
ough, was a full-length portrait of a young girl. Glossy
black curls fell over the shoulders of a white muslin
dress, tucked at the bodice, belled at the skirt. She wore
white stockings and neat black buckle shoes. Touches
of color came from the wide pink sash around her waist
and the dusky roses she carried in a basket. But this was
no demure *Pinky*.

The girl held her head high, tilting it with youthful
arrogance. The half smile spoke of devilment while the
huge gray eyes danced with both. No more than eleven
or twelve, Adam calculated. Even then, Kirby must have
been a handful.

"An adorable child, isn't she?" Kirby stood at the
doorway as she had for five full minutes. She'd enjoyed
watching and dissecting him as much as Adam had enjoyed dissecting the painting.

He stood very straight—prep school training, Kirby
decided. Yet his hands were dipped comfortably in his
pockets. Even in a casual sweater and jeans, there was
an air of formality about him. Contrasts intrigued her,
as a woman and as an artist.

Turning, Adam studied her as meticulously as he
had her portrait. The day before, he'd seen her go from

grubby urchin to sleek sophisticate. Today she was the picture of the bohemian artist. Her face was free of cosmetics and unframed as her hair hung in a ponytail down her back. She wore a shapeless black sweater, baggy, paint-streaked jeans and no shoes. To his annoyance, she continued to attract him.

She turned her head and, by accident or design, the sunlight fell over her profile. In that instant, she was breathtaking. Kirby sighed as she studied her own face. "A veritable angel."

"Apparently her father knew better."

She laughed, low and rich. His calm, dry voice pleased her enormously. "He did at that, but not everyone sees it." She was glad he had, simply because she appreciated a sharp eye and a clever mind. "Have you had breakfast?"

He relaxed. She'd turned again so that the light no longer illuminated her face. She was just an attractive, friendly woman. "No, I've been busy being awed."

"Oh, well, one should never be awed on an empty stomach. It's murder on the digestion." After pressing a button, she linked her arm through his and led him to the table. "After we've eaten, I'll take you through the house."

"I'd like that." Adam took the seat opposite her. She wore no fragrance this morning but soap—clean and sexless. It aroused nonetheless.

A woman clumped into the room. She had a long bony face, small mud-brown eyes and an unfortunate nose. Her graying hair was scraped back and bundled at the nape of her neck. The deep furrows in her brow indicated her pessimistic nature. Glancing over, Kirby smiled.

"Good morning, Tulip. You'll have to send a tray up to Papa, he won't budge out of the tower." She drew a linen napkin from its ring. "Just toast and coffee for me, and don't lecture. I'm not getting any taller."

After a grumbling disapproval, Tulip turned to Adam. His order of bacon and eggs received the same grumble before she clumped back out again.

"Tulip?" Adam cocked a brow as he turned to Kirby.

"Fits beautifully, doesn't it?" Lips sober, eyes amused, she propped her elbows on the table and dropped her face in her hands. "She's really a marvel as far as organizing. We've had a running battle over food for fifteen years. Tulip insists that if I eat, I'll grow. After I hit twenty, I figured I'd proved her wrong. I wonder why adults insist on making such absurd statements to children."

The robust young maid who'd served dinner the night before brought in coffee. She showered sunbeam smiles over Adam.

"Thank you, Polly." Kirby's voice was gentle, but Adam caught the warning glance and the maid's quick blush.

"Yes, ma'am." Without a backward glance, Polly scurried from the room. Kirby poured the coffee herself.

"Our Polly is very sweet," she began. "But she has a habit of becoming, ah, a bit too matey with two-thirds of the male population." Setting down the silver coffee urn, Kirby smiled across the table. "If you've a taste for slap and tickle, Polly's your girl. Otherwise, I wouldn't encourage her. I've even had to warn her off Papa."

The picture of the lusty young Polly with the Puck-like Fairchild zipped into Adam's mind. It lingered there a moment with perfect clarity until he roared with laughter.

Well, well, well, Kirby mused, watching him. A man who could laugh like that had tremendous potential. She wondered what other surprises he had tucked away. Hopefully she'd discover quite a few during his stay.

Picking up the cream pitcher, he added a stream to his coffee. "You have my word, I'll resist temptation."

"She's built stupendously," Kirby observed as she sipped her coffee black.

"Really?" It was the first time she'd seen his grin— quick, crooked and wicked. "I hadn't noticed."

Kirby studied him while the grin did odd things to her nervous system. Surprise again, she told herself, then reached for her coffee. "I've misjudged you, Adam," she murmured. "A definite miscalculation. You're not precisely what you seem."

He thought of the small transmitter locked in his dignified briefcase. "Is anyone?"

"Yes." She gave him a long and completely guileless look. "Yes, some people are precisely what they seem, for better or worse."

"You?" He asked because he suddenly wanted to know badly who and what she was. Not for McIntyre, not for the job, but for himself.

She was silent a moment as a quick, ironic smile moved over her face. He guessed, correctly, that she was laughing at herself. "What I seem to be today is what I am—today." With one of her lightning changes, she threw off the mood. "Here's breakfast."

They talked a little as they ate, inconsequential things, polite things that two relative strangers speak about over a meal. They'd both been raised to handle such situations—small talk, intelligent give-and-take that skimmed over the surface and meant absolutely nothing.

But Kirby found herself aware of him, more aware than she should have been. More aware than she wanted to be.

Just what kind of man was he, she wondered as he sprinkled salt on his eggs. She'd already concluded he wasn't nearly as conventional as he appeared to be— or perhaps as he thought himself to be. There was an adventurer in there, she was certain. Her only annoyance stemmed from the fact that it had taken her so long to see it.

She remembered the strength and turbulence of the kiss they'd shared. He'd be a demanding lover. And a fascinating one. Which meant she'd have to be a great deal more careful. She no longer believed he'd be easily managed. Something in his eyes...

Quickly she backed off from that line of thought. The point was, she had to manage him. Finishing off her coffee, she sent up a quick prayer that her father had the Van Gogh well concealed.

"The tour begins from bottom to top," she said brightly. Rising, she held out her hand. "The dungeons are marvelously morbid and damp, but I think we'll postpone that in respect of your cashmere sweater."

"Dungeons?" He accepted her offered arm and walked from the room with her.

"We don't use them now, I'm afraid, but if the vibrations are right, you can still hear a few moans and rattles." She said it so casually, he nearly believed her. That, he realized, was one of her biggest talents. Making the ridiculous sound plausible. "Lord Wickerton, the original owner, was quite dastardly."

"You approve?"

"Approve?" She weighed this as they walked. "Perhaps not, but it's easy to be intrigued by things that happened nearly a hundred years ago. Evil can become romantic after a certain period of time, don't you think?"

"I've never looked at it quite that way."

"That's because you have a very firm grip on what's right and what's wrong."

He stopped and, because their arms were linked, Kirby stopped beside him. He looked down at her with an intensity that put her on guard. "And you?"

She opened her mouth, then closed it again before she could say something foolish. "Let's just say I'm flexible. You'll enjoy this room," she said, pushing open a door. "It's rather sturdy and staid."

Taking the insult in stride, Adam walked through with her. For nearly an hour they wandered from room to room. It occurred to him that he'd underestimated the sheer size of the place. Halls snaked and angled, rooms popped up where they were least expected, some tiny, some enormous. Unless he got very, very lucky, Adam concluded, the job would take him a great deal of time.

Pushing open two heavy, carved doors, Kirby led him into the library. It had two levels and was the size of an average two-bedroom apartment. Faded Persian rugs were scattered over the floor. The far wall was glassed in the small diamond panes that graced most of the windows in the house. The rest of the walls were lined floor to ceiling with books. A glance showed Chaucer standing beside D. H. Lawrence. Stephen King leaned against Milton. There wasn't even the pretense of organization, but there was the rich smell of leather, dust and lemon oil.

The books dominated the room and left no space for paintings. But there was sculpture.

Adam crossed the room and lifted a figure of a stallion carved in walnut. Freedom, grace, movement, seemed to vibrate in his hands. He could almost hear the steady heartbeat against his palm.

There was a bronze bust of Fairchild on a high, round stand. The artist had captured the puckishness, the energy, but more, she'd captured a gentleness and generosity Adam had yet to see.

In silence, he wandered the room, examining each piece as Kirby looked on. He made her nervous, and she struggled against it. Nerves were something she felt rarely, and never acknowledged. Her work had been looked at before, she reminded herself. What else did an artist want but recognition? She linked her fingers and remained silent. His opinion hardly mattered, she told herself, then moistened her lips.

He picked up a piece of marble shaped into a roaring mass of flames. Though the marble was white, the fire was real. Like every other piece he'd examined, the mass of marble flames was physical. Kirby had inherited her father's gift for creating life.

For a moment, Adam forgot all the reasons he was there and thought only of the woman and the artist. "Where did you study?"

The flip remark she'd been prepared to make vanished from her mind the moment he turned and looked at her with those calm brown eyes. "école des Beaux-Arts formally. But Papa taught me always."

He turned the marble in his hands. Even a pedestrian imagination would've felt the heat. Adam could all but smell it. "How long have you been sculpting?"

"Seriously? About four years."

"Why the hell have you only had one exhibition? Why are you burying it here?"

Anger. She lifted her brow at it. She'd wondered just what sort of a temper he'd have, but she hadn't expected to see it break through over her work. "I'm having another in the spring," she said evenly. "Charles Larson's handling it." Abruptly uncomfortable, she shrugged. "Actually, I was pressured into having the other. I wasn't ready."

"That's ridiculous." He held up the marble as if she hadn't seen it before. "Absolutely ridiculous."

Why should it make her feel vulnerable to have her work in the palm of his hand? Turning away, Kirby ran a finger down her father's bronze nose. "I wasn't ready," she repeated, not sure why, when she never explained herself to anyone, she was explaining such things to him. "I had to be sure, you see. There are those who say—who'll always say—that I rode on Papa's coattails. That's to be expected." She blew out a breath, but her hand remained on the bust of her father. "I had to know differently. *I* had to know."

He hadn't expected sensitivity, sweetness, vulnerability. Not from her. But he'd seen it in her work, and he'd heard it in her voice. It moved him, every bit as much as her passion had. "Now you do."

She turned again, and her chin tilted. "Now I do." With an odd smile, she crossed over and took the marble from him. "I've never told anyone that before—not even Papa." When she looked up, her eyes were quiet, soft and curious. "I wonder why it should be you."

He touched her hair, something he'd wanted to do since he'd seen the morning sun slant on it. "I wonder why I'm glad it was."

She took a step back. There was no ignoring a longing so quick and so strong. There was no forgetting caution. "Well, we'll have to think about it, I suppose. This concludes the first part of our tour." She set the marble down and smiled easily. "All comments and questions are welcome."

He'd dipped below the surface, Adam realized, and she didn't care for it. That he understood. "Your home's...overwhelming," he decided, and made her smile broaden into a grin. "I'm disappointed there isn't a moat and dragon."

"Just try leaving your vegetables on your plate and you'll see what a dragon Tulip can be. As to the moat..." She started to shrug an apology, then remembered. "Toadstools, how could I have forgotten?"

Without waiting for an answer, she grabbed his hand and dashed back to the parlor. "No moat," she told him as she went directly to the fireplace. "But there are secret passageways."

"I should've known."

"It's been quite a while since I—" She broke off and began to mutter to herself as she pushed and tugged at the carved oak mantel. "I swear it's one of the flowers along here—there's a button, but you have to catch it just right." With an annoyed gesture, she flicked the ponytail back over her shoulder. Adam watched her long, elegant fingers push and prod. He saw that her nails were short, rounded and unpainted. A schoolgirl's nails, or a nun's. Yet the impression of sexual vitality remained. "I know it's here, but I can't quite… *Et voilà.*" Pleased with herself, Kirby stepped back as a section of paneling slid creakily aside. "Needs some oil," she decided.

"Impressive," Adam murmured, already wondering if he'd gotten lucky. "Does it lead to the dungeons?"

"It spreads out all over the house in a maze of twists and turns." Moving to the entrance with him, she peered into the dark. "There's an entrance in nearly every room. A button on the other side opens or closes the panel. The passages are horribly dark and moldy." With a shudder, she stepped back. "Perhaps that's why I forgot about them." Suddenly cold, she rubbed her hands together. "I used to haunt them as a child, drove the servants mad."

"I can imagine." But he saw the quick dread in her eyes as she looked back into the dark.

"I paid for it, I suppose. One day my flashlight went out on me and I couldn't find my way out. There're spiders down there as big as schnauzers." She laughed, but took another step back. "I don't know how long I was in there, but when Papa found me I was hysterical. Needless to say, I found other ways to terrorize the staff."

"It still frightens you."

She glanced up, prepared to brush it off. For the second time the quiet look in his eyes had her telling the simple truth. "Yes. Yes, apparently it does. Well, now that I've confessed my neurosis, let's move on."

The panel closed, grumbling in protest as she pushed the control. Adam felt rather than heard her sigh of relief. When he took her hand, he found it cold. He wanted to warm it, and her. Instead he concentrated on just what the passages could mean to him. With them he'd have access to every room without the risk of running into one of the staff or one of the Fairchilds. When an opportunity was tossed in your lap, you took it for what it was worth. He'd begin tonight.

"A delivery for you, Miss Fairchild."

Both Kirby and Adam paused on the bottom landing of the stairs. Kirby eyed the long white box the butler held in his hands. "Not again, Cards."

"It would appear so, miss."

"Galoshes." Kirby sniffed, scratched a point just under her jaw and studied the box. "I'll just have to be more firm."

"Just as you say, miss."

"Cards…" She smiled at him, and though his face remained inscrutable, Adam would have sworn he came to attention. "I know it's rude, but give them to Polly. I can't bear to look at another red rose."

"As you wish, miss. And the card?"

"Details," she muttered, then sighed. "Leave it on my desk, I'll deal with it. Sorry, Adam." Turning, she started up the stairs again. "I've been bombarded with roses for the last three weeks. I've refused to become Jared's mistress, but he's persistent." More exasperated than annoyed, she shook her head as they rounded the first curve. "I suppose I'll have to threaten to tell his wife."

"Might work," Adam murmured.

"I ask you, shouldn't a man know better by the time he hits sixty?" Rolling her eyes, she bounced up the next three steps. "I can't imagine what he's thinking of."

She smelled of soap and was shapeless in the sweater

and jeans. Moving behind her to the second story, Adam could imagine very well.

The second floor was lined with bedrooms. Each was unique, each furnished in a different style. The more Adam saw of the house, the more he was charmed. And the more he realized how complicated his task was going to be.

"The last room, my boudoir." She gave him the slow, lazy smile that made his palms itchy. "I'll promise not to compromise you as long as you're aware my promises aren't known for being kept." With a light laugh, she pushed open the door and stepped inside. "Fish fins."

"I beg your pardon?"

"Whatever for?" Ignoring him, Kirby marched into the room. "Do you see that?" she demanded. In a gesture remarkably like her father's, she pointed at the bed. A scruffy dog lay like a lump in the center of a wedding ring quilt. Frowning, Adam walked a little closer.

"What is it?"

"A dog, of course."

He looked at the gray ball of hair, which seemed to have no front or back. "It's possible."

A stubby tail began to thump on the quilt.

"This is no laughing matter, Montique. I take the heat, you know."

Adam watched the bundle shift until he could make out a head. The eyes were still hidden behind the mop of fur, but there was a little black nose and a lolling tongue. "Somehow I'd've pictured you with a brace of Afghan hounds."

"What? Oh." Giving the mop on the bed a quick pat, she turned back to Adam. "Montique doesn't belong to me, he belongs to Isabelle." She sent the dog an annoyed glance. "She's going to be very put out."

Adam frowned at the unfamiliar name. Had McIntyre missed someone? "Is she one of the staff?"

"Good grief, no." Kirby let out a peal of laughter that had Montique squirming in delight. "Isabelle serves no one. She's... Well, here she is now. There'll be the devil to pay," she added under her breath.

Shifting his head, Adam looked toward the doorway. He started to tell Kirby there was no one there when a movement caught his eye. He looked down on a large buff-colored Siamese. Her eyes were angled, icily blue and, though he hadn't considered such things before, regally annoyed. The cat crossed the threshold, sat and stared up at Kirby.

"Don't look at me like that," Kirby tossed out. "I had nothing to do with it. If he wanders in here, it has nothing to do with me." Isabelle flicked her tail and made a low, dangerous sound in her throat. "I won't tolerate your threats, and I will not keep my door locked." Kirby folded her arms and tapped a foot on the Aubusson carpet. "I refuse to change a habit of a lifetime for your convenience. You'll just have to keep a closer eye on him."

As he watched silently, Adam was certain he saw genuine temper in Kirby's eyes—the kind of temper one person aims toward another person. Gently he placed a hand on her arm and waited for her to look at him. "Kirby, you're arguing with a cat."

"Adam." Just as gently, she patted his hand. "Don't worry. I can handle it." With a lift of her brow, she turned back to Isabelle. "Take him, then, and put him on a leash if you don't want him wandering. And the next time, I'd appreciate it if you'd knock before you come into my room."

With a flick of her tail, Isabelle moved to the bed and stared up at Montique. He thumped his tail, tongue lolling, before he leaped clumsily to the floor. With a kind of jiggling trot, he followed the gliding cat from the room.

"He went with her," Adam murmured.

"Of course he did," Kirby retorted. "She has a beastly temper."

Refusing to be taken for a fool, Adam gave Kirby a long, uncompromising look. "Are you trying to tell me that the dog belongs to that cat?"

"Do you have a cigarette?" she countered. "I rarely smoke, but Isabelle affects me that way." She noted that his eyes never lost their cool, mildly annoyed expression as he took one out and lit it for her. Kirby had to swallow a chuckle. Adam was, she decided, remarkable. She drew on the cigarette and blew out the smoke without inhaling. "Isabelle maintains that Montique followed her home. I think she kidnapped him. It would be just like her."

Games, he thought again. Two could play. "And to whom does Isabelle belong?"

"Belong?" Kirby's eyes widened. "Isabelle belongs to no one but herself. Who'd want to lay claim to such a wicked creature?"

And he could play as well as anyone. Taking the cigarette from her, Adam drew in smoke. "If you dislike her, why don't you just get rid of her?"

She nipped the cigarette from his fingers again. "I can hardly do that as long as she pays the rent, can I? There, that's enough," she decided after another drag.

"I'm quite calm again." She handed him back the cigarette before she walked to the door. "I'll take you up to Papa's studio. We'll just skip over the third floor, everything's draped with dustcovers."

Adam opened his mouth, then decided that some things were best left alone. Dismissing odd cats and ugly dogs, he followed Kirby back into the hall again. The stairs continued up in a lazy arch to the third floor, then veered sharply and became straight and narrow. Kirby stopped at the transition point and gestured down the hall.

"The floor plan is the same as the second floor. There's a set of stairs at the opposite side that lead to my studio. The rest of these rooms are rarely used." She gave him the slow smile as she linked hands. "Of course, the entire floor's haunted."

"Of course." He found it only natural. Without a word, he followed her to the tower.

Chapter 3

Normalcy. Tubes of paint were scattered everywhere, brushes stood in jars. The scent of oil and turpentine hung in the air. This Adam understood—the debris and the sensuality of art.

The room was rounded with arching windows and a lofty ceiling. The floor might have been beautiful at one time, but now the wood was dull and splattered and smeared with paints and stains. Canvases were in the corners, against the walls, stacked on the floor.

Kirby gave the room a swift, thorough study. When she saw all was as it should be, the tension eased from her shoulders. Moving across the room, she went to her father.

He sat, motionless and unblinking, staring down at a partially formed mound of clay. Without speaking, Kirby walked around the worktable, scrutinizing the clay from all angles. Fairchild's eyes remained riveted on his work. After a few moments, Kirby straightened, rubbed her nose with the back of her hand and pursed her lips.

"Mmm."

"That's only your opinion," Fairchild snapped.

"It certainly is." For a moment, she nibbled on her thumbnail. "You're entitled to another. Adam, come have a look."

He sent her a killing glance that caused her to grin. Trapped by manners, he crossed the studio and looked down at the clay.

It was, he supposed, an adequate attempt—a partially formed hawk, talons exposed, beak just parted. The power, the life, that sung in his paints, and in his daughter's sculptures, just wasn't there. In vain, Adam searched for a way out.

"Hmm," he began, only to have Kirby pounce on the syllable.

"There, he agrees with me." Kirby patted her father's head and looked smug.

"What does he know?" Fairchild demanded. "He's a painter."

"And so, darling Papa, are you. A brilliant one."

He struggled not to be pleased and poked a finger into the clay. "Soon, you hateful brat, I'll be a brilliant sculptor as well."

"I'll get you some Play-Doh for your birthday," she offered, then let out a shriek as Fairchild grabbed her ear and twisted. "Fiend." With a sniff, she rubbed at the lobe.

"Mind your tongue or I'll make a Van Gogh of you."

As Adam watched, the little man cackled; Kirby,

however, froze—face, shoulders, hands. The fluidity he'd noticed in her even when she was still vanished. It wasn't annoyance, he thought, but...fear? Not of Fairchild. Kirby, he was certain, would never be afraid of a man, particularly her father. *For* Fairchild was more feasible, and just as baffling.

She recovered quickly enough and tilted her chin. "I'm going to show Adam my studio. He can settle in."

"Good, good." Because he recognized the edge to her voice, Fairchild patted her hand. "Damn pretty girl, isn't she, Adam?"

"Yes, she is."

As Kirby heaved a gusty sigh, Fairchild patted her hand again. The clay on his smeared onto hers. "See, my sweet, aren't you grateful for those braces now?"

"Papa." With a reluctant grin, Kirby laid her cheek against his balding head. "I never wore braces."

"Of course not. You inherited your teeth from me." He gave Adam a flashing smile and a wink. "Come back when you've got settled, Adam. I need some masculine company." He pinched Kirby's cheek lightly. "And don't think Adam's going to sniff around your ankles like Rick Potts."

"Adam's nothing like Rick," Kirby murmured as she picked up a rag and wiped the traces of clay from her hands. "Rick is sweet."

"She inherited her manners from the milkman," Fairchild observed.

She shot a look at Adam. "I'm sure Adam can be sweet, too." But there was no confidence in her voice. "Rick's forte is watercolor. He's the sort of man women want to mother. I'm afraid he stutters a bit when he gets excited."

"He's madly in love with our little Kirby." Fairchild would've cackled again, but for the look his daughter sent him.

"He just thinks he is. I don't encourage him."

"What about the clinch I happened in on in the library?" Pleased with himself, Fairchild turned back to Adam. "I ask you, when a man's glasses are steamed, isn't there a reason for it?"

"Invariably." He liked them, damn it, whether they were harmless lunatics or something more than harmless. He liked them both.

"You know very well that was totally one-sided." Barely shifting her stance, she became suddenly regal and dignified. "Rick lost control, temporarily. Like blowing a fuse, I suppose." She brushed at the sleeve of her sweater. "Now that's quite enough on the subject."

"He's coming to stay for a few days next week." Fairchild dropped the bombshell as Kirby walked to the door. To her credit, she barely broke stride. Adam wondered if he was watching a well-plotted game of chess or a wild version of Chinese checkers.

"Very well," Kirby said coolly. "I'll tell Rick that Adam and I are lovers and that Adam's viciously jealous, and keeps a stiletto in his left sock."

"Good God," Adam murmured as Kirby swept out of the door. "She'll do it, too."

"You can bank on it," Fairchild agreed, without disguising the glee in his voice. He loved confusion. A man of sixty was entitled to create as much as he possibly could.

The structure of the second tower studio was identical to the first. Only the contents differed. In addition to paints and brushes and canvases, there were knives, chisels and mallets. There were slabs of limestone and marble and lumps of wood. Adam's equipment was the only spot of order in the room. Cards had stacked his gear personally.

A long wooden table was cluttered with tools, wood shavings, rags and a crumpled ball of material that might've been a paint smock. In a corner was a high-tech stereo component system. An ancient gas heater was set into one wall with an empty easel in front of it.

As with Fairchild's tower, Adam understood this kind of chaos. The room was drenched with sun. It was quiet, spacious and instantly appealing.

"There's plenty of room," Kirby told him with a sweeping gesture. "Set up where you're comfortable. I don't imagine we'll get in each other's way," she said doubtfully, then shrugged. She had to make the best of it. Better for him to be here, in her way, than sharing her father's studio with the Van Gogh. "Are you temperamental?"

"I wouldn't say so," Adam answered absently as he began to unpack his equipment. "Others might. And you?"

"Oh, yes." Kirby plopped down behind the worktable and lifted a piece of wood. "I have tantrums and fits of melancholia. I hope it won't bother you." He turned to answer, but she was staring down at the wood in her hands, as if searching for something hidden inside. "I'm doing my emotions now. I can't be held responsible."

Curious, Adam left his unpacking to walk to the shelf behind her. On it were a dozen pieces in various stages. He chose a carved piece of fruitwood that had been polished. "Emotions," he murmured, running his fingers over the wood.

"Yes, that's—"

"Grief," he supplied. He could see the anguish, feel the pain.

"Yes." She wasn't sure if it pleased her or not to have him so in tune—particularly with that one piece that had cost her so much. "I've done *Joy* and *Doubt* as well. I thought to save *Passion* for last." She spread her hands under the wood she held and brought it to eye level. "This is to be *Anger.*" As if to annoy it, she tapped the wood with her fingers. "One of the seven deadly sins, though I've always thought it mislabeled. We need anger."

He saw the change in her eyes as she stared into the wood. Secrets, he thought. She was riddled with them. Yet as she sat, the sun pouring around her, the unformed wood held aloft in her hands, she seemed to be utterly, utterly open, completely readable, washed with emotion. Even as he began to see it, she shifted and broke the mood. Her smile when she looked up at him was teasing.

"Since I'm doing *Anger,* you'll have to tolerate a few bouts of temper."

"I'll try to be objective."

Kirby grinned, liking the gloss of politeness over the sarcasm. "I bet you have bundles of objectivity."

"No more than my share."

"You can have mine, too, if you like. It's very small." Still moving the wood in her hands, she glanced toward his equipment. "Are you working on anything?"

"I was." He walked around to stand in front of her. "I've something else in mind now. I want to paint you."

Her gaze shifted from the wood in her hands to his face. With some puzzlement, he saw her eyes were wary. "Why?"

He took a step closer and closed his hand over her chin. Kirby sat passively as he examined her from different angles. But she felt his fingers, each individual finger, as it lay on her skin. Soft skin, and Adam didn't bother to resist the urge to run his thumb over her cheek. The bones seemed fragile under his hands, but her eyes were steady and direct.

"Because," he said at length, "your face is fascinating. I want to paint that, the translucence, and your sexuality."

Her mouth heated under the careless brush of his fingers. Her hands tightened on the fruitwood, but her voice was even. "And if I said no?"

That was another thing that intrigued him, the trace of hauteur she used sparingly—and very successfully. She'd bring men to their knees with that look, he thought. Deliberately he leaned over and kissed her. He felt her stiffen, resist, then remain still. She was, in her own way, in her own defense, absorbing the feelings he brought to her. Her knuckles had whitened on the wood, but he didn't see. When he lifted his head, all Adam saw was the deep, pure gray of her eyes.

"I'd paint you anyway," he murmured. He left the room, giving them both time to think about it.

She did think about it. For nearly thirty minutes, Kirby sat perfectly still and let her mind work. It was a curious part of her nature that such a vibrant, restless woman could have such a capacity for stillness. When it was necessary, Kirby could do absolutely nothing while she thought through problems and looked for answers. Adam made it necessary.

He stirred something in her that she'd never felt before. Kirby believed that one of the most precious things in life was the original and the fresh. This time, however, she wondered if she should skirt around it.

She appreciated a man who took the satisfaction of his own desires for granted, just as she did. Nor was she averse to pitting herself against him. But... She couldn't quite get past the *but* in Adam's case.

It might be safer—smarter, she amended—if she concentrated on the awkwardness of Adam's presence with respect to the Van Gogh and her father's hobby. The attraction she felt was ill-timed. She touched her tongue to her top lip and thought she could taste him. Ill-timed, she thought again. And inconvenient.

Her father had better be prudent, she thought, then immediately sighed. Calling Philip Fairchild prudent was like calling Huck Finn studious. The blasted, brilliant Van Gogh was going to have to make a speedy exit. And the Titian, she remembered, gnawing on her lip. She still had to handle that.

Adam was huddled with her father, and there was nothing she could do at the moment. Just a few more days, she reminded herself. There'd be nothing more to worry about. The smile crept back to her mouth. The rest of Adam's visit might be fun. She thought of him, the serious brown eyes, the strong, sober mouth.

Dangerous fun, she conceded. But then, what was life without a bit of danger? Still smiling, she picked up her tools.

She worked in silence, in total concentration. Adam, her father, the Van Gogh were forgotten. The wood in her hand was the center of the universe. There was life there; she could feel it. It only waited for her to find the key to release it. She would find it, and the soaring satisfaction that went hand in hand with the discovery.

Painting had never given her that. She'd played at it, enjoyed it, but she'd never possessed it. She'd never been possessed by it. Art was a lover that demanded complete allegiance. Kirby understood that.

As she worked, the wood seemed to take a tentative breath. She felt suddenly, clearly, the temper she sought pushing against the confinement. Nearly—nearly free.

At the sound of her name, she jerked her head up. "Bloody murder!"

"Kirby, I'm so sorry."

"Melanie." She swallowed the abuse, barely. "I didn't hear you come up." Though she set down her tools, she continued to hold the wood. She couldn't lose it now. "Come in. I won't shout at you."

"I'm sure you should." Melanie hesitated at the doorway. "I'm disturbing you."

"Yes, you are, but I forgive you. How was New York?" Kirby gestured to a chair as she smiled at her oldest friend.

Pale blond hair was elegantly styled around a heart-shaped face. Cheekbones, more prominent than Kirby's, were tinted expertly. The Cupid's-bow mouth was carefully glossed in deep rose. Kirby decided, as she did regularly, that Melanie Burgess had the most perfect profile ever created.

"You look wonderful, Melly. Did you have fun?"

Melanie wrinkled her nose as she brushed off the seat of her chair. "Business. But my spring designs were well received."

Kirby brought up her legs and crossed them under her. "I'll never understand how you can decide in August what we should be wearing next April." She was losing the power of the wood. Telling herself it would come back, she set it on the table, within reach. "Have you done something nasty to the hemlines again?"

"You never pay any attention anyway." She gave Kirby's sweater a look of despair.

"I like to think of my wardrobe as timeless rather than trendy." She grinned, knowing which buttons to push. "This sweater's barely twelve years old."

"And looks every day of it." Knowing the game and Kirby's skill, Melanie switched tactics. "I ran into Ellen Parker at 21."

"Did you?" After lacing her hands, Kirby rested her chin on them. She never considered gossiping rude, particularly if it was interesting. "I haven't seen her for months. Is she still spouting French when she wants to be confidential?"

"You won't believe it." Melanie shuddered as she pulled a long, slender cigarette from an enameled case. "I didn't believe it myself until I saw it with my own eyes. Jerry told me. You remember Jerry Turner, don't you?"

"Designs women's underwear."

"Intimate apparel," Melanie corrected with a sigh. "Really, Kirby."

"Whatever. I appreciate nice underwear. So what did he tell you?"

Melanie pulled out a monogrammed lighter and flicked it on. She took a delicate puff. "He told me that Ellen was having an affair."

"There's news," Kirby returned dryly. With a yawn,

she stretched her arms to the ceiling and relieved the stiffness in her shoulder blades. "Is this number two hundred and three, or have I missed one?"

"But, Kirby—" Melanie tapped her cigarette for emphasis as she leaned forward "—she's having this one with her son's orthodontist."

It was the sound of Kirby's laughter that caused Adam to pause on his way up the tower steps. It rang against the stone walls, rich, real and arousing. He stood as it echoed and faded. Moving quietly, he continued up.

"Kirby, really. An orthodontist." Even knowing Kirby as well as she did, Melanie was stunned by her reaction. "It's so—so middle-class."

"Oh, Melanie, you're such a wonderful snob." She smothered another chuckle as Melanie gave an indignant huff. When Kirby smiled, it was irresistible. "It's perfectly acceptable for Ellen to have any number of affairs, as long as she keeps her choice socially prominent but an orthodontist goes beyond good taste?"

"It's not acceptable, of course," Melanie muttered, finding herself caught in the trap of Kirby's logic. "But if one is discreet, and…"

"Selective?" Kirby supplied good-naturedly. "Actually, it is rather nasty. Here's Ellen carrying on with her son's orthodontist, while poor Harold shells out a fortune for the kid's overbite. Where's the justice?"

"You say the most astonishing things."

"Orthodonture work is frightfully expensive."

With an exasperated sigh, Melanie tried another change of subject. "How's Stuart?"

Though he'd been about to enter, Adam stopped in the doorway and kept his silence. Kirby's smile had vanished. The eyes that had been alive with humor were frigid. Something hard, strong and unpleasant came into them. Seeing the change, Adam realized she'd make a formidable enemy. There was grit behind the careless wit, the raw sexuality and the eccentric-rich-girl polish. He wouldn't forget it.

"Stuart," Kirby said in a brittle voice. "I really wouldn't know."

"Oh, dear." At the arctic tone, Melanie caught her bottom lip between her teeth. "Have you two had a row?"

"A row?" The smile remained unpleasant. "One might put it that way." Something flared—the temper she'd been prodding out of the wood. With an effort, Kirby shrugged it aside. "As soon as I'd agreed to marry him, I knew I'd made a mistake. I should've dealt with it right away."

"You'd told me you were having doubts." After stubbing out her cigarette, Melanie leaned forward to take Kirby's hands. "I thought it was nerves. You'd never let any relationship get as far as an engagement before."

"It was an error in judgment." No, she'd never let a relationship get as far as an engagement. Engagements equaled commitment. Commitments were a lock, perhaps the only lock, Kirby considered sacred. "I corrected it."

"And Stuart? I suppose he was furious."

The smile that came back to Kirby's lips held no humor. "He gave me the perfect escape hatch. You know he'd been pressuring me to set a date?"

"And I know that you'd been putting him off."

"Thank God," Kirby murmured. "In any case, I'd finally drummed up the courage to renege. I think it was the first time in my life I've felt genuine guilt." Moving her shoulders restlessly, she picked up the wood again. It helped to steady her, helped her to concentrate on temper. "I went by his place, unannounced. It was a now-or-never sort of gesture. I should've seen what was up as soon as he answered the door, but I was already into my neat little speech when I noticed a few—let's say articles of intimate apparel tossed around the room."

"Oh, Kirby."

Letting out a long breath, Kirby went on. "That part of it was my fault, I suppose. I wouldn't sleep with him. There was just no driving urge to be intimate with him. No…" She searched for a word. "Heat," she decided, for lack of anything better. "I guess that's why I knew I'd never marry him. But, I was faithful." The fury whipped through her again. "I was faithful, Melly."

"I don't know what to say." Distress vibrated in her voice. "I'm so sorry, Kirby."

Kirby shook her head at the sympathy. She never looked for it. "I wouldn't have been so angry if he hadn't stood there, telling me how much he loved me, when he had another woman keeping the sheets warm. I found it humiliating."

"You have nothing to be humiliated about," Melanie returned with some heat. "He was a fool."

"Perhaps. It would've been bad enough if we'd stuck to the point, but we got off the track of love and fidelity. Things got nasty."

Her voice trailed off. Her eyes clouded over. It was time for secrets again. "I found out quite a bit that night," she murmured. "I've never thought of myself as a fool, but it seems I'd been one."

Again, Melanie reached for her hand. "It must have

been a dreadful shock to learn Stuart was unfaithful even before you were married."

"What?" Blinking, Kirby brought herself back. "Oh, that. Yes, that, too."

"Too? What else?"

"Nothing." With a shake of her head, Kirby swept it all aside. "It's all dead and buried now."

"I feel terrible. Damn it, I introduced you."

"Perhaps you should shave your head in restitution, but I'd advise you to forget it."

"Can you?"

Kirby's lips curved up, her brow lifted. "Tell me, Melly, do you still hold André Fayette against me?"

Melanie folded her hands primly. "It's been five years."

"Six, but who's counting?" Grinning, Kirby leaned forward. "Besides, who expects an oversexed French art student to have any taste?"

Melanie's pretty mouth pouted. "He was very attractive."

"But base." Kirby struggled with a new grin. "No class, Melly. You should thank me for luring him away, however unintentionally."

Deciding it was time to make his presence known, Adam stepped inside. Kirby glanced up and smiled without a trace of the ice or the fury. "Hello, Adam. Did you have a nice chat with Papa?"

"Yes."

Melanie, he decided as he glanced in her direction, was even more stunning at close quarters. Classic face, classic figure draped in a pale rose dress cut with style and simplicity. "Am I interrupting?"

"Just gossip. Melanie Burgess, Adam Haines. Adam's our guest for a few weeks."

Adam accepted the slim rose-tipped hand. It was soft and pampered, without the slight ridge of callus that Kirby's had just under the fingers. He wondered what had happened in the past twenty-four hours to make him prefer the untidy artist to the perfectly groomed woman smiling up at him. Maybe he was coming down with something.

"*The* Adam Haines?" Melanie's smile warmed. She knew of him, the irreproachable lineage and education. "Of course you are," she continued before he could comment. "This place attracts artists like a magnet. I have one of your paintings."

"Do you?" Adam lit her cigarette, then one of his own. "Which one?"

"*A Study in Blue.*" Melanie tilted her face to smile into his eyes, a neat little feminine trick she'd learned soon after she'd learned to walk.

From across the table, Kirby studied them both. Two extraordinary faces, she decided. The tips of her fingers itched to capture Adam in bronze. A year before, she'd done Melanie in ivory—smooth, cool and perfect. With Adam, she'd strive for the undercurrents.

"I wanted the painting because it was so strong," Melanie continued. "But I nearly let it go because it made me sad. You remember, Kirby. You were there."

"Yes, I remember." When she looked up at him, her eyes were candid and amused, without the traces of flirtation that flitted in Melanie's. "I was afraid she'd break down and disgrace herself, so I threatened to buy it myself. Papa was furious that I didn't."

"Uncle Philip could practically stock the Louvre already," Melanie said with a casual shrug.

"Some people collect stamps," Kirby returned, then smiled again. "The still life in my room is Melanie's work, Adam. We studied together in France."

"No, don't ask," Melanie said quickly, holding up her hand. "I'm not an artist. I'm a designer who dabbles."

"Only because you refuse to dig your toes in."

Melanie inclined her head, but didn't agree or refute. "I must go. Tell Uncle Philip I said hello. I won't risk disturbing him, as well."

"Stay for lunch, Melly. We haven't seen you in two months."

"Another time." She rose with the grace of one who'd been taught to sit and stand and walk. Adam stood with her, catching the drift of Chanel. "I'll see you this weekend at the party." With another smile, she offered Adam her hand. "You'll come, too, won't you?"

"I'd like that."

"Wonderful." Snapping open her bag, Melanie drew out thin leather gloves. "Nine o'clock, Kirby. Don't forget. Oh!" On her way to the door, she stopped, whirling back. "Oh, God, the invitations were sent out before I… Kirby, Stuart's going to be there."

"I won't pack my derringer, Melly." She laughed, but it wasn't quite as rich or quite as free. "You look as though someone's just spilled caviar on your Saint Laurent. Don't worry about it." She paused, and the chill passed quickly in and out of her eyes. "I promise you, I won't."

"If you're sure…" Melanie frowned. It was, however, not possible to discuss such a thing in depth in front of a guest. "As long as you won't be uncomfortable."

"I won't be the one who suffers discomfort." The careless arrogance was back.

"Saturday, then." Melanie gave Adam a final smile before she slipped from the room.

"A beautiful woman," Adam commented, coming back to the table.

"Yes, exceptional." The simple agreement had no undertones of envy or spite.

"How do two women, two exceptional women, of totally different types, remain friends?"

"By not attempting to change one another." She picked up the wood again and began to roll it around in her hands. "I overlook what I see as Melanie's faults, and she overlooks mine." She saw the pad and pencil in his hand and lifted a brow. "What're you doing?"

"Some preliminary sketches. What are your faults?"

"Too numerous to mention." Setting the wood down again, she leaned back.

"Any good points?"

"Dozens." Perhaps it was time to test him a bit, to see what button worked what switch. "Loyalty," she began breezily. "Sporadic patience and honesty."

"Sporadic?"

"I'd hate to be perfect." She ran her tongue over her teeth. "And I'm terrific in bed."

His gaze shifted to her bland smile. Just what game was Kirby Fairchild playing? His lips curved as easily as hers. "I bet you are."

Laughing, she leaned forward again, chin cupped in her hands. "You don't rattle easily, Adam. It makes me all the more determined to keep trying."

"Telling me something I'd already concluded isn't likely to rattle me. Who's Stuart?"

The question had her stiffening. She'd challenged him, Kirby conceded, now she had to meet one of his. "A former fiancé," she said evenly. "Stuart Hiller."

The name clicked, but Adam continued to sketch. "The same Hiller who runs the Merrick Gallery?"

"The same." He heard the tightening in her voice. For a moment he wanted to drop it, to leave her to her privacy and her anger. The job came first.

"I know him by reputation," Adam continued. "I'd planned to see the gallery. It's about twenty miles from here, isn't it?"

She paled a bit, which confused him, but when she spoke her voice was steady. "Yes, it's not far. Under the circumstances, I'm afraid I can't take you."

"You may mend your differences over the weekend." Prying wasn't his style. He had a distaste for it, particularly when it involved someone he was beginning to care about. When he lifted his gaze, however, he didn't see discomfort. She was livid.

"I think not." She made a conscious effort to relax her hands. Noting the gesture, Adam wondered how much it cost her. "It occurred to me that my name would be Fairchild-Hiller." She gave a slow, rolling shrug. "That would never do."

"The Merrick Gallery has quite a reputation."

"Yes. As a matter of fact, Melanie's mother owns it, and managed it until a couple of years ago."

"Melanie? Didn't you say her name was Burgess?"

"She was married to Carlyse Burgess—Burgess Enterprises. They're divorced."

"So, she's Harriet Merrick's daughter." The cast of players was increasing. "Mrs. Merrick's given the running of the gallery over to Hiller?"

"For the most part. She dips her hand in now and then."

Adam saw that she'd relaxed again, and concentrated on the shape of her eyes. Round? Not quite, he decided. They were nearly almond shaped, but again, not quite. Like Kirby, they were simply unique.

"Whatever my personal feelings, Stuart's a knowledgeable dealer." She gave a quick, short laugh. "Since she hired him, she's had time to travel. Harriet's just back from an African safari. When I phoned her the other day, she told me she'd brought back a necklace of crocodile teeth."

To his credit, Adam closed his eyes only briefly. "Your families are close, then. I imagine your father's done a lot of dealing through the Merrick Gallery."

"Over the years. Papa had his first exhibition there, more than thirty years ago. It sort of lifted his and Harriet's careers off at the same time." Straightening in her chair, Kirby frowned across the table. "Let me see what you've done."

"In a minute," he muttered, ignoring her outstretched hand.

"Your manners sink to my level when it's convenient, I see." Kirby plopped back in her chair. When he didn't comment, she screwed her face into unnatural lines.

"I wouldn't do that for long," Adam advised. "You'll hurt yourself. When I start in oil, you'll have to behave or I'll beat you."

Kirby relaxed her face because her jaw was stiffening. "Corkscrews, you wouldn't beat me. You have the disadvantage of being a gentleman, inside and out."

Lifting his head, he pinned her with a look. "Don't bank on it."

The look alone stopped whatever sassy rejoinder she might have made. It wasn't the look of a gentleman, but of a man who made his own way however he chose. Before she could think of a proper response, the sound of shouting and wailing drifted up the tower steps and through the open door. Kirby made no move to spring up and investigate. She merely smiled.

"I'm going to ask two questions," Adam decided. "First, what the hell is that?"

"Which that is that, Adam?" Her eyes were dove gray and guileless.

"The sound of mourning."

"Oh, that." Grinning, she reached over and snatched his sketch pad. "That's Papa's latest tantrum because his sculpture's not going well—which of course it never will. Does my nose really tilt that way?" Experimentally she ran her finger down it. "Yes, I guess it does. What was your other question?"

"Why do you say 'corkscrews' or something equally ridiculous when a simple 'hell' or 'damn' would do?"

"It has to do with cigars. You really must show these sketches to Papa. He'll want to see them."

"Cigars." Determined to have her full attention, Adam grabbed the pad away from her.

"Those big, nasty, fat ones. Papa used to smoke them by the carload. You needed a gas mask just to come in the door. I begged, threatened, even tried smoking them myself." She swallowed on that unfortunate memory. "Then I came up with the solution. Papa is a sucker."

"Is that so?"

"That is, he just can't resist a bet, no matter what the odds." She touched the wood again, knowing she'd have to come back to it later. "My language was, let's say, colorful. I can swear eloquently in seven languages."

"Quite an accomplishment."

"It has its uses, believe me. I bet Papa ten thousand dollars that I could go longer without swearing than he could without smoking. Both my language and the ozone layer have been clean for three months." Rising, Kirby circled the table. "I have the gratitude of the entire staff." Abruptly she dropped in his lap. Letting her head fall back, she wound her arms around his neck. "Kiss me again, will you? I can't resist."

There can't be another like her, Adam thought as he closed his mouth over hers. With a low sound of pleasure, Kirby melted against him, all soft demand.

Then neither of them thought, but felt only.

Desire was swift and sharp. It built and expanded so that they could wallow in it. She allowed herself the luxury, for such things were too often brief, too often hollow. She wanted the speed, the heat, the current. A risk, but life was nothing without them. A challenge, but each day brought its own. He made her feel soft, giddy, senseless. No one else had. If she could be swept away, why shouldn't she be? It had never happened before.

She needed what she'd never realized she needed from a man before: strength, solidity.

Adam felt the initial stir turn to an ache—something deep and dull and constant. It wasn't something he could resist, but something he found he needed. Desire had always been basic and simple and painless. Hadn't he known she was a woman who would make a man suffer? Knowing it, shouldn't he have been able to avoid it? But he hurt. Holding her soft and pliant in his arms, he hurt. From wanting more.

"Can't you two wait until after lunch?" Fairchild demanded from the doorway.

With a quiet sigh, Kirby drew her lips from Adam's. The taste lingered as she knew now it would. Like the wood behind her, it would be something that pulled her back again and again.

"We're coming," she murmured, then brushed Adam's mouth again, as if in promise. She turned and rested her cheek against his in a gesture he found impossibly sweet. "Adam's been sketching me," she told her father.

"Yes, I can see that." Fairchild gave a quick snort. "He can sketch you all he chooses after lunch. I'm hungry."

Chapter 4

Food seemed to soothe Fairchild's temperament. As he plowed his way through poached salmon, he went off on a long, technical diatribe on surrealism. It appeared breaking conventional thought to release the imagination had appealed to him to the extent that he'd given nearly a year of his time in study and application. With a good-humored shrug, he confessed that his attempts at surrealistic painting had been poor, and his plunge into abstraction little better.

"He's banished those canvases to the attic," Kirby told Adam as she poked at her salad. "There's one in shades of blue and yellow, with clocks of all sizes and shapes sort of melting and drooping everywhere and two left shoes tucked in a corner. He called it *Absence of Time*."

"Experimental," Fairchild grumbled, eyeing Kirby's uneaten portion of fish.

"He refused an obscene amount of money for it and locked it, like a mad relation, in the attic." Smoothly she transferred her fish to her father's plate. "He'll be sending his sculpture to join it before long."

Fairchild swallowed a bite of fish, then ground his teeth. "Heartless brat." In the blink of an eye he changed from amiable cherub to gnome. "By this time next year, Philip Fairchild's name will be synonymous with sculpture."

"Horse dust," Kirby concluded, and speared a cucumber. "That shade of pink becomes you, Papa." Leaning over, she placed a loud kiss on his cheek. "It's very close to fuchsia."

"You're not too old to forget my ability to bring out the same tone on your bottom."

"Child abuser." As Adam watched, she stood and wrapped her arms around Fairchild's neck. In the matter of love for her father, the enigma of Kirby Fairchild was easily solvable. "I'm going out for a walk before I turn yellow and dry up. Will you come?"

"No, no, I've a little project to finish." He patted her hand as she tensed. Adam saw something pass between them before Fairchild turned to him. "Take her for a walk and get on with your…sketching," he said with a cackle. "Have you asked Kirby if you can paint her yet? They all do." He stabbed at the salmon again. "She never lets them."

Adam lifted his wine. "I told Kirby I was going to paint her."

The new cackle was full of delight. Pale blue eyes lit with the pleasure of trouble brewing. "A firm hand, eh? She's always needed one. Don't know where she got such a miserable temper." He smiled artlessly. "Must've come from her mother's side."

Adam glanced up at the serene, mild-eyed woman in the portrait. "Undoubtedly."

"See that painting there?" Fairchild pointed to the portrait of Kirby as a girl. "That's the one and only time she modeled for me. I had to pay the brat scale." He gave a huff and a puff before he attacked the fish again. "Twelve years old and already mercenary."

"If you're going to discuss me as if I weren't here, I'll go fetch my shoes." Without a backward glance, Kirby glided from the room.

"Hasn't changed much, has she?" Adam commented as he drained his wine.

"Not a damn bit," Fairchild agreed proudly. "She'll lead you a merry chase, Adam, my boy. I hope you're in condition."

"I ran track in college."

Fairchild's laugh was infectious. Damn it, Adam thought again, I like him. It complicated things. From the other room he heard Kirby in a heated discussion with Isabelle. He was beginning to realize complication was the lady's middle name. What should've been a very simple job was developing layers he didn't care for.

"Come on, Adam." Kirby poked her head around the doorway. "I've told Isabelle she can come, but she and Montique have to keep a distance of five yards at all times. Papa—" she tossed her ponytail back "—I really think we ought to try raising the rent. She might look for an apartment in town."

"We should never have agreed to a long-term lease,"

Fairchild grumbled, then gave his full attention to Kirby's salmon.

Deciding not to comment, Adam rose and went outside.

It was warm for September, and breezy. The grounds around the house were alive with fall. Beds of zinnias and mums spread out helter-skelter, flowing over their borders and adding a tang to the air. Near a flaming maple, Adam saw an old man in patched overalls. With a whimsical lack of dedication, he raked at the scattered leaves. As they neared him, he grinned toothlessly.

"You'll never get them all, Jamie."

He made a faint wheezing sound that must've been a laugh. "Sooner or later, missy. There be plenty of time."

"I'll help you tomorrow."

"Ayah, and you'll be piling them up and jumping in 'em like always." He wheezed again and rubbed a frail hand over his chin. "Stick to your whittling and could be I'll leave a pile for you."

With her hands hooked in her back pockets, she scuffed at a leaf. "A nice big one?"

"Could be. If you're a good girl."

"There's always a catch." Grabbing Adam's hand, she pulled him away.

"Is that little old man responsible for the grounds?" Three acres, he calculated. Three acres if it was a foot.

"Since he retired."

"Retired?"

"Jamie retired when he was sixty-five. That was before I was born." The breeze blew strands of hair into her face and she pushed at them. "He claims to be ninety-two, but of course he's ninety-five and won't admit it." She shook her head. "Vanity."

Kirby pulled him along until they stood at a dizzying height above the river. Far below, the ribbon of water seemed still. Small dots of houses were scattered along the view. There was a splash of hues rather than distinct tones, a melding of textures.

On the ridge where they stood there was only wind, river and sky. Kirby threw her head back. She looked primitive, wild, invincible. Turning, he looked at the house. It looked the same.

"Why do you stay here?" Blunt questions weren't typical of him. Kirby had already changed that.

"I have my family, my home, my work."

"And isolation."

Her shoulders moved. Though her lashes were lowered, her eyes weren't closed. "People come here. That's not isolation."

"Don't you want to travel? To see Florence, Rome, Venice?"

From her stance on a rock, she was nearly eye level with him. When she turned to him, it was without her usual arrogance. "I'd been to Europe five times before I was twelve. I spent four years in Paris on my own when I was studying."

She looked over his shoulder a moment, at nothing or at everything, he couldn't be sure. "I slept with a Breton count in a chateau, skied in the Swiss Alps and hiked the moors in Cornwall. I've traveled, and I'll travel again. But…" He knew she looked at the house now, because her lips curved. "I always come home."

"What brings you back?"

"Papa." She stopped and smiled fully. "Memories, familiarity. Insanity."

"You love him very much." She could make things

impossibly complicated or perfectly simple. The job he'd come to do was becoming more and more of a burden.

"More than anything or anyone." She spoke quietly, so that her voice seemed a part of the breeze. "He's given me everything of importance: security, independence, loyalty, friendship, love—and the capability to give them back. I'd like to think someday I'll find someone who wants that from me. My home would be with him then."

How could he resist the sweetness, the simplicity, she could show so unexpectedly? It wasn't in the script, he reminded himself, but reached a hand to her face, just to touch. When she brought her hand to his, something stirred in him that wasn't desire, but was just as potent.

She felt the strength in him, and sensed a confusion that might have been equal to her own. Another time, she thought. Another time, it might have worked. But now, just now, there were too many other things. Deliberately she dropped her hand and turned back to the river. "I don't know why I tell you these things," she murmured. "It's not in character. Do people usually let you in on their personal thoughts?"

"No. Or maybe I haven't been listening."

She smiled and, in one of her lightning changes of mood, leaped from the rock. "You're not the type people would confide in." Casually she linked her arm through his. "Though you seem to have strong, sturdy shoulders. You're a little aloof," she decided. "And just a tad pompous."

"Pompous?" How could she allure him one instant and infuriate him the next? "What do you mean, pompous?"

Because he sounded dangerously like her father, she

swallowed. "Just a tad," she reminded him, nearly choking on a laugh. "Don't be offended, Adam. Pomposity certainly has its place in the world." When he continued to scowl down at her, she cleared her throat of another laugh. "I like the way your left brow lifts when you're annoyed."

"I'm not pompous." He spoke very precisely and watched her lips tremble with fresh amusement.

"Perhaps that was a bad choice of words."

"It was a completely incorrect choice." Just barely, he caught himself before his brow lifted. Damn the woman, he thought, and swore he wouldn't smile.

"Conventional." Kirby patted his cheek. "I'm sure that's what I meant."

"I'm sure those two words mean the same thing to you. I won't be categorized by either."

Tilting her head, she studied him. "Maybe I'm wrong," she said, to herself as much as him. "I've been wrong before. Give me a piggyback ride."

"What?"

"A piggyback ride," Kirby repeated.

"You're crazy." She might be sharp, she might be talented, he'd already conceded that, but part of her brain was permanently on holiday.

With a shrug, she started back toward the house. "I knew you wouldn't. Pompous people never give or receive piggyback rides. It's the law."

"Damn." She was doing it to him, and he was letting her. For a moment, he stuck his hands in his pockets and stood firm. Let her play her games with her father, Adam told himself. He wasn't biting. With another oath, he caught up to her. "You're an exasperating woman."

"Why, thank you."

They stared at each other, him in frustration, her in amusement, until he turned his back. "Get on."

"If you insist." Nimbly she jumped on his back, blew the hair out of her eyes and looked down. "Wombats, you're tall."

"You're short," he corrected, and hitched her to a more comfortable position.

"I'm going to be five-seven in my next life."

"You'd better add pounds as well as inches to your fantasy." Her hands were light on his shoulders, her thighs firm around his waist. Ridiculous, he thought. Ridiculous to want her now, when she's making a fool of both of you. "What do you weigh?"

"An even hundred." She sent a careless wave to Jamie.

"And when you take the ball bearings out of your pocket?"

"Ninety-six, if you want to be technical." With a laugh, she gave him a quick hug. Her laughter was warm and distracting at his ear. "You might do something daring, like not wearing socks."

"The next spontaneous act might be dropping you on your very attractive bottom."

"Is it attractive?" Idly she swung her feet back and forth. "I see so little of it myself." She held him for a moment longer because it felt so right, so good. Keep it light, she reminded herself. And watch your step. As long as she could keep him off balance, things would run smoothly. Leaning forward, she caught the lobe of his ear between her teeth. "Thanks for the lift, sailor."

Before he could respond, she'd jumped down and dashed into the house.

* * *

It was night, late, dark and quiet, when Adam sat alone in his room. He held the transmitter in his hand and found he wanted to smash it into little pieces and forget it had ever existed. No personal involvements. That was rule number one, and he'd always followed it. He'd never been tempted not to.

He'd wanted to follow it this time, he reminded himself. It just wasn't working that way. Involvement, emotion, conscience; he couldn't let any of it interfere. Staring at Kirby's painting of the Hudson, he flicked the switch.

"McIntyre?"

"Password."

"Damn it, this isn't a chapter of Ian Fleming."

"Procedure," McIntyre reminded him briskly. After twenty seconds of dead air, he relented. "Okay, okay, what've you found out?"

I've found out I'm becoming dangerously close to being crazy about a woman who makes absolutely no sense to me, he thought. "I've found out that the next time you have a brainstorm, you can go to hell with it."

"Trouble?" McIntyre's voice snapped into the receiver. "You were supposed to call in if there was trouble."

"The trouble is I like the old man and the daughter's… unsettling." An apt word, Adam mused. His system hadn't settled since he'd set eyes on her.

"It's too late for that now. We're committed."

"Yeah." He let out a breath between his teeth and blocked Kirby from his mind. "Melanie Merrick Burgess is a close family friend and Harriet Merrick's daughter. She's a very elegant designer who doesn't seem to have any deep interest in painting. At a guess I'd say she'd be very supportive of the Fairchilds. Kirby recently broke off her engagement to Stuart Hiller."

"Interesting. When?"

"I don't have a date," Adam retorted. "And I didn't like pumping her about something that sensitive." He struggled with himself as McIntyre remained silent. "Sometime during the last couple months, I'd say, no longer. She's still smoldering." And hurting, he said to himself. He hadn't forgotten the look in her eyes. "I've been invited to a party this weekend. I should meet both Harriet Merrick and Hiller. In the meantime, I've had a break here. The place is riddled with secret passages."

"With what?"

"You heard me. With some luck, I'll have easy access throughout the house."

McIntyre grunted in approval. "You won't have any trouble recognizing it?"

"If he's got it, and if it's in the house, *and* if by some miracle I can find it in this anachronism, I'll recognize it." He switched off and, resisting the urge to throw the transmitter against the wall, dropped it back in the briefcase.

Clearing his mind, Adam rose and began to search the fireplace for the mechanism.

It took him nearly ten minutes, but he was rewarded with a groaning as a panel slid halfway open. He squeezed inside with a flashlight. It was both dank and musty, but he played the light against the wall until he found the inside switch. The panel squeaked closed and left him in the dark.

His footsteps echoed and he heard the scuttering sound of rodents. He ignored both. For a moment he stopped at the wall of Kirby's room. Telling himself he was only doing his job, he took the time to find the switch. But he wondered if she was already sleeping in the big four-poster bed, under the wedding ring quilt.

He could press the button and join her. The hell with McIntyre and the job. The hell with everything but what lay beyond the wall. Procedure, he thought on an oath. He was sick to death of procedure. But Kirby had been right. Adam had a very firm grip on what was right and what was wrong.

He turned and continued down the passage.

Abruptly the corridor snaked off, with steep stone steps forking to the left. Mounting them, he found himself in another corridor. A spider scrambled on the wall as he played his light over it. Kirby hadn't exaggerated much about the size. The third story, he decided, was as good a place to start as any.

He turned the first mechanism he found and slipped through the opening. Dust and dustcovers. Moving quietly, he began a slow, methodical search.

Kirby was restless. While Adam had been standing on the other side of the wall, fighting back the urge to open the panel, she'd been pacing her room. She'd considered going up to her studio. Work might calm her—but any work she did in this frame of mind would be trash. Frustrated, she sank down on the window seat. She could see the faint reflection of her own face and stared at it.

She wasn't completely in control. Almost any other flaw would've been easier to admit. Control was essential and, under the current circumstances, vital. The problem was getting it back.

The problem was, she corrected, Adam Haines.

Attraction? Yes, but that was simple and easily dealt with. There was something more twisted into it that was anything but simple. He could involve her, and once involved, nothing would be easily dealt with.

Laying her hands on the sill, she rested her head on them. He could hurt her. That was a first—a frightening first. Not a superficial blow to the pride or ego, Kirby admitted, but a hurt down deep where it counted; where it wouldn't heal.

Obviously, she told herself, forewarned was forearmed. She just wouldn't let him involve her, therefore she wouldn't let him hurt her. And that little piece of logic brought her right back to the control she didn't have. While she struggled to methodically untangle her thoughts, the beam of headlights distracted her.

Who'd be coming by at this time of night? she wondered without too much surprise. Fairchild had a habit of asking people over at odd hours. Kirby pressed her nose to the glass. A sound, not unlike Isabelle's growl, came from her throat.

"Of all the nerve," she muttered. "Of all the bloody nerve."

Springing up, she paced the floor three times before she grabbed a robe and left the room.

Above her head, Adam was about to reenter the passageway when he, too, saw the beams. Automatically he switched off his flashlight and stepped beside the window. He watched the man step from a late-model Mercedes and walk toward the house. Interesting, Adam decided. Abandoning the passageway, he slipped silently into the hall.

The sound of voices drifted up as he eased himself into the cover of a doorway and waited. Footsteps drew nearer. From his concealment, Adam watched Cards lead a slim, dark man up to Fairchild's tower studio.

"Mr. Hiller to see you, sir." Cards gave the information as if it were four in the afternoon rather than after midnight.

"Stuart, so nice of you to come." Fairchild's voice boomed through the doorway. "Come in, come in."

After counting to ten, Adam started to move toward the door Cards had shut, but just then a flurry of white scrambled up the stairs. Swearing, he pressed back into the wall as Kirby passed, close enough to touch.

What the hell is this? he demanded, torn between frustration and the urge to laugh. Here he was, trapped in a doorway, while people crept up tower steps in the middle of the night. While he watched, Kirby gathered the skirt of her robe around her knees and tiptoed up to the tower.

It was a nightmare, he decided. Women with floating hair sneaking around drafty corridors in filmy white. Secret passages. Clandestine meetings. A normal, sensible man wouldn't be involved in it for a minute. Then again, he'd stopped being completely sensible when he'd walked in the front door.

After Kirby reached the top landing, Adam moved closer. Her attention was focused on the studio door. Making a quick calculation, Adam moved up the steps behind her, then melted into the shadows in the corner. With his eyes on her, he joined Kirby in the eavesdropping.

"What kind of fool do you think I am?" Stuart demanded. He stood beside Adam with only the wall separating them.

"Whatever kind you prefer. Makes no difference to me. Have a seat, my boy."

"Listen to me, we had a deal. How long did you think it would take before I found out you'd double-crossed me?"

"Actually I didn't think it would take you quite so long." Smiling, Fairchild rubbed a thumb over his clay hawk. "Not as clever as I thought you were, Stuart. You should've discovered the switch weeks ago. Not that it wasn't superb," he added with a touch of pride. "But a smart man would've had the painting authenticated."

Because the conversation confused her, Kirby pressed even closer to the door. She tucked her hair behind her ear as if to hear more clearly. Untended, her robe fell open, revealing a thin excuse for a nightgown and a great deal of smooth golden skin. In his corner, Adam shifted and swore to himself.

"We had a deal—" Stuart's voice rose, but Fairchild cut him off with no more than a wave of his hand.

"Don't tell me you believe in that nonsense about honor among thieves? Time to grow up if you want to play in the big leagues."

"I want the Rembrandt, Fairchild."

Kirby stiffened. Because his attention was now fully focused on the battle in the tower, Adam didn't notice. By God, he thought grimly, the old bastard did have it.

"Sue me," Fairchild invited. Kirby could hear the shrug in his voice.

"Hand it over, or I'll break your scrawny neck."

For a full ten seconds, Fairchild watched calmly as Stuart's face turned a deep, dull red. "You won't get it that way. And I should warn you that threats make me irritable. You see…" Slowly he picked up a rag and began to wipe some excess clay from his hands. "I didn't care for your treatment of Kirby. No, I didn't care for it at all."

Abruptly he was no longer the harmless eccentric. He was neither cherub nor gnome, but a man. A dangerous one. "I knew she'd never go as far as marrying you. She's far too bright. But your threats, once she told you off, annoyed me. When I'm annoyed, I tend to be vindictive. A flaw," he said amiably. "But that's just the way I'm made." The pale eyes were cold and calm on Stuart's. "I'm still annoyed, Stuart. I'll let you know when I'm ready to deal. In the meantime, stay away from Kirby."

"You're not going to get away with this."

"I hold all the cards." In an impatient gesture, he brushed Stuart aside. "I have the Rembrandt, and only I know where it is. If you become a nuisance, which you're dangerously close to becoming, I may decide to keep it. Unlike you, I have no pressing need for money." He smiled, but the chill remained in his eyes. "One should never live above one's means, Stuart. That's my advice."

Impotent, intimidated, Stuart loomed over the little man at the worktable. He was strong enough, and furious enough, to have snapped Fairchild's neck with his hands. But he wouldn't have the Rembrandt, or the money he so desperately needed. "Before we're done, you'll pay," Stuart promised. "I won't be made a fool of."

"Too late," Fairchild told him easily. "Run along now. You can find your way out without disturbing Cards, can't you?"

As if he were already alone, Fairchild went back to his hawk.

Swiftly, Kirby looked around for a hiding place. For one ridiculous moment, Adam thought she'd try to ease herself into the corner he occupied. The moment she started to cross the hall toward him, the handle of the door turned. She'd left her move too late. With her back pressed against the wall, Kirby closed her eyes and pretended to be invisible.

Stuart wrenched open the door and stalked from the room, blind with rage. Without a backward glance he plunged down the steps. His face, Adam noted as he passed, was murderous. At the moment, he lacked a weapon. But if he found one, he wouldn't hesitate.

Kirby stood, still and silent, as the footsteps receded. She sucked in a deep breath, then let it out on a huff. What now? *What now?* she thought, and wanted to just bury her face in her hands and surrender. Instead, she straightened her shoulders and went in to confront her father.

"Papa." The word was quiet and accusing. Fairchild's head jerked up, but his surprise was quickly masked by a genial smile.

"Hello, love. My hawk's beginning to breathe. Come have a look."

She took another deep breath. All of her life she'd loved him, stood by him. Adored him. None of that had ever stopped her from being angry with him. Slowly, keeping her eyes on him, she crossed the front panels of her robe and tied the sash. As she approached, Fairchild thought she looked like a gunslinger buckling on his six-gun. She wouldn't, he thought with a surge of pride, intimidate like Hiller.

"Apparently you haven't kept me up to date," she began. "A riddle, Papa. What do Philip Fairchild, Stuart Hiller and Rembrandt have in common?"

"You've always been clever at riddles, my sweet."

"*Now,* Papa."

"Just business." He gave her a quick, hearty smile as he wondered just how much he'd have to tell her.

"Let's be specific, shall we?" She moved so that only the table separated them. "And don't give me that blank, foolish look. It won't work." Bending over, she stared directly into his eyes. "I heard quite a bit while I was outside. Tell me the rest."

"Eavesdropping." He made a disapproving tsk-tsk. "Rude."

"I come by it honestly. Now tell me or I'll annihilate your hawk." Sweeping up her arm, she held her palm three inches above his clay.

"Vicious brat." With his bony fingers, he grabbed her wrist, each knowing who'd win if it came down to it. He gave a windy sigh. "All right."

With a nod, Kirby removed her hand then folded her arms under her breasts. The habitual gesture had him sighing again.

"Stuart came to me with a little proposition some time ago. You know, of course, he hasn't a cent to his name, no matter what he pretends."

"Yes, I know he wanted to marry me for my money." No one but her father would've detected the slight tightening in her voice.

"I didn't bring that up to hurt you." His hand reached for hers in the bond that had been formed when she'd taken her first breath.

"I know, Papa." She squeezed his hand, then stuck

both of hers in the pockets of her robe. "My pride suffered. It has to happen now and again, I suppose. But I don't care for humiliation," she said with sudden fierceness. "I don't care for it one bloody bit." With a toss of her head, she looked down at him. "The rest."

"Well." Fairchild puffed out his cheeks, then blew out the breath. "Among his other faults, Stuart's greedy. He needed a large sum of money, and didn't see why he had to work for it. He decided to help himself to the Rembrandt self-portrait from Harriet's gallery."

"He *stole* it?" Kirby's eyes grew huge. "Great buckets of bedbugs! I wouldn't have given him credit for that much nerve."

"He thought himself clever." Rising, Fairchild walked to the little sink in the corner to wash off his hands. "Harriet was going on her safari, and there'd be no one to question the disappearance for several weeks. Stuart's a bit dictatorial with the staff at the gallery."

"It's such a treat to flog underlings."

"In any case—" lovingly, Fairchild draped his hawk for the night "—he came to me with an offer—a rather paltry offer, too—if I'd do the forgery for the Rembrandt's replacement."

She hadn't thought he could do anything to surprise her. Certainly nothing to hurt her. "Papa, it's Harriet's Rembrandt," she said in shock.

"Now, Kirby, you know I'm fond of Harriet. Very fond." He put a comforting arm around her shoulders. "Our Stuart has a very small brain. He handed over the Rembrandt when I said I needed it to do the copy." Fairchild shook his head. "There wasn't any challenge to it, Kirby. Hardly any fun at all."

"Pity," she said dryly and dropped into a chair.

"Then I told him I didn't need the original any longer, and gave him the copy instead. He never suspected." Fairchild linked his hands behind his back and stared up at the ceiling. "I wish you'd seen it. It was superlative. It was one of Rembrandt's later works, you know. Rough textures, such luminous depth—"

"Papa!" Kirby interrupted what would've become a lecture.

"Oh, yes, yes." With an effort, Fairchild controlled himself. "I told him it'd take just a little more time to complete the copy and treat it for the illusion of age. He bought it. Gullibility," Fairchild added and clucked his tongue. "It's been almost three weeks, and he just got around to having the painting tested. I made certain it wouldn't stand up to the most basic of tests, of course."

"Of course," Kirby murmured.

"Now he has to leave the copy in the gallery. And I have the original."

She gave herself a moment to absorb all he'd told her. It didn't make any difference in how she felt. Furious. "Why, Papa? Why did you do this! It isn't like all the others. It's Harriet."

"Now, Kirby, don't lose control. You've such a nasty temper." He did his best to look small and helpless. "I'm much too old to cope with it. Remember my blood pressure."

"Blood pressure be hanged." She glared up at him with fury surging into her eyes. "Don't think you're going to get around me with that. Old?" she tossed back. "You're still your youngest child."

"I feel a spell coming on," he said, inspired by Kirby's own warning two days before. He pressed a trembling hand to his heart and staggered. "I'll end up a useless heap of cold spaghetti. Ah, the paintings I might have done. The world's losing a genius."

Clenching her fists, Kirby beat them on his worktable. Tools bounced and clattered while she let out a long wail. Protective, Fairchild placed his hands around his hawk and waited for the crisis to pass. At length, she slumped back in the chair, breathless.

"You used to do better than that," he observed. "I think you're mellowing."

"Papa." Kirby clamped her teeth to keep from grinding them. "I know I'll be forced to beat you about the head and ears, then I'll be arrested for patricide. You know I've a terror of closed-in places. I'd go mad in prison. Do you want that on your conscience?"

"Kirby, have I ever given you cause for one moment's worry?"

"Don't force me into a recital, Papa, it's after midnight. What have you done with the Rembrandt?"

"Done with it?" He frowned and fiddled with the cover of his hawk. "What do you mean, done with it?"

"Where is it?" she asked, carefully spacing the words. "You can't leave a painting like that lying around the house, particularly when you've chosen to have company."

"Company? Oh, you mean Adam. Fine boy. I'm fond of him already." His eyebrows wiggled twice. "You seem to be finding him agreeable."

Kirby narrowed her eyes. "Leave Adam out of this."

"Dear, dear, dear." Fairchild grinned lavishly. "And I thought you'd brought him up."

"Where *is* the Rembrandt?" All claim to patience disintegrated. Briefly, she considered banging her head on the table, but she'd given up that particular ploy at ten.

"Safe and secure, my sweet." Fairchild's voice was calm and pleased. "Safe and secure."

"Here? In the house?"

"Of course." He gave her an astonished look. "You don't think I'd keep it anywhere else?"

"Where?"

"You don't need to know everything." With a flourish, he whipped off his painting smock and tossed it over a chair. "Just content yourself that it's safe, hidden with appropriate respect and affection."

"Papa."

"Kirby." He smiled—a gentle father's smile. "A child must trust her parent, must abide by the wisdom of his years. You do trust me, don't you?"

"Yes, of course, but—"

He cut her off with the first bars of "Daddy's Little Girl" in a wavering falsetto.

Kirby moaned and lowered her head to the table. When would she learn? And how was she going to deal with him this time? He continued to sing until the giggles welled up and escaped. "You're incorrigible." She lifted her head and took a deep breath. "I have this terrible feeling that you're leaving out a mountain of details and that I'm going to go along with you anyway."

"Details, Kirby." His hand swept them aside. "The world's too full of details, they clutter things up. Remember, art reflects life, and life's an illusion. Come now, I'm tired." He walked to her and held out his hand. "Walk your old papa to bed."

Defeated, she accepted his hand and stood. Never, never would she learn. And always, always would she adore him. Together they walked from the room.

Adam watched as they started down the steps, arm in arm.

"Papa…" Only feet away from Adam's hiding place, Kirby stopped. "There is, of course, a logical reason for all this?"

"Kirby." Adam could see the mobile face move into calm, sober lines. "Have I ever done anything without a sensible, logical reason?"

She started with a near-soundless chuckle. In moments, her laughter rang out, rich and musical. It echoed back, faint and ghostly, until she rested her head against her father's shoulder. In the half-light, with her eyes shining, Adam thought she'd never looked more alluring. "Oh, my papa," she began in a clear contralto. "To me he is so wonderful." Linking her arm through Fairchild's, she continued down the steps.

Rather pleased with himself, and with his offspring, Fairchild joined her in his wavery falsetto. Their mixed voices drifted over Adam until the distance swallowed them.

Leaving the shadows, he stood at the head of the stairway. Once he heard Kirby's laugh, then there was silence.

"Curiouser and curiouser," he murmured.

Both Fairchilds were probably mad. They fascinated him.

Chapter 5

In the morning the sky was gray and the rain sluggish. Adam was tempted to roll over, close his eyes and pretend he was in his own well-organized home, where a housekeeper tended to the basics and there wasn't a gargoyle in sight. Partly from curiosity, partly from courage, he rose and prepared to deal with the day.

From what he'd overheard the night before, he didn't count on learning much from Kirby. Apparently she'd known less about the matter of the Rembrandt than he. Adam was equally sure that no matter how much he prodded and poked, Fairchild would let nothing slip. He might look innocent and harmless, but he was as shrewd as they came. And potentially dangerous, Adam mused, remembering how cleanly Fairchild had dealt with Hiller.

The best course of action remained the nightly

searches with the aid of the passages. The days he determined for his own sanity to spend painting.

I shouldn't be here in the first place, Adam told himself as he stood in the shower under a strong cold spray of water. If it hadn't been for the fact that Mac tantalized me with the Rembrandt, I *wouldn't* be here. The last time, he promised himself as he toweled off. The very last time.

Once the Fairchild hassle was over, painting would not only be his first order of business, it would be his only business.

Dressed, and content with the idea of ending his secondary career in a few more weeks, Adam walked down the hallway thinking of coffee. Kirby's door was wide open. As he passed, he glanced in. Frowning, he stopped, walked back and stood in the doorway.

"Good morning, Adam. Isn't it a lovely day?" She smiled, upside down, as she stood on her head in the corner.

Deliberately he glanced at the window to make sure he was on solid ground. "It's raining."

"Don't you like the rain? I do." She rubbed her nose with the back of her hand. "Look at it this way, there must be dozens of places where the sun's shining. It's all relative. Did you sleep well?"

"Yes." Even in her current position, Adam could see that her face glowed, showing no signs of a restless night.

"Come in and wait a minute, I'll go down to breakfast with you."

He walked over to stand directly in front of her. "Why are you standing on your head?"

"It's a theory of mine." She crossed her ankles

against the wall while her hair pooled onto the carpet. "Could you sit down a minute? It's hard for me to talk to you when your head's up there and mine's down here."

Knowing he'd regret it, Adam crouched. Her sweater had slipped up, showing a thin line of smooth midriff.

"Thanks. My theory is that all night I've been horizontal, and most of the day I'll be right side up. So…" Somehow she managed to shrug. "I stand on my head in the morning and before bed. That way the blood can slosh around a bit."

Adam rubbed his nose between his thumb and forefinger. "I think I understand. That terrifies me."

"You should try it."

"I'll just let my blood stagnate, thanks."

"Suit yourself. You'd better stand back, I'm coming up."

She dropped her feet and righted herself with a quick athletic agility that surprised him. Facing him, she pushed at the hair that floated into her eyes. As she tossed it back she gave him a long, slow smile.

"Your face is red," he murmured, more in his own defense than for any other reason.

"Can't be helped, it's part of the process." She'd spent a good many hours arguing with herself the night before. This morning she'd decided to let things happen as they happened. "It's the only time I blush," she told him. "So, if you'd like to say something embarrassing… or flattering…?"

Against his better judgment, he touched her, circling her waist with his hands. She didn't move back, didn't move forward, but simply waited. "Your blush is already fading, so it seems I've missed my chance."

"You can give it another try tomorrow. Hungry?"

"Yes." Her lips made him hungry, but he wasn't ready to test himself quite yet. "I want to go through your clothes after breakfast."

"Oh, really?" She drew out the word, catching her tongue between her teeth.

His brow lifted, but only she was aware of the gesture. "For the painting."

"You don't want to do a nude." The humor in her eyes faded into boredom as she drew away. "That's the usual line."

"I don't waste my time with lines." He studied her—the cool gray eyes that could warm with laughter, the haughty mouth that could invite and promise with no more than a smile. "I'm going to paint you because you were meant to be painted. I'm going to make love with you for exactly the same reason."

Her expression didn't change, but her pulse rate did. Kirby wasn't foolish enough to pretend even to herself it was anger. Anger and excitement were two different things. "How decisive and arrogant of you," she drawled. Strolling over to her dresser, she picked up her brush and ran it quickly through her hair. "I haven't agreed to pose for you, Adam, nor have I agreed to sleep with you." She flicked the brush through a last time then set it down. "In fact, I've serious doubts that I'll do either. Shall we go?"

Before she could get to the door, he had her. The speed surprised her, if the strength didn't. She'd hoped to annoy him, but when she tossed her head back to look at him, she didn't see temper. She saw cool, patient determination. Nothing could have been more unnerving.

Then he had her close, so that his face was a blur and his mouth was dominant. She didn't resist. Kirby rarely resisted what she wanted. Instead she let the heat wind through her in a slow continuous stream that was somehow both terrifying and peaceful.

Desire. Wasn't that how she'd always imagined it would be with the right man? Wasn't that what she'd been waiting for since the first moment she'd discovered herself a woman? It was here now. Kirby opened her arms to it.

His heartbeat wasn't steady, and it should have been. His mind wasn't clear, and it had to be. How could he win with her when he lost ground every time he was around her? If he followed through on his promise—or threat—that they'd be lovers, how much more would he lose? And gain, he thought as he let himself become steeped in her. The risk was worth taking.

"You'll pose for me," he said against her mouth. "And you'll make love with me. There's no choice."

That was the word that stopped her. That was the phrase that forced her to resist. She'd always have a choice. "I don't—"

"For either of us," Adam finished as he released her. "We'll decide on the clothes after breakfast." Because he didn't want to give either of them a chance to speak, he propelled her from the room.

An hour later, he propelled her back.

She'd been serene during the meal. But he hadn't been fooled. Livid was what she was, and livid was exactly how he wanted her. She didn't like to be outmaneuvered, even on a small point. It gave him a surge of satisfaction to be able to do so. The defiant, sulky look in her eyes was exactly what he wanted for the portrait.

"Red, I think," he stated. "It would suit you best."

Kirby waved a hand at her closet and flopped backward onto her bed. Staring up at the ceiling, she thought through her position. It was true she'd always refused to be painted, except by her father. She hadn't wanted anyone else to get that close to her. As an artist, she knew just how intimate the relationship was between painter and subject, be the subject a person or a bowl of fruit. She'd never been willing to share herself with anyone to that extent.

But Adam was different. She could, if she chose, tell herself it was because of his talent, and because he wanted to paint her, not flatter her. It wasn't a lie, but it wasn't quite the truth. Still, Kirby was comfortable with partial truths in certain cases. If she was honest, she had to admit that she was curious to see just how she'd look from his perspective, and yet she wasn't entirely comfortable with that.

Moving only her eyes, she watched him as he rummaged through her closet.

He didn't have to know what was going on in her head. Certainly she was skilled in keeping her thoughts to herself. It might be a challenge to do so under the sharp eyes of an artist. It might be interesting to see just how difficult she could make it for him. She folded her hands demurely on her stomach.

While Kirby was busy with her self-debate, Adam looked through an incredible variety of clothes. Some were perfect for an orphan, others for an eccentric teenager. He wondered if she'd actually worn the purple miniskirt and just how she'd looked in it. Elegant gowns from Paris and New York hung haphazardly with army surplus. If clothes reflected the person, there was more than one Kirby Fairchild. He wondered just how many she'd show him.

He discarded one outfit after another. This one was too drab, that one too chic. He found a pair of baggy overalls thrown over the same hanger with a slinky sequin dress with a two-thousand-dollar label. Pushing aside a three-piece suit perfect for an assistant D.A., he found it.

Scarlet silk. It was undoubtedly expensive, but not chic in the way he imagined Melanie Burgess would design. The square-necked bodice tapered to a narrow waist before the material flared into a full skirt. There were flounces at the hem and underskirts of white and black and fuchsia. The sleeves were short and puffed, running with stripes of the same colors. It was made for a wealthy gypsy. It was perfect.

"This." Adam carried it to the bed and stood over Kirby. With a frown, she continued to stare up at the ceiling. "Put it on and come up to the studio. I'll do some sketches."

She spoke without looking at him. "Do you realize that not once have you asked me to pose for you? You told me you wanted to paint me, you told me you were going to paint me, but you've never *asked* if you could paint me." With her hands still folded, one finger began to tap. "Instinct tells me you're basically a gentleman, Adam. Perhaps you've just forgotten to say please."

"I haven't forgotten." He tossed the dress across the bottom of the bed. "But I think you hear far too many pleases from men. You're a woman who brings men to their knees with the bat of an eye. I'm not partial to kneeling." No, he wasn't partial to kneeling, and it was becoming imperative that he handle the controls, for both of them. Bending over, he put his hands on either side of her head then sat beside her. "And I'm just as used to getting my own way as you are."

She studied him, thinking over his words and her position. "Then again, I haven't batted my eyes at you yet."

"Haven't you?" he murmured.

He could smell her, that wild, untamed fragrance that was suited to isolated winter nights. Her lips pouted, not by design, but mood. It was that that tempted him. He had to taste them. He did so lightly, as he'd intended. Just a touch, just a taste, then he'd go about his business. But her mouth yielded to him as the whole woman hadn't. Or perhaps it conquered.

Desire scorched him. Fire was all he could relate to. Flames and heat and smoke. That was her taste. Smoke and temptation and a promise of unreasonable delights.

He tasted, but it was no longer enough. He had to touch.

Her body was small, delicate, something a man might fear to take. He did, but no longer for her sake. For his own. Small and delicate she might be, but she could slice a man in two. Of that he was certain. But as he touched, as he tasted, he didn't give a damn.

Never had he wanted a woman more. She made him feel like a teenager in the back seat of a car, like a man paying for the best whore in a French bordello, like a husband nuzzling into the security of a wife. Her complexities were more erotic than satin and lace and smoky light—the soft, agile mouth, the strong, determined hands. He wasn't certain he'd ever escape from either. In possessing her, he'd invite an endless cycle of complications, of struggles, of excitement. She was an opiate. She was a dive from a cliff. If he wasn't careful, he was going to overdose and hit the rocks.

It cost him more than he would have believed to draw back. She lay with her eyes half closed, her mouth just parted. Don't get involved, he told himself frantically. Get the Rembrandt and walk away. That's what you came to do.

"Adam…" She whispered his name as if she'd never said it before. It felt so beautiful on her tongue. The only thought that stayed with her was that no one had ever made her feel like this. No one else ever would. Something was opening inside her, but she wouldn't fight it. She'd give. The innocence in her eyes was real, emotional not physical. Seeing it, Adam felt desire flare again.

She's a witch, he told himself. Circe. Lorelei. He had to pull back before he forgot that. "You'll have to change."

"Adam…" Still swimming, she reached up and touched his face.

"Emphasize your eyes." He stood before he could take the dive.

"My eyes?" Mind blank, body throbbing, she stared up at him.

"And leave your hair loose." He strode to the door as she struggled up to her elbows. "Twenty minutes."

She wouldn't let him see the hurt. She wouldn't allow herself to feel the rejection. "You're a cool one, aren't you?" she said softly. "And as smooth as any I've ever run across. You might find yourself on your knees yet."

She was right—he could've strangled her for it. "That's a risk I'll have to take." With a nod, he walked through the door. "Twenty minutes," he called back.

Kirby clenched her fists together then slowly relaxed them. "On your knees," she promised herself. "I swear it."

* * *

Alone in Kirby's studio, Adam searched for the mechanism to the passageway. He looked mainly from curiosity. It was doubtful he'd need to rummage through a room that he'd been given free run in, but he was satisfied when he located the control. The panel creaked open, as noisily as all the others he'd found. After a quick look inside, he shut it again and went back to the first order of business—painting.

It was never a job, but it wasn't always a pleasure. The need to paint was a demand that could be soft and gentle, or sharp and cutting. Not a job, but work certainly, sometimes every bit as exhausting as digging a trench with a pick and shovel.

Adam was a meticulous artist, as he was a meticulous man. Conventional, as Kirby had termed him, perhaps. But he wasn't rigid. He was as orderly as she wasn't, but his creative process was remarkably similar to hers. She might stare at a piece of wood for an hour until she saw the life in it. He would do the same with a canvas. She would feel a jolt, a physical release the moment she saw what she'd been searching for. He'd feel that same jolt when something would leap out at him from one of his dozens of sketches.

Now he was only preparing, and he was as calm and ordered as his equipment. On an easel he set the canvas, blank and waiting. Carefully, he selected three pieces of charcoal. He'd begin with them. He was going over his first informal sketches when he heard her footsteps.

She paused in the doorway, tossed her head and stared at him. With deliberate care, he set his pad back on the worktable.

Her hair fell loose and rich over the striped silk

shoulders. At a movement, the gold hoops at her ears and the half-dozen gold bracelets on her arm jangled. Her eyes, darkened and sooty, still smoldered with temper. Without effort, he could picture her whirling around an open fire to the sound of violins and tambourines.

Aware of the image she projected, Kirby put both hands on her hips and walked into the room. The full scarlet skirt flowed around her legs. Standing in front of him, she whirled around twice, turning her head each time so that she watched him over her shoulder. The scent of wood smoke and roses flowed into the room.

"You want to paint Katrina's picture, eh?" Her voice lowered into a sultry Slavic accent as she ran a fingertip down his cheek. Insolence, challenge, and then a laugh that skidded warm and dangerous over his skin. "First you cross her palm with silver."

He'd have given her anything. What man wouldn't? Fighting her, fighting himself, he pulled out a cigarette. "Over by the east window," he said easily. "The light's better there."

No, he wouldn't get off so easy. Behind the challenge and the insolence, her body still trembled for him. She wouldn't let him know it. "How much you pay?" she demanded, swirling away in a flurry of scarlet and silk. "Katrina not come free."

"Scale." He barely resisted the urge to grab her by the hair and drag her back. "And you won't get a dime until I'm finished."

In an abrupt change, Kirby brushed and smoothed her skirts. "Is something wrong?" she asked mildly. "Perhaps you don't like the dress after all."

He crushed out his cigarette in one grinding motion. "Let's get started."

"I thought we already had," she murmured. Her eyes were luminous and amused. He wanted to choke her every bit as much as he wanted to crawl for her. "You insisted on painting."

"Don't push me too far, Kirby. You have a tendency to bring out my baser side."

"I don't think I can be blamed for that. Maybe you've locked it up too long." Because she'd gotten precisely the reaction she'd wanted, she became completely co-operative. "Now, where do you want me to stand?"

"By the east window."

Tie score, she thought with satisfaction as she obliged him.

He spoke only when he had to—tilt your chin higher, turn your head. Within moments he was able to turn the anger and the desire into concentration. The rain fell, but its sound was muffled against the thick glass windows. With the tower door nearly closed, there wasn't another sound.

He watched her, studied her, absorbed her, but the man and the artist were working together. Perhaps by putting her on canvas, he'd understand her...and himself. Adam swept the charcoal over the canvas and began.

Now she could watch him, knowing that he was turned inward. She'd seen dozens of artists work; the old, the young, the talented, the amateur. Adam was, as she'd suspected, different.

He wore a sweater, one he was obviously at home in, but no smock. Even as he sketched he stood straight, as though his nature demanded that he remain always alert. That was one of the things she'd noticed about him first.

He was always watching. A true artist did, she knew, but there seemed to be something more.

She called him conventional, knowing it wasn't quite true. Not quite. What was it about him that didn't fit into the mold he'd been fashioned for? Tall, lean, attractive, aristocratic, wealthy, successful, and…daring? That was the word that came to mind, though she wasn't completely sure why.

There was something reckless about him that appealed to her. It balanced the maturity, the dependability she hadn't known she'd wanted in a man. He'd be a rock to hold on to during an earthquake. And he'd be the earthquake. She was, Kirby realized, sinking fast. The trick would be to keep him from realizing it and making a fool of herself. Still, beneath it all, she liked him. That simple.

Adam glanced up to see her smiling at him. It was disarming, sweet and uncomplicated. Something warned him that Kirby without guards was far more dangerous than Kirby with them. When she let hers drop, he put his in place.

"Doesn't Hiller paint a bit?"

He saw her smile fade and tried not to regret it. "A bit."

"Haven't you posed for him?"

"No."

"Why not?"

The ice that came into her eyes wasn't what he wanted for the painting. The man and artist warred as he continued to sketch. "Let's say I didn't care much for his work."

"I suppose I can take that as a compliment to mine."

She gave him a long, neutral look. "If you like."

Deceit was part of the job, he reminded himself. What he'd heard in Fairchild's studio left him no choice. "I'm surprised he didn't make an issue of it, being in love with you."

"He wasn't." She bit off the words, and ice turned to heat.

"He asked you to marry him."

"One hasn't anything to do with the other."

He looked up and saw she said exactly what she meant. "Doesn't it?"

"I agreed to marry him without loving him."

He held the charcoal an inch from the canvas, forgetting the painting. "Why?"

While she stared at him, he saw the anger fade. For a moment she was simply a woman at her most vulnerable. "Timing," she murmured. "It's probably the most important factor governing our lives. If it hadn't been for timing, Romeo and Juliet would've raised a half-dozen children."

He was beginning to understand, and understanding only made him more uncomfortable. "You thought it was time to get married?"

"Stuart's attractive, very polished, charming, and I'd thought harmless. I realized the last thing I wanted was a polished, charming, harmless husband. Still, I thought he loved me. I didn't break the engagement for a long time because I thought he'd make a convenient husband, and one who wouldn't demand too much." It sounded empty. It had been empty. "One who'd give me children."

"You want children?"

The anger was back, quickly. "Is there something wrong with that?" she demanded. "Do you think it strange that I'd want a family?" She made a quick, furious movement that had the gold jangling again. "This might come as a shock, but I have needs and feelings almost like a real person. And I don't have to justify myself to you."

She was halfway to the door before he could stop her. "Kirby, I'm sorry." When she tried to jerk out of his hold, he tightened it. "I *am* sorry."

"For what?" she tossed back.

"For hurting you," he murmured. "With stupidity."

Her shoulders relaxed under his hands, slowly, so that he knew it cost her. Guilt flared again. "All right. You hit a nerve, that's all." Deliberately she removed his hands from her shoulders and stepped back. He'd rather she'd slapped him. "Give me a cigarette, will you?"

She took one from him and let him light it before she turned away again. "When I accepted Stuart's proposal—"

"You don't have to tell me anything."

"I don't leave things half done." Some of the insolence was back when she whirled back to him. For some reason it eased Adam's guilt. "When I accepted, I told Stuart I wasn't in love with him. It didn't seem fair otherwise. If two people are going to have a relationship that means anything, it has to start out honestly, don't you think?"

He thought of the transmitter tucked into his briefcase. He thought of McIntyre waiting for the next report. "Yes."

She nodded. It was one area where she wasn't flexible. "I told him that what I wanted from him was fidelity and children, and in return I'd give him those things and as much affection as I could." She toyed with the cigarette, taking one of her quick, nervous drags. "When I realized things just wouldn't work for either of us that way, I went to see him. I didn't do it carelessly, casually. It was very difficult for me. Can you understand that?"

"Yes, I understand that."

It helped, she realized. More than Melanie's sympathy, more even than her father's unspoken support, Adam's simple understanding helped. "It didn't go well. I'd known there'd be an argument, but I hadn't counted on it getting so out of hand. He made a few choice remarks on my maternal abilities and my track record. Anyway, with all the blood and bone being strewn about, the real reason for him wanting to marry me came out."

She took a last puff on the cigarette and crushed it out before she dropped into a chair. "He never loved me. He'd been unfaithful all along. I don't suppose it mattered." But she fell silent, knowing it did. "All the time he was pretending to care for me, he was using me." When she looked up again, the hurt was back in her eyes. She didn't know it—she'd have hated it. "Can you imagine how it feels to find out that all the time someone was holding you, talking with you, he was thinking of how you could be useful?" She picked up the piece of half-formed wood that would be her anger. "Useful," she repeated. "What a nasty word. I haven't bounced back from it as well as I should have."

He forgot McIntyre, the Rembrandt and the job he still had to do. Walking over, he sat beside her and closed his hand over hers. Under them was her anger. "I can't imagine any man thinking of you as useful."

When she looked up, her smile was already spreading. "What a nice thing to say. The perfect thing." Too perfect for her rapidly crumbling defenses. Because she knew it would take so little to have her turning to him now and later, she lightened the mood. "I'm glad you're going to be there Saturday."

"At the party?"

"You can send me long, smoldering looks and everyone'll think I jilted Stuart for you. I'm fond of petty revenge."

He laughed and brought her hands to his lips. "Don't change," he told her with a sudden intenseness that had her uncertain again.

"I don't plan on it. Adam, I— Oh, chicken fat, what're you doing here? This is a private conversation."

Wary, Adam turned his head and watched Montique bounce into the room. "He won't spread gossip."

"That isn't the point. I've told you you're not allowed in here."

Ignoring her, Montique scurried over and with an awkward leap plopped into Adam's lap. "Cute little devil," Adam decided as he scratched the floppy ears.

"Ah, Adam, I wouldn't do that."

"Why?"

"You're only asking for trouble."

"Don't be absurd. He's harmless."

"Oh, yes, he is. *She* isn't." Kirby nodded her head toward the doorway as Isabelle slinked through. "Now you're in for it. I warned you." Tossing back her head, Kirby met Isabelle's cool look equally. "I had nothing to do with it."

Isabelle blinked twice, then shifted her gaze to Adam. Deciding her responsibility had ended, Kirby sighed and rose. "There's nothing I can do," she told Adam and patted his shoulder. "You asked for it." With this, she swept out of the room, giving the cat a wide berth.

"I didn't ask him to come up here," Adam began, scowling down at Isabelle. "And there can't be any harm in— Oh, God," he murmured. "She's got me doing it."

Chapter 6

"Let's walk," Kirby demanded when the afternoon grew late and Fairchild had yet to budge from his studio. Nor would he budge, she knew, until the Van Gogh was completed down to the smallest detail. If she didn't get out and forget about her father's pet project for a while, she knew she'd go mad.

"It's raining," Adam pointed out as he lingered over coffee.

"You mentioned that before." Kirby pushed away her own coffee and rose. "All right then, I'll have Cards bring you a lap robe and a nice cup of tea."

"Is that a psychological attack?"

"Did it work?"

"I'll get a jacket." He strode from the room, ignoring her quiet chuckle.

When they walked outside, the fine misting rain fell

over them. Leaves streamed with it. Thin fingers of fog twisted along the ground. Adam hunched inside his jacket, thinking it was miserable weather for a walk. Kirby strolled along with her face lifted to the sky.

He'd planned to spend the afternoon on the painting, but perhaps this was better. If he was going to capture her with colors and brush strokes, he should get to know her better. No easy task, Adam mused, but a strangely appealing one.

The air was heavy with the fragrance of fall, the sky gloomy. For the first time since he'd met her, Adam sensed a serenity in Kirby. They walked in silence, with the rain flowing over them.

She was content. It was an odd feeling for her to identify as she felt it so rarely. With her hand in his, she was content to walk along as the fog moved along the ground and the chilly drizzle fell over them. She was glad of the rain, of the chill and the gloom. Later, there would be time for a roaring fire and warm brandy.

"Adam, do you see the bed of mums over there?"

"Hmm?"

"The mums, I want to pick some. You'll have to be the lookout."

"Lookout for what?" He shook wet hair out of his eyes.

"For Jamie, of course. He doesn't like anyone messing with his flowers."

"They're your flowers."

"No, they're Jamie's."

"He works for you."

"What does that have to do with it?" She put a hand on his shoulder as she scanned the area. "If he catches me, he'll get mad, then he won't save me any leaves. I'll be quick—I've done this before."

"But if you—"

"There's no time to argue. Now, you watch that window there. He's probably in the kitchen having coffee with Tulip. Give me a signal when you see him."

Whether he went along with her because it was simpler, or because he was getting into the spirit of things despite himself, Adam wasn't sure. But he walked over to the window and peeked inside. Jamie sat at a huge round table with a mug of coffee in both frail hands. Turning, he nodded a go-ahead to Kirby.

She moved like lightning, dashing to the flower bed and plucking at stems. Dark and wet, her hair fell forward to curtain her face as she loaded her arms with autumn flowers. She should be painted like this, as well, Adam mused. In the fog, with her arms full of wet flowers. Perhaps it would be possible to capture those odd little snatches of innocence in the portrait.

Idly he glanced back in the window. With a ridiculous jolt of panic, he saw Jamie rise and head for the kitchen door. Forgetting logic, Adam dashed toward her.

"He's coming."

Surprisingly swift, Kirby leaped over the bed of flowers and kept on going. Even though he was running full stride, Adam didn't catch her until they'd rounded the side of the house. Giggling and out of breath, she collapsed against him.

"We made it!"

"Just," he agreed. His own heart was thudding—from the race? Maybe. He was breathless—from the game? Perhaps. But they were wet and close and the fog was rising. It didn't seem he had a choice any longer.

With his eyes on hers, he brushed the dripping hair back from her face. Her cheeks were cool, wet and smooth. Yet her mouth, when his lowered to it, was warm and waiting.

She hadn't planned it this way. If she'd had the time to think, she'd have said she didn't want it this way. She didn't want to be weak. She didn't want her mind muddled. It didn't seem she had a choice any longer.

He could taste the rain on her, fresh and innocent. He could smell the sharp tang of the flowers that were crushed between them. He couldn't keep his hands out of her hair, the soft, heavy tangle of it. He wanted her closer. He wanted all of her, not in the way he'd first wanted her, but in every way. The need was no longer the simple need of a man for woman, but of him for her. Exclusive, imperative, impossible.

She'd wanted to fall in love, but she'd wanted to plan it out in her own way, in her own time. It wasn't supposed to happen in a crash and a roar that left her trembling. It wasn't supposed to happen without her permission. Shaken, Kirby drew back. It wasn't going to happen until she was ready. That was that. Nerves taut again, she made herself smile.

"It looks like we've done a good job of squashing them." When he would've drawn her back, Kirby thrust the flowers at him. "They're for you."

"For me?" Adam looked down at the mums they held between them.

"Yes, don't you like flowers?"

"I like flowers," he murmured. However unintentionally, she'd moved him as much with the gift as with the kiss. "I don't think anyone's given me flowers before."

"No?" She gave him a long, considering look. She'd

been given floods of them over the years, orchids, lilies, roses and more roses, until they'd meant little more than nothing. Her smile came slowly as she touched a hand to his chest. "I'd've picked more if I'd known."

Behind them a window was thrown open. "Don't you know better than to stand in the rain and neck?" Fairchild demanded. "If you want to nuzzle, come inside. I can't stand sneezing and sniffling!" The window shut with a bang.

"You're terribly wet," Kirby commented, as if she hadn't noticed the steadily falling rain. She linked her arm with his and walked to the door that was opened by the ever-efficient Cards.

"Thank you." Kirby peeled off her soaking jacket. "We'll need a vase for the flowers, Cards. They're for Mr. Haines's room. Make sure Jamie's not about, will you?"

"Naturally, miss." Cards took both the dripping jackets and the dripping flowers and headed back down the hall.

"Where'd you find him?" Adam wondered aloud. "He's incredible."

"Cards?" Like a wet dog, Kirby shook her head. "Papa brought him back from England. I think he was a spy, or maybe it was a bouncer. In either case, it's obvious he's seen everything."

"Well, children, have you had a nice holiday?" Fairchild bounced out of the parlor. He wore a paint-streaked shirt and a smug smile. "My work's complete, and now I'm free to give my full attention to my sculpting. It's time I called Victor Alvarez," he murmured. "I've kept him dangling long enough."

"He'll dangle until after coffee, Papa." She sent her

father a quick warning glance Adam might've missed if he hadn't been watching so closely. "Take Adam in the parlor and I'll see to it."

She kept him occupied for the rest of the day. Deliberately, Adam realized. Something was going on that she didn't want him getting an inkling of. Over dinner, she was again the perfect hostess. Over coffee and brandy in the parlor, she kept him entertained with an in-depth discussion on baroque art. Though her conversations and charm were effortless, Adam was certain there was an underlying reason. It was one more thing for him to discover.

She couldn't have set the scene better, he mused. A quiet parlor, a crackling fire, intelligent conversation. And she was watching Fairchild like a hawk.

When Montique entered, the scene changed. Once again, the scruffy puppy leaped into Adam's lap and settled down.

"How the hell did he get in here?" Fairchild demanded.

"Adam encourages him," Kirby stated as she sipped at her brandy. "We can't be held responsible."

"I should say not!" Fairchild gave both Adam and Montique a steely look. "And if that—that creature threatens to sue again, Adam will have to retain his own attorney. I won't be involved in a legal battle, particularly when I have my business with Senhor Alvarez to complete. What time is it in Brazil?"

"Some time or other," Kirby murmured.

"I'll call him immediately and close the deal before we find ourselves slapped with a summons."

Adam sat back with his brandy and scratched Montique's ears. "You two don't seriously expect me to believe you're worried about being sued by a cat?"

Kirby ran a fingertip around the rim of her snifter. "I don't think we'd better tell him about what happened last year when we tried to have her evicted."

"No!" Fairchild leaped up and shuffled before he darted to the door. "I won't discuss it. I won't remember it. I'm going to call Brazil."

"Ah, Adam…" Kirby trailed off with a meaningful glance at the doorway.

Adam didn't have to look to know that Isabelle was making an entrance.

"I won't be intimidated by a cat."

"I'm sure that's very stalwart of you." Kirby downed the rest of her drink then rose. "Just as I'm sure you'll understand if I leave you to your courage. I really have to reline my dresser drawers."

For the second time that day, Adam found himself alone with a dog and cat.

A half hour later, after he'd lost a staring match with Isabelle, Adam locked his door and contacted McIntyre. In the brief, concise tones that McIntyre had always admired, Adam relayed the conversation he'd overheard the night before.

"It fits," McIntyre stated. Adam could almost see him rubbing his hands together. "You've learned quite a bit in a short time. The check on Hiller reveals he's living on credit and reputation. Both are running thin. No idea where Fairchild's keeping it?"

"I'm surprised he doesn't have it hanging in full view." Adam lit a cigarette and frowned at the Titian across the room. "It would be just like him. He mentioned a Victor Alvarez from Brazil a couple of times. Some kind of deal he's cooking."

"I'll see what I can dig up. Maybe he's selling the Rembrandt."

"He hardly needs the money."

"Some people never have enough."

"Yeah." But it didn't fit. It just didn't fit. "I'll get back to you."

Adam brooded, but only for a few moments. The sooner he had something tangible, the sooner he could untangle himself. He opened the panel and went to work.

In the morning, Kirby posed for Adam for more than two hours without the slightest argument. If he thought her cooperation and her sunny disposition were designed to confuse him, he was absolutely right. She was also keeping him occupied while Fairchild made the final arrangements for the disposal of the Van Gogh.

Adam had worked the night before until after midnight, but had found nothing. Wherever Fairchild had hidden the Rembrandt, he'd hidden it well. Adam's search of the third floor was almost complete. It was time to look elsewhere.

"Hidden with respect and affection," he remembered. In all probability that would rule out the dungeons and the attic. Chances were he'd have to give them some time, but he intended to concentrate on the main portion of the house first. His main objective would be Fairchild's private rooms, but when and how he'd do them he had yet to determine.

After the painting session was over and Kirby went back to her own work, Adam wandered around the first floor. There was no one to question his presence. He was a guest and he was trusted. He was supposed to be, he reminded himself when he became uncomfortable. One of the reasons McIntyre had drafted him for this particular job was because he would have easy access to the Fairchilds and the house. He was, socially and professionally, one of them. They'd have no reason to be suspicious of a well-bred, successful artist whom they'd welcomed into their own home. And the more Adam tried to justify his actions, the more the guilt ate at him.

Enough, he told himself as he stared out at the darkening sky. He'd had enough for one day. It was time he went up and changed for Melanie Burgess's party. There he'd meet Stuart Hiller and Harriet Merrick. There were no emotional ties there to make him feel like a spy and a thief. Swearing at himself, he started up the stairs.

"Excuse me, Mr. Haines." Impatient, Adam turned and looked down at Tulip. "Were you going up?"

"Yes." Because he stood on the bottom landing blocking her way, he stood aside to let her pass.

"You take this up to her then, and see she drinks it." Tulip shoved a tall glass of milky white liquid into his hand. "All," she added tersely before she clomped back toward the kitchen.

Where did they get their servants? Adam wondered, frowning down at the glass in his hands. And why, for the love of God, had he let himself be ordered around by one? When in Rome, he supposed, and started up the steps again.

The *she* obviously meant Kirby. Adam sniffed doubtfully at the glass as he knocked on her door.

"You can bring it in," she called out, "but I won't drink it. Threaten all you like."

All right, he decided, and pushed her door open. The bedroom was empty, but he could smell her.

"Do your worst," she invited. "You can't intimidate me with stories of intestinal disorders and vitamin deficiencies. I'm healthy as a horse."

The warm, sultry scent flowed over him. Glass in hand, he walked through and into the bathroom where the steam rose up, fragrant and misty as a rain forest. With her hair pinned on top of her head, Kirby lounged in a huge sunken tub. Overhead, hanging plants dripped down, green and moist. White frothy bubbles floated in heaps on the surface of the water.

"So she sent you, did she?" Unconcerned, Kirby rubbed a loofah sponge over one shoulder. The bubbles, she concluded, covered her with more modesty than most women at the party that night would claim. "Well, come in then, and stop scowling at me. I won't ask you to scrub my back."

He thought of Cleopatra, floating on her barge. Just how many men other than Caesar and Antony had she driven mad? He glanced at the long mirrored wall behind the sink. It was fogged with the steam that rose in visible columns from her bath. "Got the water hot enough?"

"Do you know what that is?" she demanded, and plucked her soap from the dish. The cake was a pale, pale pink and left a creamy lather on her skin. "It's a filthy-tasting mixture Tulip tries to force on me periodically. It has raw eggs in it and other vile things." Making a face she lifted one surprisingly long leg out of the bath and soaped it. "Tell me the truth, Adam, would you voluntarily drink raw eggs?"

He watched her run soap and fingertips down her calf. "I can't say I would."

"Well, then." Satisfied, she switched legs. "Down the drain with it."

"She told me to see that you drank it. All," he added, beginning to enjoy himself.

Her lower lip moved forward a bit as she considered. "Puts you in an awkward position, doesn't it?"

"A position in any case."

"Tell you what, I'll have a sip. Then when she asks if I drank it I can say I did. I'm trying to cut down on my lying."

Adam handed her the glass, watching as she sipped and grimaced. "I'm not sure you're being truthful this way."

"I said cutting down, not eliminating. Into the sink," she added. "Unless you'd care for the rest."

"I'll pass." He poured it out then sat on the lip of the tub.

Surprised by the move, she tightened her fingers on the soap. It plopped into the water. "Hydrophobia," she muttered. "No, don't bother, I'll find it." Dipping her hand in, she began to search. "You'd think they could make a soap that wasn't forever leaping out of your hands." Grateful for the distraction, she gripped the soap again. "Aha. I appreciate your bringing me that revolting stuff, Adam. Now if you'd like to run along…"

"I'm in no hurry." Idly he picked up her loofah. "You mentioned something about scrubbing your back."

"Robbery!" Fairchild's voice boomed into the room just ahead of him. "Call the police. Call the FBI. Adam, you'll be a witness." He nodded, finding nothing odd in the audience to his daughter's bath.

"I'm so glad I have a large bathroom," she murmured. "Pity I didn't think to serve refreshments." Relieved by the interruption, she ran the soap down her arm. "What's been stolen, Papa? The Monet street scene, the Renoir portrait? I know, your sweat socks."

"My black dinner suit!" Dramatically he pointed a finger to the ceiling. "We'll have to take fingerprints."

"Obviously stolen by a psychotic with a fetish for formal attire," Kirby concluded. "I love a mystery. Let's list the suspects." She pushed a lock of hair out of her eyes and leaned back—a naked, erotic Sherlock Holmes. "Adam, have you an alibi?"

With a half smile, he ran the damp abrasive sponge through his hands. "I've been seducing Polly all afternoon."

Her eyes lit with amusement. She'd known he had potential. "That won't do," she said soberly. "It wouldn't take above fifteen minutes to seduce Polly. You have a black dinner suit, I suppose."

"Circumstantial evidence."

"A search warrant," Fairchild chimed in, inspired. "We'll get a search warrant and go through the entire house."

"Time-consuming," Kirby decided. "Actually, Papa, I think we'd best look to Cards."

"The butler did it." Fairchild cackled with glee, then immediately sobered. "No, no, my suit would never fit Cards."

"True. Still, as much as I hate to be an informer, I overheard Cards telling Tulip he intended to take your suit."

"Trust," Fairchild mumbled to Adam. "Can't trust anyone."

"His motive was sponging and pressing, I believe." She sank down to her neck and examined her toes. "He'll crumble like a wall if you accuse him. I'm sure of it."

"Very well." Fairchild rubbed his thin, clever hands together. "I'll handle it myself and avoid the publicity."

"A brave man," Kirby decided as her father strode out of the room. Relaxed and amused, she smiled at Adam. "Well, my bubbles seem to be melting, so we'd better continue this discussion some other time."

Reaching over, Adam yanked the chain and drew the old-fashioned plug out of the stupendous tub. "The time's coming when we're going to start—and finish— much more than a conversation."

Wary, Kirby watched her water level and last defense recede. When cornered, she determined, it was best to be nonchalant. She tried a smile that didn't quite conceal the nerves. "Let me know when you're ready."

"I intend to," he said softly. Without another word, he rose and left her alone.

Later, when he descended the stairs, Adam grinned when he heard her voice.

"Yes, Tulip, I drank the horrid stuff. I won't disgrace you by fainting in the Merrick living room from malnutrition." The low rumble of response that followed was dissatisfied. "Cricket wings, I've been walking in heels for half my life. They're not six inches, they're three. And I'll still have to look up at everyone over twelve. Go bake a cake, will you?"

He heard Tulip's mutter and sniff before she stomped out of the room and passed him.

"Adam, thank God. Let's go before she finds something else to nag me about."

Her dress was pure, unadorned white, thin and floaty. It covered her arms, rose high at the throat, as modest as a nun's habit, as sultry as a tropical night. Her hair fell, black and straight over the shoulders.

Tossing it back, she picked up a black cape and swirled it around her. For a moment she stood, adjusting it while the light from the lamps flitted over the absence of color. She looked like a Manet portrait— strong, romantic and timeless.

"You're a fabulous-looking creature, Kirby."

They both stopped, staring. He'd given compliments before, with more style, more finesse, but he'd never meant one more. She'd been flattered by princes, in foreign tongues and with smooth deliveries. It had never made her stomach flutter.

"Thank you," she managed. "So're you." No longer sure it was wise, she offered her hand. "Are you ready?"

"Yes. Your father?"

"He's already gone," she told him as she walked toward the door. And the sooner they were, the better. She needed a little more time before she was alone with him again. "We don't drive to parties together, especially to Harriet's. He likes to get there early and usually stays longer, trying to talk Harriet into bed. I've had my car brought around." She shut the door and led him to a silver Porsche. "I'd rather drive than navigate, if you don't mind."

But she didn't wait for his response as she dropped into the driver's seat. "Fine," Adam agreed.

"It's a marvelous night." She turned the key in the ignition. The power vibrated under their feet. "Full moon, lots of stars." Smoothly she released the brake, engaged the clutch and pressed the accelerator. Adam was tossed against the seat as they roared down the drive.

"You'll like Harriet," Kirby continued, switching gears as Adam stared at the blurring landscape. "She's like a mother to me." When they came to the main road, Kirby downshifted and swung to the left, tires squealing. "You met Melly, of course. I hope you won't desert me completely tonight after seeing her again."

Adam braced his feet against the floor. "Does anyone notice her when you're around?" And would they make it to the Merrick home alive?

"Of course." Surprised by the question, she turned to look at him.

"Good God, watch where you're going!" None too gently, he pushed her head around.

"Melly's the most perfectly beautiful woman I've ever known." Downshifting again, Kirby squealed around a right turn then accelerated. "She's a very clever designer and very, very proper. Wouldn't even take a settlement from her husband when they divorced. Pride, I suppose, but then she wouldn't need the money. There's a marvelous view of the Hudson coming up on your side, Adam." Kirby leaned over to point it out. The car swerved.

"I prefer seeing it from up here, thanks," Adam told her as he shoved her back in her seat. "Do you always drive this way?"

"Yes. There's the road you take to the gallery," she continued. She waved her hand vaguely as the car whizzed by an intersection. Adam glanced down at the speedometer.

"You're doing ninety."

"I always drive slower at night."

"There's good news." Muttering, he flicked on the lighter.

"There's the house up ahead." She raced around an ess curve. "Fabulous when it's all lit up this way."

The house was white and stately, the type you expected to see high above the riverbank. It glowed with elegance from dozens of windows. Without slackening pace, Kirby sped up the circular drive. With a squeal of brakes, and a muttered curse from Adam, she stopped the Porsche at the front entrance.

Reaching over, Adam pulled the keys from the ignition and pocketed them. "I'm driving back."

"How thoughtful." Offering her hand to the valet, Kirby stepped out. "Now I won't have to limit myself to one drink. Champagne," she decided, moving up the steps beside him. "It seems like a night for it."

The moment the door opened, Kirby was enveloped by a flurry of dazzling, trailing silks. "Harriet." Kirby squeezed the statuesque woman with flaming red hair. "It's wonderful to see you, but I think I'm being gnawed by the denture work of your crocodile."

"Sorry, darling." Harriet held her necklace and drew back to press a kiss to each of Kirby's cheeks. She was an impressive woman, full-bodied in the style Rubens had immortalized. Her face was wide and smooth, dominated by deep green eyes that glittered with silver on the lids. Harriet didn't believe in subtlety. "And this must be your houseguest," she continued with a quick sizing up of Adam.

"Harriet Merrick, Adam Haines." Kirby grinned and pinched Harriet's cheek. "And behave yourself, or Papa'll have him choosing weapons."

"Wonderful idea." With one arm still linked with Kirby's, Harriet twined her other through Adam's. "I'm sure you have a fascinating life story to tell me, Adam."

"I'll make one up."

"Perfect." She liked the look of him. "We've a crowd already, though they're mostly Melanie's stuffy friends."

"Harriet, you've got to be more tolerant."

"No, I don't." She tossed back her outrageous hair. "I've been excruciatingly polite. Now that you're here, I don't have to be."

"Kirby." Melanie swept into the hall in an ice-blue sheath. "What a picture you make. Take her cloak, Ellen, though it's a pity to spoil that effect." Smiling, she held out a hand to Adam as the maid slipped Kirby's cloak off her shoulders. "I'm so glad you came. We've some mutual acquaintances here, it seems. The Birminghams and Michael Towers from New York. You remember Michael, Kirby?"

"The adman who clicks his teeth?"

Harriet let out a roar of laughter while Adam struggled to control his. With a sigh, Melanie led them toward the party. "Try to behave, will you?" But Adam wasn't certain whether she spoke to Kirby or her mother.

This was the world he was used to—elegant people in elegant clothes having rational conversations. He'd been raised in the world of restrained wealth where champagne fizzed quietly and dignity was as essential as the proper alma mater. He understood it, he fit in.

After fifteen minutes, he was separated from Kirby and bored to death.

"I've decided to take a trek through the Australian bush," Harriet told Kirby. She fingered her necklace of crocodile teeth. "I'd love you to come with me. We'd have such fun brewing a billy cup over the fire."

"Camping?" Kirby asked, mulling it over. Maybe what she needed was a change of scene, after her father settled down.

"Give it some thought," Harriet suggested. "I'm not planning on leaving for another six weeks. Ah, Adam." Reaching out, she grabbed his arm. "Did Agnes Birmingham drive you to drink? No, don't answer. It's written all over your face, but you're much too polite."

He allowed himself to be drawn between her and Kirby, where he wanted to be. "Let's just say I was looking for more stimulating conversation. I've found it."

"Charming." She decided she liked him, but would reserve judgment a bit longer as to whether he'd suit her Kirby. "I admire your work, Adam. I'd like to put the first bid in on your next painting."

He took glasses from a passing waiter. "I'm doing a portrait of Kirby."

"She's posing for you?" Harriet nearly choked on her champagne. "Did you chain her?"

"Not yet." He gave Kirby a lazy glance. "It's still a possibility."

"You have to let me display it when it's finished." She might've been a woman who ran on emotion on many levels, but the bottom line was art, and the business of it. "I can promise to cause a nasty scene if you refuse."

"No one does it better," Kirby toasted her.

"You'll have to see the portrait of Kirby that Philip painted for me. She wouldn't sit for it, but it's brilliant." She toyed with the stem of her glass. "He painted it when she returned from Paris—three years ago, I suppose."

"I'd like to see it. I'd planned on coming by the gallery."

"Oh, it's here, in the library."

"Why don't you two just toddle along then?" Kirby suggested. "You've been talking around me, you might as well desert me physically, as well."

"Don't be snotty," Harriet told her. "You can come, too. And I… Well, well," she murmured in a voice suddenly lacking in warmth. "Some people have no sense of propriety."

Kirby turned her head, just slightly, and watched Stuart walk into the room. Her fingers tightened on the glass, but she shrugged. Before the movement was complete, Melanie was at her side.

"I'm sorry, Kirby. I'd hoped he wouldn't come after all."

In a slow, somehow insolent gesture, Kirby pushed her hair behind her back. "If it had mattered, I wouldn't have come."

"I don't want you to be embarrassed," Melanie began, only to be cut off by a quick and very genuine laugh.

"When have you ever known me to be embarrassed?"

"Well, I'll greet him, or it'll make matters worse." Still, Melanie hesitated, obviously torn between loyalty and manners.

"I'll fire him, of course," Harriet mused when her daughter went to do her duty. "But I want to be subtle about it."

"Fire him if you like, Harriet, but not on my account." Kirby drained her champagne.

"It appears we're in for a show, Adam." Harriet tapped a coral fingertip against her glass. "Much to Melanie's distress, Stuart's coming over."

Without saying a word, Kirby took Adam's cigarette.

"Harriet, you look marvelous." The smooth, cultured voice wasn't at all like the tone Adam had heard in Fairchild's studio. "Africa agreed with you."

Harriet gave him a bland smile. "We didn't expect to see you."

"I was tied up for a bit." Charming, elegant, he turned to Kirby. "You're looking lovely."

"So are you," she said evenly. "It seems your nose is back in joint." Without missing a beat, she turned to Adam. "I don't believe you've met. Adam, this is Stuart Hiller. I'm sure you know Adam Haines's work, Stuart."

"Yes, indeed." The handshake was polite and meaningless. "Are you staying in our part of New York long?"

"Until I finish Kirby's portrait," Adam told him and had the dual satisfaction of seeing Kirby grin and Stuart frown. "I've agreed to let Harriet display it in the gallery."

With that simple strategy, Adam won Harriet over.

"I'm sure it'll be a tremendous addition to our collection." Even a man with little sensitivity wouldn't have missed the waves of resentment. For the moment, Stuart ignored them. "I wasn't able to reach you in Africa, Harriet, and things have been hectic since your return. The Titian woman has been sold to Ernest Myerling."

As he lifted his glass, Adam's attention focused on Kirby. Her color drained, slowly, degree by degree until her face was as white as the silk she wore.

"I don't recall discussing selling the Titian," Harriet countered. Her voice was as colorless as Kirby's skin.

"As I said, I couldn't reach you. As the Titian isn't listed under your personal collection, it falls among the saleable paintings. I think you'll be pleased with the price." He lit a cigarette with a slim silver lighter. "Myerling did insist on having it tested. He's more interested in investment than art, I'm afraid. I thought you'd want to be there tomorrow for the procedure."

Oh, God, oh, my God! Panic, very real and very strong, whirled through Kirby's mind. In silence, Adam watched the fear grow in her eyes.

"Tested!" Obviously insulted, Harriet seethed. "Of all the gall, doubting the authenticity of a painting from my gallery. The Titian should not have been sold without my permission, and certainly not to a peasant."

"Testing isn't unheard-of, Harriet." Seeing a hefty commission wavering, Stuart soothed, "Myerling's a businessman, not an art expert. He wants facts." Taking a long drag, he blew out smoke. "In any case, the paperwork's already completed and there's nothing to be done about it. The deal's a fait accompli, hinging on the test results."

"We'll discuss this in the morning." Harriet's voice lowered as she finished off her drink. "This isn't the time or place."

"I—I have to freshen my drink," Kirby said suddenly. Without another word, she spun away to work her way through the crowd. The nausea, she realized, was a direct result of panic, and the panic was a long way from over. "Papa." She latched on to his arm and pulled him out of a discussion on Dali's versatility. "I have to talk to you. Now."

Hearing the edge in her voice, he let her drag him from the room.

Chapter 7

Kirby closed the doors of Harriet's library behind her and leaned back against them. She didn't waste any time. "The Titian's being tested in the morning. Stuart sold it."

"Sold it!" Fairchild's eyes grew wide, his face pink. "Impossible. Harriet wouldn't sell the Titian."

"She didn't. She was off playing with lions, remember?" Dragging both hands through her hair, she tried to speak calmly. "Stuart closed the deal, he just told her."

"I told you he was a fool, didn't I? Didn't I?" Fairchild repeated as he started dancing in place. "I told Harriet, too. Would anyone listen? No, not Harriet." He whirled around, plucked up a pencil from her desk and broke it in two. "She hires the idiot anyway and goes off to roam the jungle."

"There's no use going over that again!" Kirby snapped at him. "We've got to deal with the results."

"There wouldn't be any results if I'd been listened to. Stubborn woman falling for a pretty face. That's all it was." Pausing, he took a deep breath and folded his hands. "Well," he said in a mild voice, "this is a problem."

"Papa, this isn't an error in your checkbook."

"But it can be handled, probably with less effort. Any way out of the deal?"

"Stuart said the paperwork had been finalized. And it's Myerling," she added.

"That old pirate." He scowled a moment and gave Harriet's desk a quick kick. "No way out of it," Fairchild concluded. "On to the next step. We exchange them." He saw by Kirby's nod that she'd already thought of it. There was a quick flash of pride before anger set in. The round, cherubic face tightened. "By God, Stuart's going to pay for making me give up that painting."

"Very easily said, Papa." Kirby walked into the room until she stood toe to toe with him. "But who was it who settled Adam in the same room with the painting? Now we're going to have to get it out of his room, then get the copy from the gallery in without him knowing there's been a switch. I'm sure you've noticed Adam's not a fool."

Fairchild's eyebrows wiggled. His lips curved. He rubbed his palms together. "A plan."

Knowing it was too late for regrets, Kirby flopped into a chair. "We'll phone Cards and have him put the painting in my room before we get back."

He approved this with a brief nod. "You have a marvelous criminal mind, Kirby."

She had to smile. A sense of adventure was already spearing through the panic. "Heredity," she told her father. "Now, here's my idea...." Lowering her voice, she began the outline.

"It'll work," Fairchild decided a few moments later.

"That has yet to be seen." It sounded plausible enough, but she didn't underestimate Adam Haines. "So there's nothing to be done but to do it."

"And do it well."

Her agreement was a careless shrug of her shoulders. "Adam should be too tired to notice that the Titian's gone, and after I make the exchange at the gallery, I'll slip it back into his room. Sleeping pills are the only way." She stared down at her hands, dissatisfied, but knowing it was the only way out. "I don't like doing this to Adam."

"He'll just get a good night's sleep." Fairchild sat on the arm of her chair. "We all need a good night's sleep now and again. Now we'd better go back or Melanie'll send out search parties."

"You go first." Kirby let out a deep breath. "I'll phone Cards and tell him to get started."

Kirby waited until Fairchild had closed the doors again before she went to the phone on Harriet's desk. She didn't mind the job she had to do, in fact she looked forward to it. Except for Adam's part. It couldn't be helped, she reminded herself, and gave Cards brief instructions.

Now, she thought as she replaced the receiver, it was too late to turn back. The die, so to speak, had been cast. The truth was, the hastily made plans for the evening would prove a great deal more interesting than a party.

While she hesitated a moment longer, Stuart opened the door, then closed it softly behind him.

"Kirby." He crossed to her with a half smile on his face. His patience had paid off now that he'd found her alone. "We have to talk."

Not now, she thought on a moment's panic. Didn't she have enough to deal with? Then she thought of the way he'd humiliated her. The way he'd lied. Perhaps it was better to get everything over with at once.

"I think we said everything we had to say at our last meeting."

"Not nearly everything."

"Redundancy bores me," she said mildly. "But if you insist, I'll say this. It's a pity you haven't the money to suit your looks. Your mistake, Stuart, was in not making me want you—not the way you wanted me." Deliberately her voice dropped, low and seductive. She hadn't nearly finished paying him back. "You could deceive me about love, but not about lust. If you'd concentrated on that instead of greed, you might've had a chance. You are," she continued softly, "a liar and a cheat, and while that might've been an interesting diversion for a short time, I thank God you never got your hands on me or my money."

Before she could sweep around him, he grabbed her arm. "You'd better remember your father's habits before you sling mud."

She dropped her gaze to his hand, then slowly raised it again. It was a look designed to infuriate. "Do you honestly compare yourself with my father?" Her fury came out on a laugh, and the laugh was insult itself. "You'll never have his style, Stuart. You're second-rate, and you'll always be second-rate."

He brought the back of his hand across her face hard enough to make her stagger. She didn't make a sound. When she stared up at him, her eyes were slits, very dark, very dangerous slits. The pain meant nothing, only that he'd caused it and she had no way to pay him back in kind. Yet.

"You prove my point," Kirby said evenly as she brushed her fingers over her cheek. "Second-rate."

He wanted to hit her again, but balled his hands into fists. He needed her, for the moment. "I'm through playing games, Kirby. I want the Rembrandt."

"I'd take a knife to it before I saw Papa hand it over to you. You're out of your class, Stuart." She didn't bother to struggle when he grabbed her arms.

"Two days, Kirby. You tell the old man he has two days or it's you who'll pay."

"Threats and physical abuse are your only weapons." Abruptly, with more effort than she allowed him to see, Kirby turned her anger to ice. "I've weapons of my own, Stuart, infinitely more effective. And if I chose to drop to gutter tactics, you haven't the finesse to deal with me." She kept her eyes on his, her body still. He might curse her, but Stuart knew the truth when he heard it. "You're a snake," she added quietly. "And you can't stay off your belly for long. The fact that you're stronger than I is only a temporary advantage."

"Very temporary," Adam said as he closed the door at his back. His voice matched Kirby's chill for chill. "Take your hands off her."

Kirby felt the painful grip on her arms relax and watched Stuart struggle with composure. Carefully he straightened his tie. "Remember what I said, Kirby. It could be important to you."

"You remember how Byron described a woman's revenge," she countered as she rubbed the circulation back into her arms. "'Like a tiger's spring—deadly, quick and crushing.'" She dropped her arms to her sides. "It could be important to you." Turning, she walked to the window and stared out at nothing.

Adam kept his hand on the knob as Stuart walked to the door. "Touch her again and you'll have to deal with me." Slowly Adam turned the knob and opened the door. "That's something else for you to remember." The sounds of the party flowed in, then silenced again as he shut the door at Stuart's back.

"Well," he began, struggling with his own fury. "I guess I should be grateful I don't have an ex-fiancée hanging around." He'd heard enough to know that the Rembrandt had been at the bottom of it, but he pushed that aside and went to her. "He's a poor loser, and you're amazing. Most women would have been weeping or pleading. You stood there flinging insults."

"I don't believe in pleading," she said as lightly as she could. "And Stuart would never reduce me to tears."

"But you're trembling," he murmured as he put his hands on her shoulders.

"Anger." She drew in a deep breath and let it out slowly. She didn't care to show a weakness, not to anyone. "I appreciate the white-knight routine."

He grinned and kissed the top of her head. "Any time. Why don't we…" He trailed off as he turned her to face him. The mark of Stuart's hand had faded to a dull, angry red, but it was unmistakable. When Adam touched his fingers to her cheek, his eyes were cold. Colder and more dangerous than she'd ever seen them. Without a word, he spun around and headed for the door.

"No!" Desperation wasn't characteristic, but she felt it now as she grabbed his arm. "No, Adam, don't. Don't get involved." He shook her off, but she sprinted to the door ahead of him and stood with her back pressed against it. The tears she'd been able to control with Stuart now swam in her eyes. "Please, I've enough on my conscience without dragging you into this. I live my life as I choose, and what I get from it is of my own making."

He wanted to brush her aside and push through the crowd outside the door until he had his hands on Stuart. He wanted, more than he'd ever wanted anything, the pleasure of smelling the other man's blood. But she was standing in front of him, small and delicate, with tears in her eyes. She wasn't the kind of woman tears came easily to.

"All right." He brushed one from her cheek and made a promise on it. Before it was over, he would indeed smell Stuart Hiller's blood. "You're only postponing the inevitable."

Relieved, she closed her eyes a moment. When she opened them again, they were still damp, but no longer desperate. "I don't believe in the inevitable." She took his hand and brought it to her cheek, holding it there a moment until she felt the tension drain from both of them. "You must've come in to see my portrait. It's there, above the desk."

She gestured, but he didn't take his eyes from hers. "I'll have to give it a thorough study, right after I give my attention to the original." He gathered her close and just held her. It was, though neither one of them had known it, the perfect gesture of support. Resting her head against his shoulder, she thought of peace, and she thought of the plans that had already been put into motion.

"I'm sorry, Adam."

He heard the regret in her voice and brushed his lips over her hair. "What for?"

"I can't tell you." She tightened her arms around his waist and clung to him as she had never clung to anyone. "But I am sorry."

The drive away from the Merrick estate was more sedate than the approach. Kirby sat in the passenger seat. Under most circumstances, Adam would've attributed her silence and unease to her scene with Hiller. But he remembered her reaction at the mention of the sale of a Titian.

What was going on in that kaleidoscope brain of hers? he wondered. And how was he going to find out? The direct approach, Adam decided, and thought fleetingly that it was a shame to waste the moonlight. "The Titian that's been sold," he began, pretending he didn't see Kirby jolt. "Has Harriet had it long?"

"The Titian." She folded her hands in her lap. "Oh, years and years. Your Mrs. Birmingham's shaped like a zucchini, don't you think?"

"She's not my Mrs. Birmingham." A new game, he concluded, and relaxed against the seat. "It's too bad it was sold before I could see it. I'm a great admirer of Titian. The painting in my room's exquisite."

Kirby let out a sound that might have been a nervous giggle. "The one at the gallery is just as exquisite," she told him. "Ah, here we are, home again. Just leave the car out front," she said, half relieved, half annoyed, that the next steps were being put into play. "Cards will see to it. I hope you don't mind coming back early, Adam. There's Papa," she added as she stepped from the car. "He must've struck out with Harriet. Let's have a nightcap, shall we?"

She started up the steps without waiting for his agreement. Knowing he was about to become a part of some hastily conceived plan, he went along. It's all too pat, he mused as Fairchild waited at the door with a genial smile.

"Too many people," Fairchild announced. "I much prefer small parties. Let's have a drink in the parlor and gossip."

Don't look so bloody anxious, Kirby thought, and nearly scowled at him. "I'll go tell Cards to see to the Rolls and my car." Still, she hesitated as the men walked toward the parlor. Adam caught the indecision in her eyes before Fairchild cackled and slapped him on the back.

"And don't hurry back," he told Kirby. "I've had enough of women for a while."

"How sweet." The irony and strength came back into her voice. "I'll just go in and eat Tulip's lemon trifle. All," she added as she swept past.

Fairchild thought of his midnight snack with regret. "Brat," he muttered. "Well, we'll have Scotch instead."

Adam dipped his hands casually in his pockets and watched every move Fairchild made. "I had a chance to see Kirby's portrait in Harriet's library. It's marvelous."

"One of my best, if I say so myself." Fairchild lifted the decanter of Chivas Regal. "Harriet's fond of my brat, you know." In a deft move, Fairchild slipped two pills from his pocket and dropped them into the Scotch.

Under normal circumstances Adam would've missed it. Clever hands, he thought as intrigued as he was amused. Very quick, very agile. Apparently they wanted him out of the way. He was going to find it a challenge to pit himself against both of them. With a smile, he accepted the drink, then turned to the Corot landscape behind him.

"Corot's treatment of light," Adam began, taking a small sip. "It gives all of his work such deep perspective."

No ploy could've worked better. Fairchild was ready to roll. "I'm very partial to Corot. He had such a fine hand with details without being finicky and obscuring the overall painting. Now the leaves," he began, and set down his drink to point them out. While the lecture went on, Adam set down his own drink, picked up Fairchild's and enjoyed the Scotch.

Upstairs Kirby found the Titian already wrapped in heavy paper. "Bless you, Cards," she murmured. She checked her watch and made herself wait a full ten minutes before she picked up the painting and left the room. Quietly she moved down the back stairs and out to where her car waited.

In the parlor, Adam studied Fairchild as he sat in the corner of the sofa, snoring. Deciding the least he could do was to make his host more comfortable, Adam started to swing Fairchild's legs onto the couch. The sound of a car engine stopped him. Adam was at the window in time to see Kirby's Porsche race down the drive.

"You're going to have company," he promised her. Within moments, he was behind the wheel of the Rolls.

The surge of speed added to Kirby's sense of adventure. She drove instinctively while she concentrated on her task for the evening. It helped ease the guilt over Adam, a bit.

A quarter mile from the gallery, she stopped and parked on the side of the road. Grateful that the Titian was relatively small, though the frame added weight, she gathered it up again and began to walk. Her heels echoed on the asphalt.

Clouds drifted across the moon, obscuring the light then freeing it again. With her cape swirling around her, Kirby walked into the cover of trees that bordered the gallery. The light was dim, all shadows and secrets. Up ahead came the low moan of an owl. Tossing back her hair, she laughed.

"Perfect," she decided. "All we need is a rumble of thunder and a few streaks of lightning. Skulking through the woods on a desperate mission," she mused. "Surrounded by the sounds of night." She shifted the bundle in her arms and continued on. "What one does for those one loves."

She could see the stately red brick of the gallery through the trees. Moonlight slanted over it. Almost there, she thought with a quick glance at her watch. In an hour she'd be back home—and perhaps she'd have the lemon trifle after all.

A hand fell heavily on her shoulder. Her cape spread out like wings as she whirled. Great buckets of blood, she thought as she stared up at Adam.

"Out for a stroll?" he asked her.

"Why, hello, Adam." Since she couldn't disappear,

she had to face him down. She tried a friendly smile. "What are you doing out here?"

"Following you."

"Flattering. But wasn't Papa entertaining you?"

"He dozed off."

She stared up at him a moment, then let out a breath. A wry smile followed it. "I suppose he deserved it. I hope you left him comfortable."

"Enough. Now what's in the package?"

Though she knew it was useless, she fluttered her lashes. "Package?"

He tapped his finger on the wrapping.

"Oh, this package. Just a little errand I have to run. It's getting late, shouldn't you be starting back?"

"Not a chance."

"No." She moved her shoulders. "I thought not."

"What's in the package, Kirby, and what do you intend to do with it?"

"All right." She thrust the painting into his arms because hers were tiring. When the jig was up, you had to make the best of it. "I suppose you deserve an explanation, and you won't leave until you have one anyway. It has to be the condensed version, Adam, I'm running behind schedule." She laid a hand on the package he held. "This is the Titian woman, and I'm going to put it in the gallery."

He lifted a brow. He didn't need Kirby to tell him that he held a painting. "I was under the impression that the Titian woman was in the gallery."

"No…" She drew out the word. If she could have thought of a lie, a half-truth, a fable, she'd have used it. She could only think of the truth. "This is a Titian," she told him with a nod to the package. "The painting in the gallery is a Fairchild."

He let the silence hang a moment while the moonlight filtered over her face. She looked like an angel… or a witch. "Your father forged a Titian and palmed it off on the gallery as an original?"

"Certainly not!" Indignation wasn't feigned. Kirby bit back on it and tried to be patient. "I won't tell you any more if you insult my father."

"I don't know what came over me."

"All right then." She leaned back against a tree. "Perhaps I should start at the beginning."

"Good choice."

"Years ago, Papa and Harriet were vacationing in Europe. They came across the Titian, each one swearing they'd seen it first. Neither one would give way, and it would've been criminal to let the painting go altogether. They compromised." She gestured at the package. "Each paid half, and Papa painted a copy. They rotate ownership of the original every six months, alternating with the copy, if you get the drift. The stipulation was that neither of them could claim ownership. Harriet kept hers in the gallery—not listing it as part of her private collection. Papa kept it in a guest room."

He considered for a moment. "That's too ridiculous for you to have made up."

"Of course I didn't make it up." As it could, effectively, her bottom lip pouted. "Don't you trust me?"

"No. You're going to do a lot more explaining when we get back."

Perhaps, Kirby thought. And perhaps not.

"Now just how do you intend to get into the gallery?"

"With Harriet's keys."

"She gave you her keys?"

Kirby let out a frustrated breath. "Pay attention, Adam. Harriet's furious about Stuart selling the painting, but until she studies the contracts there's no way to know how binding the sale is. It doesn't look good, and we can't take a chance on having the painting tested— my father's painting, that is. If the procedure were sophisticated enough, it might prove that the painting's not sixteenth-century."

"Harriet's aware that a forgery's hanging in her gallery?"

"An emulation, Adam."

"And are there any other...emulations in the Merrick Gallery?"

She gave him a long, cool look. "I'm trying not to be annoyed. All of Harriet's paintings are authentic, as is her half of the Titian."

"Why didn't she replace it herself?"

"Because," Kirby began and checked her watch. Time was slipping away from her. "Not only would it have been difficult for her to disappear from the party early as we did, but it would've been awkward altogether. The night watchman could report to Stuart that she came to the gallery in the middle of the night carrying a package. He might put two and two together. Yes, even he might add it up."

"So what'll the night watchman have to say about Kirby Fairchild coming into the gallery in the middle of the night?"

"He won't see us." Her smile was quick and very, very smug.

"Us?"

"Since you're here." She smiled at him again, and

meant it. "I've told you everything, and being a gentleman you'll help me make the switch. We'll have to work quickly. If we're caught, we'll just brazen it out. You won't have to do anything, I'll handle it."

"You'll handle it." He nodded at the drifting clouds. "We can all sleep easy now. One condition." He stopped her before she could speak. "When we're done, if we're not in jail or hospitalized, I want to know it all. If we are in jail, I'll murder you as slowly as possible."

"That's two conditions," she muttered. "But all right."

They watched each other a moment, one wondering how much would have to be divulged, one wondering how much could be learned. Both found the deceit unpleasant.

"Let's get it done." Adam gestured for her to go first.

Kirby walked across the grass and went directly to the main door. From the deep pocket of her cloak, she drew out keys.

"These two switch off the main alarm," she explained as she turned keys in a series of locks. "And these unbolt the door." She smiled at the faint click of tumblers. Turning, she studied Adam, standing behind her in his elegant dinner suit. "I'm so glad we dressed for it."

"Seems right to dress formally when you're breaking into a distinguished institution."

"True." Kirby dropped the keys back in her pocket. "And we do make a rather stunning couple. The Titian hangs in the west room on the second floor. The watchman has a little room in the back, here on the main floor. I assume he drinks black coffee laced with rum and reads pornographic magazines. I would. He's supposed to make rounds hourly, though there's no way to be certain he's diligent."

"And what time does he make them, if he does?"

"On the hour—which gives us twenty minutes." She glanced at her watch and shrugged. "That's adequate, though if you hadn't pressed for details we'd've had more time. Don't scowl," she added. She pressed her finger to her lips and slipped through the door.

From out of the depths of her pocket came a flashlight. They followed the narrow beam over the carpet. Together they moved up the staircase.

Obviously she knew the gallery well. Without hesitation, she moved through the dark, turning on the second floor and marching down the corridor without breaking rhythm. Her cape swirled out as she pivoted into a room. In silence she played her light over paintings until it stopped on the copy of the Titian that had hung in Adam's room.

"There," Kirby whispered as the light shone on the sunset hair Titian had immortalized. The light was too poor for Adam to be certain of the quality, but he promised himself he'd examine it minutes later.

"It's not possible to tell them apart—not even an expert." She knew what he was thinking. "Harriet's a respected authority, and she couldn't. I'm not sure the tests wouldn't bear it out as authentic. Papa has a way of treating the paints." She moved closer so that her light illuminated the entire painting. "Papa put a red circle on the back of the copy's frame so they could be told apart. I'll take the package now," she told him briskly. "You can get the painting down." She knelt and began to unwrap the painting they'd brought with them. "I'm glad you happened along," she decided. "Your height's going to be an advantage when it comes to taking down and putting up again."

Adam paused with the forgery in his hands. Throttling her would be too noisy at the moment, he decided. But later… "Let's have it then."

In silence they exchanged paintings. Adam replaced his on the wall, while Kirby wrapped the other. After she'd tied the string, she played the light on the wall again. "It's a bit crooked," she decided. "A little to the left."

"Look, I—" Adam broke off at the sound of a faint, tuneless whistle.

"He's early!" Kirby whispered as she gripped the painting. "Who expects efficiency from hired help these days?"

In a quick move, Adam had the woman, the painting and himself pressed against the wall by the archway. Finding herself neatly sandwiched, and partially smothered, Kirby held back a desperate urge to giggle. Certain it would annoy Adam, she held her breath and swallowed.

The whistle grew louder.

In her mind's eye, Kirby pictured the watchman strolling down the corridor, pausing to shine his light here and there as he walked. She hoped, for the watchman's peace of mind and Adam's disposition, the search was cursory.

Adam felt her trembling and held her tighter. Somehow he'd manage to protect her. He forgot that she'd gotten him into the mess in the first place. Now his only thought was to get her out of it.

A beam of light streamed past the doorway, with the whistle close behind. Kirby shook like a leaf. The light bounced into the room, sweeping over the walls in a curving arch. Adam tensed, knowing discovery was inches away. The light halted, rested a moment, then streaked away over its original route. And there was darkness.

They didn't move, though Kirby wanted to badly, with the frame digging into her back. They waited, still and silent, until the whistling receded.

Because her light trembling had become shudder after shudder, Adam drew her away to whisper reassurance. "It's all right. He's gone."

"You were wonderful." She covered her mouth to muffle the laughter. "Ever thought about making breaking and entering a hobby?"

He slid the painting under one arm, then took a firm grip on hers. When the time was right, he'd pay her back for this one. "Let's go."

"Okay, since it's probably a bad time to show you around. Pity," she decided. "There are some excellent engravings in the next room, and a really marvelous still life Papa painted."

"Under his own name?"

"Really, Adam." They paused at the hallway to make certain it was clear. "That's tacky."

They didn't speak again until they were hidden by the trees. Then Adam turned to her. "I'll take the painting and follow you back. If you go over fifty, I'll murder you."

She stopped when they reached the cars, then threw him off balance with suddenly serious eyes. "I appreciate everything, Adam. I hope you don't think too badly of us. It matters."

He ran a finger down her cheek. "I've yet to decide what I think of you."

Her lips curved up at the corners. "That's all right then. Take your time."

"Get in and drive," he ordered before he could forget what had to be resolved. She had a way of making a man forget a lot of things. Too many things.

The trip back took nearly twice the time, as Kirby stayed well below the speed limit. Again she left the Porsche out front, knowing Cards would handle the details. Once inside, she went straight to the parlor.

"Well," she mused as she looked at her father. "He seems comfortable enough, but I think I'll just stretch him out."

Adam leaned against the doorjamb and waited as she settled her father for the night. After loosening his tie and pulling off his shoes, she tossed her cape over him and kissed his balding head. "Papa," she murmured. "You've been outmaneuvered."

"We'll talk upstairs, Kirby. Now."

Straightening, Kirby gave Adam a long, mild look. "Since you ask so nicely." She plucked a decanter of brandy and two glasses from the bar. "We may as well be sociable during the inquisition." She swept by him and up the stairs.

Chapter 8

Kirby switched on the rose-tinted bedside lamp before she poured brandy. After handing Adam a snifter, she kicked off her shoes and sat cross-legged on the bed. She watched as he ripped off the wrapping and examined the painting.

Frowning, he studied the brush strokes, the use of color, the Venetian technique that had been Titian's. Fascinating, he thought. Absolutely fascinating. "This is a copy?"

She had to smile. She warmed the brandy between her hands but didn't drink. "Papa's mark's on the frame."

Adam saw the red circle but didn't find it conclusive. "I'd swear it was authentic."

"So would anyone."

He propped the painting against the wall and turned

to her. She looked like an Indian priestess—the night-fall of hair against the virgin white silk. With an enigmatic smile, she continued to sit in the lotus position, the brandy cupped in both hands.

"How many other paintings in your father's collection are copies?"

Slowly she lifted the snifter and sipped. She had to work at not being annoyed by the question, telling herself he was entitled to ask. "All of the paintings in Papa's collection are authentic. Excepting now this Titian." She moved her shoulders carelessly. It hardly mattered at this point.

"When you spoke of his technique in treating paints for age, you didn't give the impression he'd only used it on one painting."

What had given her the idea he wouldn't catch on to a chance remark like that one? she wondered. The fat's in the fire in any case, she reminded herself. And she was tired of trying to dance around it. She swirled her drink and red and amber lights glinted against the glass.

"I trust you," she murmured, surprising them both. "But I don't want to involve you, Adam, in something you'll regret knowing about. I really want you to understand that. Once I tell you, it'll be too late for regrets."

He didn't care for the surge of guilt. Who was deceiving whom now? his conscience demanded of him. And who'd pay the price in the end? "Let me worry about that," he stated, dealing with Kirby now and saving his conscience for later. He swallowed brandy and let the heat ease through him. "How many copies has your father done?"

"Ten—no, eleven," she corrected, and ignored his

quick oath. "Eleven, not counting the Titian, which falls into a different category."

"A different category," he murmured. Crossing the room, he splashed more brandy into his glass. He was certain to need it. "How is this different?"

"The Titian was a personal agreement between Harriet and Papa. Merely a way to avoid bad feelings."

"And the others?" He sat on a fussily elegant Queen Anne chair. "What sort of arrangements did they entail?"

"Each is individual, naturally." She hesitated as she studied him. If they'd met a month from now, would things have been different? Perhaps. Timing again, she mused and sipped the warming brandy. "To simplify matters, Papa painted them, then sold them to interested parties."

"Sold them?" He stood because he couldn't be still. Wishing it had been possible to stop her before she'd begun, he started to pace the room. "Good God, Kirby. Don't you understand what he's done? What he's doing? It's fraud, plain and simple."

"I wouldn't call it fraud," she countered, giving her brandy a contemplative study. It was, after all, something she'd given a great deal of thought to. "And certainly not plain or simple."

"What then?" If he'd had a choice, he'd have taken her away then and there—left the Titian, the Rembrandt and her crazy father in the ridiculous castle and taken off. Somewhere. Anywhere.

"Fudging," Kirby decided with a half smile.

"Fudging," he repeated in a quiet voice. He'd forgotten she was mad as well. "Fudging. Selling counterfeit paintings for large sums of money to the unsuspecting is fudging? Fixing a parking ticket's fudging." He paced another moment, looking for answers. "Damn it, his work's worth a fortune. Why does he do it?"

"Because he can," she said simply. She spread one hand, palm out. "Papa's a genius, Adam. I don't say that just as his daughter, but as a fellow artist. With the genius comes a bit of eccentricity, perhaps." Ignoring the sharp sound of derision, she went on. "To Papa, painting's not just a vocation. Art and life are one, interchangeable."

"I'll go along with all that, Kirby, but it doesn't explain why—"

"Let me finish." She had both hands on the snifter again, resting it in her lap. "One thing Papa can't tolerate is greed, in any form. To him greed isn't just the worship of money, but the hoarding of art. You must know his collection's constantly being lent out to museums and art schools. Though he has strong feelings that art belongs in the private sector, as well as public institutions, he hates the idea of the wealthy buying up great art for investment purposes."

"Admirable, Kirby. But he's made a business out of selling fraudulent paintings."

"Not a business. He's never benefited financially." She set her glass aside and clasped her hands together. "Each prospective buyer of one of Papa's emulations is first researched thoroughly." She waited a beat. "By Harriet."

He nearly sat back down again. "Harriet Merrick's in on all of this?"

"All of this," she said mildly, "has been their joint hobby for the last fifteen years."

"Hobby," he murmured and did sit.

"Harriet has very good connections, you see. She makes certain the buyer is very wealthy and that he or she lives in a remote location. Two years ago, Papa sold an Arabian sheik a fabulous Renoir. It was one of my favorites. Anyway—" she continued, getting up to freshen Adam's drink, then her own "—each buyer would also be known for his or her attachment to money, and/or a complete lack of any sense of community spirit or obligation. Through Harriet, they'd learn of Papa's ownership of a rare, officially undiscovered artwork."

Taking her own snifter, she returned to her position on the bed while Adam remained silent. "At the first contact, Papa is always uncooperative without being completely dismissive. Gradually he allows himself to be worn down until the deal's made. The price, naturally, is exorbitant, otherwise the art fanciers would be insulted." She took a small sip and enjoyed the warm flow of the brandy. "He deals only in cash, so there's no record. Then the paintings float off to the Himalayas or Siberia or somewhere to be kept in seclusion. Papa then donates the money anonymously to charity."

Taking a deep breath at the end of her speech, Kirby rewarded herself with more brandy.

"You're telling me that he goes through all that, all the work, all the intrigue, for nothing?"

"I certainly am not." Kirby shook her head and leaned forward. "He gets a great deal. He gets satisfaction, Adam. What else is necessary after all?"

He struggled to remember the code of right and wrong. "Kirby, he's stealing!"

Kirby tilted her head and considered. "Who caught your support and admiration, Adam? The Sheriff of Nottingham or Robin Hood?"

"It's not the same." He dragged a hand through his hair as he tried to convince them both. "Damn it, Kirby, it's not the same."

"There's a newly modernized pediatric wing at the local hospital," she began quietly. "A little town in Appalachia has a new fire engine and modern equipment. Another, in the dust bowl, has a wonderful new library."

"All right." He rose again to cut her off. "In fifteen years I'm sure there's quite a list. Maybe in some strange way it's commendable, but it's also illegal, Kirby. It has to stop."

"I know." Her simple agreement broke his rhythm. With a half smile, Kirby moved her shoulders. "It was fun while it lasted, but I've known for some time it had to stop before something went wrong. Papa has a project in mind for a series of paintings, and I've convinced him to begin soon. It should take him about five years and give us a breathing space. But in the meantime, he's done something I don't know how to cope with."

She was about to give him more. Even before she spoke, Adam knew Kirby was going to give him all her trust. He sat in silence, despising himself, as she told him everything she knew about the Rembrandt.

"I imagine part of it's revenge on Stuart," she continued, while Adam smoked in silence and she again swirled her brandy without drinking. "Somehow Stuart found out about Papa's hobby and threatened exposure the night I broke our engagement. Papa told me not to worry, that Stuart wasn't in a position to make waves. At the time I had no idea about the Rembrandt business."

She was opening up to him, no questions, no hesitation. He was going to probe, God help him, he hadn't a choice. "Do you have any idea where he might've hidden it?"

"No, but I haven't looked." When she looked at him, she wasn't the sultry gypsy or the exotic princess. She was only a daughter concerned about an adored father. "He's a good man, Adam. No one knows that better than I. I know there's a reason for what he's done, and for the time being, I have to accept that. I don't expect you to share my loyalty, just my confidence." He didn't speak, and she took his silence for agreement. "My main concern now is that Papa's underestimating Stuart's ruthlessness."

"He won't when you tell him about the scene in the library."

"I'm not going to tell him. Because," she continued before Adam could argue, "I have no way of predicting his reaction. You may have noticed, Papa's a very volatile man." Tilting her glass, she met his gaze with a quick change of mood. "I don't want you to worry about all this, Adam. Talk to Papa about it if you like. Have a chat with Harriet, too. Personally, I find it helpful to tuck the whole business away from time to time and let it hibernate. Like a grizzly bear."

"Grizzly bear."

She laughed and rose. "Let me get you some more brandy."

He stopped her with a hand on her wrist. "Have you told me everything?"

With a frown, she brushed at a speck of lint on the bedspread. "Did I mention the Van Gogh?"

"Oh, God." He pressed his fingers to his eyes. Somehow he'd hoped there'd be an end without really believing it. "What Van Gogh?"

Kirby pursed her lips. "Not exactly a Van Gogh."

"Your father?"

"His latest. He's sold it to Victor Alvarez, a coffee baron in South America." She smiled as Adam said nothing and stared straight ahead. "The working conditions on his farm are deplorable. Of course, there's nothing we can do to remedy that, but Papa's already allocated the purchase price for a school somewhere in the area. It's his last for several years, Adam," she added as he sat with his fingers pressed against his eyes. "And really, I think he'll be pleased that you know all about everything. He'd love to show this painting to you. He's particularly pleased with it."

Adam rubbed his hands over his face. It didn't surprise him to hear himself laughing. "I suppose I should be grateful he hasn't decided to do the ceiling in the Sistine Chapel."

"Only after he retires," Kirby put in cheerfully. "And that's years off yet."

Not certain whether she was joking or not, he let it pass. "I've got to give all this a little time to settle."

"Fair enough."

He wasn't going back to his room to report to McIntyre, he decided as he set his brandy aside. He wasn't ready for that yet, so soon after Kirby shared it all with him without questions, without limitations. It wasn't possible to think about his job, or remember outside obligations, when she looked at him with all her trust. No, he'd find a way, somehow, to justify what he chose to do in the end. Right and wrong weren't so well defined now.

Looking at her, he needed to give, to soothe, to show her she'd been right to give him that most precious of gifts—unqualified trust. Perhaps he didn't deserve it, but he needed it. He needed her.

Without a word, he pulled her into his arms and crushed his mouth to hers, no patience, no requests. Before either of them could think, he drew down the zipper at the back of her dress.

She wanted to give to him—anything, everything he wanted. She didn't want to question him but to forget all the reasons why they shouldn't be together. It would be so easy to drown in the flood of feeling that was so new and so unique. And yet, anything real, anything strong, was never easy. She'd been taught from an early age that the things that mattered most were the hardest to obtain. Drawing back, she determined to put things back on a level she could deal with.

"You surprise me," she said with a smile she had to work at.

He pulled her back. She wouldn't slip away from him this time. "Good."

"You know, most women expect a seduction, no matter how perfunctory."

The amusement might be in her eyes, but he could feel the thunder of her heart against his. "Most women aren't Kirby Fairchild." If she wanted to play it lightly, he'd do his damnedest to oblige her—as long as the result was the same. "Why don't we call this my next spontaneous act?" he suggested, and slipped her dress down her shoulders. "I wouldn't want to bore you with a conventional pursuit."

How could she resist him? The hands light on her skin, the mouth that smiled and tempted? She'd never hesitated about taking what she wanted…until now. Perhaps the time had come for the chess game to stop at a stalemate, with neither winning all and neither losing anything.

Slowly she smiled and let her dress whisper almost soundlessly to the floor.

He found her a treasure of cool satin and warm flesh. She was as seductive, as alluring, as he'd known she'd be. Once she'd decided to give, there were no restrictions. In a simple gesture she opened her arms to him and they came together.

Soft sighs, low murmurs, skin against skin. Moonlight and the rose tint from the lamp competed, then merged, as the mattress yielded under their weight. Her mouth was hot and open, her arms were strong. As she moved under him, inviting, taunting, he forgot how small she was.

Everything. All. Now. Needs drove them both to take without patience, and yet… Somehow, beneath the passion, under the heat, was a tenderness neither had expected from the other.

He touched. She trembled. She tasted. He throbbed. They wanted until the air seemed to spark with it. With each second both of them found more of what they'd needed, but the findings brought more greed. Take, she seemed to say, then give and give and give.

She had no time to float, only to throb. For him. From him. Her body craved—*yearn* was too soft a word. She required him, something unique for her. And he, with a kiss, with a touch of his hand, could raise her up to planes she'd only dreamed existed. Here was the completion, here was the delight, she'd hoped for without truly believing in. This was what she'd wanted so desperately in her life but had never found. Here and now. Him. There was and needed to be nothing else.

He edged toward madness. She held him, hard and tight, as they swung toward the edge together. Together was all she could think. Together.

Quiet. It was so quiet there might never have been such a thing as sound. Her hair brushed against his cheek. Her hand, balled into a loose fist, lay over his heart. Adam lay in the silence and hurt as he'd never expected to hurt.

How had he let it happen? Control? What had made him think he had control when it came to Kirby? Somehow she'd wrapped herself around him, body and mind, while he'd been pretending he'd known exactly what he'd been doing.

He'd come to do a job, he reminded himself. He still had to do it, no matter what had passed between them. Could he go on with what he'd come to do, and protect her? Was it possible to split himself in two when his road had always been so straight? He wasn't certain of anything now, but the tug-of-war he'd lose whichever way the game ended. He had to think, create the distance he needed to do so. Better for both of them if he started now.

But when he shifted away, she held him tighter. Kirby lifted her head so that moonlight caught in her eyes and mesmerized him. "Don't go," she murmured. "Stay and sleep with me. I don't want it to end yet."

He couldn't resist her now. Perhaps he never would. Saying nothing, Adam drew her close again and closed his eyes. For a little while he could pretend tomorrow would take care of itself.

Sunlight woke her, but Kirby tried to ignore it by piling pillows on top of her head. It didn't work for long. Resigned, she tossed them on the floor and lay quietly, alone.

She hadn't heard Adam leave, nor had she expected him to stay until morning. As it was, she was grateful to have woken alone. Now she could think.

How was it she'd given her complete trust to a man she hardly knew? No answer. Why hadn't she evaded his questions, skirted her way around certain facts as she was well capable of doing? No answer.

It wasn't true. Kirby closed her eyes a moment, knowing she'd been more honest with Adam than she was being with herself. She knew the answer.

She'd given him more than she'd ever given to any man. It had been more than a physical alliance, more than a few hours of pleasure in the night. The essence of self had been shared with him. There was no taking it back now, even if both of them would have preferred it.

Unknowingly, he'd taken her innocence. Emotional virginity was just as real, just as vital, as the physical. And it was just as impossible to reclaim. She, thinking of the night, knew that she had no desire to go back. Now they would both move forward to whatever waited for them.

Rising, she prepared to face the day.

Upstairs in Fairchild's studio, Adam studied the rural landscape. He could feel the agitation and drama. The serene scene leaped with frantic life. Vivid, real, disturbing. Its creator stood beside him, not the Vincent van Gogh who Adam would've sworn had wielded the brush and pallette, but Philip Fairchild.

"It's magnificent," Adam murmured. The compliment was out before he could stop it.

"Thank you, Adam. I'm fond of it." Fairchild spoke as a man who'd long before accepted his own superiority and the responsibility that came with it.

"Mr. Fairchild—"

"Philip," Fairchild interrupted genially. "No reason for formality between us."

Somehow Adam felt even the casual intimacy could complicate an already hopelessly tangled situation. "Philip," he began again, "this is fraud. Your motives might be sterling, but the result remains fraud."

"Absolutely." Fairchild bobbed his head in agreement. "Fraud, misrepresentation, a bald-faced lie without a doubt." He lifted his arms and let them fall. "I'm stripped of defenses."

Like hell, Adam thought grimly. Unless he was very much mistaken, he was about to be treated to the biggest bag of pure, classic bull on record.

"Adam…" Fairchild drew out the name and steepled his hands. "You're an astute man, a rational man. I pride myself on being a good judge of character." As if he were very old and frail, Fairchild lowered himself into a chair. "Then, again, you're imaginative and open-minded—that shows in your work."

Adam reached for the coffee Cards had brought up. "So?"

"Your help with our little problem last night—and your skill in turning my own plot against me—leads me to believe you have the ability to adapt to what some might term the unusual."

"Some might."

"Now." Accepting the cup Adam handed him, Fairchild leaned back. "You tell me Kirby filled you in on everything. Odd, but we'll leave that for now." He'd already drawn his own conclusions there and found them to his liking. He wasn't about to lose on other points. "After what you've been told, can you find one iota of selfishness in my enterprise? Can you see my motive as anything but humanitarian?" On a roll, Fairchild set down his cup and let his hands fall between his bony knees. "Small, sick children, and those less fortunate than ourselves, have benefited from my hobby. Not one dollar have I kept, not a dollar, a franc, a sou. Never, never have I asked for credit or honor that, naturally, society would be anxious to bestow on me."

"You haven't asked for the jail sentence they'd bestow on you, either."

Fairchild tilted his head in acknowledgment but didn't miss a beat. "It's my gift to mankind, Adam. My payment for the talent awarded to me by a higher power. These hands..." He held them up, narrow, gaunt and oddly beautiful. "These hands hold a skill I'm obliged to pay for in my own way. This I've done." Bowing his head, Fairchild dropped them into his lap. "However, if you must condemn me, I understand."

Fairchild looked, Adam mused, like a stalwart Christian faced by pagan lions: firm in his belief, resigned to his fate. "One day," Adam murmured, "your halo's going to slip and strangle you."

"A possibility." Grinning, he lifted his head again. "But in the meantime, we enjoy what we can. Let's have one of those Danishes, my boy."

Wordlessly, Adam handed him the tray. "Have you considered the repercussions to Kirby if your...hobby is discovered?"

"Ah." Fairchild swallowed pastry. "A straight shot to my Achilles' heel. Naturally both of us know that Kirby can meet any obstacle and find a way over, around or through it." He bit off more Danish, enjoying the tang of raspberry. "Still, merely by being, Kirby demands emotion of one kind or another. You'd agree?"

Adam thought of the night, and what it had changed in him. "Yes."

The brief, concise answer was exactly what Fairchild had expected. "I'm taking a hiatus from this business for various reasons, the first of which is Kirby's position."

"And her position as concerns the Merrick Rembrandt?"

"A different kettle of fish." Fairchild dusted his fingers on a napkin and considered another pastry. "I'd like to share the ins and outs of that business with you, Adam, but I'm not free to just yet." He smiled and gazed over Adam's head. "One could say I've involved Kirby figuratively, but until things are resolved, she's a minor player in the game."

"Are you casting as well as directing this performance, Papa?" Kirby walked into the room and picked up the Danish Fairchild had been eyeing. "Did you sleep well, darling?"

"Like a rock, brat," he muttered, remembering the confusion of waking up on the sofa under her cape. He didn't care to be outwitted, but was a man who acknowledged a quick mind. "I'm told your evening activities went well."

"The deed's done." She glanced at Adam before resting her hands on her father's shoulders. The bond was there, unbreakable. "Maybe I should leave the two of you alone for a while. Adam has a way of digging out information. You might tell him what you won't tell me."

"All in good time." He patted her hands. "I'm devoting the morning to my hawk." Rising, he went to uncover his clay, an obvious dismissal. "You might give Harriet a call and tell her all's well before you two amuse yourselves."

Kirby held out her hand. "Have you any amusements in mind, Adam?"

"As a matter of fact…" He went with the impulse and kissed her as her father watched and speculated. "I had a session of oils and canvas in mind. You'll have to change."

"If that's the best you can do. Two hours only," she warned as they walked from the room. "Otherwise my rates go up. I have my own work, you know."

"Three."

"Two and a half." She paused at the second-floor landing.

"You looked like a child this morning," he murmured, and touched her cheek. "I couldn't bring myself to wake you." He left his hand there only a moment, then moved away. "I'll meet you upstairs."

Kirby went to her room and tossed the red dress on the bed. While she undressed with one hand, she dialed the phone with the other.

"Harriet, it's Kirby to set your mind at rest."

"Clever child. Was there any trouble?"

"No." She wiggled out of her jeans. "We managed."

"We? Did Philip go with you?"

"Papa was snoozing on the couch after Adam switched drinks."

"Oh, dear." Amused, Harriet settled back. "Was he very angry?"

"Papa or Adam?" Kirby countered, then shrugged.

"No matter, in the end they were both very reasonable. Adam was a great help."

"The test isn't for a half hour. Give me the details."

Struggling in and out of clothes, Kirby told her everything.

"Marvelous!" Pleased with the drama, Harriet beamed at the phone. "I wish I'd done it. I'll have to get to know your Adam better and find some spectacular way of showing him my gratitude. Do you think he'd like the crocodile teeth?"

"Nothing would please him more."

"Kirby, you know how grateful I am to you." Harriet's voice was abruptly serious and maternal. "The situation's awkward to say the least."

"The contract's binding?"

"Yes." She let out a sigh at the thought of losing the Titian. "My fault. I should've explained to Stuart that the painting wasn't to be sold. Philip must be furious with me."

"You can handle him. You always do."

"Yes, yes. Lord knows what I'd do without you, though. Poor Melly just can't understand me as you do."

"She's just made differently." Kirby stared down at the floor and tried not to think about the Rembrandt and the guilt it brought her. "Come to dinner tonight, Harriet, you and Melanie."

"Oh, I'd love to, darling, but I've a meeting. Tomorrow?"

"Fine. Shall I call Melly, or will you speak with her?"

"I'll see her this afternoon. Take care and do thank Adam for me. Damn shame I'm too old to give him anything but crocodile teeth."

With a laugh, Kirby hung up.

* * *

The sun swept over her dress, shooting it with flames or darkening it to blood. It glinted from the rings at her ears, the bracelets on her arms. Knowing the light was as perfect as it would ever be, Adam worked feverishly.

He was an artist of subtle details, one who used light and shadow for mood. In his portraits he strove for an inner reality, the truth beneath the surface of the model. In Kirby he saw the essence of woman—power and frailty and that elusive, mystical quality of sex. Aloof, alluring. She was both. Now, more than ever, he understood it.

Hours passed without him giving them a thought. His model, however, had a different frame of mind.

"Adam, if you'll consult your watch, you'll see I've given you more than the allotted time already."

He ignored her and continued to paint.

"I can't stand here another moment." She let her arms drop from their posed position, then wiggled them from the shoulders down. "As it is, I'll probably never pole-vault again."

"I can work on the background awhile," he muttered. "I need another three hours in the morning. The light's best then."

Kirby bit off a retort. Rudeness was something to be expected when an artist was taken over by his art. Stretching her muscles, she went to look over his shoulder.

"You've a good hand with light," she decided as she studied the emerging painting. "It's very flattering, certainly, rather fiery and defiant with the colors you've chosen." She looked carefully at the vague lines of her face, the tints and hues he was using to create her on canvas. "Still, there's a fragility here I don't quite understand."

"Maybe I know you better than you know yourself." He never looked at her, but continued to paint. In not looking, he didn't see the stunned expression or the gradual acceptance.

Linking her hands together, Kirby wandered away. She'd have to do it quickly, she decided. It needed to be done, to be said. "Adam…"

An inarticulate mutter. His back remained to her.

Kirby took a deep breath. "I love you."

"Mmm-hmm."

Some women might've been crushed. Others would've been furious. Kirby laughed and tossed back her hair. Life was never what you expected. "Adam, I'd like just a moment of your attention." Though she continued to smile, her knuckles turned white. "I'm in love with you."

It got through on the second try. His brush, tipped in coral, stopped in midair. Very slowly, he set it down and turned. She was looking at him, the half smile on her face, her hands linked together so tightly they hurt. She hadn't expected a response, nor would she demand one.

"I don't tell you that to put pressure on you, or to embarrass you." Nerves showed only briefly as she moistened her lips. "It's just that I think you have a right to know." Her words began to spill out quickly. "We haven't known each other for long, I know, but I suppose it just happens this way sometimes. I couldn't do anything about it. I don't expect anything from you, permanently or temporarily." When he still didn't speak, she felt a jolt of panic she didn't know how to deal with. Had she ruined it? Now the smile didn't reach her eyes.

"I've got to change," she said lightly. "You've made me miss lunch as it is."

She was nearly to the door before he stopped her. As he took her shoulders, he felt her tense. And as he felt it, he understood she'd given him everything that was in her heart. Something he knew instinctively had never been given to any other man.

"Kirby, you're the most exceptional woman I've ever known."

"Yes, someone's always pointing that out." She had to get through the door and quickly. "Are you coming down, or shall I have a tray sent up?"

He lowered his head to the top of hers and wondered how things had happened so quickly, so finally. "How many people could make such a simple and unselfish declaration of love, then walk away without asking for anything? From the beginning you haven't done one thing I'd've expected." He brushed his lips over her hair, lightly, so that she hardly felt it. "Don't I get a chance to say anything?"

"It's not necessary."

"Yes, it is." Turning her, he framed her face with his hands. "And I'd rather have my hands on you when I tell you I love you."

She stood very straight and spoke very calmly. "Don't feel sorry for me, Adam. I couldn't bear it."

He started to say all the sweet, romantic things a woman wanted to hear when love was declared. All the traditional, normal words a man offered when he offered himself. They weren't for Kirby. Instead he lifted a brow. "If you hadn't counted on being loved back, you'll have to adjust."

She waited a moment because she had to be certain.

She'd take the risk, take any risk, if she was certain. As she looked into his eyes, she began to smile. The tension in her shoulders vanished. "You've brought it on yourself."

"Yeah. I guess I have to live with it."

The smile faded as she pressed against him. "Oh, God, Adam, I need you. You've no idea how much."

He held her just as tightly, just as desperately. "Yes, I do."

Chapter 9

To love and to be loved in return. It was bewildering to Kirby, frightening, exhilarating. She wanted time to experience it, absorb it. Understanding it didn't matter, not now, in the first rush of emotion. She only knew that although she'd always been happy in her life, she was being offered more. She was being offered laughter at midnight, soft words at dawn, a hand to hold and a life to share. The price would be a portion of her independence and the loyalty that had belonged only to her father.

To Kirby, love meant sharing, and sharing had no restrictions. Whatever she had, whatever she felt, belonged to Adam as much as to herself. Whatever happened between them now, she'd never be able to change that. No longer able to work, she went down from her studio to find him.

The house was quiet in the early-evening lull with the staff downstairs making the dinner preparations and gossiping. Kirby had always liked this time of day—after a long, productive session in her studio, before the evening meal. These were the hours to sit in front of a roaring fire, or walk along the cliffs. Now there was someone she needed to share those hours with. Stopping in front of Adam's door, she raised a hand to knock.

The murmur of voices stopped her. If Adam had her father in another discussion, he might learn something more about the Rembrandt that would put her mind at ease. While she hesitated, the thumping of the front door knocker vibrated throughout the house. With a shrug, she turned away to answer.

Inside his room, Adam shifted the transmitter to his other hand. "This is the first chance I've had to call in. Besides, there's nothing new."

"You're supposed to check in every night." Annoyed, McIntyre barked into the receiver. "Damn it, Adam, I was beginning to think something had happened to you."

"If you knew these people, you'd realize how ridiculous that is."

"They don't suspect anything?"

"No." Adam swore at the existence of this job.

"Tell me about Mrs. Merrick and Hiller."

"Harriet's charming and flamboyant." He wouldn't say harmless. Though he thought of what he and Kirby had done the night before, he left it alone. Adam had already rationalized the entire business as having nothing to do with his job. Not specifically. That was enough to justify his keeping it from McIntyre. Instead, Adam would tell him what Adam felt applied and nothing more. "Hiller's very smooth and a complete phony. I walked in on him and Kirby in time to keep him from shoving her around."

"What was his reason?"

"The Rembrandt. He doesn't believe her father's keeping her in the dark about it. He's the kind of man who thinks you can always get what you want by knocking the other person around—if they're smaller."

"Sounds like a gem." But he'd heard the change in tone. If Adam was getting involved with the Fairchild woman... No. McIntyre let it go. That they didn't need. "I've got a line on Victor Alvarez."

"Drop it." Adam kept his voice casual, knowing full well just how perceptive Mac could be. "It's a wild-goose chase. I've already dug it up and it doesn't have anything to do with the Rembrandt."

"You know best."

"Yeah." McIntyre, he knew, would never understand Fairchild's hobby. "Since we agree about that, I've got a stipulation."

"Stipulation?"

"When I find the Rembrandt, I handle the rest my own way."

"What do you mean your own way? Listen, Adam—"

"My way," Adam cut him off. "Or you find someone else. I'll get it back for you, Mac, but after I do, the Fairchilds are kept out of it."

"Kept out?" McIntyre exploded so that the receiver crackled with static. "How the hell do you expect me to keep them out?"

"That's your problem. Just do it."

"The place is full of crazies," McIntyre muttered. "Must be contagious."

"Yeah. I'll get back to you." With a grin, Adam switched off the transmitter.

Downstairs, Kirby opened the door and looked into the myopic, dark-framed eyes of Rick Potts. Knowing his hand would be damp with nerves, she held hers out. "Hello, Rick. Papa told me you were coming to visit."

"Kirby." He swallowed and squeezed her hand. Just the sight of her played havoc with his glands. "You look mar-marvelous." He thrust drooping carnations into her face.

"Thank you." Kirby took the flowers Rick had partially strangled and smiled. "Come, let me fix you a drink. You've had a long drive, haven't you? Cards, see to Mr. Potts's luggage, please," she continued without giving Rick a chance to speak. He'd need a little time, she knew, to draw words together. "Papa should be down soon." She found a club soda and poured it over ice. "He's been giving a lot of time to his new project; I'm sure he'll want to discuss it with you." After handing him his drink, she gestured to a chair. "So, how've you been?"

He drank first, to separate his tongue from the roof of his mouth. "Fine. That is, I had a bit of a cold last week, but I'm much better now. I'd never come to see you if I had any germs."

She turned in time to hide a grin and poured herself a glass of Perrier. "That's very considerate of you, Rick."

"Have you—have you been working?"

"Yes, I've nearly done enough for my spring showing."

"It'll be wonderful," he told her with blind loyalty. Though he recognized the quality of her work, the more powerful pieces intimidated him. "You'll be staying in New York?"

"Yes." She walked over to sit beside him. "For a week."

"Then maybe—that is, I'd love to, if you had the time, of course, I'd like to take you to dinner." He gulped down club soda. "If you had an evening free."

"That's very sweet of you."

Astonished, he gaped, pupils dilating. From the doorway, Adam watched the puppylike adulation of the lanky, somewhat untidy man. In another ten seconds, Adam estimated, Kirby would have him at her feet whether she wanted him there or not.

Kirby glanced up, and her expression changed so subtly Adam wouldn't have noticed if he hadn't been so completely tuned in to her. "Adam." If there'd been relief in her eyes, her voice was casual. "I was hoping you'd come down. Rick, this is Adam Haines. Adam, I think Papa mentioned Rick Potts to you the other day."

The message came across loud and clear. Be kind. With an easy smile, Adam accepted the damp handshake. "Yes, Philip said you were coming for a few days. Kirby tells me you work in watercolors."

"She did?" Nearly undone by the fact that Kirby would speak of him at all, Rick simply stood there a moment.

"We'll have to have a long discussion after dinner." Rising, Kirby began to lead Rick gently toward the door. "I'm sure you'd like to rest a bit after your drive. You can find the way to your room, can't you?"

"Yes, yes, of course."

Kirby watched him wander down the hall before she turned back. She walked back to Adam and wrapped her arms around him. "I hate to repeat myself, but I love you."

He framed her face with his hands and kissed her softly, lightly, with the promise of more. "Repeat yourself as often as you like." He stared down at her, suddenly and completely aroused by no more than her smile. He pressed his mouth into her palm with a restraint that left her weak. "You take my breath away," he murmured. "It's no wonder you turn Rick Potts to jelly."

"I'd rather turn you to jelly."

She did. It wasn't an easy thing to admit. With a half smile, Adam drew her away. "Are you really going to tell him I'm a jealous lover with a stiletto?"

"It's for his own good." Kirby picked up her glass of Perrier. "He's always so embarrassed after he loses control. Did you learn any more from Papa?"

"No." Puzzled, he frowned. "Why?"

"I was coming to see you right before Rick arrived. I heard you talking."

She slipped a hand into his and he fought to keep the tension from being noticeable. "I don't want to press things now." That much was the truth, he thought fiercely. That much wasn't a lie.

"No, you're probably right about that. Papa tends to get obstinate easily. Let's sit in front of the fire for a little while," she said as she drew him over to it. "And do nothing."

He sat beside her, holding her close, and wished things were as simple as they seemed.

Hours went by before they sat in the parlor again, but they were no longer alone. After an enormous meal, Fairchild and Rick settled down with them to continue the ongoing discussion of art and technique. Assisted by two glasses of wine and half a glass of brandy, Rick began to heap praise on Kirby's work. Adam recognized the warning signals of battle—Fairchild's pink ears and Kirby's guileless eyes.

"Thank you, Rick." With a smile, Kirby lifted her brandy. "I'm sure you'd like to see Papa's latest work. It's an attempt in clay. A bird or something, isn't it, Papa?"

"A bird? A bird?" In a quick circle, he danced around the table. "It's a hawk, you horrid girl. A bird of prey, a creature of cunning."

A veteran, Rick tried to soothe. "I'd love to see it, Mr. Fairchild."

"And so you will." In one dramatic gulp, Fairchild finished off his drink. "I intend to donate it to the Metropolitan."

Whether Kirby's snort was involuntary or contrived, it produced results.

"Do you mock your father?" Fairchild demanded. "Have you no faith in these hands?" He held them out, fingers spread. "The same hands that held you fresh from your mother's womb?"

"Your hands are the eighth wonder of the world," Kirby told him. "However…" She set down her glass, sat back and crossed her legs. Meticulously she brought her fingers together and looked over them. "From my observations, you have difficulty with your structure. Perhaps with a few years of practice, you'll develop the knack of construction."

"Structure?" he sputtered. "Construction?" His eyes narrowed, his jaw clenched. "Cards!" Kirby sent him an easy smile and picked up her glass again. "Cards!"

"Yes, Mr. Fairchild."

"Cards," Fairchild repeated, glaring at the dignified butler, who stood waiting in the doorway.

"Yes, Mr. Fairchild."

"Cards!" He bellowed and pranced.

"I believe Papa wants a deck of cards—Cards," Kirby explained. "Playing cards."

"Yes, miss." With a slight bow, Cards went to get some.

"What's the matter with that man?" Fairchild muttered. In hurried motions, he began to clear off a small table. Exquisite Wedgwood and delicate Venetian glass were dumped unceremoniously on the floor. "You'd think I didn't make myself clear."

"It's so hard to get good help these days," Adam said into his glass.

"Your cards, Mr. Fairchild." The butler placed two sealed decks on the table before gliding from the room.

"Now I'll show you about construction." Fairchild pulled up a chair and wrapped his skinny legs around its legs. Breaking the seal on the first deck, he poured the cards on the table. With meticulous care, he leaned one card against another and formed an arch. "A steady hand and a discerning eye," Fairchild mumbled as he began slowly, and with total intensity, to build a house of cards.

"That should keep him out of trouble for a while," Kirby declared. Sending Adam a wink, she turned to Rick and drew him into a discussion on mutual friends.

An hour drifted by over brandy and quiet conversation. Occasionally there was a mutter or a grumble from the architect in the corner. The fire crackled. When

Montique entered and jumped into Adam's lap, Rick paled and sprang up.

"You shouldn't do that. She'll be here any second." He set down his glass with a clatter. "Kirby, I think I'll go up. I want to start work early."

"Of course." She watched his retreat before turning to Adam. "He's terrified of Isabelle. Montique got into his room when he was sleeping and curled on his pillow. Isabelle woke Rick with some rather rude comments while she stood on his chest. I'd better go up and make sure everything's in order." She rose, then bent over and kissed him lightly.

"That's not enough."

"No?" The slow smile curved her lips. "Perhaps we'll fix that later. Come on, Montique, let's go find your wretched keeper."

"Kirby…" Adam waited until both she and the puppy were at the doorway. "Just how much rent does Isabelle pay?"

"Ten mice a month," she told him soberly. "But I'm going to raise it to fifteen in November. Maybe she'll be out by Christmas." Pleased with the thought, she led Montique away.

"A fascinating creature, my Kirby," Fairchild commented.

Adam crossed the room and stared down at the huge, erratic card structure Fairchild continued to construct. "Fascinating."

"She's a woman with much below the surface. Kirby can be cruel when she feels justified. I've seen her squash a six-foot man like a bug." He held a card between the index fingers of both hands, then slowly lowered it into place. "You'll notice, however, that her attitude toward Rick is invariably kind."

Though Fairchild continued to give his full attention to his cards, Adam knew it was more than idle conversation. "Obviously she doesn't want to hurt him."

"Exactly." Fairchild began to patiently build another wing. Unless Adam was very much mistaken, the cards were slowly taking on the lines of the house they were in. "She'll take great care not to because she knows his devotion to her is sincere. Kirby's a strong, independent woman. Where her heart's involved, however, she's a marshmallow. There are a handful of people on this earth she'd sacrifice anything she could for. Rick's one of them—Melanie and Harriet are others. And myself." He held a card on the tops of his fingers as if weighing it. "Yes, myself," he repeated softly. "Because of this, the circumstances of the Rembrandt are very difficult for her. She's torn between separate loyalties. Her father, and the woman who's been her mother most of her life."

"You do nothing to change it," Adam accused. Irrationally he wanted to sweep the cards aside, flatten the meticulously formed construction. He pushed his hands into his pockets, where they balled into fists. Just how much could he berate Fairchild, when he was deceiving Kirby in nearly the same way? "Why don't you give her some explanation? Something she could understand?"

"Ignorance is bliss," Fairchild stated calmly. "In this case, the less Kirby knows, the simpler things are for her."

"You've a hell of a nerve, Philip."

"Yes, yes, that's quite true." He balanced more cards, then went back to the subject foremost in his mind. "There've been dozens of men in Kirby's life. She could choose and discard them as other women do clothing. Yet, in her own way, she was always cautious. I think Kirby believed she wasn't capable of loving a man and had decided to settle for much, much less by agreeing to marry Stuart. Nonsense, of course." Fairchild picked up his drink and studied his rambling card house. "Kirby has a great capacity for love. When she loves a man, she'll love with unswerving devotion and loyalty. And when she does, she'll be vulnerable. She loves intensely, Adam."

For the first time, he raised his eyes and met Adam's. "When her mother died, she was devastated. I wouldn't want to live to see her go through anything like that again."

What could he say? Less than he wanted to, but still only the truth. "I don't want to hurt Kirby. I'll do everything I can to keep from hurting her."

Fairchild studied him a moment with the pale blue eyes that saw deep and saw much. "I believe you, and hope you find a way to avoid it. Still, if you love her, you'll find a way to mend whatever damage is done. The game's on, Adam, the rules set. They can't be altered now, can they?"

Adam stared down at the round face. "You know why I'm here, don't you?"

With a cackle, Fairchild turned back to his cards. Yes, indeed, Adam Haines was sharp, he thought, pleased. Kirby had called it from the beginning. "Let's just say for now that you're here to paint and to…observe. Yes, to observe." He placed another card. "Go up to her now, you've my blessing if you feel the need for it. The game's nearly over, Adam. Soon enough we'll have to pick up the pieces. Love's tenuous when it's new, my boy. If you want to keep her, be as stubborn as she is. That's my advice."

In long, methodical strokes, Kirby pulled the brush through her hair. She'd turned the radio on low so that the hot jazz was hardly more than a pulse beat. At the sound of a knock, she sighed. "Rick, you really must go to bed. You'll hate yourself in the morning."

Adam pushed open the door. He took a long look at the woman in front of the mirror, dressed in wisps of beige silk and ivory lace. Without a word, he closed and latched the door behind him.

"Oh, my." Setting the brush on her dresser, Kirby turned around with a little shudder. "A woman simply isn't safe these days. Have you come to have your way with me—I hope?"

Adam crossed to her. Letting his hands slide along the silk, he wrapped his arms around her. "I was just passing through." When she smiled, he lowered his mouth to hers. "I love you, Kirby. More than anyone, more than anything." Suddenly his mouth was fierce, his arms were tight. "Don't ever forget it."

"I won't." But her words were muffled against his mouth. "Just don't stop reminding me. Now..." She drew away, inches only, and slowly began to loosen his tie. "Maybe I should remind you."

He watched his tie slip to the floor just before she began to ease his jacket from his shoulders. "It might be a good idea."

"You've been working hard," she told him as she tossed his jacket in the general direction of a chair. "I think you should be pampered a bit."

"Pampered?"

"Mmm." Nudging him onto the bed, she knelt to take off his shoes. Carelessly she let them drop, followed by his socks, before she began to massage his feet. "Pampering's good for you in small doses."

He felt the pleasure spread through him at the touch that could almost be described as motherly. Her hands were soft, with that ridge of callus that proved they weren't idle. They were strong and clever, belonging both to artist and to woman. Slowly she slid them up his legs, then down—teasing, promising, until he wasn't certain whether to lay back and enjoy, or to grab and take. Before he could do either, Kirby stood and began to unbutton his shirt.

"I like everything about you," she murmured as she tugged the shirt from the waistband of his slacks. "Have I mentioned that?"

"No." He let her loosen the cuffs and slip the shirt from him. Taking her time, Kirby ran her hands up his rib cage to his shoulders. "The way you look." Softly she pressed a kiss to his cheek. "The way you feel." Then the other. "The way you think." Her lips brushed over his chin. "The way you taste." Unhooking his slacks, she drew them off, inch by slow inch. "There's nothing about you I'd change."

She straddled him and began to trace long, lingering kisses over his face and neck. "Once when I wondered about falling in love, I decided there simply wasn't a man I'd like well enough to make it possible." Her mouth paused just above his. "I was wrong."

Soft, warm and exquisitely tender, her lips met his. Pampering...the word drifted through his mind as she gave him more than any man could expect and only a few might dream of. The strength of her body and her mind, the delicacy of both. They were his, and he didn't have to ask. They'd be his as long as his arms could hold her and open wide enough to give her room.

Knowing only that she loved, Kirby gave. His body heated beneath hers, lean and hard. Disciplined. Somehow the word excited her. He knew who he was and what he wanted. He'd work for both. And he wouldn't demand that she lose any part of what she was to suit that.

His shoulders were firm. Not so broad they would overwhelm her, but wide enough to offer security when she needed it. She brushed her lips over them. There were muscles in his arms, but subtle, not something he'd flex to show her his superiority, but there to protect if she chose to be protected. She ran her fingers over them. His hands were clever, elegantly masculine. They wouldn't hold her back from the places she had to go, but they would be there, held out, when she returned. She pressed her mouth to one, then the other.

No one had ever loved him just like this—patiently, devotedly. He wanted nothing more than to go on feeling those long, slow strokes of her fingers, those moist, lingering traces of her lips. He felt each in every pore. A total experience. He could see the glossy black fall of her hair as it tumbled over his skin and hear the murmur of her approval as she touched him.

The house was quiet again, but for the low, simmering sound of the music. The quilt was soft under his back. The light was dim and gentle—the best light for lovers. And while he lay, she loved him until he was buried under layer upon layer of pleasure. This he would give back to her.

He could touch the silk, and her flesh, knowing

that both were exquisite. He could taste her lips and know that he'd never go hungry as long as she was there. When he heard her sigh, he knew he'd be content with no other sound. The need for him was in her eyes, clouding them, so that he knew he could live with little else as long as he could see her face.

Patience began to fade in each of them. He could feel her body spring to frantic life wherever he touched. He could feel his own strain from the need only she brought to him. Desperate, urgent, exclusive. If he'd had only a day left to live, he'd have spent every moment of it there, with Kirby in his arms.

She smelled of wood smoke and musky flowers, of woman and of sex, ripe and ready. If he'd had the power, he'd have frozen time just then, as she loomed above him in the moonlight, eyes dark with need, skin flashing against silk.

Then he drew the silk up and over her head so that he could see her as he swore no man would ever see her again. Her hair tumbled down, streaking night against her flesh. Naked and eager, she was every primitive fantasy, every midnight dream. Everything.

Her lips were parted as the breath hurried between them. Passion swamped her so that she shuddered and rushed to take what she needed from him—for him. Everything. Everything and more. With a low sound of triumph, Kirby took him inside her and led the way. Fast, furious.

Her body urged her on relentlessly while her mind exploded with images. Such color, such sound. Such frenzy. Arched back, she moved like lightning, hardly aware of how tightly his hands gripped her hips. But she heard him say her name. She felt him fill her.

The first crest swamped her, shocking her system then thrusting her along to more, and more and more. There was nothing she couldn't have and nothing she wouldn't give. Senseless, she let herself go.

With his hands on her, with the taste of her still on his lips, Adam felt his system shudder on the edge of release. For a moment, only a moment, he held back. He could see her above him, poised like a goddess, flesh damp and glowing, hair streaming back as she lifted her hands to it in ecstasy. This he would remember always.

The moon was no longer full, but its light was soft and white. They were still on top of the quilt, tangled close as their breathing settled. As she lay over him, Adam thought of everything Fairchild had said. And everything he could and couldn't do about it.

Slowly their systems settled, but he could find none of the answers he needed so badly. What answers would there be based on lies and half-truths?

Time. Perhaps time was all he had now. But how much or how little was no longer up to him. With a sigh, he shifted and ran a hand down her back.

Kirby rose on an elbow. Her eyes were no longer clouded, but saucy and clear. She smiled, touched a fingertip to her own lips and then to his. "Next time you're in town, cowboy," she drawled as she tossed her hair over her shoulder, "don't forget to ask for Lulu."

She'd expected him to grin, but he grabbed her hair and held her just as she was. There was no humor in his eyes, but the intensity she'd seen when he held a paintbrush. His muscles had tensed, she could feel it.

"Adam?"

"No, don't." He forced his hand to relax, then stroked

her cheek. It wouldn't be spoiled by the wrong word, the wrong move. "I want to remember you just like this. Fresh from loving, with moonlight on your hair."

He was afraid, unreasonably, that he'd never see her like that again—with that half smile inches away from his face. He'd never feel the warmth of her flesh spread over his with nothing, nothing to separate them.

The panic came fast and was very real. Unable to stop it, Adam pulled her against him and held her as if he'd never let her go.

Chapter 10

After thirty minutes of posing, Kirby ordered herself not to be impatient. She'd agreed to give Adam two hours, and a bargain was a bargain. She didn't want to think about the time she had left to stand idle, so instead tried to concentrate on her plans for sculpting once her obligation was over. Her *Anger* was nearly finished.

But the sun seemed too warm and too bright. Every so often her mind would go oddly blank until she pulled herself back just to remember where she was.

"Kirby." Adam called her name for the third time and watched as she blinked and focused on him. "Could you wait until the session's over before you take a nap?"

"Sorry." With an effort, she cleared her head and smiled at him. "I was thinking of something else."

"Don't think at all if it puts you to sleep," he muttered, and slashed scarlet across the canvas. It was right, so right. Nothing he'd ever done had been as right as this painting. The need to finish it was becoming obsessive. "Tilt your head to the right again. You keep breaking the pose."

"Slave driver." But she obeyed and tried to concentrate.

"Cracking the whip's the only way to work with you." With care, he began to perfect the folds in the skirt of her dress. He wanted them soft, flowing, but clearly defined. "You'd better get used to posing for me. I've already several other studies in mind that I'll start after we're married."

Giddiness washed over her. She felt it in waves— physical, emotional—she couldn't tell one from the other. Without thinking, she dropped her arms.

"Damn it, Kirby." He started to swear at her again when he saw how wide and dark her eyes were. "What is it?"

"I hadn't thought…I didn't realize that you…" Lifting a hand to her spinning head, she walked around the room. The bracelets slid down to her elbow with a musical jingle. "I need a minute," she murmured. Should she feel as though someone had cut off her air? As if her head was three feet above her shoulders?

Adam watched her for a moment. She didn't seem quite steady, he realized. And there was an unnaturally high color in her cheeks. Standing, he took her hand and held her still. "Are you ill?"

"No." She shook her head. She was never ill, Kirby reminded herself. Just a bit tired—and, perhaps for the first time in her life, completely overwhelmed. She took a deep breath, telling herself she'd be all right in a moment. "I didn't know you wanted to marry me, Adam."

Was that it? he wondered as he ran the back of his hand over her cheek. Shouldn't she have known? And yet, he remembered, everything had happened so fast. "I love you." It was simple for him. Love led to marriage and marriage to family. But how could he have forgotten Kirby wasn't an ordinary woman and was anything but simple? "You accused me of being conventional," he reminded her, and ran his hands down her hair to her shoulders. "Marriage is a very conventional institution." And one she might not be ready for, he thought with a quick twinge of panic. He'd have to give her room if he wanted to keep her. But how much room did she need, and how much could he give?

"I want to spend my life with you." Adam waited until her gaze had lifted to his again. She looked stunned by his words—a woman like her, Adam thought. Beautiful, sensuous, strong. How was it a woman like Kirby would be surprised to be wanted? Perhaps he'd moved too quickly, and too clumsily. "Any way you choose, Kirby. Maybe I should've chosen a better time, a better place, to ask rather than assume."

"It's not that." Shaky, she lifted a hand to his face. It was so solid, so strong. "I don't need that." His face blurred a moment, and, shaking her head, she moved away again until she stood where she'd been posing. "I've had marriage proposals before—and a good many less binding requests." She managed a smile. He wanted her, not just for today, but for the tomorrows, as well. He wanted her just as she was. She felt the tears well up, of love, of gratitude, but blinked them back. When wishes came true it was no time for tears. "This is the one I've been waiting for all of my life, I just didn't expect to be so flustered."

Relieved, he started to cross to her. "I'll take that as a good sign. Still, I wouldn't mind a simple yes."

"I hate to do anything simple."

She felt the room lurch and fade, then his hands on her shoulders.

"Kirby— Good God, there's gas leaking!" As he stood holding her up, the strong, sweet odor rushed over him. "Get out! Get some air! It must be the heater." Giving her a shove toward the door, he bent over the antiquated unit.

She stumbled across the room. The door seemed miles away, so that when she finally reached it she had only the strength to lean against the heavy wood and catch her breath. The air was cleaner there. Gulping it in, Kirby willed herself to reach for the knob. She tugged, but it held firm.

"Damn it, I told you to get out!" He was already choking on the fumes when he reached her. "The gas is pouring out of that thing!"

"I can't open the door!" Furious with herself, Kirby pulled again. Adam pushed her hands away and yanked himself. "Is it jammed?" she murmured, leaning against him. "Cards will see to it."

Locked, he realized. From the outside. "Stay here." After propping her against the door, Adam picked up a chair and smashed it against the window. The glass cracked, but held. Again, he rammed the chair, and again, until with a final heave, the glass shattered. Moving quickly, he went back for Kirby and held her head near the jagged opening.

"Breathe," he ordered.

For the moment she could do nothing else but gulp

fresh air into her lungs and cough it out again. "Some-one's locked us in, haven't they?"

He'd known it wouldn't take her long once her head had cleared. Just as he knew better than to try to evade. "Yes."

"We could shout for hours." She closed her eyes and concentrated. "No one would hear us, we're too isolated up here." With her legs unsteady, she leaned against the wall. "We'll have to wait until someone comes to look for us."

"Where's the main valve for that heater?"

"Main valve?" She pressed her fingers to her eyes and forced herself to think. "I just turn the thing on when it's cold up here…. Wait. Tanks—there are tanks out in back of the kitchen." She turned back to the bro-ken window again, telling herself she couldn't be sick. "One for each tower and for each floor."

Adam glanced at the small, old-fashioned heater again. It wouldn't take much longer, even with the bro-ken window. "We're getting out of here."

"How?" If she could just lie down—just for a min-ute… "The door's locked. I don't think we'd survive a jump into Jamie's zinnias," she added, looking down to where the chair had landed. But he wasn't listening to her. When Kirby turned, she saw Adam running his hand over the ornate trim. The panel yawned open. "How'd you find that one?"

He grabbed her by the elbow and pulled her for-ward. "Let's go."

"I can't." With the last of her strength, Kirby braced her hands against the wall. Fear and nausea doubled at the thought of going into the dark, dank hole in the wall. "I can't go in there."

"Don't be ridiculous."

When he would've pulled her through, Kirby jerked away and backed up. "No, you go. I'll wait for you to come around and open the door."

"Listen to me." Fighting the fumes, he grabbed her shoulders. "I don't know how long it'd take me to find my way through that maze in the dark."

"I'll be patient."

"You could be dead," he countered between his teeth. "That heater's unstable—if there's a short this whole room would go up! You've already taken in too much of the gas."

"I won't go in!" Hysteria bubbled, and she didn't have the strength or the wit to combat it. Her voice rose as she stumbled back from him. "I can't go in, don't you understand?"

"I hope you understand this," he muttered, and clipped her cleanly on the jaw. Without a sound, she collapsed into his arms. Adam didn't hesitate. He tossed her unceremoniously over his shoulder and plunged into the passageway.

With the panel closed to cut off the flow of gas, the passage was in total darkness. With one arm holding Kirby in place, Adam inched along the wall. He had to reach the stairs, and the first mechanism. Groping, testing each step, he hugged the wall, knowing what would happen to both of them if he rushed and plunged them headlong down the steep stone stairway.

He heard the skitter of rodents and brushed spiderwebs out of his face. Perhaps it was best that Kirby was unconscious, he decided. He'd get her through a lot easier carrying her than he would dragging her.

Five minutes, then ten, then at last his foot met empty space.

Cautiously, he shifted Kirby on his shoulder, pressed the other to the wall, and started down. The steps were stone, and treacherous enough with a light. In the dark, with no rail for balance, they were deadly. Fighting the need to rush, Adam checked himself on each step before going on to the next. When he reached the bottom, he went no faster, but began to trace his hand along the wall, feeling for a switch.

The first one stuck. He had to concentrate just to breathe. Kirby swayed on his shoulder as he maneuvered the sharp turn in the passage. Swearing, Adam moved forward blindly until his fingers brushed over a second lever. The panel groaned open just enough for him to squeeze himself and his burden through. Blinking at the sunlight, he dashed around dust-covered furniture and out into the hall.

When he reached the second floor and passed Cards, he didn't break stride. "Turn off the gas to Kirby's studio from the main valve," he ordered, coughing as he moved by. "And keep everyone away from there."

"Yes, Mr. Haines." Cards continued to walk toward the main stairway, carrying his pile of fresh linens.

When Adam reached her room, he laid Kirby on the bed, then opened the windows. He stood there a moment, just breathing, letting the air rush over his face and soothe his eyes. His stomach heaved. Forcing himself to take slow, measured breaths, he leaned out. When the nausea passed, he went back to her.

The high color had faded. Now she was as pale as the quilt. She didn't move. Hadn't moved, he remembered, since he'd hit her. With a tremor, he pressed his fingers to her throat and felt a slow, steady pulse. Quickly he went into the bathroom and soaked a cloth with cold water. As he ran it over her face, he said her name.

She coughed first, violently. Nothing could've relieved him more. When her eyes opened, she stared at him dully.

"You're in your room," he told her. "You're all right now."

"You hit me."

He grinned because there was indignation in her voice. "I thought you'd take a punch better with a chin like that. I barely tapped you."

"So you say." Gingerly she sat up and touched her chin. Her head whirled once, but she closed her eyes and waited for it to pass. "I suppose I had it coming. Sorry I got neurotic on you."

He let his forehead rest against hers. "You scared the hell out of me. I guess you're the only woman who's received a marriage proposal and a right jab within minutes of each other."

"I hate to do the ordinary." Because she needed another minute, she lay back against the pillows. "Have you turned off the gas?"

"Cards is seeing to it."

"Of course." She said this calmly enough, then began to pluck at the quilt with her fingers. "As far as I know, no one's tried to kill me before."

It made it easier, he thought, that she understood and accepted that straight off. With a nod, he touched a hand to her cheek. "First we call a doctor. Then we call the police."

"I don't need a doctor. I'm just a little queasy now,

it'll pass." She took both his hands and held them firmly. "And we can't call the police."

He saw something in her eyes that nearly snapped his temper. Stubbornness. "It's the usual procedure after attempted murder, Kirby."

She didn't wince. "They'll ask annoying questions and skulk all over the house. It's in all the movies."

"This isn't a game." His hands tightened on hers. "You could've been killed—would've been if you'd been in there alone. I'm not giving him another shot at you."

"You think it was Stuart." She let out a long breath. Be objective, she told herself. Then you can make Adam be objective. "Yes, I suppose it was, though I wouldn't have thought him ingenious enough. There's no one else who'd want to hurt me. Still, we can't prove a thing."

"That has yet to be seen." His eyes flashed a moment as he thought of the satisfaction he'd get from beating a confession out of Hiller. She saw it. She understood it.

"You're more primitive than I'd imagined." Touched, she traced her finger down his jaw. "I didn't know how nice it would be to have someone want to vanquish dragons for me. Who needs a bunch of silly police when I have you?"

"Don't try to outmaneuver me."

"I'm not." The smile left her eyes and her lips. "We're not in the position to call the police. I couldn't answer the questions they'd ask, don't you see? Papa has to resolve the business of the Rembrandt, Adam. If everything came out now, he'd be hopelessly compromised. He might go to prison. Not for anything," she said softly. "Not for anything would I risk that."

"He won't," Adam said shortly. No matter what strings he'd have to pull, what dance he'd have to perform, he'd see to it that Fairchild stayed clear. "Kirby, do you think your father would continue with whatever he's plotting once he knew of this?"

"I couldn't predict his reaction." Weary, she let out a long breath and tried to make him understand. "He might destroy the Rembrandt in a blind rage. He could go after Stuart single-handed. He's capable of it. What good would any of that do, Adam?" The queasiness was passing, but it had left her weak. Though she didn't know it, the vulnerability was her best weapon. "We have to let it lie for a while longer."

"What do you mean, let it lie?"

"I'll speak to Papa—tell him what happened in my own way, so that he doesn't overreact. Harriet and Melanie are coming to dinner tonight. It has to wait until tomorrow."

"How can he sit down and have dinner with Harriet when he has stolen something from her?" Adam demanded. "How can he do something like this to a friend?"

Pain shot into her eyes. Deliberately she lowered them, but he'd already seen it. "I don't know."

"I'm sorry."

She shook her head. "No, you have no reason to be. You've been wonderful through all of this."

"No, I haven't." He pressed the heels of his hands to his eyes.

"Let me be the judge of that. And give me one more day." She touched his wrists and waited until he lowered his hands. "Just one more day, then I'll talk to Papa. Maybe we'll get everything straightened out."

"That much, Kirby. No more." He had some thinking of his own to do. Perhaps one more night would give him some answers. "Tomorrow you tell Philip everything, no glossing over the details. If he doesn't agree to resolve the Rembrandt business then, I'm taking over."

She hesitated a minute. She'd said she trusted him. It was true. "All right."

"And I'll deal with Hiller."

"You're not going to fight with him."

Amused, he lifted a brow. "No?"

"Adam, I won't have you bruised and bloodied. That's it."

"Your confidence in me is overwhelming."

With a laugh, she sat up again and threw her arms around him. "My hero. He'd never lay a hand on you."

"I beg your pardon, Miss Fairchild."

"Yes, Cards." Shifting her head, Kirby acknowledged the butler in the doorway.

"It seems a chair has somehow found its way through your studio window. Unfortunately, it landed in Jamie's bed of zinnias."

"Yes, I know. I suppose he's quite annoyed."

"Indeed, miss."

"I'll apologize, Cards. Perhaps a new lawn mower… You'll see to having the window repaired?"

"Yes, miss."

"And have that heater replaced by something from the twentieth-century," Adam added. He watched as Cards glanced at him then back at Kirby.

"As soon as possible, please, Cards."

With a nod, the butler backed out of the doorway.

"He takes his orders from you, doesn't he?" Adam commented as the quiet footsteps receded. "I've seen the subtle nods and looks between the two of you."

She brushed a smudge of dirt on the shoulder of his shirt. "I've no idea what you mean."

"A century ago, Cards would've been known as the queen's man." When she laughed at the term, he eased her back on the pillows. "Rest," he ordered.

"Adam, I'm fine."

"Want me to get tough again?" Before she could answer, he covered her mouth with his, lingering. "Turn the batteries down awhile," he murmured. "I might have to call the doctor after all."

"Blackmail." She brought his mouth back to hers again. "But maybe if you rested with me..."

"Rest isn't what would happen then." He drew away as she grumbled a protest.

"A half hour."

"Fine. I'll be back."

She smiled and let her eyes close. "I'll be waiting."

It was too soon for stars, too late for sunbeams. From a window in the parlor, Adam watched the sunset hold off twilight just a few moments longer.

After reporting the attempt on Kirby's life to McIntyre, he'd found himself suddenly weary. Half lies, half truths. It had to end. It would end, he decided, tomorrow. Fairchild would have to see reason, and Kirby would be told everything. The hell with McIntyre, the job and anything else. She deserved honesty along with everything else he wanted to give her. Everything else, he realized, would mean nothing to Kirby without it.

The sun lowered further and the horizon exploded with rose-gold light. He thought of the Titian woman. She'd understand, he told himself. She had to understand. He'd make her understand. Thinking to check on her again, Adam turned from the window.

When he reached her room, he heard the sound of running water. The simple, natural sound of her humming along with her bath dissolved his tension. He thought about joining her, then remembered how pale and tired she'd looked. Another time, he promised both of them as he shut the door to her room again. Another time he'd have the pleasure of lounging in the big marble tub with her.

"Where's that wretched girl?" Fairchild demanded from behind him. "She's been hiding out all day."

"Having a bath," Adam told him.

"She'd better have a damn good explanation, that's all I have to say." Looking grim, Fairchild reached for the doorknob. Adam blocked the door automatically.

"For what?"

Fairchild glared at him. "My shoes."

Adam looked down at Fairchild's small stockinged feet. "I don't think she has them."

"A man tugs himself into a restraining suit, chokes himself with a ridiculous tie, then has no shoes." Fairchild pulled at the knot around his neck. "Is that justice?"

"No. Have you tried Cards?"

"Cards couldn't get his big British feet in my shoes." Then he frowned and pursed his lips. "Then again, he did have my suit."

"I rest my case."

"The man's a kleptomaniac," Fairchild grumbled as he wandered down the hall. "I'd check my shorts if I were you. No telling what he'll pick up next. Cocktails in a half hour, Adam. Hustle along."

Deciding a quiet drink was an excellent idea after the day they'd put in, Adam went to change. He was adjusting the knot in his own tie when Kirby knocked. She opened it without waiting for his answer, then stood a moment, deliberately posed in the doorway—head thrown back, one arm raised high on the jamb, the other at her hip. The slinky jumpsuit clung to every curve, falling in folds from her neck and dispensing with a back altogether. At her ears, emeralds the size of quarters picked up the vivid green shade. Five twisted, gold chains hung past her waist.

"Hello, neighbor." Glittering and gleaming, she crossed to him. Adam put a finger under her chin and studied her face. As an artist, she knew how to make use of the colors of a makeup palette. Her cheeks were tinted with a touch of bronze, her lips just a bit darker. "Well?"

"You look better," he decided.

"That's a poor excuse for a compliment."

"How do you feel?"

"I'd feel a lot better if you'd stop examining me as though I had a rare terminal disease and kiss me as you're supposed to." She twisted her arms around his neck and let her lashes lower.

It was them he kissed first, softly, with a tenderness that had her sighing. Then his lips skimmed down, over her cheeks, gently over her jawline.

"Adam…" His name was only a breath on the air as his mouth touched hers. She wanted it all now. Instantly. She wanted the fire and flash, the pleasure and the passion. She wanted that calm, spreading contentment that only he could give to her. "I love you," she murmured. "I love you until there's nothing else but that."

"There is nothing else but that," he said, almost fiercely. "We've a lifetime for it." He drew her away so he could bring both of her hands to his lips. "A lifetime, Kirby, and it isn't long enough."

"Then we'll have to start soon." She felt the giddiness again, the light-headedness, but she wouldn't run from it. "Very soon," she added. "But we have to wait at least until after dinner. Harriet and Melanie should be here any minute."

"If I had my choice, I'd stay with you alone in this room and make love until sunrise."

"Don't tempt me to tarnish your reputation." Because she knew she had to, she stepped back and finished adjusting his tie herself. It was a brisk, womanly gesture he found himself enjoying. "Ever since I told Harriet about your help with the Titian, she's decided you're the greatest thing since peanut butter. I wouldn't want to mess that up by making you late for dinner."

"Then we'd better go now. Five more minutes alone with you and we'd be a lot more than late." When she laughed, he linked her arm through his and led her from the room. "By the way, your father's shoes were stolen."

To the casual observer, the group in the parlor would have seemed a handful of elegant, cosmopolitan people. Secure, friendly, casually wealthy. Looking beyond the sparkle and glitter, a more discerning eye might have seen the pallor of Kirby's skin that her careful application of makeup disguised. Someone looking closely might have noticed that her friendly nonsense covered a discomfort that came from battling loyalties.

To someone from the outside, the group might have taken on a different aspect if the canvas were stretched. Rick's stuttering nerves were hardly noticed by those in the parlor. As was Melanie's subtle disdain for him. Both were the expected. Fairchild's wolfish grins and Harriet's jolting laughter covered the rest.

Everyone seemed relaxed, except Adam. The longer it went on, the more he wished he'd insisted that Kirby postpone the dinner party. She looked frail. The more energy she poured out, the more fragile she seemed to him. And touchingly valiant. Her devotion to Harriet hadn't been lip service. Adam could see it, hear it. When she loved, as Fairchild had said, she loved completely. Even the thought of the Rembrandt would be tearing her in two. Tomorrow. By the next day, it would be over.

"Adam." Harriet took his arm as Kirby poured after-dinner drinks. "I'd love to see Kirby's portrait."

"As soon as it's finished you'll have a private viewing." And until the repairs in the tower were complete, he thought, he was keeping all outsiders away.

"I'll have to be content with that, I suppose." She pouted a moment, then forgave him. "Sit beside me," Harriet commanded and spread the flowing vermilion of her skirt on the sofa. "Kirby said I could flirt with you."

Adam noticed that Melanie turned a delicate pink at her mother's flamboyance. Unable to resist, he lifted Harriet's hand to his lips. "Do I need permission to flirt with you?"

"Guard your heart, Harriet," Kirby warned as she set out drinks.

"Mind your own business," Harriet tossed back. "By the way, Adam, I'd like you to have my necklace of crocodile teeth as a token of my appreciation."

"Good heavens, Mother." Melanie sipped at her blackberry brandy. "Why would Adam want that hideous thing?"

"Sentiment," she returned without blinking an eye. "Adam's agreed to let me exhibit Kirby's portrait, and I want to repay him."

The old girl's quick, Adam decided as she sent him a guileless smile, and Melanie's been kept completely in the dark about the hobby her mother shares with Fairchild. Studying Melanie's cool beauty, Adam decided her mother knew best. She'd never react as Kirby did. Melanie could have their love and affection, but secrets were kept within the triangle. No, he realized, oddly pleased. It was now a rectangle.

"He doesn't have to wear it," Harriet went on, breaking into his thoughts.

"I should hope not," Melanie put in, rolling her eyes at Kirby.

"It's for good luck." Harriet sent Kirby a glance, then squeezed Adam's arm. "But perhaps you have all the luck you need."

"Perhaps my luck's just beginning."

"How quaintly they speak in riddles." Kirby sat on the arm of Melanie's chair. "Why don't we ignore them?"

"Your hawk's coming along nicely, Mr. Fairchild," Rich hazarded.

"Aha!" It was all Fairchild needed. Bursting with good feelings, he treated Rick to an in-depth lecture on the use of calipers.

"Rick's done it now," Kirby whispered to Melanie. "Papa has no mercy on a captive audience."

"I didn't know Uncle Philip was sculpting."

"Don't mention it," Kirby said quickly. "You'll never escape." Pursing her lips, she looked down at Melanie's elegant dark rose dress. The lines flowed fluidly with the flash of a studded buckle at the waist. "Melly, I wonder if you'd have time to design a dress for me."

Surprised, Melanie glanced up. "Oh course, I'd love to. But I've been trying to talk you into it for years and you've always refused to go through the fittings."

Kirby shrugged. A wedding dress was a different matter, she mused. Still, she didn't mention her plans with Adam. Her father would know first. "I usually buy on impulse, whatever appeals at the time."

"From Goodwill to Rive Gauche," Melanie murmured. "So this must be special."

"I'm taking a page from your book," Kirby evaded. "You know I've always admired your talent, I just knew I wouldn't have the patience for all the preliminaries." She laughed. "Do you think you can design a dress that'd make me look demure?"

"Demure?" Harriet cut in, pouncing on the word. "Poor Melanie would have to be a sorceress to pull that off. Even as a child in that sweet little muslin you looked capable of battling a tribe of Comanches. Philip, you must let me borrow that painting of Kirby for the gallery."

"We'll see." His eyes twinkled. "You'll have to soften me up a bit first. I've always had a deep affection for that painting." With a hefty sigh, he leaned back with his drink. "Its value goes below the surface."

"He still begrudges me my sitting fee." Kirby sent her father a sweet smile. "He forgets I never collected for any of the others."

"You never posed for the others," Fairchild reminded her.

"I never signed a release for them, either."

"Melly posed for me out of the goodness of her heart."

"Melly's nicer than I am," Kirby said simply. "I like being selfish."

"Heartless creature," Harriet put in mildly. "It's so selfish of you to teach sculpture in the summer to those handicapped children."

Catching Adam's surprised glance, Kirby shifted uncomfortably. "Harriet, think of my reputation."

"She's sensitive about her good deeds," Harriet told Adam with a squeeze for his knee.

"I simply had nothing else to do." With a shrug, Kirby turned away. "Are you going to Saint Moritz this year, Melly?"

Fraud, Adam thought as he watched her guide the subject away from herself. A beautiful, sensitive fraud. And finding her so, he loved her more.

By the time Harriet and Melanie rose to leave, Kirby was fighting off a raging headache. Too much strain, she knew, but she wouldn't admit it. She could tell herself she needed only a good night's sleep, and nearly believe it.

"Kirby." Harriet swirled her six-foot shawl over her shoulder before she took Kirby's chin in her hand. "You look tired, and a bit pale. I haven't seen you look pale since you were thirteen and had the flu. I remember you swore you'd never be ill again."

"After that disgusting medicine you poured down my throat, I couldn't afford to. I'm fine." But she threw her arms around Harriet's neck and held on. "I'm fine, really."

"Mmm." Over her head, Harriet frowned at Fairchild. "You might think about Australia. We'll put some color in your cheeks."

"I will. I love you."

"Go to sleep, child," Harriet murmured.

The moment the door was closed, Adam took Kirby's arm. Ignoring her father and Rick, he began to pull her up the stairs. "You belong in bed."

"Shouldn't you be dragging me by the hair instead of the arm?"

"Some other time, when my intentions are less peaceful." He stopped outside her door. "You're going to sleep."

"Tired of me already?"

The words were hardly out of her mouth when his covered it. Holding her close, he let himself go for a moment, releasing the needs, the desires, the love. He could feel her heart thud, her bones melt. "Can't you see how tired I am of you?" He kissed her again with his hands framing her face. "You must see how you bore me."

"Anything I can do?" she murmured, slipping her hands under his jacket.

"Get some rest." He took her by the shoulders. "This is your last opportunity to sleep alone."

"Am I sleeping alone?"

It wasn't easy for him. He wanted to devour her, he wanted to delight her. He wanted, more than anything else, to have a clean slate between them before they made love again. If she hadn't looked so weary, so worn, he'd have told her everything then and there. "This may come as a shock to you," he said lightly. "But you're not Wonder Woman."

"Really?"

"You're going to get a good night's sleep. Tomorrow." He took her hands and the look, the sudden intenseness, confused her. "Tomorrow, Kirby, we have to talk."

"About what?"

"Tomorrow," he repeated before he could change his mind. "Rest now." He gave her a nudge inside. "If you're not feeling any better tomorrow, you're going to stay in bed and be pampered."

She managed one last wicked grin. "Promise?"

Chapter 11

It was clear after Kirby had tossed in bed and fluffed up her pillow for more than an hour that she wasn't going to get the rest everyone seemed to want for her. Her body was dragging, but her mind refused to give in to it.

She tried. For twenty minutes she recited dull poetry. Closing her eyes, she counted five hundred and twenty-seven camels. She turned on her bedside radio and found chamber music. She was, after all of it, wide awake.

It wasn't fear. If Stuart had indeed tried to kill her, he'd failed. She had her own wits, and she had Adam. No, it wasn't fear.

The Rembrandt. She couldn't think of anything else after seeing Harriet laughing, after remembering how Harriet had nursed her through the flu and had given her a sweet and totally unnecessary woman-to-woman talk when she'd been a girl.

Kirby had grieved for her own mother, and though she'd died when Kirby had been a child, the memory remained perfectly clear. Harriet hadn't been a substitute. Harriet had simply been Harriet. Kirby loved her for that alone.

How could she sleep?

Annoyed, Kirby rolled over on her back and stared at the ceiling. Maybe, just maybe, she could make use of the insomnia and sort it all out and make some sense out of it.

Her father, she was certain, would do nothing to hurt Harriet without cause. Was revenge on Stuart cause enough? After a moment, she decided it didn't follow.

Harriet had gone to Africa—that was first. It had been nearly two weeks after that when Kirby had broken her engagement with Stuart. Afterward she had told her father of Stuart's blackmail threats and he'd been unconcerned. He'd said, Kirby remembered, that Stuart wasn't in any position to make waves.

Then it made sense to assume they'd already begun plans to switch the paintings. Revenge was out.

Then why?

Not for money, Kirby thought. Not for the desire to own the painting himself. That wasn't his way—she knew better than anyone how he felt about greed. But then, stealing from a friend wasn't his way either.

If she couldn't find the reason, perhaps she could find the painting itself.

Still staring at the ceiling, she began to go over everything her father had said. So many ambiguous comments, she mused. But then, that was typical of him. In the house—that much was certain. In the house, hidden with appropriate affection and respect. Just how many hundreds of possibilities could she sort through in one night?

She blew out a disgusted breath and rolled over again. With a last thump for her pillow, she closed her eyes. The yawn, she felt, was a hopeful sign. As she snuggled deeper, a tiny memory probed.

She'd think about it tomorrow.... No, now, she thought, and rolled over again. She'd think about it now. What was it her father had been saying to Adam when she'd walked into his studio the night after the Titian switch? Something... Something...about involving her figuratively.

"Root rot," she muttered, and squeezed her eyes shut in concentration. "What the devil was that supposed to mean?" Just as she was about to give up, the idea seeped in. Her eyes sprang open as she sprang up. "It'd be just like him!"

Grabbing a robe, she dashed from the room.

For a moment in the hall she hesitated. Perhaps she should wake Adam and tell him of her theory. Then again, it was no more than that, and he hadn't had the easiest day of it, either. If she produced results, then she'd wake him. And if she was wrong, her father would kill her.

She made a quick trip to her father's studio, then went down to the dining room.

On neither trip did she bother with lights. She wanted no one to pop out of their room and ask what she was up to. Carrying a rag, a bottle and a stack of newspapers, she went silently through the dark. Once she'd reached the dining room, she turned on the lights. No one would investigate downstairs except Cards. He'd never question her. She worked quickly.

Kirby spread the newspapers in thick pads on the dining room table. Setting the bottle and the rag on them, she turned to her own portrait.

"You're too clever for your own good, Papa," she murmured as she studied the painting. "I'd never be able to tell if this was a duplicate. There's only one way."

Once she'd taken the portrait from the wall, Kirby laid it on the newspaper. "Its value goes below the surface," she murmured. Isn't that what he'd said to Harriet? And he'd been smug. He'd been smug right from the start. Kirby opened the bottle and tipped the liquid onto the rag. "Forgive me, Papa," she said quietly.

With the lightest touch—an expert's touch—she began to remove layers of paint in the lower corner. Minutes passed. If she was wrong, she wanted the damage to be minimal. If she was right, she had something priceless in her hands. Either way, she couldn't rush.

She dampened the rag and wiped again. Her father's bold signature disappeared, then the bright summer grass beneath it, and the primer.

And there, beneath where there should have been only canvas, was a dark, somber brown. One letter, then another, appeared. It was all that was necessary.

"Great buckets of blood," she murmured. "I was right."

Beneath the feet of the girl she'd been was Rembrandt's signature. She'd go no further. As carefully as she'd unstopped it, Kirby secured the lid of the bottle.

"So, Papa, you put Rembrandt to sleep under a copy of my portrait. Only you would've thought to copy yourself to pull it off."

"Very clever."

Whirling, Kirby looked behind her into the dark

outside the dining room. She knew the voice; it didn't frighten her. As her heart pounded, the shadows moved. What now? she asked herself quickly. Just how would she explain it?

"Cleverness runs in the family, doesn't it, Kirby?"

"So I'm told." She tried to smile. "I'd like to explain. You'd better come in out of the dark and sit down. It could take—" She stopped as the first part of the invitation was accepted. She stared at the barrel of a small polished revolver. Lifting her gaze from it, she stared into clear, delicate blue eyes. "Melly, what's going on?"

"You look surprised. I'm glad." With a satisfied smile, Melanie aimed the gun at Kirby's head. "Maybe you're not so clever after all."

"Don't point that at me."

"I intend to point it at you." She lowered the gun to chest level. "And I'll do more than point it if you move."

"Melly." She wasn't afraid, not yet. She was confused, even annoyed, but she wasn't afraid of the woman she'd grown up with. "Put that thing away and sit down. What're you doing here this time of night?"

"Two reasons. First, to see if I could find any trace of the painting you've so conveniently found for me. Second, to finish the job that was unsuccessful this morning."

"This morning?" Kirby took a step forward then froze when she heard the quick, deadly click. Good God, could it actually be loaded? "Melly…"

"I suppose I must have miscalculated a bit or you'd be dead already." The elegant rose silk whispered as she shrugged. "I know the passages very well. Remember, you used to drag me around in them when we were children—before you went in with a faulty flashlight. I'd changed the batteries in it, you see. I'd never told you about that, had I?" She laughed as Kirby remained silent. "I used the passages this morning. Once I was sure you and Adam were settled in, I went out and turned on the gas by the main valve—I'd already broken the switch on the unit."

"You can't be serious." Kirby dragged a hand through her hair.

"Deadly serious, Kirby."

"Why?"

"Primarily for money, of course."

"Money?" She would've laughed, but her throat was closing. "But you don't need money."

"You're so smug." The venom came through. Kirby wondered that she'd never heard it before. "Yes, I need money."

"You wouldn't take a settlement from your ex-husband."

"He wouldn't give me a dime," Melanie corrected. "He cut me off, and as he had me cold on adultery, I wasn't in a position to take him to court. He let me get a quiet, discreet divorce so that our reputations wouldn't suffer. And except for one incident, I'd been very discreet. Stuart and I were always very careful."

"Stuart?" Kirby lifted a hand to rub at her temple. "You and Stuart?"

"We've been lovers for over three years. Questions are just buzzing around in your head, aren't they?" Enjoying herself, Melanie stepped closer. The whiff of Chanel followed her. "It was more practical for us if we pretended to be just acquaintances. I convinced Stuart to ask you to marry him. My inheritance has dwindled to next to nothing. Your money would have met Stuart's and my tastes very nicely. And we'd have got close to Uncle Philip."

She ignored the rest and homed in on the most important. "What do you want from my father?"

"I found out about the little game he and Mother indulged in years ago. Not all the details, but enough to know I could use it if I had to. I thought it was time to use your father's talent for my own benefit."

"You made plans to steal from your own mother."

"Don't be so self-righteous." Her voice chilled. The gun was steady. "Your father betrayed her without a murmur, then double-crossed us in the bargain. Now you've solved that little problem for me." With her free hand, she gestured to the painting. "I should be grateful I failed this morning. I'd still be looking for the painting."

Somehow, some way, she'd deal with this. Kirby started with the basics. "Melly, how could you hurt me? We've been friends all our lives."

"Friends?" The word sounded like an obscenity. "I've hated you for as long as I can remember."

"No—"

"Hated," Melanie repeated, coldly this time and with the ring of truth. "It was always you people flocked around, always you men preferred. My own mother preferred you."

"That's not true." Did it go so deep? Kirby thought with a flood of guilt. Should she have seen it before? "Melly—" But as she started forward, Melanie gestured with the gun.

"'Melanie, don't be so stiff and formal.… Melanie, where's your sense of humor?'" Her eyes narrowed into slits. "She never came right out and said I should be more like you, but that's what she wanted."

"Harriet loves you—"

"Love?" Melanie cut Kirby off with a laugh. "I don't give a damn for love. It won't buy what I need. You may have taken my mother, but that was a minor offense. The men you snatched from under my nose time and time again is a bigger one."

"I never took a man from you. I've never shown an interest in anyone you were serious about."

"There have been dozens," Melanie corrected. Her voice was as brittle as glass. "You'd smile and say something stupid and I'd be forgotten. You never had my looks, but you'd use that so-called charm and lure them away, or you'd freeze up and do the same thing."

"I might've been friendly to someone you cared for," Kirby said quickly. "If I froze it was to discourage them. Good God, Melly, I'd never have done anything to hurt you. I love you."

"I've no use for your love any longer. It served its purpose well enough." She smiled slowly as tears swam in Kirby's eyes. "My only regret is that you didn't fall for Stuart. I wanted to see you fawn over him, knowing he preferred me—married you only because I wanted it. When you came to see him that night, I nearly came out of the bedroom just for the pleasure of seeing your face. But…" She shrugged. "We had long-range plans."

"You used me," Kirby said quietly when she could no longer deny it. "You had Stuart use me."

"Of course. Still, it wasn't wise of me to come back from New York for the weekend to be with him."

"Why, Melanie? Why have you pretended all these years?"

"You were useful. Even as a child I knew that. Later, in Paris, you opened doors for me, then again in New York. It was even due to you that I spent a year of luxury with Carlyse. You wouldn't sleep with him and you wouldn't marry him. I did both."

"And that's all?" Kirby murmured. "That's all?"

"That's all. You're not useful any longer, Kirby. In fact, you're an inconvenience. I'd planned your death as a warning to Uncle Philip, now it's just a necessity."

She wanted to turn away, but she needed to face it. "How could I have known you all my life and not seen it? How could you have hated me and not shown it?"

"You let emotions rule your life, I don't. Pick up the painting, Kirby." With the gun, she gestured. "And be careful with it. Stuart and I have been offered a healthy sum for it. If you call out," she added, "I'll shoot you now and be in the passage with the painting before anyone comes down."

"What are you going to do?"

"We're going into the passage. You're going to have a nasty spill, Kirby, and break your neck. I'm going to take the painting home and wait for the call to tell me of your accident."

She'd stall. If only she'd woken Adam… No, if she'd woken him, he, too, would have a gun pointed at him. "Everyone knows how I feel about the passages."

"It'll be a mystery. When they find the empty space on the wall, they'll know the Rembrandt was responsible. Stuart should be the first target, but he's out of town and has been for three days. I'll be devastated by the death of my oldest and dearest friend. It'll take months in Europe to recover from the grief."

"You've thought this out carefully." Kirby rested

against the table. "But are you capable of murder, Melly?" Slowly she closed her fingers around the bottle, working off the top with her thumb. "Face-to-face murder, not remote-control like this morning."

"Oh, yes." Melanie smiled beautifully. "I prefer it. I feel better with you knowing who's going to kill you. Now pick up the painting, Kirby. It's time."

With a jerk of her arm, Kirby tossed the turpentine mixture, splattering it on Melanie's neck and dress. When Melanie tossed up her hand in protection, Kirby lunged. Together they fell in a rolling heap onto the floor, the gun pressed between them.

"What do you mean Hiller's been in New York since yesterday?" Adam demanded. "What happened this morning wasn't an accident. He had to have done it."

"No way." In a few words McIntyre broke Adam's theory. "I have a good man on him. I can give you the name of Hiller's hotel. I can give you the name of the restaurant where he had lunch and what he ate while you were throwing chairs through windows. He's got his alibi cold, Adam, but it doesn't mean he didn't arrange it."

"Damn." Adam lowered the transmitter while he rearranged his thinking. "It gives me a bad feeling, Mac. Dealing with Hiller's one thing, but it's a whole new story if he has a partner or he's hired a pro to do his dirty work. Kirby needs protection, official protection. I want her out."

"I'll work on it. The Rembrandt—"

"I don't give a damn about the Rembrandt," Adam tossed back. "But it'll be in my hands tomorrow if I have to hang Fairchild up by his thumbs."

McIntyre let out a sigh of relief. "That's better. You were making me nervous thinking you were hung up on the Fairchild woman."

"I am hung up on the Fairchild woman," Adam returned mildly. "So you'd better arrange for—" He heard the shot. One, sharp and clean. It echoed and echoed through his head. "*Kirby!*" He thought of nothing else as he dropped the open transmitter on the floor and ran.

He called her name again as he raced downstairs. But his only answer was silence. He called as he rushed like a madman through the maze of rooms downstairs, but she didn't call back. Nearly blind with terror, his own voice echoing back to mock him, he ran on, slamming on lights as he went until the house was lit up like a celebration. Racing headlong into the dining room, he nearly fell over the two figures on the floor.

"Oh, my God!"

"I've killed her! Oh, God, Adam, help me! I think I've killed her!" With tears streaming down her face, Kirby pressed a blood-soaked linen napkin against Melanie's side. The stain spread over the rose silk of the dress and onto Kirby's hand.

"Keep the pressure firm." He didn't ask questions, but grabbed a handful of linen from the buffet behind him. Nudging Kirby aside, he felt for a pulse. "She's alive." He pressed more linen to Melanie's side. "Kirby—"

Before he could speak again, there was chaos. The rest of the household poured into the dining room from every direction. Polly let out one squeal that never ended.

"Call an ambulance," Adam ordered Cards, even as

the butler turned to do so. "Shut her up, or get her out," he told Rick, nodding to Polly.

Recovering quickly, Fairchild knelt beside his daughter and the daughter of his closest friend. "Kirby, what happened here?"

"I tried to take the gun from her." She struggled to breathe as she looked down at the blood on her hands. "We fell. I don't—Papa, I don't even know which one of us pulled the trigger. Oh, God, I don't even know."

"Melanie had a gun?" Steady as a rock, Fairchild took Kirby's shoulders and turned her to face him. "Why?"

"She hates me." Her voice shook, then leveled as she stared into her father's face. "She's always hated me, I never knew. It was the Rembrandt, Papa. She'd planned it all."

"Melanie?" Fairchild glanced beyond Kirby to the unconscious figure on the floor. "She was behind it." He fell silent, only a moment. "How bad, Adam?"

"I don't know, damn it. I'm an artist, not a doctor." There was fury in his eyes and blood on his hands. "It might've been Kirby."

"Yes, you're right." Fairchild's fingers tightened on his daughter's shoulder. "You're right."

"I found the Rembrandt," Kirby murmured. If it was shock that was making her light-headed, she wouldn't give in to it. She forced herself to think and to speak clearly.

Fairchild looked at the empty space on the wall, then at the table where the painting lay. "So you did."

With a cluck of her tongue, Tulip pushed Fairchild aside and took Kirby by the arm. Ignoring everyone else, she pulled Kirby to her feet. "Come with me, lovie. Come along with me now, that's a girl."

Feeling helpless, Adam watched Kirby being led away while he fought to stop the bleeding. "You'd better have a damn good explanation," he said between his teeth as his gaze swept over Fairchild.

"Explanations don't seem to be enough at this point," he murmured. Very slowly he rose. The sound of sirens cut through the quiet. "I'll phone Harriet."

Almost an hour had passed before Adam could wash the blood from his hands. Unconscious still, Melanie was speeding on her way to the hospital. His only thought was for Kirby now, and he left his room to find her. When he reached the bottom landing, he came upon an argument in full gear. Though the shouting was all one-sided, the noise vibrated through the hall.

"I want to see Adam Haines and I want to see him immediately!"

"Gate-crashing, Mac?" Adam moved forward to stand beside Cards.

"Adam, thank God." The small, husky man with the squared-off face and disarming eyes ran a hand through his disheveled mat of hair. "I didn't know what'd happened to you. Tell this wall to move aside, will you?"

"It's all right, Cards." He drew an expressionless stare. "He's not a reporter. I know him."

"Very well, sir."

"What the hell's going on?" McIntyre demanded when Cards walked back down the hall. "Who just got carted out of here in an ambulance? Damn it, Adam, I thought it might be you. Last thing I know, you're shouting and breaking transmission."

"It's been a rough night." Putting a hand on his shoul-

der, Adam led him into the parlor. "I need a drink."
Going directly to the bar, Adam poured, drank and
poured again. "Drink up, Mac," he invited. "This has
to be better than the stuff you've been buying in that
little motel down the road. Philip," he continued as Fairchild walked into the room, "I imagine you could use
one of these."

"Yes." With a nod of acknowledgment for McIntyre,
and no questions, Fairchild accepted the glass Adam
offered.

"We'd better sit down. Philip Fairchild," Adam went
on as Fairchild settled himself, "Henry McIntyre, in-
vestigator for the Commonwealth Insurance company."

"Ah, Mr. McIntyre." Fairchild drank half his Scotch
in one gulp. "We have quite a bit to discuss. But first,
Adam, satisfy my curiosity. How did you become involved with the investigation?"

"It's not the first time I've worked for Mac, but it's
the last." He sent McIntyre a quiet look that was lined
in steel. "There's a matter of our being cousins," he
added. "Second cousins."

"Relatives." Fairchild smiled knowingly, then gave
McIntyre a charming smile.

"You knew why I was here," Adam said. "How?"

"Well, Adam, my boy, it's nothing to do with your
cleverness." Fairchild tossed off the rest of the Scotch,
then rose to fill his glass again. "I was expecting someone to come along. You were the only one who did." He
sat back down with a sigh. "Simple as that."

"Expecting?"

"Would someone tell me who was in that ambulance?" McIntyre cut in.

"Melanie Burgess." Fairchild looked into his Scotch.

"Melly." It would hurt, he knew, for a long time. For himself, for Harriet and for Kirby. It was best to begin to deal with it. "She was shot when Kirby tried to take her gun away—the gun she was pointing at my daughter."

"Melanie Burgess," McIntyre mused. "It fits with the information I got today. Information," he added to Adam, "I was about to give you when you broke transmission. I'd like it from the beginning, Mr. Fairchild. I assume the police are on their way."

"Yes, no way around that." Fairchild sipped at his Scotch and deliberated on just how to handle things. Then he saw he no longer had McIntyre's attention. He was staring at the doorway.

Dressed in jeans and a white blouse, Kirby stood just inside the room. She was pale, but her eyes were dark. She was beautiful. It was the first thing McIntyre thought. The second was that she was a woman who could empty a man's mind the way a thirsty man empties a bottle.

"Kirby." Adam was up and across the room. He had his hands on hers. Hers were cold, but steady. "Are you all right?"

"Yes. Melanie?"

"The paramedics handled everything. I got the impression the wound wasn't as bad as it looked. Go lie down," he murmured. "Forget it for a while."

"No." She shook her head and managed a weak smile. "I'm fine, really. I've been washed and patted and plied with liquor, though I wouldn't mind another. The police will want to question me." Her gaze drifted to McIntyre. She didn't ask, but simply assumed he was with the police. "Do you need to talk to me?"

It wasn't until then he realized he'd been staring.

Clearing his throat, McIntyre rose. "I'd like to hear your father's story first, Miss Fairchild."

"Wouldn't we all?" Struggling to find some balance, she walked to her father's chair. "Are you going to come clean, Papa, or should I hire a shady lawyer?"

"Unnecessary, my sweet." He took her hand and held it. "The beginning," he continued with a smile for McIntyre. "It started, I suppose, a few days before Harriet flew off to Africa. She's an absentminded woman. She had to return to the gallery one night to pick up some papers she'd forgotten. When she saw the light in Stuart's office, she started to go in and scold him for working late. Instead she eavesdropped on his phone conversation and learned of his plans to steal the Rembrandt. Absentminded but shrewd, Harriet left and let Stuart think his plans were undetected." He grinned and squeezed Kirby's hand. "An intelligent woman, she came directly to a friend known for his loyalty and his sharp mind."

"Papa." With a laugh of relief, she bent over and kissed his head. "You were working together, I should've known."

"We developed a plan. Perhaps unwisely, we decided not to bring Kirby into it." He looked up at her. "Should I apologize?"

"Never."

But the fingers brushing over her hand said it for him. "Kirby's relationship with Stuart helped us along in that decision. And her occasional shortsightedness. That is, when she doesn't agree with my point of view."

"I might take the apology after all."

"In any case." Rising, Fairchild began to wander around the room, hands clasped behind his back. His version of Sherlock Holmes, Kirby decided, and settled back for the show. "Harriet and I both knew Stuart wasn't capable of constructing and carrying through on a theft like this alone. Harriet hadn't any idea whom he'd been talking to on the phone, but my name had been mentioned. Stuart had said he'd, ah, 'feel me out on the subject of producing a copy of the painting.'" His face fell easily into annoyed lines. "I've no idea why he should've thought a man like me would do something so base, so dishonest."

"Incredible," Adam murmured, and earned a blinding smile from father and daughter.

"We decided I'd agree, after some fee haggling. I'd then have the original in my possession while palming the copy off on Stuart. Sooner or later, his accomplice would be forced into the open to try to recover it. Meanwhile, Harriet reported the theft, but refused to file a claim. Instead she demanded that the insurance company act with discretion. Reluctantly she told them of her suspicion that I was involved, thereby ensuring that the investigation would be centered around me, and by association, Stuart and his accomplice. I concealed the Rembrandt behind a copy of a painting of my daughter, the original of which is tucked away in my room. I'm sentimental."

"Why didn't Mrs. Merrick just tell the police and the insurance company the truth?" McIntyre demanded after he'd worked his way through the explanation.

"They might have been hasty. No offense," Fairchild added indulgently. "Stuart might've been caught, but his accomplice would probably have gotten away. And, I confess, it was the intrigue that appealed to both of us. It was irresistible. You'll want to corroborate my story, of course."

"Of course," McIntyre agreed, and wondered if he could deal with another loony.

"We'd have done things differently if we'd had any idea that Melanie was involved. It's going to be difficult for Harriet." Pausing, he aimed a long look at McIntyre that was abruptly no-nonsense. "Be careful with her. Very careful. You might find our methods unorthodox, but she's a mother who's had two unspeakable shocks tonight: her daughter's betrayal and the possibility of losing her only child." He ran a hand over Kirby's hair as he stopped by her. "No matter how deep the hurt, the love remains, doesn't it, Kirby?"

"All I feel is the void," she murmured. "She hated me, and I think, I really think, she wanted me dead more than she wanted the painting. I wonder…I wonder just how much I'm to blame for that."

"You can't blame yourself for being, Kirby." Fairchild cupped her chin. "You can't blame a tree for reaching for the sun or another for rotting from within. We make our own choices and we're each responsible for them. Blame and credit belong to the individual. You haven't the right to claim either from someone else."

"You won't let me cover the hurt with guilt." After a long breath she rose and kissed his cheek. "I'll have to deal with it." Without thinking, she held out a hand for Adam before she turned to McIntyre. "Do you need a statement from me?"

"No, the shooting's not my jurisdiction, Miss Fairchild. Just the Rembrandt." Finishing off the rest of his Scotch he rose. "I'll have to take it with me, Mr. Fairchild."

All graciousness, Fairchild spread his arms wide. "Perfectly understandable."

"I appreciate your cooperation." If he could call it that. With a weary smile, he turned to Adam. "Don't worry, I haven't forgotten your terms. If everything's as he says, I should be able to keep them out of it officially, as we agreed the other day. Your part of the job's over, and all in all you handled it well. So, I'll be sorry if you're serious about not working for me anymore. You got the Rembrandt back, Adam. Now I've got to get started on untangling the red tape."

"Job?" Going cold, Kirby turned. Her hand was still linked in Adam's, but she felt it go numb as she drew it slowly away. "Job?" she repeated, pressing the hand to her stomach as if to ward off a blow.

Not now, he thought in frustration, and searched for the words he'd have used only a few hours later. "Kirby—"

With all the strength she had left, all the bitterness she'd felt, she brought her hand across his face. "Bastard," she whispered. She fled at a dead run.

"Damn you, Mac." Adam raced after her.

Chapter 12

Adam caught up to her just as Kirby started to slam her bedroom door. Shoving it open, he pushed his way inside. For a moment, they only stared at each other.

"Kirby, let me explain."

"No." The wounded look had been replaced by glacial anger. "Just get out. All the way out, Adam—of my house and my life."

"I can't." He took her by the shoulders, but her head snapped up, and the look was so cold, so hard, he dropped his hands again. It was too late to explain the way he'd planned. Too late to prevent the hurt. Now he had to find the way around it. "Kirby, I know what you must be thinking. I want—"

"Do you?" It took all of her effort to keep her voice from rising. Instead it was cool and calm. "I'm going to tell you anyway so we can leave everything neat and tidy." She faced him because she refused to turn her back on the pain or on the betrayal. "I'm thinking that I've never detested anyone more than I detest you at this moment. I'm thinking Stuart and Melanie could take lessons on using people from you. I'm thinking how naive I was, how stupid, to have believed there was something special about you, something stable and honest. And I wonder how I could've made love with you and never seen it. Then again, I didn't see it in Melanie, either. I loved and trusted her." Tears burned behind her eyes but she ignored them. "I loved and trusted you."

"Kirby..."

"Don't touch me." She backed away, but it was the tremor in her voice, not the movement, that stopped him from going to her. "I don't ever want to feel your hands on me again." Because she wanted to weep, she laughed, and the sound was as sharp as a knife. "I've always admired a really good liar, Adam, but you're the best. Every time you touched me, you lied. You prostituted yourself in that bed." She gestured toward it and wanted to scream. She wanted to fling herself on it and weep until she was empty. She stood, straight as an arrow. "You lay beside me and said all the things I wanted to hear. Do you get extra points for that, Adam? Surely that was above and beyond the call of duty."

"Don't." He'd had enough. Enough of her cold, clear look, her cold, clear words. "You know there was no dishonesty there. What happened between us had nothing to do with the rest."

"It has everything to do with it."

"No." He'd take everything else she could fling at him, but not that. She'd changed his life with hardly more than a look. She had to know it. "I should never have put my hands on you, but I couldn't stop myself. I wanted you. I needed you. You have to believe that."

"I'll tell you what I believe," she said quietly, because every word he spoke was another slice into her heart. She'd finished with being used. "You came here for the Rembrandt, and you meant to find it no matter who or what you had to go through. My father and I were means to an end. Nothing more, nothing less."

He had to take it, had to let her say it, but there'd be no lies between them any longer. "I came for the Rembrandt. When I walked through the door I only had one priority, to find it. But I didn't know you when I walked through the door. I wasn't in love with you then."

"Is this the part where you say everything changed?" she demanded, falling back on fury. "Shall we wait for the violins?" She was weakening. She turned away and leaned on the post of the bed. "Do better, Adam."

She could be cruel. He remembered her father's warning. He only wished he believed he had a defense. "I can't do better than the truth."

"Truth? What the hell do you know about truth?" She whirled back around, eyes damp now and shimmering with heat. "I stood here in this room and told you everything, everything I knew about my father. I trusted you with his welfare, the most important thing in my life. Where was your truth then?"

"I had a commitment. Do you think it was easy for me to sit here and listen, knowing I couldn't give you what you were giving me?"

"Yes." Her tone was dead calm, but her eyes were fierce. "Yes, I think it was a matter of routine for you. If you'd told me that night, the next day or the next,

I might've believed you. If I'd heard it from you, I might've forgiven you."

Timing. Hadn't she told him how vital timing could be? Now he felt her slipping away from him, but he had nothing but excuses to give her. "I was going to tell you everything, start to finish, tomorrow."

"Tomorrow?" Slowly she nodded. "Tomorrows are very convenient. A pity for us all how rarely they come."

All the warmth, all the fire, that had drawn him to her was gone. He'd only seen this look on her face once before—when Stuart had backed her into a corner and she'd had no escape. Stuart had used physical dominance, but it was no prettier than the emotional pressure Adam knew he used. "I'm sorry, Kirby. If I'd taken the risk and told you this morning, it would've been different for all of us."

"I don't want your apology!" The tears beat her and poured out. She'd sacrificed everything else, now her pride was gone, as well. "I thought I'd found the man I could share my life with. I fell in love with you in the flash of an instant. No questions, no doubts. I believed everything you said to me. I gave you everything I had. In all my life no one's been allowed to know me as you did. I entrusted you with everything I am and you used me." Turning, she pressed her face into the bedpost.

He had, he couldn't deny it even to himself. He'd used her, as Stuart had used her. As Melanie had used her. Loving her made no difference, yet he had to hope it made all the difference. "Kirby." It took all the strength he had not to go to her, comfort her, but he'd only be comforting himself if he put his arms around her now. "There's nothing you can say to me I haven't said to myself. I came here to do a job, but I fell in love with you. There wasn't any warning for me, either. I know I've hurt you. There's nothing I can do to turn back the clock."

"Do you expect me to fall into your arms? Do you expect me to say nothing else matters but us?" She turned, and though her cheeks were still damp, her eyes were dry. "It all matters," she said flatly. "Your job's finished here, Adam. You've recovered your Rembrandt. Take it, you earned it."

"You're not going to cut me out of your life."

"You've done that for me."

"No." The fury and frustration took over so that he grabbed her arm and jerked her against him. "No, you'll have to adjust to the way things are, because I'm coming back." He ran his hands down her hair, and they weren't steady. "You can make me suffer. By God, you can do it. I'll give you that, Kirby, but I'll be back."

Before his anger could push him too far, he whirled around and left her alone.

Fairchild was waiting for him, sitting calmly in the parlor by the fire. "I thought you'd need this." Without getting up, he gestured to the glass of Scotch on the table beside him. He waited until Adam had tossed it back. He didn't need to be told what had passed between them. "I'm sorry. She's hurt. Perhaps in time the wounds will close and she'll be able to listen."

Adam's knuckles whitened on the glass. "That's what I told her, but I didn't believe it. I betrayed her." His glance lowered and settled on the older man. "And you."

"You did what you had to do. You had a part to play." Fairchild spread his hands on his knees and stared at them, thinking of his own part. "She would've dealt with it, Adam. She's strong enough. But even Kirby has a breaking point. Melanie... It was too soon after Melanie."

"She won't let me comfort her." It was that anguish that had him turning to stare out of the window. "She looks so wounded, and my being here only makes it harder for her." Steadying himself, he stared out at nothing. "I'll be out as soon as I can pack." He turned, his head only, and looked at the small, balding man in front of the fire. "I love her, Philip."

In silence Fairchild watched Adam walk away. For the first time in his six decades he felt old. Old and tired. With a deep, deep sigh he rose and went to his daughter.

He found her curled on her bed, her head cradled by her knees and arms. She sat silent and unmoving and, he knew, utterly, utterly beaten. When he sat beside her, her head jerked up. Slowly, with his hand stroking her hair, her muscles relaxed.

"Do we ever stop making fools of ourselves, Papa?"

"You've never been a fool."

"Oh, yes, yes, it seems I have." Settling her chin on her knees, she stared straight ahead. "I lost our bet. I guess you'll be breaking open that box of cigars you've been saving."

"I think we can consider the extenuating circumstances."

"How generous of you." She tried to smile and failed. "Aren't you going to the hospital to be with Harriet?"

"Yes, of course."

"You'd better go then. She needs you."

His thin, bony hand continued to stroke her hair. "Don't you?"

"Oh, Papa." Tears came in a flood as she turned into his arms.

* * *

Kirby followed Cards downstairs as he carried her bags. In the week since the discovery of the Rembrandt she'd found it impossible to settle. She found no comfort in her art, no comfort in her home. Everything here held memories she could no longer deal with. She slept little and ate less. She knew she was losing touch with the person she was, and so she'd made plans to force herself back.

She opened the door for Cards and stared out at the bright, cheery morning. It made her want to weep.

"I don't know why a sensible person would get up at this ridiculous hour to drive to the wilderness."

Kirby forced back the gloom and turned to watch her father stride down the stairs in a ratty bathrobe and bare feet. What hair he had left was standing on end. "The early bird gathers no moss," she told him. "I want to get to the lodge and settle in. Want some coffee?"

"Not while I'm sleeping," he muttered as she nuzzled his cheek. "I don't know what's wrong with you, going off to that shack in the Himalayas."

"It's Harriet's very comfortable cabin in the Adirondacks, twenty miles from Lake Placid."

"Don't nitpick. You'll be alone."

"I've been alone before," she reminded him. "You're annoyed because you won't have anyone but Cards to shout at for a few weeks."

"He never shouts back." But even as he grumbled, Fairchild was studying Kirby's face. The shadows were still under her eyes and the loss of weight was much too apparent. "Tulip should go with you. Someone has to make you eat."

"I'm going to do that. Mountain air should make

me ravenous." When he continued to frown at her, she touched his cheek. "Don't worry, Papa."

"I am worried." Taking her shoulders, he held her at arm's length. "For the first time in your life, you're causing me genuine concern."

"A few pounds, Papa."

"Kirby." He cupped her face in his strong, thin hand. "You have to talk to Adam."

"No!" The word came out violently. With an effort, she drew a steadying breath. "I've said all I want to say to Adam. I need time and some solitude, that's all."

"Running away, Kirby?"

"As fast as I can. Papa, Rick proposed to me again before he left."

"What the hell does that have to do with anything?" he demanded. "He always proposes to you before he leaves."

"I nearly said yes." She lifted her hands to his, willing him to understand. "I nearly said yes because it seemed an easy way out. I'd have ruined his life."

"What about yours?"

"I have to glue the pieces back together. Papa, I'll be fine. It's Harriet who needs you now."

He thought of his friend, his oldest and closest friend. He thought of the grief. "Melanie's going to Europe when she's fully recovered."

"I know." Kirby tried not to remember the gun, or the hate. "Harriet told me. She'll need both of us when Melly's gone. If I can't help myself, how can I help Harriet?"

"Melanie won't see Harriet. The girl's destroying herself with hate." He looked at his own daughter, his pride, his treasure. "The sooner Melanie's out of the hospital and thousands of miles away, the better it'll be for everyone."

She knew what he'd done, how he'd fought against his feelings about Melanie to keep from causing either her or Harriet more grief. He'd comforted them both without releasing his own fury. She held him tightly a moment, saying nothing. Needing to say nothing.

"We all need some time," she murmured. When she drew away, she was smiling. She wouldn't leave him with tears in her eyes. "I'll cloister myself in the wilderness and sculpt while you pound on your hawk."

"Such a wicked tongue in such a pretty face."

"Papa..." Absently she checked the contents of her purse. "Whatever painting you do will be done under your own name?" When he didn't answer, she glanced up, narrowing her eyes. "Papa?"

"All my paintings will be Fairchilds. Haven't I given you my word?" He sniffed and looked injured. Kirby began to feel alarmed.

"This obsession with sculpting," she began, eyeing him carefully. "You don't have it in your head to attempt an emulation of a Rodin or Cellini?"

"You ask too many questions," he complained as he nudged her toward the door. "The day's wasting away, better get started. Don't forget to write."

Kirby paused on the porch and turned back to him. "It'll take you years," she decided. "If you ever acquire the talent. Go ahead and play with your hawk." She kissed his forehead. "I love you, Papa."

He watched her dart down the steps and into her car. "One should never interfere in the life of one's child," he murmured. Smiling broadly, he waved goodbye. When she was out of sight, he went directly to the phone.

* * *

The forest had always appealed to her. In mid-autumn, it shouted with life. The burst of colors were a last swirling fling before the trees went into the final cycle. It was an order Kirby accepted—birth, growth, decay, rebirth. Still, after three days alone, she hadn't found her serenity.

The stream she walked past rushed and hissed. The air was brisk and tangy. She was miserable.

She'd nearly come to terms with her feelings about Melanie. Her childhood friend was ill, had been ill for a long, long time and might never fully recover. It hadn't been a betrayal any more than cancer was a betrayal. But it was a malignancy Kirby knew she had to cut out of her life. She'd nearly accepted it, for Melanie's sake and her own.

She could come to terms with Melanie, but she had yet to deal with Adam. He'd had no illness, nor a lifetime of resentments to feed it. He'd simply had a job to do. And that was too cold for her to accept.

With her hands in her pockets, she sat down on a log and scowled into the water. Her life, she admitted, was a mess. She was a mess. And she was damn sick of it.

She tried to tell herself she'd put Adam out of her life. She hadn't. Yes, she'd refused to listen to him. She'd made no attempt to contact him. It wasn't enough. It wasn't enough, Kirby decided, because it left things unfinished. Now she'd never know if he'd had any real feelings for her. She'd never know if, even briefly, he'd belonged to her.

Perhaps it was best that way.

Standing, she began to walk again, scuffing the leaves that danced around her feet. She was tired of herself. Another first. It wasn't going to go on, she determined. Whatever the cost, she was going to whip Kirby Fairchild back into shape. Starting now. At a brisk pace, she started back to the cabin.

She liked the way it looked, set deep in the trees by itself. The roof was pitched high and the glass sparkled. Today, she thought as she went in through the back door, she'd work. After she'd worked, she'd eat until she couldn't move.

Peeling off her coat as she went, she walked directly to the worktable she'd set up in the corner of the living room. Without looking around, she tossed the coat aside and looked at her equipment. She hadn't touched it in days. Now she sat and picked up a formless piece of wood. This was to be her *Passion*. Perhaps now more than ever, she needed to put that emotion into form.

There was silence as she explored the feel and life of the wood in her hands. She thought of Adam, of the nights, the touches, the tastes. It hurt. Passion could. Using it, she began to work.

An hour slipped by. She only noticed when her fingers cramped. With a sigh, she set the wood down and stretched them. The healing had begun. She could be certain of it now. "A start," she murmured to herself. "It's a start."

"It's *Passion*. I can already see it."

The knife slipped out of her hand and clattered on the table as she whirled. Across the room, calmly sitting in a faded wingback chair, was Adam. She'd nearly sprung out of the chair to go to him before she stopped herself. He looked the same, just the same. But nothing was. That she had to remember.

"How did you get in here?"

He heard the ice in her voice. But he'd seen her eyes. In that one instant, she'd told him everything he'd ached for. Still, he knew she couldn't be rushed. "The front door wasn't locked." He rose and crossed to her. "I came inside to wait for you, but when you came in, you looked so intense; then you started right in. I didn't want to disturb your work." When she said nothing, he picked up the wood and turned it over in his hand. He thought it smoldered. "Amazing," he murmured. "Amazing what power you have." Just holding it made him want her more, made him want what she'd put into the wood. Carefully he set it down again, but his eyes were just as intense when he studied her. "What the hell've you been doing? Starving yourself?"

"Don't be ridiculous." She stood and walked away from him, but she didn't know where to go.

"Am I to blame for that, too?"

His voice was quiet, serious. She'd never be able to resist that tone. Gathering her strength, she turned back to him. "Did Tulip send you to check up on me?"

She was too thin. Damn it. Had the pounds melted off her? She was so small. How could she be so small and look so arrogant? He wanted to go to her. Beg. He was nearly certain she'd listen now. Yet she wouldn't want it that way. Instead, he tucked his hands in his pockets and rocked back on his heels. "This is a cozy little place. I wandered around a bit while you were out."

"Glad you made yourself at home."

"It's everything Harriet said it would be." He looked at her again and smiled. "Isolated, cozy, charming."

She lifted a brow. It was easiest with the distance between them. "You've spoken to Harriet?"

"I took your portrait to the gallery."

Emotion came and went again in her eyes. Picking up a small brass pelican, she caressed it absently. "My portrait?"

"I promised her she could exhibit it when I'd finished." He watched her nervous fingers run over the brass. "It wasn't difficult to finish without you. I saw you everywhere I looked."

Quickly she turned to walk to the front wall. It was all glass, open to the woods. No one could feel trapped with that view. Kirby clung to it. "Harriet's having a difficult time."

"The strain shows a bit." In her, he thought, and in you. "I think it's better for her that Melanie won't see her at this point. With Stuart out of the way, the gallery's keeping Harriet busy." He stared at her back, trying to imagine what expression he'd find on her face. "Why aren't you pressing charges, Kirby?"

"For what purpose?" she countered. She set the piece of brass down. A crutch was a crutch, and she was through with them. "Both Stuart and Melanie are disgraced, banished from the elite that means so much to them. The publicity's been horrid. They have no money, no reputation. Isn't that punishment enough?"

"Melanie tried to kill you. Twice." Suddenly furious at the calm, even tone, he went to her and spun her around. "Damn it, Kirby, she wanted you dead!"

"It was she who nearly died." Her voice was still even, but she took a step back, from him. "The police have to accept my story that the gun went off accidentally, even if others don't. I could have sent Melly to jail. Wouldn't I feel avenged watching Harriet suffer?"

Adam forced back the impatience and stared through the glass. "She's worried about you."

"Harriet?" Kirby shrugged. "There's no need. When you see her, tell her I'm well."

"You can tell her yourself when we get back."

"We?" The lightest hint of temper entered her voice. Nothing could have relieved him more. "I'm going to be here for some time yet."

"Fine. I've nothing better to do."

"That wasn't an invitation."

"Harriet already gave me one," he told her easily. He gave the room another sweeping glance while Kirby smoldered. "The place looks big enough for two."

"That's where you're wrong, but don't let me spoil your plans." She spun on her heel and headed for the stairs. Before she'd gotten five feet, his fingers curled around her arm and held her still. When she whirled, he saw that his gypsy was back.

"You don't really think I'd let you leave? Kirby, you disappoint me."

"You don't *let* me do anything, Adam. Nor do you prevent me from doing anything."

"Only when it's necessary." While she stood rigid, he put his hands on her shoulders. "You're going to listen to me this time. And you're going to start listening in just a minute."

He pressed his mouth to hers as he'd needed to for weeks. She didn't resist. Nor did she respond. He could feel her fighting the need to do both. He could press her, he knew, and she'd give in to him. Then he might never really have her. Slowly their gazes locked; he straightened.

"You're nearly through making me suffer," he murmured. "I've paid, Kirby, in every moment I haven't been with you. Through every night you haven't been beside me. When are you going to stop punishing me?"

"I don't want to punish you." It was true. She'd already forgiven him. Yet, her confidence, that strong, thin shield she'd always had, had suffered an enormous blow. This time when she stepped back he didn't try to stop her. "I know we parted badly. Maybe it'd be best if we just admitted we'd both made a mistake and left it at that. I realize you did what you had to do. I've always done the same. It's time I got on with my life and you with yours."

He felt a quick jiggle of panic. She was too calm, much too calm. He wanted emotion from her, any kind she'd give. "What sort of life would either of us have without the other?"

None. But she shook her head. "I said we made a mistake—"

"And now you're going to tell me you don't love me?"

She looked straight at him and opened her mouth. Weakening, she shifted her gaze to just over his shoulder. "No, I don't love you, Adam. I'm sorry."

She'd nearly cut him off at the knees. If she hadn't looked away at the last instant, it would've been over for him. "I'd've thought you could lie better than that." In one move he closed the distance between them. His arms were around her, firm, secure. The same, she thought. Nothing had changed after all. "I've given you two weeks, Kirby. Maybe I should give you more time, but I can't." He buried his face in her hair while she squeezed her eyes shut. She'd been wrong, she remembered. She'd been wrong about so many things. Could this be right?

"Adam, please…"

"No, no more. I love you." He drew away, barely resisting the need to shake her. "I love you and you'll have to get used to it. It isn't going to change."

She curled her hand into a fist before she could stroke his cheek. "I think you're getting pompous again."

"Then you'll have to get used to that, too. Kirby..." He framed her face with his hands. "How many ways would you like me to apologize?"

"No." Shaking her head she moved away again. She should be able to think, she warned herself. She had to think. "I don't need apologies, Adam."

"You wouldn't," he murmured. Forgiveness would come as easily to her as every other emotion. "Your father and I had a long talk before I drove up here."

"Did you?" She gave her attention to a bowl of dried flowers. "How nice."

"He's given me his word he'll no longer...emulate paintings."

With her back to him, she smiled. The pain vanished without her realizing it, and with it, the doubts. They loved. There was so little else in life. Still smiling, Kirby decided she wouldn't tell Adam of her father's ambition with sculpting. Not just yet. "I'm glad you convinced him," she said with her tongue in her cheek.

"He decided to concede the point to me, since I'm going to be a member of the family."

With a flutter of her lashes, she turned. "How lovely. Is Papa adopting you?"

"That wasn't precisely the relationship we discussed." Crossing to her, he took her into his arms again. This time he felt the give and the strength. "Tell me again that you don't love me."

"I don't love you," she murmured, and pulled his mouth to hers. "I don't want you to hold me." Her arms wound around his neck. "I don't want you to kiss me again. Now." Her lips clung to his, opening, giving. As the heat built, he groaned and drew her in.

"Obstinate, aren't you?" he muttered.

"Invariably."

"But are you going to marry me?"

"On my terms."

When her head tilted back, he ran kisses up the length of her throat. "Which are?"

"I may come easy, but I don't come free."

"What do you want, a marriage settlement?" On a half laugh, he drew away. She was his, whoever, whatever she was. He'd never let her go again. "Can't you think of anything but money?"

"I'm fond of money—and we still have to discuss my sitting fee. However…" She drew a deep breath. "My terms for marriage are four children."

"Four?" Even knowing Kirby, he'd been caught off guard. "Four children?"

She moistened her lips but her voice was strong. "I'm firm on that number, Adam. The point's non-negotiable." Then her eyes were young and full of needs. "I want children. Your children."

Every time he thought he loved her completely, he found he could love her more. Still more. "Four," he repeated with a slow nod. "Any preference to gender?"

The breath she'd been holding came out on a laugh. No, she hadn't been wrong. They loved. There was very little else. "I'm flexible, though a mix of some sort would be nice." She tossed her head back and smiled up at him. "What do you think?"

He swept her into his arms then headed for the stairs. "I think we'd better get started."

* * * * *

STORM WARNING

For Mom,
who wouldn't let my brothers clobber me—
even when I deserved it.

Chapter 1

The Pine View Inn was nestled comfortably in the Blue Ridge Mountains. After leaving the main road, the meandering driveway crossed a narrow ford just wide enough for one car. The inn was situated a short distance beyond the ford.

It was a lovely place, full of character, the lines so clean they disguised the building's rambling structure. It was three stories high, built of brick that had been weathered to a soft rose, the facade interspersed with narrow, white-shuttered windows. The hipped roof had faded long ago to a quiet green, and three straight chimneys rose from it. A wide wooden porch made a white skirt around the entire house and doors opened out to it from all four sides.

The surrounding lawn was smooth and well tended. There was less than an acre, house included, before the trees and outcroppings of rock staked their claim on the land. It was as if nature had decided that the house could have this much and no more. The effect was magnificent. The house and mountains stood in peaceful coexistence, neither detracting from the other's beauty.

As she pulled her car to the informal parking area at the side of the house, Autumn counted five cars, including her aunt's vintage Chevy. Though the season was still weeks off, it appeared that the inn already had several guests.

There was a light April chill in the air. The daffodils had yet to open, and the crocuses were just beginning to fade. A few azalea buds showed a trace of color. The day was poised and waiting for spring. The higher, surrounding mountains clung to their winter brown, but touches of green were creeping up them. It wouldn't be gloomy brown and gray for long.

Autumn swung her camera case over one shoulder and her purse over the other—the purse was of secondary importance. Two large suitcases also had to be dragged from the trunk. After a moment's struggle, she managed to arrange everything so that she could take it all in one load, then mounted the steps. The door, as always, was unlocked.

There was no one about. The sprawling living room which served as a lounge was empty, though a fire crackled in the grate. Setting down her cases, Autumn entered the room. Nothing had changed.

Rag rugs dotted the floor; hand-crocheted afghans were draped on the two patchworked sofas. At the windows were chintz priscillas and the Hummel collection was still on the mantel. Characteristically, the room was neat, but far from orderly. There were magazines here and there, an overflowing sewing basket, a group of pillows piled for comfort rather than style on the windowseat. The ambience was friendly with a faintly distracted charm. Autumn thought with a smile that the room suited her aunt perfectly.

She felt an odd pleasure. It was always reassuring to find that something loved hasn't changed. Taking a last quick glance around the room, she ran a hand through her hair. It hung past her waist and was tousled from the long drive with open windows. She gave idle consideration to digging out a brush, but promptly forgot when she heard footsteps down the hall.

"Oh, Autumn, there you are." Typically, her aunt greeted her as though Autumn had just spent an hour at the local supermarket rather than a year in New York. "I'm glad you got in before dinner. We're having pot roast, your favorite."

Not having the heart to remind her aunt that pot roast was her brother Paul's favorite, Autumn smiled. "Aunt Tabby, it's so good to see you!" Quickly she walked over and kissed her aunt's cheek. The familiar scent of lavender surrounded her.

Aunt Tabby in no way resembled the cat her name brought to mind. Cats are prone to snobbishness, disdainfully tolerating the rest of the world. They are known for speed, agility and cunning. Aunt Tabby was known for her vague meanderings, disjointed conversations and confused thinking. She had no guile. Autumn adored her.

Drawing her aunt away, Autumn studied her closely. "You look wonderful." It was invariably true. Aunt Tabby's hair was the same deep chestnut as her niece's, but it was liberally dashed with gray. It suited her. She wore it short, curling haphazardly around her small round face. Her features were all small-scaled—mouth, nose, ears, even her hands and feet. Her eyes were a mistily faded blue. Though she was halfway through her fifties, her skin refused to wrinkle; it was smooth as a girl's. She stood a half-foot shorter than Autumn and was pleasantly round and soft. Beside her, Autumn felt like a gangly toothpick. Autumn hugged her again, then kissed her other cheek. "Absolutely wonderful."

Aunt Tabby smiled up at her. "What a pretty girl you are. I always knew you would be. But so awfully thin." She patted Autumn's cheek and wondered how many calories were in pot roast.

With a shrug, Autumn thought of the ten pounds she had gained when she'd stopped smoking. She had lost them again almost as quickly.

"Nelson always was thin," Aunt Tabby added, thinking of her brother, Autumn's father.

"Still is," Autumn told her. She set her camera case on a table and grinned at her aunt. "Mom's always threatening to sue for divorce."

"Oh well." Aunt Tabby clucked her tongue and looked thoughtful. "I don't think that's wise after all the years they've been married." Knowing the jest had been lost, Autumn merely nodded in agreement. "I gave you the room you always liked, dear. You can still see the lake from the window. The leaves will be full soon though, but... Remember when you fell in when you were a little girl? Nelson had to fish you out."

"That was Will," Autumn reminded her, thinking back on the day her younger brother had toppled into the lake.

"Oh?" Aunt Tabby looked faintly confused a moment, then smiled disarmingly. "He learned to swim quite well, didn't he? Such an enormous young man now. It always surprised me. There aren't any children with us at the moment," she added, flowing from sentence to sentence with her own brand of logic.

"I saw several cars. Are there many people here?" Autumn stretched her cramped muscles as she wandered the room. It smelled of sandalwood and lemon oil.

"One double and five singles," she told her. "One of the singles is French and quite fond of my apple pie. I must go check on my blueberry cobbler," she announced suddenly. "Nancy is a marvel with a pot roast, but helpless with baking. George is down with a virus."

She was already making for the door as Autumn tried to puzzle out the last snatch of information.

"I'm sorry to hear that," she replied with what she hoped was appropriate sympathy.

"I'm a bit shorthanded at the moment, dear, so perhaps you can manage your suitcases yourself. Or you can wait for one of the gentlemen to come in."

George, Autumn remembered. Gardener, bellboy and bartender.

"Don't worry, Aunt Tabby. I can manage."

"Oh, by the way, Autumn." She turned back, but Autumn knew her aunt's thoughts were centered on the fate of her cobbler. "I have a little surprise for you— oh, I see Miss Bond is coming in." Typically, she interrupted herself, then smiled. "She'll keep you company. Dinner's at the usual time. Don't be late."

Obviously relieved that both her cobbler and her niece were about to be taken care of, she bustled off, her heels tapping cheerfully on the hardwood floor.

Autumn turned to watch her designated companion enter through the side door. She found herself gaping.

Julia Bond. Of course, Autumn recognized her instantly. There could be no other woman who possessed such shimmering, golden beauty. How many times had she sat in a crowded theater and watched Julia's charm and talent transcend the movie screen? In person, in the flesh, her beauty didn't diminish. It sparkled, all the more alive in three dimensions.

Small, with exquisite curves just bordering on lush, Julia Bond was a magnificent example of womanhood at its best. Her cream-colored linen slacks and vivid blue cashmere sweater set off her coloring to perfection. Pale golden hair framed her face like sunlight. Her eyes were a deep summer blue. The full, shapely mouth lifted into a smile even as the famous brows arched. For a moment, Julia stood, fingering her silk scarf. Then she spoke, her voice smoky, exactly as Autumn had known it would be. "What fabulous hair."

It took Autumn a moment to register the comment. Her mind was blank at seeing Julia Bond step into her aunt's lounge as casually as she would have strolled into the New York Hilton. The smile, however, was full of charm and so completely unaffected that Autumn was able to form one in return.

"Thank you. I'm sure you're used to being stared at, Miss Bond, but I apologize anyway."

Julia sat, with a grace that was at once insolent and admirable, in a wingback chair. Drawing out a long, thin cigarette, she gave Autumn a full-power smile. "Actors adore being stared at. Sit down." She gestured. "I have a feeling I've at last found someone to talk to in this place."

Autumn's obedience was automatic, a tribute to the actress's charm.

"Of course," Julia continued, still studying Autumn's face, "you're entirely too young and too attractive." Settling back, she crossed her legs. Somehow, she managed to transform the wingback chair, with the small darning marks in the left arm, into a throne. "Then your coloring and mine offset each other nicely. How old are you, darling?"

"Twenty-five." Captivated, Autumn answered without thinking.

Julia laughed, a low bubbling sound that flowed and ebbed like a wave. "Oh, so am I. Perennially." She tossed her head in amusement, then left it cocked to the side. Autumn's fingers itched for her camera. "What's your name, darling, and what brings you to solitude and pine trees?"

"Autumn," she responded as she pushed her hair off her shoulders. "Autumn Gallegher. My aunt owns the inn."

"Your aunt?" Julia's face registered surprise and more amusement. "That dear fuzzy little lady is your aunt?"

"Yes." A grin escaped at the accuracy of the description. "My father's sister." Relaxed, Autumn leaned back. She was doing her own studying, thinking in angles and shadings.

"Incredible," Julia decided with a shake of her head. "You don't look like her. Oh, the hair," she corrected with an envious glance. "I imagine hers was once your color. Magnificent. I know women who would kill for that shade, and you seem to have about three feet of it." With a sigh, she drew delicately on her cigarette. "So, you've come to pay your aunt a visit."

There was nothing condescending in her attitude. Her eyes were interested and Autumn began to find her not only charming but likable. "For a few weeks. I haven't seen her in nearly a year. She wrote and asked me to come down, so I'm taking my vacation all at one time."

"What do you do?" Julia pursed her lips. "Model?"

"No." Autumn's laughter came quickly at the thought of it. "I'm a photographer."

"Photographer!" Julia exclaimed. She glowed with pleasure. "I'm very fond of photographers. Vanity, I suppose."

"I imagine photographers are fond of you for the same reason."

"Oh, my dear." When Julia smiled, Autumn recognized both pleasure and amusement. "How sweet."

"Are you alone, Miss Bond?" Her sense of curiosity was ingrained. Autumn had already forgotten to be overwhelmed.

"Julia, please, or you'll remind me of the half-decade that separates our ages. The color of that sweater suits you," she commented, eyeing Autumn's crewneck. "I never could wear gray. Sorry, darling," she apologized with a lightning-quick smile. "Clothes are a weakness of mine. Am I alone?" The smile deepened. "Actually, this little hiatus is a mixture of business and pleasure. I'm in between husbands at the moment—a glorious interlude." Julia tossed her head. "Men are delightful, but husbands can be dreadfully inhibiting. Have you ever had one?"

"No." The grin was irrepressible. From the tone, Julia might have asked if Autumn had ever owned a cocker spaniel.

"I've had three." Julia's eyes grew wicked and delighted. "In this case, the third was *not* the charm. Six months with an English baron was quite enough."

Autumn remembered the photos she had seen of Julia with a tall, aristocratic Englishman. She had worn tweed brilliantly.

"I've taken a vow of abstinence," Julia continued. "Not against men—against marriage."

"Until the next time?" Autumn ventured.

"Until the next time," Julia agreed with a laugh. "At the moment, I'm here for platonic purposes with Jacques LeFarre."

"The producer?"

"Of course." Again, Autumn felt the close scrutiny. "He'll take one look at you and decide he has a new star on the horizon. Still, that might be an interesting diversion." She frowned a moment, then shrugged it away. "The other residents of your aunt's cozy inn have offered little in the way of diversions thus far."

"Oh?" Automatically, Autumn shook her head as Julia offered her a cigarette.

"We have Dr. and Mrs. Spicer," Julia began. One perfectly shaped nail tapped against the arm of her chair. There was something different in her attitude now. Autumn was sensitive to moods, but this was too subtle a change for her to identify. "The doctor himself might be interesting," Julia continued. "He's very tall and nicely built, smoothly handsome with just the right amount of gray at the temples."

She smiled. Just then Autumn thought Julia resembled a very pretty, well-fed cat.

"The wife is short and unfortunately rather dumpy. She spoils whatever attractiveness she might have with a continually morose expression." Julia demonstrated it with terrifying skill. Autumn's laughter burst out before she could stop it.

"How unkind," Autumn chided, smiling still.

"Oh, I know." A graceful hand waved in dismissal. "I have no patience for women who let themselves go, then look daggers at those who don't. He's fond of fresh air and walking in the woods, and she grumbles and mopes along after him." Julia paused, giving Autumn a wary glance. "How do you feel about walking?"

"I like it." Hearing the apology in her voice, Autumn grinned.

"Oh well." Julia shrugged at eccentricities. "It takes all kinds. Next, we have Helen Easterman." The oval, tinted nails began to tap again. Her eyes drifted from Autumn's to the view out the window. Somehow, Autumn didn't think she was seeing mountains and pine trees. "She says she's an art teacher, taking time off to sketch nature. She's rather attractive, though a bit over-ripe, with sharp little eyes and an unpleasant smile. Then, there's Steve Anderson." Julia gave her slow, cat smile again. Describing men, Autumn mused, was more to her taste. "He's rather delicious. Wide shoulders, California blond hair. Nice blue eyes. And he's embarrassingly rich. His father owns, ah…"

"Anderson Manufacturing?" Autumn prompted and was rewarded with a beam of approval.

"How clever of you."

"I heard something about Steve Anderson aiming for a political career."

"Mmm, yes. It would suit him." Julia nodded. "He's very well-mannered and has a disarmingly boyish smile—that's always a political asset."

"It's a sobering thought that government officials are elected on their smiles."

"Oh, politics." Julia wrinkled her nose and shrugged away the entire profession. "I had an affair with a senator once. Nasty business, politics." She laughed at some private joke.

Not certain whether her comment had been a romantic observation or a general one, Autumn didn't pursue it. "So far," Autumn said, "it seems an unlikely menagerie for Julia Bond and Jacques LeFarre to join."

"Show business." With a smile, she lit another cigarette, then waved it at Autumn. "Stick with photography, Autumn, no matter what promises Jacques makes you. We're here due to a whim of the last and most interesting character in our little play. He's a genius of a writer. I did one of his screenplays a few years back. Jacques wants to produce another, and he wants me for the lead." She dragged deep on the cigarette. "I'm willing—really good scripts aren't that easy to come by—but our writer is in the middle of a novel. Jacques thinks the novel could be turned into a screenplay, but our genius resists. He told Jacques he was coming here to write in peace for a few weeks, and that he'd think it over. The charming LeFarre talked him into allowing us to join him for a few days."

Autumn was both fascinated and confused. Her question was characteristically blunt. "Do you usually chase writers around this way? I'd think it would be more the other way around."

"And you'd be right," Julia said flatly. With only the movement of her eyebrows, her expression turned haughty. "But Jacques is dead set on producing this man's work, and he caught me at a weak moment. I had just finished reading one of the most appalling scripts. Actually," she amended with a grimace, "three of the most appalling scripts. My work feeds me, but I won't do trash. So…" Julia smiled and moved her hands. "Here I am."

"Chasing a reluctant writer."

"It has its compensations."

I'd like to shoot her with the sun at her back. Low sun, just going down. The contrasts would be perfect. Autumn pulled herself back from her thoughts and caught up with Julia's conversation. "Compensations?" she repeated.

"The writer happens to be incredibly attractive, in that carelessly rugged sort of way that no one can pull off unless he's born with it. A marvelous change of pace," she added with a wicked gleam, "from English barons. He's tall and bronzed with black hair that's just a bit too long and always disheveled. It makes a woman itch to get her fingers into it. Best, he has those dark eyes that say 'go to hell' so eloquently. He's an arrogant devil." Her sigh was pure feminine approval. "Arrogant men are irresistible, don't you think?"

Autumn murmured something while she tried to block out the suspicions Julia's words were forming. It had to be someone else, she thought frantically. Anyone else.

"And, of course, Lucas McLean's talent deserves a bit of arrogance."

The color drained from Autumn's face and left it stiff. Waves of almost forgotten pain washed over her. *How could it hurt so much after all this time?* She had built the wall so carefully, so laboriously—how could it crumble into dust at the sound of a name? She wondered, dully, what sadistic quirk of fate had brought Lucas McLean back to torment her.

"Why, darling, what's the matter?"

Julia's voice, mixed with concern and curiosity, penetrated. As if coming up for air, Autumn shook her head. "Nothing." She shook her head again and swallowed. "It was just a surprise to hear that Lucas McLean is here." Drawing a deep breath, she met Julia's eyes. "I knew him...a long time ago."

"Oh, I see."

And she did see, Autumn noted, very well. Sympathy warred with speculation in both her face and voice. Autumn shrugged, determined to treat it lightly.

"I doubt he remembers me." Part of her prayed with fervor it was true, while another prayed at cross-purposes. Would he forget? she wondered. Could he?

"Autumn, darling, yours is a face no man is likely to forget." Through a mist of smoke, Julia studied her. "You were very young when you fell in love with him?"

"Yes." Autumn was trying, painfully, to rebuild her protective wall and wasn't surprised by the question. "Too young, too naive." She managed a brittle smile and for the first time in six months accepted a cigarette. "But I learn quickly."

"It seems the next few days might prove interesting, after all."

"Yes." Autumn's agreement lacked enthusiasm. "So it does." She needed time to be alone, to steady herself. "I have to take my bags up," she said as she rose.

While Autumn stretched her slender arms toward the ceiling, Julia smiled. "I'll see you at dinner."

Nodding, Autumn gathered up her camera case and purse and left the room.

In the hall, she struggled with her suitcases, camera and purse before beginning the task of transporting them up the stairs. Throughout the slow trek up the stairs, Autumn relieved tension by muttering and swearing. *Lucas McLean,* she thought and banged a suitcase against her shin. She nearly convinced herself that her ill humor was a result of the bruise she'd just given herself. Out of breath and patience, she reached the hallway outside her room and dumped everything on the floor with an angry thud.

"Hello, Cat. No bellboy?"

The voice—and the ridiculous nickname—knocked a few of her freshly mortared bricks loose. After a brief hesitation, Autumn turned to him. The pain wouldn't show on her face. She'd learned that much. But the pain was there, surprisingly real and physical. It reminded her of the day her brother had swung a baseball bat into her stomach when she had been twelve. *I'm not twelve now,* she reminded herself. She met Lucas's arrogant smile with one of her own.

"Hello, Lucas. I heard you were here. The Pine View Inn is bursting with celebrities."

He was the same, she noted. Dark and lean and male. There was a ruggedness about him, accented by rough black brows and craggy, demanding features that couldn't be called handsome. Oh, no, that was much too tame a word for Lucas McLean. Arousing, irresistible. Fatal. Those words suited him better.

His eyes were nearly as black as his hair. They kept secrets easily. He carried himself well, with a negligent grace that was natural rather than studied. His not-so-subtle masculine power drifted with him as he ambled closer and studied her.

It was then that Autumn noticed how hellishly tired he looked. There were shadows under his eyes. He needed a shave. The creases in his cheeks were deeper than she remembered—and she remembered very well.

"You look like yesterday." He grabbed a handful of her hair as he fastened his eyes on hers. She wondered how she could have ever thought herself over him. No woman ever got over Lucas. Sheer determination kept her eyes level.

"You," she countered as she opened her door, "look like hell. You need some sleep."

Lucas leaned on the doorjamb before she could drag her cases inside and slam the door. "Having trouble with one of my characters," he said smoothly. "She's a tall, willowy creature with chestnut hair that ripples down her back. Narrow hipped, with legs that go right up to her waist."

Bracing herself, Autumn turned back and stared at him. Carefully, she erased any expression from her face.

"She has a child's mouth," he continued, dropping his glance to hers a moment. "And a small nose, somewhat at odds with high, elegant cheekbones. Her skin is ivory with touches of warmth just under the surface. Her eyes are long lidded and ridiculously lashed—green that melts into amber, like a cat's."

Without comment, she listened to his description of herself. She gave him a bored, disinterested look he would never have seen on her face three years before. "Is she the murderer or the corpse?" It pleased Autumn to see his brows lift in surprise before they drew together in a frown.

"I'll send you a copy when it's done." He searched

her face, then a shutter came down, leaving his expression unreadable. That, too, she noted, hadn't changed.

"You do that." After giving her cases a superhuman tug, jettisoning them into her room, Autumn rested against the door. Her smile had no feeling. "You'll have to excuse me, Lucas, I've had a long drive and want a bath."

She closed the door firmly and with finality, in his face.

Autumn's movements then became brisk. There was unpacking to do and a bath to draw and a dress to choose for dinner. Those things would give her time to recover before she allowed herself to think, to feel. When she slipped into lingerie and stockings, her nerves were steadier. The worst of it had been weathered. Surely, she mused, the first meeting, the first exchange of words were the most difficult. She had seen him. She had spoken to him. She had survived. Success made her bold. For the first time in nearly two years, Autumn allowed herself to remember.

She had been so much in love. Her assignment had been an ordinary one—a picture layout of mystery novelist Lucas McLean. The result had been six months of incredible joy followed by unspeakable hurt.

He had overwhelmed her. She'd never met anyone like him. She knew now that there was no one else like him. He was a law unto himself. He had been brilliant, compelling, selfish and moody. After the first shock of learning he was interested in her, Autumn had floated along on a cloud of wonder and admiration. And love.

His arrogance, as Julia had said, was irresistible. His phone calls at three in the morning had been treasured. The last time she had been held in his arms, experiencing the wild demands of his mouth, had been as exciting as the first. She had tumbled into his bed like a ripe peach, giving up her innocence with the freedom that comes with blind, trusting love.

She remembered he'd never said the words she wanted to hear. She'd told herself she had no need for them—words weren't important. There were unexpected boxes of roses, surprise picnics on the beach with wine in paper cups and lovemaking that was both intense and all-consuming. What did she need with words? When the end had come it had been swift—but far from painless.

Autumn put his distraction, his moodiness down to trouble with the novel he was working on. It didn't occur to her that he'd been bored. It was her habit to fix dinner on Wednesdays at his home. It was a small, private evening, one she prized above all others. Her arrival was so natural to her, so routine, that when she entered his living room and found him dressed in dinner clothes, she only thought he had decided to add a more formal atmosphere to their quiet dinner.

"Why, Cat, what are you doing here?" The unexpected words were spoken so easily, she merely stared. "Ah, it's Wednesday, isn't it?" There was a slight annoyance in his tone, as though he had forgotten a dentist appointment. "I completely forgot. I'm afraid I've made other plans."

"Other plans?" she echoed. Comprehension was still a long way off.

"I should have phoned you and saved you the trip. Sorry, Cat, I'm just leaving."

"Leaving?"

"I'm going out." He moved across the room and

stared at her. She shivered. No one's eyes could be as warm—or as cold—as Lucas McLean's. "Don't be difficult, Autumn, I don't want to hurt you any more than is necessary."

Feeling the tears of realization rush out, she shook her head and fought against acceptance. The tears sent him into a fury.

"Stop it! I haven't the time to deal with weeping. Just pack it in. Chalk it up to experience. God knows you need it."

Swearing, he stomped away to light a cigarette. She had stood there, weeping without sound.

"Don't make a fool of yourself, Autumn." The calm, rigid voice was more frightening to her than his anger. At least anger was an emotion. "When something's over, you forget it and move on." He turned back with a shrug. "That's life."

"You don't want me anymore?" She stood meekly, like a dog who waits to feel the lash again. Her vision was too clouded with tears to see his expression. For a moment, he was silent.

"Don't worry, Cat," he answered in a careless, brutal voice. "Others will."

She turned and fled. It had taken over a year before he had stopped being the first thing in her mind every morning.

But she had survived, she reminded herself. She slipped into a vivid green dress. And I'll keep right on surviving. She knew she was basically the same person who had fallen in love with Lucas, but now she had a more polished veneer. Innocence was gone, and it would take more than Lucas McLean to make a fool of her again. She tossed her head, satisfied with the memory of her reception to him. That had given him a bit of a surprise. No, Autumn Gallegher was no one's fool any longer.

Her thoughts drifted to her aunt's odd assortment of guests. She wondered briefly why the rich and famous were gathering here instead of at some exclusive resort. Dismissing the thought with a shrug, she reminded herself it was dinnertime. Aunt Tabby had told her not to be late.

Chapter 2

It was a strange assortment to find clustered in the lounge of a remote Virginia inn: an award-winning writer, an actress, a producer, a wealthy California businessman, a successful cardiovascular surgeon and his wife, an art teacher who wore St. Laurent. Before Autumn's bearings were complete, she found herself enveloped in them. Julia pounced on her possessively and began introductions. Obviously, Julia enjoyed her prior claim and the center-stage position it gave her. Whatever embarrassment Autumn might have felt at being thrust into the limelight was overridden by amusement at the accuracy of Julia's earlier descriptions.

Dr. Robert Spicer was indeed smoothly handsome. He was drifting toward fifty and bursting with health. He wore a casually expensive green cardigan with brown leather patches at the elbows. His wife, Jane, was also as Julia had described: unfortunately dumpy. The small smile she gave Autumn lasted about two seconds before her face slipped back into the dissatisfied grooves that were habitual. She cast dark, bad-tempered glances at her husband while he gave Julia the bulk of his attention.

Watching them, Autumn could find little sympathy for Jane and no disapproval for Julia—no one disapproves of a flower for drawing bees. Julia's attraction was just as natural, and just as potent.

Helen Easterman was attractive in a slick, practiced fashion. The scarlet of her dress suited her, but struck a jarring note in the simply furnished lounge. Her face was perfectly made-up and reminded Autumn of a mask. As a photographer, she knew the tricks and secrets of cosmetics. Instinctively, Autumn avoided her.

In contrast, Steve Anderson was all charm. Good looks, California style, as Julia had said. Autumn liked the crinkles at the corners of his eyes and his careless chic. He wore chinos easily. From his bearing, she knew he would wear black tie with equal aplomb. If he chose a political career, she mused, he should make his way very well.

Julia had offered no description of Jacques LeFarre. What Autumn knew of him came primarily from either the gossip magazines or his films. He was smaller than she had imagined, barely as tall as she, but with a wiry build. His features were strong and he wore his brown hair brushed back from his forehead where three worry lines had been etched. She liked the trim moustache over his mouth, and the way he lifted her hand to kiss it when they were introduced.

"Well, Autumn," Steve began with a smile. "I'm playing bartender in George's absence. What can I fix you?"

"Vodka Collins, easy on the vodka," Lucas answered. Autumn gave up the idea of ignoring him.

"Your memory's improved," she said coolly.

"So's your wardrobe." He ran a finger down the collar of her dress. "I remember when it ran to jeans and old sweaters."

"I grew up." Her eyes were as steady and as measuring as his.

"So I see."

"Ah, you have met before," Jacques put in. "But this is fascinating. You are old friends?"

"Old friends?" Lucas repeated before Autumn could speak. He studied her with infuriating amusement. "Would you say that was an accurate description, Cat?"

"Cat?" Jacques frowned a moment. "Ah, the eyes, *oui*." Pleased, he brushed his index finger over his moustache. "It suits. What do you think, *chérie?*" He turned to Julia, who seemed to be enjoying herself watching the unfolding scene. "She's enchanting, and her voice is quite good."

"I've already warned Autumn about you," Julia drawled, then gave Robert Spicer a glorious smile.

"Ah, Julia," Jacques said mildly, "how wicked of you."

"Autumn works the other side of the camera," Lucas stated. Knowing his eyes had been on her the entire time, Autumn was grateful when Steve returned with her drink. "She's a photographer."

"Again, I'm fascinated." Autumn's free hand was captured in Jacques's. "Tell me why you are behind the camera instead of in front of it? Your hair alone would cause poets to run for their pens."

No woman was immune to flattery with a French accent, and Autumn smiled fully into his eyes. "I doubt I could stand still long enough to begin with."

"Photographers can be quite useful," Helen Easterman stated suddenly. Lifting a hand, she patted her dark, sleek cap of hair. "A good, clear photograph is an invaluable tool…to an artist."

An awkward pause followed the statement. Tension entered the room, so out of place in the comfortable lounge with its chintz curtains that Autumn thought it must be her imagination. Helen smiled into the silence and sipped her drink. Her eyes swept over the others, inclusively, never centering on one.

Autumn knew there was something here which isolated Helen and set her apart from the rest. Messages were being passed without words, though there was no way for Autumn to tell who was communicating what to whom. The mood changed swiftly as Julia engaged Robert Spicer in bright conversation. Jane Spicer's habitual frown became more pronounced.

The easy climate continued as they went in to dinner. Sitting between Jacques and Steve, Autumn was able to add to her education as she observed Julia flirting simultaneously with Lucas and Robert. She was, in Autumn's opinion, magnificent. Even through the discomfort of seeing Lucas casually return the flirtation, she had to admire Julia's talent. Her charm and beauty were insatiable. Jane ate in sullen silence.

Dreary woman, Autumn mused, then wondered what her own reaction would be if it were her husband so enchanted. Action, she decided, not silence. I'd simply claw her eyes out. The image of dumpy Jane wrestling with the elegant Julia made her smile. Even as she enjoyed the notion, she looked up to find Lucas's eyes on her.

His brows were lifted at an angle she knew meant amusement. Autumn turned her attention to Jacques.

"Do you find many differences in the movie industry here in America, Mr. LeFarre?"

"You must call me Jacques." His smile caused the tips of his moustache to rise. "There are differences, yes. I would say that Americans are more…adventurous than Europeans."

Autumn lifted her shoulders and smiled. "Maybe because we're a mixture of nationalities. Not watered down. Just Americanized."

"Americanized." Jacques tried out the word and approved it. His grin was younger than his smile, less urbane. "Yes, I would say I feel Americanized in California."

"Still, California's only one aspect of the country," Steve put in. "And I wouldn't call L.A. or southern California particularly typical." Autumn watched his eyes flick over her hair. His interest brought on a small flutter of response that pleased her. It proved that she was still a woman, open to a man—not just one man. "Have you ever been to California, Autumn?"

"I lived there…once." Her response to Steve, and the need to prove something to herself, urged her to turn her eyes to Lucas. Their gazes locked and held for one brief instant. "I relocated in New York three years ago."

"There was a family here from New York," Steve went on. If he'd noticed the look that had passed, he gave no sign. Yes, a good politician, Autumn thought again. "They just checked out this morning. The woman was one of those robust types with energy pouring out of every cell. She needed it," he added with a smile that was for Autumn alone. "She had three boys. Triplets. I think she said they were eleven."

"Oh, those beastly children!" Julia switched her attention from Robert and looked across the table. She rolled her summer blue eyes. "Running around like a pack of monkeys. Worse, you could never tell which one of them it was zooming by or leaping down. They did everything in triplicate." She shuddered and lifted her water glass. "They ate like elephants."

"Running and eating are part of childhood," Jacques commented with a shake of his head. "Julia," he told Autumn with a conspirator's wink, "was born twenty-one and beautiful."

"Anyone with manners is born twenty-one," Julia countered. "Being beautiful was simply a bonus." Her eyes were laughing now. "Jacques is crazy about kids," she informed Autumn. "He has three specimens of his own."

Interested, Autumn turned to him. She'd never thought of Jacques LeFarre in terms other than his work. "I'm crazy about them, too," she confessed and shot Julia a grin. "What sort of specimens do you have?"

"Boys," he answered. Autumn found the fondness in his eyes curiously touching. "They are like a ladder." With his hand, he formed imaginary steps. "Seven, eight and nine years. They live in France with my wife—my ex-wife." He frowned, then smoothed it away. Autumn realized how the worry lines in his brow had been formed.

"Jacques actually wants custody of the little monsters." Julia's look was more tolerant than her words. Here, Autumn saw, affection transcended flirtation. "Even though I hold your sanity suspect, Jacques, I'm forced to admit you make a better father than Claudette makes a mother."

"Custody suits are sensitive matters," Helen announced from the end of the table. She drank from her water glass, peering over the rim with small, sharp eyes. The look that she sent Jacques seemed to brush everyone else out of her line of vision. "It's so important that any…unsuitable information doesn't come to light."

Tension sprang back. Autumn felt the Frenchman stiffen beside her. But there was more. Undercurrents flowed up and down the long pine table. It was impossible not to feel them, though there was nothing tangible, nothing solid. Instinctively, Autumn's eyes sought Lucas's. There was nothing there but the hard, unfathomable mask she had seen too often in the past.

"Your aunt serves such marvelous meals, Miss Gallegher." With a puzzling, satisfied smirk, Helen shifted her attention to Autumn.

"Yes." She blundered into the awful silence. "Aunt Tabby gives food a high rating of importance."

"Aunt Tabby?" Julia's rich laugh warred with the tension, and won. The air was instantly lighter. "What a wonderful name. Did you know Autumn has an Aunt Tabby when you christened her Cat, Lucas?" She stared up at him, her eyes wide and guileless. Autumn was reminded of a movie Julia had been in, in which she played the innocent ingenue to perfection.

"Lucas and I didn't know each other well enough to discuss relatives." Autumn's voice was easy and careless and pleased her very much. So did Lucas's barely perceptible frown.

"Actually," he replied, recovering quickly, "we were too occupied to discuss family trees." He sent her a smile which sneaked through her defenses. Autumn's pulse hammered. "What did we talk about in those days, Cat?"

"I've forgotten," she murmured, knowing she had lost the edge before she'd really held it. "It was a long time ago."

Aunt Tabby bustled in with her prize cobbler.

There was music on the stereo and a muted fire in the hearth when they returned to the lounge. The scene, if Autumn could have captured it on film, was one of relaxed camaraderie. Steve and Robert huddled over a chessboard while Jane made her discontented way through a magazine. Even without a photographer's eye for color, Autumn knew the woman should never wear brown. She felt quite certain that Jane invariably would.

Lucas sprawled on the sofa. Somehow, he always managed to relax in a negligent fashion without seeming sloppy; there was always an alertness about him, energy simmering right under the surface. Autumn knew he watched people without being obvious—not because he cared if he made them uncomfortable, he didn't in the least—it was simply something he was able to do. And in watching them, he was able to learn their secrets. An obsessive writer, he drew his characters from flesh and blood. With no mercy, Autumn recalled.

At the moment, he seemed content with his conversation with Julia and Jacques. They flanked him on the sofa and spoke with the ease that came from familiarity; they shared the same world.

But it's not my world, Autumn reminded herself. I only pretended it was for a little while. I only pretended he was mine for a little while. She had been right when she told Lucas she had grown up. Pretend games were for children.

Yet, Autumn thought as she sat back and observed, there was a game of some sort going on here. There was a faint glistening of unease superimposed over the homey picture. Always attuned to contrasts, she could sense it, feel it. They're not letting me in on the rules, she mused, and found herself grateful. She didn't want to play. Making her excuses to no one in particular, Autumn slipped from the room to find her aunt.

Whatever tension she had felt evaporated the moment Autumn stepped into her aunt's room.

"Oh, Autumn." Aunt Tabby lifted her glasses from her nose and let them dangle from a chain around her neck. "I was just reading a letter from your mother. I'd forgotten it was here until this minute. She says by the time I read this, you'll be here. And here you are." Smiling, she patted Autumn's hand. "Debbie always was so clever. Did you enjoy your pot roast, dear?"

"It was lovely, Aunt Tabby, thank you."

"We'll have to have it once a week while you're with us." Autumn smiled and thought of how she liked spaghetti. Paul probably gets spaghetti on his visits, she mused. "I'll just make a note of that, else it'll slip right through my mind." Autumn recalled that Aunt Tabby's notes were famous for their ability to slip into another dimension, and felt more hopeful. "Where are my glasses?" Aunt Tabby murmured, puckering her impossibly smooth brow. Standing, she rummaged through her desk, lifting papers and peering under books. "They're never where you leave them."

Autumn lifted the dangling glasses from her aunt's bosom, then perched them on her nose. After blinking a moment, Aunt Tabby smiled in her vague fashion.

"Isn't that strange?" she commented. "They were here all along. You're just as clever as your mother."

Autumn couldn't resist giving her a bone-crushing hug. "Aunt Tabby, I adore you!"

"You always were such a sweet child." She patted Autumn's cheek, then moved away, leaving the scent of lavender and talc hanging in the air. "I hope you like your surprise."

"I'm sure I will."

"You haven't seen it yet?" Her small mouth pouted in thought. "No, I'm quite sure I haven't shown you yet, so you can't know if you like it. Did you and Miss Bond have a nice chat? Such a lovely lady. I believe she's in show business."

Autumn's smile was wry. There was no one, she thought, absolutely no one like Aunt Tabby. "Yes, I believe she is. I've always admired her."

"Oh, have you met before?" Aunt Tabby asked absently as she shuffled the papers on her desk back into her own particular order. "I suppose I'd better show you now while I have it on my mind."

Autumn tried to keep up with her aunt's thought processes, but it had been a year since her last visit and she was rusty. "Show me what, Aunt Tabby?"

"Oh now, it wouldn't be a surprise if I told you, would it?" Playfully, she shook her finger under Autumn's nose. "You'll just have to be patient and come along with me." With this, she bustled from the room.

Autumn followed, deducing they were again discussing the surprise. She had to shorten her gait to match her aunt's. Autumn usually moved in a loose-limbed stride, a result of leanness and lengthy legs, while her aunt scuttled unrhythmically. Like a rabbit, Autumn thought, that dashes out in the road then can't make up its mind which way to run. As they walked, Aunt Tabby muttered about bed linen. Autumn's thoughts drifted irresistibly to Lucas.

"Now, here we are." Aunt Tabby stopped. She gave the door an expectant smile. The door itself, Autumn recalled, led to a sitting room long since abandoned and converted into a storage room. It was a convenient place for cleaning supplies, as it adjoined the kitchen. "Well," Aunt Tabby said, beaming, "what do you think?"

Searching for the right comment, Autumn realized the surprise must be inside. "Is my surprise in there, Aunt Tabby?"

"Yes, of course, how silly." She clucked her tongue. "You won't know what it is until I open the door."

With this indisputable logic, she did.

When the lights were switched on, Autumn stood stunned. Where she had expected to see mops, brooms and buckets was a fully equipped darkroom. Every detail, every piece of apparatus stood neat and orderly in front of her. Her voice had been left outside the door.

"Well, what do you think?" Aunt Tabby repeated. She moved around the room, stopping now and again to peer at bottles of developing fluid, tongs and trays. "It all looks so technical and scientific to me." The enlarger caused her to frown and tilt her head. "I'm sure I don't understand a thing about it."

"Oh, Aunt Tabby." Autumn's voice finally joined her body. "You shouldn't have."

"Oh dear, is something wrong with it? Nelson told me you developed your own film, and the company that brought in all these things assured me everything was proper. Of course…" Her voice wavered in doubt. "I really don't know a thing about it."

Her aunt looked so distressed, Autumn nearly wept with love. "No, Aunt Tabby, it's perfect. It's wonderful." She enveloped the small, soft body in her arms. "I meant that you shouldn't have done this for me. All the trouble and the expense."

"Oh, is that all?" Aunt Tabby interrupted. Her distress dissolved as she beamed around the room again. "Well, it was no trouble at all. These nice young men came in and did all the work. As for the expense, well…" She shrugged her rounded shoulders. "I'd rather see you enjoy my money now than after I'm dead."

Sometimes, Autumn thought, the fuzzy little brain shot straight through to sterling sense. "Aunt Tabby." She framed her aunt's face with her hands. "I've never had a more wonderful surprise. Thank you."

"You just have a good time with it." Aunt Tabby's cheeks grew rosy with pleasure when Autumn kissed them, and she eyed the chemicals and trays again. "I don't suppose you'll blow anything up."

Knowing this wasn't a pun, and that her aunt was concerned about explosions in her vague way, Autumn assured her she would not. Satisfied, Aunt Tabby then bustled off, leaving Autumn to explore on her own.

For more than an hour, Autumn lost herself in what

she knew best. Photography, started as a hobby when she had been a child, had become both craft and profession. The chemicals and complicated equipment were no strangers to her. Here, in a darkroom, or with a camera in her hands, she knew exactly who she was and what she wanted. This was where she had learned control— the same control she knew she had to employ over her thoughts of Lucas. She was no longer a dewy-eyed girl, ready to follow the crook of a finger. She was a professional woman with a growing reputation in her field. She had to hang on to that now, as she had for three years. There was no going back to yesterday.

Pleasantly weary after rearranging the darkroom to her own preference, Autumn wandered into the kitchen to fix herself a solitary cup of tea. The moon was round and white with a thin cloud drifting over it. Unexpectedly, a shudder ran through her, quick and chilling. The odd feeling she had sensed several times that evening came back. She frowned. Imagination? Autumn knew herself well enough to admit she had her share. It was part of her art. But this was different.

Discovering Lucas at the inn had jolted her system, and her emotions had been strained. That, she decided, was all that was wrong. The tension she had felt earlier was her own tension; the strain, her own strain. Dumping the remaining tea into the sink, she decided that what she needed was a good night's sleep. No dreams, she ordered herself firmly. She'd had her fill of dreams three years before.

The house was quiet now. Moonlight filtered in, leaving the corners shadowed. The lounge was dark, but as she passed, Autumn heard muted voices. She hesitated a moment, thinking to stop and say good-night, then she detected the subtle signs that told her this wasn't a conversation, but an argument. There was anger in the hushed, sexless voices. The undistinguishable words were quick, staccato and passionate. She walked by quickly, not wanting to overhear a private battle. A brief oath shot out, steeped in temper, elegant in French.

Climbing the stairs, Autumn smothered a grin. Jacques, she concluded, was probably losing patience with Lucas's artistic stubbornness. For entirely malicious reasons, she hoped the Frenchman gave him an earful.

It wasn't until she was halfway down the hall to her room that Autumn saw that she'd been wrong. Even Lucas McLean couldn't be two places at once. And he was definitely in this one. In the doorway of another room, Lucas was locked in a very involved embrace with Julia Bond.

Autumn knew how his arms would feel, how his mouth would taste. She remembered it all, completely, as if no years had come between to dull the sensations. She knew how his hand would trail up the back until he cupped around the neck. And that his fingers wouldn't be gentle. No, there were no gentle caresses from Lucas.

There was no need for her to worry about being seen. Both Lucas and Julia were totally focused on each other. Autumn was certain that the roof could have toppled over their heads, and they would have remained unmoving and entwined. The pain came back, hatefully, in full force.

Hurrying by, she gave vent to hideous and unwelcome jealousy by slamming her door.

Chapter 3

The forest was morning fresh. It held a tranquility that was full of tangy scents and bird song. To the east, the sky was filled with scuttling rags of white clouds. An optimist, Autumn put her hopes in them and ignored the dark, threatening sky in the west. Streaks of red still crowned the peaks of the mountains. Gently, the color faded to pink before it surrendered to blue.

The light was good, filtering through the white clouds and illuminating the forest. The leaves weren't full enough to interfere with the sun, only touching the limbs of trees with dots of green. Sometimes strong, the breeze bent branches and tugged at Autumn's hair. She could smell spring.

Wood violets popped out unexpectedly, the purple dramatic against the moss. She saw her first robin marching importantly on the ground, listening for worms. Squirrels scampered up trees, down trees and over the mulch of last year's leaves.

Autumn had intended to walk to the lake, hoping to catch a deer at early watering, but when her camera insisted on planting itself in front of her face again and again, she didn't resist. She ambled along, happy in the solitude and in tune with nature.

In New York, she never truly felt alone—lonely sometimes, but not solitary. The city intruded. Now, cocooned by mountains and trees, she realized how much she'd needed to feel alone. To recharge. Since leaving California and Lucas, Autumn hadn't permitted herself time alone. There had been a void that had to be filled, and she'd filled it with people, with work, with noise—anything that would keep her mind busy. She'd used the pace of the city. It had been necessary. Now, she wanted the pace of the mountains.

In the distance, the lake shimmered. Reflections of the surrounding mountains and trees were mirrored in the water, reversed and shadowy. There were no deer, but as she drew closer, Autumn noticed two figures circling the far side. The ridge where she stood was some fifty feet above the small valley which held the lake. The view was spectacular.

The lake itself stretched in a wide finger, about a hundred feet in length, forty in width. The breeze that caught at Autumn's hair where she strode didn't reach down to the water; its surface was clear and still. The opaque water gradually darkened towards the center, warning of dangerous depths.

Autumn forgot the people walking around the lake, her mind fully occupied with angles and depths of field and shutter speeds. The distance was too great for her to make them out even if she had been interested.

The sun continued its rise, and Autumn was content. She stopped only to change film. As she replaced the roll, she noted that the lake was now deserted. The light was wrong for the mood she wanted and, turning, she began her leisurely journey back to the inn.

This time, the stillness of the forest seemed different. The sun was brighter, but she felt an odd disquiet she hadn't experienced in the paler light of dawn. Foolishly, she looked back over her shoulder, then told herself she was an idiot. Who would be following her? And why? Yet the feeling persisted.

The serenity had vanished. Autumn forced herself to put aside an impulsive desire to run back to the inn where there would be people and coffee brewing. She wasn't a child to take flight at the thought of ogres or gnomes. To prove to herself that her fantasies hadn't affected her, she forced herself to stop and take the time to perfect a shot of a cooperative squirrel. A faint rustle of dead leaves came from behind her and terror brought her scrambling to her feet.

"Well, Cat, still attached to a camera?"

Blood pounding in her head, Autumn stared at Lucas. His hands were tucked comfortably into the pockets of his jeans as he stood directly in front of her. For a moment, she couldn't speak. The fear had been sharp and real.

"What do you mean by sneaking up behind me that way?" When it returned, her voice was furious. She was annoyed that she'd been foolish enough to be frightened, and angry that he'd been the one to frighten her. She pushed her hair back and glared at him.

"I see you've finally developed the temper to match your hair," he observed in a lazy voice. He crossed the slight distance between them and stood close. Autumn had also developed pride and refused to back away.

"It gets particularly nasty when someone spoils a shot." It was a simple matter to blame her reaction on his interference with her work. Not for a moment would she amuse him by confessing fear.

"You're a bit jumpy, Cat." The devil himself could take lessons on smiling from Lucas McLean, she thought bitterly. "Do I make you nervous?"

His dark hair curled in a confused tangle around his lean face, and his eyes were dark and confident. It was the confidence, she told herself, that she cursed him for. "Don't flatter yourself," she tossed back. "I don't recall you ever being one for morning hikes, Lucas. Have you developed a love of nature?"

"I've always had a fondness for nature." He was studying her with deep, powerful eyes while his mouth curved into a smile. "I've always had a penchant for picnics."

The pain started, a dull ache in her stomach. She could remember the gritty feel of sand under her legs, the tart taste of wine on her tongue and the scent of the ocean everywhere. She forced her gaze to stay level with his. "I lost my taste for them." She turned in dismissal, but he fell into step beside her. "I'm not going straight back," she informed him. The chill in her voice would have discouraged anyone else. Stopping, she took an off-center picture of a blue jay.

"I'm in no hurry," he returned easily. "I've always enjoyed watching you work. It's fascinating how absorbed you become." He watched her back, and let his eyes run down the length of her hair. "I believe you could be snapping a charging rhino and not give an inch until you'd perfected the shot." There was a slight pause as she remained turned away from him. "I saw that photo you took of a burned-out tenement in New York. It was remarkable. Hard, clean and desperate."

Wary of the compliment, Autumn faced him. She knew Lucas wasn't generous with praise. Hard, clean and desperate, she thought. He had chosen the words perfectly. She didn't like discovering that his opinion still mattered. "Thank you." She turned back to focus on a grouping of trees. "Still having trouble with your book?"

"More than I'd anticipated," he muttered. Suddenly, he swooped her hair up into his hands. "I never could resist it, could I?" She continued to give her attention to the trees. Her answer was an absent shrug, but she squeezed her eyes tightly shut a moment. "I've never seen another woman with hair like yours. I've looked, God knows, but the shade is always wrong, or the texture or the length." There was a seductive quality in his voice. Autumn stiffened against it. "It's unique. A fiery waterfall in the sun, deep and vibrant spilling over a pillowcase."

"You always had a gift for description." She adjusted her lens without the vaguest idea of what she was doing. Her voice was detached, faintly bored, while she prayed for him to go. Instead, his grip tightened on her hair. In a swift move, he whirled her around and tore the camera from her hands.

"Damn it, don't use that tone with me. Don't turn your back on me. Don't ever turn your back on me."

She remembered the dark expression and uncertain

temper well. There'd been a time when she would have dissolved when faced with them. But not anymore, she thought fleetingly. Not this time.

"I don't cringe at being sworn at these days, Lucas." She tossed her head, lifting her chin. "Why don't you save your attention for Julia? I don't want it."

"So." His smile was light and amused in a rapid-fire change. "It was you. No need to be jealous, Cat. The lady made the move, not I."

"Yes, I noticed your mad struggle for release." Even as she spoke, she regretted the words. Annoyed, Autumn pushed away, but was only caught closer. His scent teased her senses and reminded her of things she'd rather forget. "Listen, Lucas," she ground out slowly as both anger and longing rose inside her. "It took me six months to realize what a bastard you are, and I've had three years to cement that realization. I'm a big girl now, and not susceptible to your abundant charms. Now, take your hands off me and get lost."

"Learned to sink your teeth in, have you, Cat?" To her mounting fury, his expression was more amused than insulted. His eyes lowered to her mouth for a moment, lingered then lifted. "Not malleable anymore, but just as fascinating."

Because his words hurt more than she had thought possible, she hurled a stream of abuse at him.

His laughter cut off her torrent like a slap. Abandoning verbal protest, Autumn began to struggle with a wild, furious rage. Abruptly, he molded her against him. Tasting of punishment and possession, his mouth found hers. The heat was blinding.

The old, churning need fought its way to the surface. For three years she had starved, and now all that hunger spilled out in response. There was no hesitation as her arms found their way around his neck. Eager for more, her lips parted. His mouth was urgent and bruising. The pain was like heaven, and she begged for more. Her blood was flowing again. Lucas let his mouth roam over her face, then come back to hers with new demands. Autumn met them and fretted for more. Time flew backward, then forward again before he lifted his face.

His eyes were incredibly dark, opaque with a passion she recognized. For the first time she felt the faint throbbing where his hands gripped her and his hold eased to a caress. The taste of him lingered on her lips.

"It's still there, Cat," Lucas murmured. With easy familiarity, he combed his fingers through her hair. "Still there."

All at once, pain and humiliation coursed through her. She pulled away fiercely and swung out a hand. He caught her wrist and, frustrated, she drew back with her other hand. His reflexes were too sharp, and she was denied any satisfaction. With both wrists captured, she could only stand struggling, her breath ragged. Tears burned at her throat, but she refused to acknowledge them. He won't make me cry, she vowed fiercely. He won't see me cry again.

In silence, Lucas watched her battle for control. There was no sound in the forest but Autumn's own jerking breaths. When she could speak, her voice was hard and cold. "There's a difference between love and lust, Lucas. Even you should know one from the other. What's there now may be the same for you, but not for me. I loved you. I *loved* you." The words were an accusation in their repetition. His brows drew together as his gaze grew intense. "You took it all once—my love, my innocence, my pride—then you tossed them back in my face. You can't have them back. The first is dead, the second's gone and the third belongs to me."

For a moment, they both were still. Slowly, without taking his eyes from hers, Lucas released her wrists. He didn't speak, and his expression told her nothing. Refusing to run from him a second time, Autumn turned and walked away. Only when she was certain he wasn't following did she allow her tears their freedom. Her statements about pride and innocence had been true. But her love was far from dead. It was alive, and it hurt.

As the red bricks of the inn came into view, Autumn dashed the drops away. There would be no wallowing in what was over. Loving Lucas changed nothing, any more than it had changed anything three years before. But she'd changed. He wouldn't find her weeping, helpless and—as he had said himself—malleable.

Disillusionment had given her strength. He could still hurt her. She'd learned that quickly. But he could no longer manipulate her as he had once. Still, the encounter with him had left her shaken, and she wasn't pleased when Helen approached from a path to the right.

It was impossible, without being pointedly rude, for Autumn to veer off and avoid her. Instead, she fixed a smile on her face. When Helen turned her head, the livid bruise under her eye became noticeable. Autumn's smile faded into quick concern.

"What happened?" The bruise looked painful and aroused Autumn's sympathy.

"I walked into a branch." Helen gave a careless shrug as she lifted her fingers to stroke the mark. "I'll have to be more careful in the future."

Perhaps it was her turmoil over Lucas that made

Autumn detect some hidden shade of meaning in those words, but Helen seemed to mean more than she said. Certainly the eyes which met Autumn's were as hot and angry as the bruise. And the mark itself, Autumn mused, looked more like the result of contact with a violent hand than with any stray branch. She pushed the thought aside. Who would have struck Helen? she asked herself. And why would she cover up the abuse? Her own carelessness made more sense.

"It looks nasty," Autumn commented as they began to walk toward the inn. "You'll have to do something about it. Aunt Tabby should have something to ease the soreness."

"Oh, I intend to do something about it," Helen muttered, then gave Autumn her sharp-eyed smile. "I know just the thing. Out early taking pictures?" she asked while Autumn tried to ignore the unease her words brought. "I've always found people more interesting subjects than trees. I'm especially fond of candid shots." She began to laugh at some private joke. It was the first time Autumn had heard her laugh, and she thought how suited the sound was to Helen's smile. They were both unpleasant.

"Were you down at the lake earlier?" Autumn recalled the two figures she had spotted. To her surprise, Helen's laughter stopped abruptly. Her eyes grew sharper.

"Did you see someone?"

"No," she began, confused by the harshness of the question. "Not exactly. I saw two people by the lake, but I was too far away to see who they were. I was taking pictures from the ridge."

"Taking pictures," Helen repeated. Her mouth pursed

as if she were considering something carefully. She began to laugh again with a harsh burst of sound.

"Well, well, such good humor for such early risers." Julia drifted down the porch steps. Her brow lifted as she studied Helen's cheek. Autumn wondered if the actress's shudder was real or affected. "Good heavens, what have you done to yourself?"

Helen's amusement seemed to have passed. She gave Julia a quick scowl, then fingered the bruise again. "Walked into a branch," she muttered before she stalked up the steps and disappeared inside.

"A fist more likely," Julia commented, and smiled. With a shrug, she dismissed Helen and turned to Autumn. "The call of the wild beckoned to you, too? It seems everyone but me was tramping through forests and over mountains at the cold light of dawn. It's so difficult being sane when one is surrounded by insanity."

Autumn had to smile. Julia looked like a sunbeam. In direct contrast to her own rough jeans and jacket, Julia wore delicate pink slacks and a thin silk blouse flocked with roses. The white sandals she wore wouldn't last fifty yards in the woods. Whatever resentment Autumn had felt for the actress attracting Lucas vanished under her open warmth.

"There are some," Autumn remarked mildly, "who might accuse you of laziness."

"Absolutely," Julia agreed with a nod and a smile. "When I'm not working, I wallow in sloth. If I don't get going again soon, my blood will stop flowing." She gave Autumn a shrewd glance. "Looks like you walked into a rather large branch yourself."

Bewilderment crossed Autumn's face briefly. Julia's eyes, she discovered, were very discerning. The traces of tears hadn't evaporated as completely as Autumn would have liked. Helplessly she moved her shoulders. "I heal quickly."

"Brave child. Come, tell mama all about it." Julia's eyes were sympathetic, balancing the stinging lightness of the words. Linking her arm through Autumn's, she began to walk across the lawn.

"Julia…" Autumn shook her head. Inner feelings were private. She'd broken the rule for Lucas, and wasn't certain she could do so again.

"Autumn." The refusal was firmly interrupted. "You do need to talk. You might not think that you look stricken, but you do." Julia sighed with perfect finesse. "I really don't know why I've become so fond of you; it's totally against my policy. Beautiful women tend to avoid or dislike other beautiful women, especially younger ones."

The statement completely robbed Autumn of speech. The idea of the exquisite, incomparable Julia Bond placing herself on a physical plane anywhere near Autumn's own seemed ludicrous to her. It was one matter to hear the actress speak casually of her own beauty, and quite another for her to speak of Autumn's. Julia's voice flowed over the gaping silence.

"Maybe it's the exposure to those two other females—one so dull and the other so nasty—but I've developed an affection for you." The breeze tugged at her hair, lifting it up so that the sunlight streamed through it. Absently, Julia tucked a strand behind her ear. On the lobe a diamond sparkled. Autumn thought it incongruous that they were walking arm in arm among her aunt's struggling daffodils.

"You're also a kind person," Julia went on. "I don't

know a great many kind people." She turned to Autumn so that her exquisite profile became her exquisite full face. "Autumn, darling, I always pry, but I also know how to keep a confidence."

"I'm still in love with him," Autumn blurted out, then followed that rash statement with a deep sigh. Before she knew it, words were tumbling out. She left out nothing, from the beginning to the end, to the new beginning when he had come back into her life the day before. She told Julia everything. Once she'd begun, no effort was needed. She didn't have to think, only feel, and Julia listened. The quality of her listening was so perfect, Autumn all but forgot she was there.

"The monster," Julia said, but with no malice. "You'll find all men, those marvelous creatures, are basically monsters."

Who was Autumn to argue with an expert? As they walked on in silence, she realized that she did feel better. The rawness was gone.

"The main trouble is, of course, that you're still mad about him. Not that I blame you," Julia added when Autumn made a small sound of distress. "Lucas is quite a man. I had a tiny sample last night, and I was impressed." Julia spoke so casually of the passion Autumn had witnessed, it was impossible to be angry. "Lucas is a talented man," Julia went on. By her smile, Autumn knew that Julia was very much aware of the struggle that was going on within Autumn. "He's also arrogant, selfish and used to being obeyed. It's easy for me to see that, because I am, too. We're alike. I doubt very much if we could even enjoy a pleasant affair. We'd be clawing at each other before the bed was turned down."

Autumn found no response to make to the image this produced, and merely walked on.

"Jacques is more my type," Julia mused. "But his attentions are committed elsewhere." She frowned, and Autumn sensed that her thoughts had drifted to something quite different. "Anyway." Julia made an impatient gesture. "You just have to make up your mind what you want. Obviously, Lucas wants you back, at least for as long as it suits him."

Autumn tried to ignore the sting of honesty and just listened.

"Knowing that, you could enjoy a stimulating relationship with him, with your eyes open."

"I can't do that, Julia. The knowing won't stop the hurting. I'm not sure I can survive another…relationship with Lucas. And he'd know I was still in love with him." A flash frame of their parting scene three years before jumped into her mind. "I won't be humiliated again. Pride's the only thing I have left that isn't his already."

"Love and pride don't belong together." Julia patted Autumn's hand. "Well then, you'll have to barricade yourself against the assault. I'll run interference for you."

"How will you do that?"

"Darling!" She lifted her brow as the slow, cat smile drifted to her lips.

Autumn had to laugh. It all seemed so absurd. She lifted her face to the sky. The black clouds were winning after all. For a moment, they blotted out the sun and warmth. "Looks like rain."

Her gaze shifted back to the inn. The windows were black and empty. The struggling light fell gloomily over the bricks and turned the white porch and shutters gray.

Behind the building, the sky was like slate. The mountains were colorless and oppressive. She felt a tickle at the back of her neck. To her puzzlement, Autumn found she didn't want to go back inside.

Just as quickly, the clouds shifted, letting the sun pour out through the opening. The windows blinked with light. The shadows vanished. Chiding herself for another flight of fancy, Autumn walked back to the inn with Julia.

Only Jacques joined them for breakfast. Helen was nowhere in sight, and Steve and the Spicers were apparently still hiking. Autumn trained her thoughts away from Lucas. Her appetite, as usual, was unimpaired and outrageous. She put away a healthy portion of bacon, eggs, coffee and muffins while Julia nibbled on a single piece of thin toast and sent her envious scowls.

Jacques seemed preoccupied. His charm was costing him visible effort. Memory of the muffled argument in the lounge came to Autumn's mind. Idly, she began to speculate on who he had been annoyed with. Thinking it over, the entire matter struck her as odd. Jacques LeFarre didn't seem to be the sort of man who would argue with a veritable stranger, yet, as Autumn knew, both Lucas and Julia had been preoccupied elsewhere.

Appearing totally at ease, Julia rambled on about a mutual friend in the industry. But she's an actress, Autumn reminded herself. A good one. She could easily know the cause of last night's animosity and never show a sign. Jacques, however, wasn't an actor. The distress was there; anger lay just beneath the polished charm. Autumn wondered at it throughout the meal, then dismissed it from her mind as she left to find her aunt. After all, she reflected, it wasn't any of her business.

Aunt Tabby was, as Autumn had known she would be, fussing with Nancy the cook over the day's menu. Keeping silent, Autumn let the story unfold. It seemed that Nancy had planned on chicken while Aunt Tabby was certain they had decided on pork. While the argument raged, Autumn helped herself to another cup of coffee. Through the window, she could see the thick, roiling clouds continue their roll from the west.

"Oh, Autumn, did you have a nice walk?" When she turned, Autumn found her aunt smiling at her. "Such a nice morning, a shame it's going to rain. But that's good for the flowers, isn't it? Sweet little things. Did you sleep well?"

After a moment, Autumn decided to answer only the final question. There was no use confusing her aunt. "Wonderfully, Aunt Tabby. I always sleep well when I visit you."

"It's the air," the woman replied. Her round little face lit with pleasure. "I think I'll make my special chocolate cake for tonight. That should make up for the rain."

"Any hot coffee, Aunt Tabby?" Lucas swept into the kitchen as if he enjoyed the privilege daily. As always, when he came into a room, the air charged. This phenomenon Autumn could accept. The casual use of her aunt's nickname was more perplexing.

"Of course, dear, just help yourself." Aunt Tabby gestured vaguely toward the stove, her mind on chocolate cake. Autumn's confusion grew as Lucas strode directly to the proper cupboard, retrieved a cup and proceeded to fix himself a very homey cup of coffee.

He drank, leaning against the counter. The eyes that met Autumn's were very cool. All traces of anger and passion were gone, as if they had never existed. His rough black brows lifted as she continued to stare. The damnable devil smile tugged at his mouth.

"Oh, is that your camera, dear?" Aunt Tabby's voice broke into her thoughts. Autumn lowered her eyes.

The camera still hung around her neck, so much a part of her that she'd forgotten it was there.

"My, my, so many numbers. It looks complicated." Aunt Tabby peered at it through narrowed eyes, forgetting the glasses that dangled from her chain. "I have a very nice one, Autumn. You're welcome to use it whenever you like." After giving the Nikon another dubious glance, she beamed up with her misty smile. "You just push a little red button, and the picture pops right out. You can see if you've cut off someone's head or have your thumb in the corner right away, so you can take another picture. And you don't have to grope around in that darkroom either. I don't know how you see what you're doing in there." Her brows drew close, and she tapped a finger against her cheek. "I'm almost certain I can find it."

Autumn grinned. She was compelled to subject her aunt to yet another bear hug. Over the gray-streaked head, Autumn saw that Lucas was grinning as well. It was the warm, natural grin which came to his face so rarely. For a moment, she found she could smile back at him without pain.

Chapter 4

When the rain came, it didn't begin with the slow drip-drop of an April shower. As the sky grew hazy, the light in the lounge became dim. Everyone was back and the inn was again filled with its odd assortment of guests.

Steve, expanding on his role of bartender, had wandered to the kitchen to get coffee. Robert Spicer had trapped Jacques in what seemed to be a technical explanation of open-heart surgery. During the discussion, Julia sat beside him, hanging on every word—or seeming to. Autumn knew better. Occasionally, Julia sent messages across to her with her extraordinary eyes. She was enjoying herself immensely.

Jane sat sullen over a novel Autumn was certain was riddled with explicit sex. She wore dull brown again, slacks and a sweater. Helen, her bruise livid, smoked quietly in long, deep drags. She reminded Autumn eerily of Alice in Wonderland's caterpillar. Once or twice, Autumn found Helen's sharp eyes on her. The speculative smile left her confused and uncomfortable.

Lucas wasn't there. He was upstairs, Autumn knew, hammering away at his typewriter. She hoped it would keep him busy for hours. Perhaps he'd even take his meals in his room.

Abruptly, the dim light outdoors was snuffed out, and the room plunged into gloom. The warmth fled with it. Autumn shuddered with a sharp premonition of dread. The feeling surprised her, as storms had always held a primitive appeal for her. For a heartbeat, there was no sound, then the rain began with a gushing explosion. With instant force, instant fury, it battered against the windows, punctuated by wicked flashes of lightning.

"A spring shower in the mountains," Steve observed. He paused a moment in the doorway with a large tray balanced in his hands. The friendly scent of coffee entered with him.

"More like special effects," Julia returned. With a flutter of her lashes, she cuddled toward Robert. "Storms are so terrifying and moving. I find myself longing to be frightened."

It was straight out of *A Long Summer's Evening,* Autumn noted, amused. But the doctor seemed too overcome with Julia's ingenuous eyes to recognize the line. Autumn wanted to laugh badly. When Julia cuddled even closer and sent her a wink, Autumn's eyes retreated to the ceiling.

Jane wasn't amused. Autumn noticed she was no longer sullen but smoldering. Perhaps she had claws after all, Autumn thought, and felt she would like her better for it. It might be wise, she mused as Steve passed her a cup of coffee, if Julia concentrated on him rather than the doctor.

"Cream, no sugar, right?" Steve smiled down at her with his California blue eyes. Autumn's lips curved in response. He was a man with the rare ability to make a woman feel pampered without being patronizing. She admired him for it.

"Right. You've got a better memory than George." Her eyes smiled at him over the rim of her cup. "You serve with such style, too. Have you been in this line of work long?"

"I'm only here on a trial basis," he told her with a grin. "Please pass your comments on to the management."

Lightning speared through the gloom again. Jacques shifted in his seat as thunder rumbled and echoed through the room. "With such a storm, is it not possible to lose power?" he addressed Autumn.

"We often lose power." Her answer, accompanied by an absent shrug, brought on varying reactions.

Julia found the idea marvelous—candlelight was so wonderfully romantic. At the moment, Robert couldn't have agreed more. Jacques appeared not to care one way or the other. He lifted his hands in a Gallic gesture, indicating his acceptance of fate.

Steve and Helen seemed inordinately put out, though his comments were milder than hers. He mumbled once about inconveniences, then stalked over to the window to stare out at the torrent of wind and rain. Helen was livid.

"I didn't pay good money to grope around in the dark and eat cold meals." Lighting another cigarette with a swift, furious gesture, she glared at Autumn. "It's in-

tolerable that we should have to put up with such ineffi-
ciency. Your aunt will certainly have to make the proper
adjustments. I for one won't pay these ridiculous prices,
then live like a pioneer." She waved her cigarette, preparing to continue, but Autumn cut her off. She aimed
the cold, hard stare she had recently developed.

"I'm sure my aunt will give your complaints all the
consideration they warrant." Turning pointedly away,
she allowed Helen's sharp little darts to bounce off her.
"Actually," she told Jacques, noting his smile of approval, "we have a generator. My uncle was as practical as Aunt Tabby is…"

"Charming," Steve supplied, and instantly became
her friend.

After she'd finished beaming at him, Autumn continued. "If we lose main power, we switch over to the
generator. With that, we can maintain essential power
with little inconvenience."

"I believe I'll have candles in my room anyway,"
Julia decided. She gave Robert an under-the-lashes
smile as he lit her cigarette.

"Julia should have been French," Jacques commented. His moustache tilted at the corner. "She's an
incurable romantic."

"Too much…romance," Helen murmured, "can be
unwise." Her eyes swept the room, then focused on
Julia.

Before Autumn's astonished gaze, Julia transformed
from mischievous angel to tough lady. "I've always
found that only idiots think they're wise." Statement
made, she melted back into a celestial being so quickly,
Autumn blinked.

Seeing her perform on the screen was nothing compared to a live show. It occurred to Autumn that she had no inkling which woman was the real Julia Bond—if indeed she was either. The notion germinated that she really didn't know any of the people in that room. They were all strangers.

The air was still vibrating with the uncomfortable silence when Lucas entered. He seemed impervious to the swirling tension. Helplessly, Autumn's eyes locked on his. He came to her, ignoring the others in his cavalier fashion. The devil smile was on his face.

She felt a tremor when she couldn't stop the room from receding, leaving only him in her vision. Something of that fear must have been reflected in her face.

"I'm not going to eat you, Cat," Lucas murmured. Against the violent sounds of the storm, his voice was low, only for her. "Do you still like to walk in the rain?" The question was offhand, and didn't require an answer as he searched her face. "I remember when you did." He paused when she said nothing. "Your aunt sent you this." Lucas held out his hand, and Autumn's gaze dropped to it. Tension dissolved into laughter. "I haven't heard that in a long time," Lucas said softly.

She lifted her eyes to his again. He was studying her with a complete, singleminded intensity. "No?" As she accepted Aunt Tabby's famous red-button camera, her shoulders moved in a careless shrug. "Laughing's quite a habit of mine."

"Aunt Tabby says for you to have a good time with it." Dismissively, he turned his back on her and walked to the coffeepot.

"What have you got there, Autumn?" Julia demanded, her eyes following Lucas's progress.

Flourishing the camera, Autumn used a sober, didactic tone. "This, ladies and gentlemen, is the latest technological achievement in photography. At the mere touch of a button, friends and loved ones are beamed inside and spewed out onto a picture which develops before your astonished eyes. No focusing, no need to consult your light meter. The button is faster than the brain. Why, a child of five can operate it while riding his tricycle."

"It should be known," Lucas inserted in a dry voice, "that Autumn is a photographic snob." He stood by the window, carelessly drinking coffee while he spoke to the others. His eyes were on Autumn. "If it doesn't have interchangeable lenses and filters, multispeed shutters and impossibly complicated operations, it isn't a camera, but a toy."

"I've noticed her obsession," Julia agreed. She sent him a delicious look before she turned to Autumn. "She wears that black box like other women wear diamonds. She was actually tramping through the forest at the break of dawn, snapping pictures of chipmunks and bunnies."

With a good-natured grin, Autumn lifted the camera and snapped Julia's lovely face.

"Really, darling," Julia said with a professional toss of the head. "You might have given me the chance to turn my best side."

"You haven't got a best side," Autumn countered.

Julia smiled, obviously torn between amusement and insult while Jacques exploded with laughter. "And I thought she was such a sweet child," she murmured.

"In my profession, Miss Bond," Autumn returned gravely, "I've had occasion to photograph a fair number of women. This one you shoot from the left profile, that one from the right, another straight on. Still another from an upward angle, and so on." Pausing a moment, she gave Julia's matchless face a quick, critical survey. "I could shoot you from any position, any angle, any light, and the result would be equally wonderful."

"Jacques." Julia placed a hand on his arm. "We really must adopt this girl. She's invaluable for my ego."

"Professional integrity," Autumn claimed before placing the quickly developing snapshot on the table. She aimed Aunt Tabby's prize at Steve.

"You should be warned that with a camera of any sort in her hands, Autumn becomes a dangerous weapon." Lucas moved closer. He lifted the snap of Julia and studied it.

Autumn frowned as she remembered the innumerable photographs she had taken of him. Under the pretext that they were art, she'd never disposed of them. She'd snapped and focused and crouched around him until, exasperated, he'd dislodged the camera from her hands and effectively driven photography from her mind.

Lucas saw the frown. With his eyes dark and unreadable, he reached down to tangle his fingers in her hair. "You never could teach me how to take a proper picture, could you, Cat?"

"No." The battle with the growing ache made her voice brittle. "I never taught you anything, Lucas. But I learned quite a bit."

"I've never been able to master anything but a one-button job myself." Steve ambled over. Autumn's camera sat on the table beside her. Picking it up, he examined it as if it were a strange contraption from the outer reaches of space. "How can you remember what all these numbers are for?"

When he perched on the arm of her chair, Autumn grasped at the diversion. She began a lesson in basic photography. Lucas wandered back to the coffeepot, obviously bored. From the corner of her eye, Autumn noticed Julia gliding to join him. Within moments, her hand was tucked into his arm, and he no longer appeared bored. Gritting her teeth, Autumn began to give Steve a more involved lesson.

Lucas and Julia left, arm in arm, ostensibly for Julia to nap and Lucas to work. Autumn's eyes betrayed her by following them.

When she dragged her attention back to Steve, she caught his sympathetic smile. That he understood her feelings was too obvious. Cursing herself, she resumed her explanations of f-stops, grateful that Steve picked up the conversation as if there had been no lull.

The afternoon wore on. It was a long, dreary day with rain beating against windows. Lightning and thunder came and went, but the wind built in force until it was one continuous moan. Robert tended the fire until flames crackled and spit. The cheery note this might have brought to the room was negated by Jane's sullenness and Helen's pacing. The air was tight.

Evading Steve's suggestion of cards, Autumn sought the peace and activity of her darkroom. As she closed and locked the door behind her, the headache which had started to build behind her temples eased.

This room was without tensions. Her senses picked up no nagging, intangible disturbances here, but were clear and ready to work. Step by step, she took her film through the first stages of development, preparing chemicals, checking temperatures, setting timers. Growing absorbed, she forgot the battering storm.

While it was necessary, Autumn worked in a total absence of light. Her fingers were her eyes at this stage and she worked quickly. Over the muffled sound of the storm, she heard a faint rattle. She ignored it, busy setting the timer for the next stage of developing. When the sound came again, it annoyed her.

Was it the doorknob? she wondered. Had she remembered to lock the door? All she needed at that point was for some layman to blunder in and bring damaging light with him.

"Leave the door alone," she called out just as the radio she had switched on for company went dead. There went the power, she concluded. Standing in the absolute darkness, Autumn sighed as the rattle came again.

Was it someone at the door, or just someone in the kitchen? Curious and annoyed, she walked in the direction of the door to make sure it was locked. Her steps were confident. She knew every inch of the room now. Suddenly, to her astonishment, pain exploded inside her head. Lights flashed and fractured before the darkness again became complete.

"Autumn, Autumn, open your eyes." Though the sound was far off and muffled, she heard the command in the tone. She resisted it. The nearer she came to consciousness, the more hideous grew the throbbing in her head. Oblivion was painless.

"Open your eyes." The voice was clearer now and more insistent. Autumn moaned.

Reluctantly, she opened her eyes as hands brushed the hair from her face. For a moment, she felt them linger against her cheek. Lucas came into focus gradually, dimming and receding until she forced him back, clear and sharp.

"Lucas?" Disoriented, Autumn could not think beyond his name. It seemed to satisfy him.

"That's better," he said with approval. Before any protest could be made, he kissed her hard, with a briefness that spoke of past intimacy. "You had me worried there a minute. What the hell did you do to yourself?"

The accusation was typical of him. She barely noticed it. "Do?" Autumn lifted a hand to touch the spot on her head where the pain was concentrated. "What happened?"

"That's my question, Cat. No, don't touch the lump." He caught her hand in his and held it. "It'll only hurt more if you do. I'm curious as to how you came by it, and why you were lying in a heap on the floor."

It was difficult to keep clear of the mists in her brain. Autumn tried to center in on the last thing she remembered. "How did you get in?" she demanded, remembering the rattling knob. "Hadn't I locked the door?" It came to her slowly that he was cradling her in his arms, holding her close against his chest. She struggled to sit up. "Were you rattling at the door?"

"Take it easy," he ordered as she groaned with the movement.

Autumn squeezed her eyes shut against the pounding in her head. "I must have walked into the door," she murmured, wondering at the quality of her clumsiness.

"You walked into the door and knocked yourself unconscious?" She couldn't tell if Lucas was angry or amused. The ache in her head kept her from caring one way or the other. "Strange, I don't recall you possessing that degree of uncoordination."

"It was dark," she grumbled, coherent enough to feel embarrassed. "If you hadn't been rattling around at the door..."

"I wasn't rattling around at your door," he began, but she cut him off with a startled gasp.

"The lights!" For a second time, she tried to struggle away from him. "You turned on the lights!"

"It was a mad impulse when I saw you crumpled on the floor," he returned dryly. Without any visible effort, he held her still. "I wanted to see the extent of the damage."

"My film!" Her glare was as accusing as her voice, but he responded with laughter.

"The woman's a maniac."

"Let go of me, will you?" Her anger made her less than gracious. Pushing away, she scrambled to her feet. At her movement, the pain grew to a crashing roar. She staggered under it.

"For God's sake, Autumn." Lucas rose and gripped her shoulders, steadying her. "Stop behaving like an imbecile over a few silly pictures."

This statement, under normal conditions, would have been unwise. In her present state of mind, it was a declaration of war. Pain was eclipsed by a pure silver streak of fury. She whirled on him.

"You never could see my work as anything but silly pictures, could you? You never saw me as anything but a silly child, diverting for a while, but eventually boring. You always hated being bored, didn't you, Lucas?" She made a violent swipe at the hair that fell over her eyes. "You sit with your novels and bask in the adulation you get and look down your nose at the rest of us. You're not the only person in the world with talent, Lucas. My abilities are just as creative as yours, and my pictures give me as much fulfillment as your silly little books."

For a moment, he stood in silence, studying her with a frown. When he did speak, his voice was oddly weary. "All right, Autumn, now that you've gotten that out, you'd better get yourself some aspirin."

"Just leave me alone!" She shook off the hand he put on her arm. Turning, she started to take her camera from the shelf she had placed it on before beginning her work. Glancing down at the table, she flared again. "What do you mean by messing around with my equipment? You've exposed an entire roll of film!" Seething with fury, she whirled on him. "It isn't enough to interrupt my work by fooling around at the door, then turn on the lights and ruin what I've started. You have to put your hands into something you know nothing about."

"I told you before, I wasn't fooling around at your door." His eyes were darkening dangerously. "I came back after the power went out and the generator switched on. The door was open, and you were lying in a heap in the middle of the floor. I never touched your damned film."

There was ice in his voice now to go with the heat in his eyes but Autumn was too infuriated to be touched by either. "Foolish as it may seem," he continued, "my concern and attention were on you." Moving toward her, he glanced down at the confusion on her work table. "I don't suppose it occurred to you that in the dark you disturbed the film yourself?"

"Don't be absurd." Her professional ability was again insulted, but he cut off her retort in a voice filled with strained patience. Autumn pondered on it. As she remembered, Lucas had no patience at all.

"Autumn, I don't know what happened to your film. I didn't get any farther into the room than the spot where you were lying. I won't apologize for switching on the lights; I'd do precisely the same thing again." He circled her neck with his fingers and his words took on the old caressing note she remembered. "I happen to think your welfare is more important than your pictures."

Suddenly, her interest in the film waned. She wanted only to escape from him, and the feelings he aroused in her so effortlessly. Programmed response, she told herself. The soft voice and gentle hands tripped the release, and she went under.

"You're pale," Lucas muttered, abruptly dropping his hands and stuffing them into his pockets. "Dr. Spicer can take a look at you."

"No, I don't need—" She got no farther. He grabbed her arms with quicksilver fury.

"Damn it, Cat, must you argue with everything I say? Is there no getting past the hate you've built up for me?" He gave a quick shake. The pain rolled and spun in her head. For an instant, his face went out of focus as dizziness blurred her vision. Swearing with short, precise expertise, he pulled her close against him until the faintness passed. In a swift move, he lifted her into his arms. "You're pale as a ghost," he muttered. "Like it or not, you're going to see the doctor. You can vent your venom on him for a while."

By the time Autumn realized he was carrying her to her room, her temper had ebbed. There was only a dull, wicked ache and the weariness. Flagging, she rested her head against his shoulder and surrendered. This wasn't the time to think about the darkroom door or how it had come to be opened. It wasn't the time to think of how she had managed to walk into it like a perfect fool. This wasn't the time to think at all.

Accepting the fact that she had no choice, Autumn closed her eyes and allowed Lucas to take over. She kept them closed when she felt him lower her to the bed, but she knew he stood looking down at her a moment. She knew too that he was frowning.

The sound of his footsteps told her that he had walked into the adjoining bathroom. The faint splash of water in the sink sounded like a waterfall to her throbbing head. In a moment, there was a cool cloth over the ache in her forehead. Opening her eyes, Autumn looked into his.

"Lie still," he ordered curtly. Lucas brooded down at her with an odd, enigmatic expression. "I'll get Spicer," he muttered abruptly. Turning on his heel, he strode to the door.

"Lucas." Autumn stopped him because the cool cloth had brought back memories of all the gentle things he had ever done. He'd had his gentle moments, though she'd tried hard to pretend he hadn't. It had seemed easier.

When he turned back, impatience was evident in the very air around him. What a man of contradictions he was, she mused. Intemperate, with barely any middle ground at all.

"Thank you," she said, ignoring his obvious desire to be gone. "I'm sorry I shouted at you. You're being very kind."

Lucas leaned against the door and stared back at her. "I've never been kind." His voice was weary again.

Autumn found it necessary to force back the urge to go to him, wipe away his lines of fatigue. He sensed her thoughts, and his eyes softened briefly. On his mouth moved one of his rare, disarming smiles.

"My God, Cat, you always were so incredibly sweet. So terrifyingly warm."

With that, he left her.

Chapter 5

Autumn was staring at the ceiling when Robert entered. Shifting her eyes, she looked at his black bag dubiously. She'd never cared for what doctors carried inside those innocent-looking satchels.

"A house call," she said and managed a smile. "The eighth wonder of the world. I didn't think you'd have your bag with you on vacation."

He was quick enough to note her uneasy glance. "Do you travel without your camera?"

"Touché." She told herself to relax and not to be a baby.

"I don't think we'll need to operate." He sat on the bed and removed the cloth Lucas had placed there. "Mmm, that's going to be colorful. Is your vision blurred?"

"No."

His hands were surprisingly soft and gentle, reminding Autumn of her father's. She relaxed further and answered his questions on dizziness, nausea and so forth while watching his face. He was different, she noted. The competence was still there, but his dapper self-presentation had been replaced by a quiet compassion. His voice was kind, she thought, and so were his eyes. He was well suited to his profession.

"How'd you come by this, Autumn?" As he asked he reached in his bag and her attention switched to his hands. He removed cotton and a bottle, not the needle she'd worried about.

She wrinkled her nose ruefully. "I walked into a door."

He shook his head with a laugh, and began to bathe the bruise. "A likely story."

"And embarrassingly true. In the darkroom," she added. "I must have misjudged the distance."

His eyes shifted and studied hers a moment before they returned to her forehead. "You struck me as a woman who kept her eyes open," he said a bit grimly, Autumn thought, before he smiled again. "It's just a bump," he told her and held her hand. "Though my diagnosis won't make it hurt any less."

"It's only an agonizing ache now," Autumn returned, trying for lightness. "The cannons have stopped going off."

With a chuckle, he reached into his bag again. "We can do something about smaller artillery."

"Oh." She eyed the bottle of pills he held and frowned. "I was going to take some aspirin."

"You don't put a forest fire out with a water pistol." He smiled at her again and shook out two pills.

"They're very mild, Autumn. Take these and rest for an hour or two. You can trust me," he added with exaggerated gravity as her brows stayed lowered. "Even though I am a surgeon."

"Okay." His eyes convinced her and she smiled back, accepting the glass of water and pills. "You're not going to take out my appendix or anything, are you?"

"Not on vacation." He waited until she had swallowed the medication, then pulled a light blanket over her. "Rest," he ordered and left her.

The next time Autumn opened her eyes, the room was in shadows. Rest? she thought and shifted under the blanket. I've been unconscious. How long? She listened. The storm was still raging, whipping against her windows with a fury she'd been oblivious to. Carefully, she pushed herself into a sitting position. Her head didn't pound, but a touch of her fingers assured her she hadn't dreamed up the entire incident. Her next thought was entirely physical—she discovered she was starving.

Rising, she took a quick glance in the mirror, decided she didn't like what she saw and went in search of food and company. She found them both in the dining room. Her timing was perfect.

"Autumn." It was Robert who spotted her first. "Feeling better?"

She hesitated a moment, embarrassed. Hunger was stronger, however, and the scent of Nancy's chicken was too tempting. "Much," she told him. She glanced at Lucas, but he said nothing, only watched her. The gentleness she had glimpsed so briefly before might have been an illusion. His eyes were dark and hard. "I'm starving," she confessed as she took her seat.

"Good sign. Any more pain?"

"Only in my pride." Forging ahead, she began to fill her plate. "Clumsiness isn't a talent I like to brag about, and walking into a door is such a tired cliché. I wish I'd come up with something more original."

"It's odd." Jacques twirled his fork by the stem as he studied her. "It doesn't seem to me that you would have the power enough to knock yourself unconscious."

"An amazon," Autumn explained and let the chicken rest for a delicious moment on her tongue.

"She eats like one," Julia commented. Autumn glanced over in time to catch the speculative look on her face before it vanished into a smile. "I gain weight watching her."

"Metabolism," Autumn claimed and took another forkful of chicken. "The real tragedy is that I lost the two rolls of film I shot on the trip from New York."

"Perhaps we're in for a series of accidents." Helen's voice was as hard as her eyes as they swept the table. "Things come in threes, don't they?" No one answered and she went on, fingering her own bruise. "It's hard to say what might happen next."

Autumn had come to detest the odd little silences that followed Helen's remarks, the fingers of tension that poked holes in the normalcy of the situation. On impulse, she broke her rule and started a conversation with Lucas.

"What would you do with this setting, Lucas?" She turned to him, but found no change in his expression. He's watching all of us, she thought. Just watching. Shaking off her unease, Autumn continued. "Nine people—ten really, counting the cook—isolated in a remote country inn, a storm raging. The main power's already snuffed out. The phone's likely to be next."

"The phone's already out," Steve told her. Autumn drew out a dramatic "Ah."

"And the ford, of course, is probably impassable." Robert winked at her, falling in with the theme.

"What more could you ask for?" Autumn demanded of Lucas. Lightning flashed, as if on cue.

"Murder." Lucas uttered the six-letter word casually, but it hung in the air as all eyes turned to him. Autumn shuddered involuntarily. It was the response she'd expected, yet she felt a chill on hearing it. "But, of course," he continued as the word still whispered in the air, "it's a rather overly obvious setting for my sort of work."

"Life is sometimes obvious, is it not?" Jacques stated. A small smile played on his mouth as he lifted his glass of golden-hued wine.

"I could be very effective," Julia mused. "Gliding down dark passageways in flowing white." She placed her elbows on the table, folded her hands and rested her chin on them. "The flame of my candle flickering into the shadows while the murderer waits with a silk scarf to cut off my life."

"You'd make a lovely corpse," Autumn told her.

"Thank you, darling." She turned to Lucas. "I'd much rather remain among the living, at least until the final scene."

"You die so well." Steve grinned across the table at her. "I was impressed by your Lisa in *Hope Springs*."

"What sort of murder do you see, Lucas?" Steve was eating little, Autumn noted; he preferred the wine. "A crime of passion or revenge? The impulsive act of a discarded lover or the evil workings of a cool, calculating mind?"

"Aunt Tabby could sprinkle an exotic poison over the

food and eliminate us one by one," Autumn suggested as she dipped into the mashed potatoes.

"Once someone's dead, they're no more use." Helen brought the group's attention back to her. "Murder is a waste. You gain more by keeping someone alive. Alive and vulnerable." She shot Lucas a look. "Don't you agree, Mr. McLean?"

Autumn didn't like the way she smiled at him. *Cool and calculating.* Jacques's words repeated in her mind. Yes, she mused, this was a cool and calculating woman. In the silence, Autumn shifted her gaze to Lucas.

His face held the faintly bored go-to-hell look she knew so well. "I don't think murder is always a waste." Again, his voice was casual, but Autumn, in tune with him, saw the change in his eyes. They weren't bored, but cold as ice. "The world would gain much by the elimination of some." He smiled, and it was deadly.

They no longer seemed to be speaking hypothetically. Shifting her gaze to Helen, Autumn saw the quick fear. *But it's just a game,* she told herself frantically and looked at Julia. The actress was smiling, but there was none of her summer warmth in it. She was enjoying watching Helen flutter like a moth on a pin. Noting Autumn's expression of dismayed shock, Julia changed the subject without a ripple.

After dinner, the group loitered in the lounge, but the storm, which continued unabated, was wearing on the nerves. Only Julia and Lucas seemed unaffected. Autumn noted how they huddled together in a corner, apparently enthralled with each other's company. Julia's laughter was low and rich over the sound of rain. Once, she watched Lucas pinch a strand of the pale hair between his fingers. Autumn turned away. Julia ran interference expertly, and the knowledge depressed her.

The Spicers, without Julia as a distraction, sat together on the sofa nearest the fire. Though their voices were low, Autumn sensed the strain of a domestic quarrel. She moved farther out of earshot. A bad time, she decided, for Jane to confront Robert on his fascination with Julia when the actress was giving another man the benefit of her attentions. When they left, Jane's face was no longer sullen, but simply miserable. Julia never glanced in their direction, but leaned closer to Lucas and murmured something in his ear that made him laugh. Autumn found she, too, wanted out of the room.

It has nothing to do with Lucas, she told herself as she moved down the hall. I just want to say good-night to Aunt Tabby. Julia's doing precisely what I want her to—keeping Lucas entertained. He never even looked at me once Julia stepped in between. Shaking off the hurt, Autumn opened the door to her aunt's room.

"Autumn, dear! Lucas told me you bumped your head." Aunt Tabby stopped clucking over her laundry list and rose to peer at the bruise. "Oh, poor thing. Do you want some aspirin? I have some somewhere."

Though she appreciated Lucas's consideration in giving her aunt a watered-down version, Autumn wondered at the ease of their relationship. It didn't seem quite in character for Lucas McLean to bother overmuch with a vague old woman whose claim to fame was a small inn and a way with chocolate cake.

"No, Aunt Tabby, I'm fine. I've already taken something."

"That's good." She patted Autumn's hand and

frowned briefly at the bruise. "You'll have to be more careful, dear."

"I will. Aunt Tabby…" Autumn poked idly at the papers on her aunt's desk. "How well do you know Lucas? I don't recall you ever calling a roomer by his first name." She knew there was no use in beating around the bush with her aunt. It would produce the same results as reading *War and Peace* in dim light—a headache and confusion.

"Oh, now that depends, Autumn. Yes, that really does depend." Aunt Tabby gently removed her papers from Autumn's reach before she focused on a spot in the ceiling. Autumn knew this meant she was thinking. "There's Mrs. Nollington. She has a corner room every September. I call her Frances and she calls me Tabitha. Such a nice woman. A widow from North Carolina."

"Lucas calls you Aunt Tabby," Autumn pointed out before her aunt could get going on Frances Nollington.

"Yes, dear, quite a number of people do. You do."

"Yes, but—"

"And Paul and Will," Aunt Tabby continued blithely. "And the little boy who brings the eggs. And…oh, several people. Yes, indeed, several people. Did you enjoy your dinner?"

"Yes, very much. Aunt Tabby," Autumn continued, determined that tenacity would prevail. "Lucas seems very much at home here."

"Oh, I am glad!" She beamed at her niece as she took Autumn's hand and patted it. "I do try so hard to make everyone feel at home. It always seems a shame to have to make them pay, but…" She glanced down at her laundry bills and began to mutter.

Give up, Autumn told herself. She kissed her aunt's cheek and left her to her towels and pillowcases.

It was growing late when Autumn finished putting her darkroom back in order. She left the door open this time and kept all the lights on. The echo of rain followed her inside as it beat on the kitchen windows. Other than its angry murmur, the house was silent.

No, Autumn thought, old houses are never silent. They creak and whisper, but the groaning boards and settling didn't disturb her. She liked the humming quality of the silence. Absorbed and content, she emptied trays and replaced bottles. She threw her ruined film into the wastecan with a sigh.

That hurts a bit, she thought, but there's nothing to be done about it. Tomorrow, she decided, she'd develop the film she'd taken that morning—the lake, the early sun, the mirrored trees. It would put her in a better frame of mind. Stretching her back, she lifted her hair from her neck, feeling pleasantly tired.

"I remember you doing that in the mornings."

Autumn whirled, her hair flying out from her shoulders as quick fear brought her heart to her throat. Pushing strands from her face, she stared at Lucas.

He leaned against the open doorway, a cup of coffee in his hand. His eyes locked on hers without effort.

"You'd pull up your hair, then let it fall, tumbling down your back until I ached to get my hands on it." His voice was deep and strangely raw. Autumn couldn't speak at all. "I often wondered if you did it on purpose, just to drive me mad." As he studied her face, he frowned, then lifted the coffee to his lips. "But, of course you didn't. I've never known anyone else who could arouse with such innocence."

"What are you doing here?" The trembling in her voice took some of the power out of the demand.

"Remembering."

Turning, she began to juggle bottles, jumbling them out of their carefully organized state. "You always were clever with words, Lucas." Cooler now that she wasn't facing him, she meticulously studied a bottle of bath soap. "I suppose you have to be in your profession."

"I'm not writing at the moment."

It was easier to deliberately misunderstand him. "Your book still giving trouble?" Turning, Autumn again noticed the signs of strain and fatigue on his face. Sympathy and love flared up, and she struggled to bank them down. His eyes were much too keen. "You might have more success if you'd get a good night's sleep." She gestured toward the cup in his hands. "Coffee's not going to help."

"Perhaps not." He drained the cup. "But it's wiser than bourbon."

"Sleep's better than both." She shrugged her shoulders carelessly. Lucas's habits were no longer her concern. "I'm going up." Autumn walked toward him, but he stayed where he was, barring the door. She pulled up sharply. They were alone. The ground floor was empty but for them and the sound of rain.

"Lucas." She sighed sharply, wanting him to think her impatient rather than vulnerable. "I'm tired. Don't be troublesome."

His eyes smoldered at her tone. Though Autumn remained calm, she could feel her knees turning to water. The dull, throbbing ache was back in her head. When he moved aside, she switched off the lights, then brushed past him. Swiftly, he took her arm, preventing what she had thought was going to be an easy exit.

"There'll come a time, Cat," he murmured, "when you won't walk away so easily."

"Don't threaten me with your overactive masculinity." Her temper rose and she forgot caution. "I'm immune now."

She was jerked against him. All she could see was his fury. "I've had enough of this."

His mouth took hers roughly; she could taste the infuriated desire. When she struggled, he pinned her back against the wall, holding her arms to her sides and battering at her will with his mouth alone. She could feel herself going under and hating herself for it as much, she told herself, as she hated him. His lips didn't soften, even when her struggles ceased. He took and took as the anger vibrated between them.

Her heart was thudding wildly, and she could feel the mad pace of his as they pressed together. Passion was all-encompassing, and her back was to the wall. There's no escape, she thought dimly. There's never been any escape from him. No place to run. No place to hide. She began to tremble with fear and desire.

Abruptly he pulled away. His eyes were so dark, she saw nothing but her own reflection. I'm lost in him, she thought. I've always been lost in him. Then he was shaking her, shocking a gasp out of her.

"Watch how far you push," he told her roughly. "Damn it, you'd better remember I haven't any scruples. I know how to deal with people who pick fights with me." He stopped, but his fingers still dug into her skin. "I'll take you, Cat, take you kicking and screaming if you push me much further."

Too frightened by the rage she saw in his face to think of pride, she twisted away. She flew down the hall and up the stairs.

Chapter 6

Autumn reached her door, out of breath and fighting tears. He shouldn't be allowed to do this to her. She couldn't allow it. Why had he barged back into her life this way? Just when she was beginning to get over him. *Liar.* The voice was clear as crystal inside her head. You've never gotten over him. Never. But I will. She balled her hands into fists as she stood outside her door and caught her breath. I will get over him.

Hearing the sound of his footsteps on the stairs, she fumbled with the doorknob. She didn't want to deal with him again tonight. Tomorrow was soon enough.

Something was wrong. Autumn knew it the moment she opened her door and stumbled into the dark. The scent of perfume was so strong, her head whirled with it. She groped for the light and when it flashed on, she gave a small sound of despair.

The drawers and closet had been turned out and her clothes were tossed and scattered across the room. Some were ripped and torn, others merely lay in heaps. Her jewelry had been dumped from its box and tossed indiscriminately over the mounds of clothes. Bottles of cologne and powder had been emptied out and flung everywhere. Everything—every small object or personal possession—had been abused or destroyed.

She stood frozen in shock and disbelief. The wrong room, she told herself dumbly. This had to be the wrong room. But the lawn print blouse with its sleeve torn at the shoulder had been a Christmas gift from Will. The sandals, flung into a corner and slashed, she had bought herself in a small shop off Fifth Avenue the summer before.

"No." She shook her head as if that would make it all go away. "It's not possible."

"Good God!" Lucas's voice came from behind her. Autumn turned to see him staring into her room.

"I don't understand." The words were foolish, but they were all she had. Slowly, Lucas shifted his attention to her face. She made a helpless gesture. "Why?"

He came to her, and with his thumb brushed a tear from her cheek. "I don't know, Cat. First we have to find out who."

"But it's—it's so spiteful." She wandered through the rubble of her things, still thinking she must be dreaming. "No one here would have any reason to do this to me. You'd have to hate someone to do this, wouldn't you? No one here has any reason to hate me. No one even knew me before last night."

"Except me."

"This isn't your style." She pressed her fingers to

her temple and struggled to understand. "You'd find a more direct way of hurting me."

"Thanks."

Autumn looked over at him and frowned, hardly aware of what was being said. His expression was brooding as he studied her face. She turned away. She wasn't up to discussing Lucas McLean. Then she saw it.

"Oh, *no!*"

Scrambling on all fours, Autumn worked her way over the mangled clothes and began pushing at the tangled sheets of her bed. Her hands shook as she reached for her camera. The lens was shattered, with spiderweb cracks spreading over the surface. The back was broken, hanging drunkenly on one hinge. The film streamed out like the tail of a kite. Exposed. Ruined. The mirror was crushed. With a moan, she cradled it in her hands and began to weep.

Her clothes and trinkets meant nothing, but the Nikon was more to her than a single-reflex camera. It was as much a part of her as her hands. With it, she had taken her first professional picture. Its mutilation was rape.

Her face was suddenly buried against a hard chest. She made no protest as Lucas's arms came around her, but wept bitterly. He said nothing, offered no comforting words, but his hands were unexpectedly gentle, his arms strong.

"Oh, Lucas." She drew away from him with a sigh. "It's so senseless."

"There's sense to it somewhere, Cat. There always is."

She looked back up at him. "Is there?" His eyes were keeping their secrets so she dropped her own back to her mangled camera. "Well, if someone wanted to hurt me, this was the right way."

Her fingers clenched on the camera. She was suddenly, fiercely angry; it pushed despair and tears out of her mind. Her body flooded with it. She wasn't going to sit and weep any longer. She was going to do something. Pushing her camera into Lucas's hands, Autumn scrambled to her feet.

"Wait a minute." He grabbed her hand before she could rush from the room. "Where are you going?"

"To drag everyone out of bed," she snapped at him, jerking her hand. "And then I'm going to break someone's neck."

He didn't have an easy time subduing her. Ultimately, he pinned her by wrapping his arms around her and holding her against him. "You probably could." There was a touch of surprised admiration in his tone, but it brought her no pleasure.

"Watch me," she challenged.

"Calm down first." He tightened his grip as she squirmed against him.

"I want—"

"I know what you want, Cat, and I don't blame you. But you have to think before you rush in."

"I don't have anything to think about," she tossed back. "Someone's going to pay for this."

"All right, fair enough. Who?"

His logic annoyed her, but succeeded in taking her temper from boil to simmer. "I don't know yet." With an effort, she managed to take a deep breath.

"That's better." He smiled and kissed her lightly. "Though your eyes are still lethal enough." He loosened his grip, but kept a hold on her arm. "Just keep your claws sheathed, Cat, until we find out what's going on. Let's go knock on a few doors."

Julia's room adjoined hers, so Autumn steered there first. Her rage was now packed in ice. Systematic, she told herself, aware of Lucas's grip. All right, we'll be systematic until we find out who did it. And then...

She knocked sharply on Julia's door. After the second knock, Julia answered with a soft, husky slur.

"Get up, Julia," Autumn demanded. "I want to talk to you."

"Autumn, darling." Her voice evoked a picture of Julia snuggling into her pillows. "Even I require beauty sleep. Go away like a good girl."

"Up, Julia," Autumn repeated, barely restraining herself from shouting. "Now."

"Goodness, aren't we grumpy. I'm the one who's being dragged from my bed."

She opened the door, a vision in a white lace negligee, her hair a tousled halo around her face, her eyes dark and heavy with sleep.

"Well, I'm up." Julia gave Lucas a slow, sensual smile and ran a hand through her hair. "Are we going to have a party?"

"Someone tore my room apart," Autumn stated bluntly. She watched Julia's attention switch from the silent flirtation with Lucas to her.

"What?" The catlike expression had melted into a frown of concentration. An actress, Autumn reminded herself. She's an actress and don't forget it.

"My clothes were pulled out and ripped, tossed around the room. My camera's broken." She swallowed on this. It was the most difficult to accept.

"That's crazy." Julia was no longer leaning provocatively against the door, but standing straight. "Let me see." She brushed past them and hurried down the hall. Stopping in the doorway of Autumn's room, she stared. Her eyes, when they turned back, were wide with shock. "Autumn, how awful!" She came back and slipped an arm around Autumn's waist. "How perfectly awful. I'm so sorry."

Sincerity, sympathy, shock. They were all there. Autumn wanted badly to believe them.

"Who would have done that?" she demanded of Lucas. Autumn saw that Julia's eyes were angry now. She was again the tough lady Autumn had glimpsed briefly that afternoon.

"We intend to find out. We're going to wake the others." Something passed between them. Autumn saw it flash briefly, then it was gone.

"All right," Julia said. "Then let's do it." She pushed her hair impatiently behind her ears. "I'll get the Spicers, you get Jacques and Steve. You," she continued to Autumn, "wake up Helen."

Her tone carried enough authority that Autumn found herself turning down the hall to Helen's room. She could hear the pounding, the answering stirs and murmurs from behind her. Reaching Helen's door, Autumn banged against it. This, at least, she thought, was progress. Lucas was right. We need a trial before we can hang someone.

Her knock went unanswered. Annoyed, Autumn rapped again. She wasn't in the mood to be ignored. Now there was more activity behind her as people came out of their rooms to stare at the disaster in hers.

"Helen!" She knocked again with fraying patience. "Come out here." She pushed the door open. It would give her some satisfaction to drag at least one person from bed. Ruthlessly, she switched on the light. "Helen, I—"

Helen wasn't in bed. Autumn stared at her, too shocked to feel horror. She was on the floor, but she wasn't sleeping. She was done with sleeping. Was that blood? Autumn thought in dumb fascination. She took a step forward before the reality struck her.

Horror gripped her throat, denying her the release of screaming. Slowly, she backed away. It was a nightmare. Starting with her room, it was all a nightmare. None of it was real. Lucas's careless voice played back in her head. *Murder.* Autumn shook her head as she backed into a wall. No, that was only a game. She heard a voice shouting in terror for Lucas, not even aware it was her own. Then blessedly, her hands came up to cover her eyes.

"Get her out of here." Lucas's rough command floated through Autumn's brain. She was trapped in a fog of dizziness. Arms came round her and led her from the room.

"Oh my God." Steve's voice was unsteady. When Autumn found the strength to look up at him, his face was ashen. She struggled against the faintness and buried her face in his chest. When was she going to wake up?

Confusion reigned around her. She heard disembodied voices as she drifted from horror to shock. There were Julia's smoky tones, Jane's gravelly voice and Jacques's rapid French-English mixture. Then Lucas's voice joined in—calm, cool, like a splash of cold water.

"She's dead. Stabbed. The phone's out so I'm going into the village to get the police."

"Murdered? She was murdered? Oh God!" Jane's

voice rose, then became muffled. Raising her head, Autumn saw Jane being held tightly against her husband.

"I think, as a precaution, Lucas, no one should leave the inn alone." Robert took a deep breath as he cradled his wife. "We have to face the implications."

"I'll go with him." Steve's voice was strained and uneven. "I could use the fresh air."

With a curt nod, Lucas focused on Autumn. His eyes never left hers as he spoke to Robert. "Have you got something to put her out? She can double up with Julia tonight."

"I'm fine." Autumn managed to speak as she drew back from Steve's chest. "I don't want anything." It wasn't a dream, but real, and she had to face it. "Don't worry about me, it's not me. I'm all right." Hysteria was bubbling, and she bit down on her lip to cut it off.

"Come on, darling." Julia's arm replaced Steve's. "We'll go downstairs and sit down for a while. She'll be all right."

"I want—"

"I said she'll be all right," Julia cut off Lucas's protest sharply. "I'll see to her. Do what you have to do." Before he could speak again, she led Autumn down the staircase.

"Sit down," she ordered, nudging Autumn onto the sofa. "You could use a drink."

Looking up, Autumn saw Julia's face hovering over hers. "You're pale," she said stupidly before the brandy burned her throat and brought the world into focus with a jolt.

"I'm not surprised," Julia murmured and sank down on the low table in front of Autumn. "Better?" she asked when Autumn lifted the snifter again.

"Yes, I think so." She took a deep breath and focused on Julia's eyes. "It's really happening, isn't it? She's really lying up there."

"It's happening." Julia drained her own brandy. Color seeped gradually into her cheeks. "The bitch finally pushed someone too far."

Stunned by the hardness of Julia's voice, Autumn could only stare. Calmly, Julia set down her glass.

"Listen." Her tone softened, but her eyes were still cold. "You're a strong lady, Autumn. You've had a shock, a bad one, but you won't fall apart."

"No." Autumn tried to believe it, then said with more strength, "No, I won't fall apart."

"This is a mess, and you have to face it." Julia paused, then leaned closer. "One of us killed her."

Part of her had known it, but the rest had fought against the knowledge, blocking it out. Now that it had been said in cool, simple terms, there was no escape from it. Autumn nodded again and swallowed the remaining brandy in one gulp.

"She got what she deserved."

"Julia!" Jacques strode into the room. His face was covered with horror and disapproval.

"Oh, Jacques, thank God. Give me one of those horrible French cigarettes. Give one to Autumn, too. She could use it."

"Julia." He obeyed her automatically. "You musn't speak so now."

"I'm not a hypocrite." Julia drew deeply on the cigarette, shuddered, then drew again. "I detested her. The police will find out soon enough why we all detested her."

"*Nom de Dieu!* How can you speak so calmly of it?"

Jacques exploded in a quick, passionate rage Autumn hadn't thought him capable of. "The woman is dead, murdered. You didn't see the cruelty of it. I wish to God I had not."

Autumn drew hard on her cigarette, trying to block out the picture that flashed back into her mind. She gasped and choked on the power of the smoke.

"Autumn, forgive me." Jacques's anger vanished as he sat down beside her and draped an arm over her shoulders. "I shouldn't have reminded you."

"No." She shook her head, then crushed out the cigarette. It wasn't going to help. "Julia's right. It has to be faced."

Robert entered, but his normally swinging stride was slow and dragging. "I gave Jane a sedative." With a sigh, he too made for the brandy. "It's going to be a long night."

The room grew silent. The rain, so much a part of the night, was no longer noticeable. Jacques paced the room, smoking continually while Robert kindled a fresh fire. The blaze, bright and crackling, brought no warmth. Autumn's skin remained chilled. In defense, she poured herself another brandy but found she couldn't drink it.

Julia remained seated. She smoked in long, slow puffs. The only outward sign of her agitation was the continual tapping of a pink-tipped nail against the arm of her chair. The tapping, the crackling, the hiss of rain, did nothing to diminish the overwhelming power of the silence.

When the front door opened with a click and a thud, all eyes flew toward the sound. Strings of tension tightened and threatened to snap. Autumn waited to see Lucas's face. It would be all right, somehow, as long as she could see his face.

"Couldn't get through the ford," he stated shortly as he came into the room. He peeled off a sopping jacket, then made for the community brandy.

"How bad is it?" Robert looked from Lucas to Steve, then back to Lucas. Already, the line of command had been formed.

"Bad enough to keep us here for a day or two," Lucas informed him. He swallowed a good dose of the brandy, then stared out the window. There was nothing to see but the reflection of the room behind him. "That's if the rain lets up by morning." Turning, he locked onto Autumn, making a long, thorough study. Again he had, in his way, pushed everyone from the room but the two of them.

"The phones," she blurted out, needing to say something, anything. "We could have phone service by tomorrow."

"Don't count on it." Lucas ran a hand through his dripping hair, showering the room with water. "According to the car radio, this little spring shower is the backlash of a tornado. The power's out all over this part of the state." He lit a cigarette with a shrug. "We'll just have to wait and see."

"Days." Steve flopped down beside Autumn, his face still gray. She gave him her unwanted brandy. "It could be days."

"Lovely." Rising, Julia went to Lucas. She plucked the cigarette from his fingers and drew on it. "Well." She stared at him. "What the hell do we do now?"

"First we lock and seal off Helen's room." Lucas lit another cigarette. His eyes stayed on Julia's. "Then we get some sleep."

Chapter 7

Sometime during the first murky light of dawn, Autumn did sleep. She'd passed the night lying wide-eyed, listening to the sound of Julia's gentle breathing beside her. Though she'd envied her ability to sleep, Autumn had fought off the drowsiness. If she closed her eyes, she might see what she'd seen when she opened Helen's door. When her eyes did close, however, the sleep was dreamless—the total oblivion of exhaustion.

It might have been the silence that woke her. Suddenly, she found herself awake and sitting straight up in bed. Confused, she stared around her.

Julia's disorder greeted her. Silk scarves and gold chains were draped here and there. Elegant bottles cluttered the bureau. Small, incredibly high Italian heels littered the floor. Memory returned.

With a sigh, Autumn rose, feeling a bit ridiculous

in Julia's black silk nightgown; it neither suited nor fit. After seeing herself in the mirror, Autumn was glad Julia had already awakened and gone. She didn't want to wear any of the clothes that might have survived the attack on her room, and prepared to change back into yesterday's shirt and jeans.

A note lay on them. The elegant, sloping print could only have been Julia's:

Darling, help yourself to some undies and a blouse or sweater. I'm afraid my slacks won't fit you. You're built like a pencil. You don't wear a bra, and in any case, the idea of you filling one of mine is ridiculous.

J.

Autumn laughed, as Julia had intended. It felt so good, so normal, that she laughed again. Julia had known exactly how I'd feel, Autumn realized, and a wave of gratitude swept through her for the simple gesture. She showered, letting the water beat hot against her.

Coming back to the bedroom, Autumn pulled out a pair of cobwebby panties. There was a stack of them in misted pastels that she estimated would cost as much as a wide-angle lens. She tugged on one of Julia's sweaters, then pushed it up to her elbows—it was almost there in any case. Leaving the room, she kept her eyes firmly away from Helen's door.

"Autumn, I was hoping you'd sleep longer."

She paused at the foot of the stairs and waited for Steve to reach her. His face was sleep shadowed and older than it had been the day before. A fragment of his boyish smile touched his lips for her, but his eyes didn't join in.

"You don't look as if you got much," he commented and lifted a finger to her cheek.

"I doubt any of us did."

He draped an arm over her shoulder. "At least the rain's slowed down."

"Oh." Realization slowly seeped in and Autumn gave a weak laugh. "I knew there was something different. The quiet woke me. Where is…" She hesitated as Lucas's name trembled on her tongue. "Everyone?" she amended.

"In the lounge," he told her, but steered her toward the dining room. "Breakfast first. I haven't eaten myself, and you can't afford to drop any weight."

"How charming of you to remind me." She managed a friendly grimace. If he could make the effort to be normal, so could she. "Let's eat in the kitchen, though."

Aunt Tabby was there, as usual, giving instructions to a much subdued Nancy. She turned as they entered, then enfolded Autumn in her soft, lavender-scented arms.

"Oh, Autumn, what a dreadful tragedy. I don't know what to make of it." Autumn squeezed her. Here was something solid to hold on to. "Lucas said someone killed the poor thing, but that doesn't seem possible, does it?" Drawing back, Aunt Tabby searched Autumn's face. "You didn't sleep well, dear. Only natural. Sit down and have your breakfast. It's the best thing to do."

Aunt Tabby could, Autumn mused, so surprisingly cut through to the quick when she needed to. She began to bustle around the room, murmuring to Nancy as Autumn and Steve sat at the small kitchen table.

There were simple, normal sounds and scents. Bacon, coffee, the quick sizzle of eggs. It was, Autumn had to agree, the best thing to do. The food, the routine, would bring some sense of order. And with the order, she'd be able to think clearly again.

Steve sat across from her, sipping coffee while she toyed with her eggs. She simply couldn't summon her usual appetite, and turned to conversation instead. The questions she asked Steve about himself were general and inane, but he picked up the effort and went with it. She realized, as she nibbled without interest on a piece of toast, that they were supporting each other.

Autumn discovered he was quite well traveled. He'd crisscrossed all over the country performing various tasks in his role as troubleshooter for his father's conglomerate. He treated wealth with the casual indifference of one who has always had it, but she sensed a knowledge and a dedication toward the company which had provided him with it. He spoke of his father with respect and admiration.

"He's sort of a symbol of success and ingenuity," Steve said, pushing his own half-eaten breakfast around his plate. "He worked his way up the proverbial ladder. He's tough." He grinned and shrugged. "He's earned it."

"How does he feel about you going into politics?"

"He's all for it." Steve glanced down at her plate and sent her a meaningful look. Autumn only smiled and shook her head. "Anyway, he's always encouraged me to 'go for what I want and I better be good at it.'" He grinned again. "He's tough, but since I am good at it and intend to keep it that way, we'll both be satisfied. I like paperwork." He gestured with both hands. "Organizing. Refining the system from within the system."

"That can't be as easy as it sounds," Autumn commented, encouraging his enthusiasm.

"No, but—" He shook his head. "Don't get me started. I'll make a speech." He finished off his second cup of coffee. "I'll be making enough of those when I get back to California and my campaign officially starts."

"It just occurs to me that you, Lucas, Julia and Jacques are all from California." Autumn pushed her hair behind her back and considered the oddity. "It's strange that so many people from the coast would be here at one time."

"The Spicers, too," Aunt Tabby added from across the room, deeply involved in positioning pies in the oven. "Yes, I'm almost sure Dr. Spicer told me they were from California. So warm and sunny there. Well—" she patted the range as if to give it the confidence it needed to handle her pies "—I must see to the rooms now. I moved you next door to Lucas, Autumn. Such a terrible thing about your clothes. I'll have them cleaned for you."

"I'll help you, Aunt Tabby." Pushing away her plate, Autumn rose.

"Oh no, dear, the cleaners will do it."

Smiling wasn't as difficult as Autumn had thought. "I meant with the rooms."

"Oh…" Aunt Tabby trailed off and clucked her tongue. "I do appreciate it, Autumn, I really do, but…" She looked up with a touch of distress in her eyes. "I have my own system, you see. You'd just confuse me. It's all done with numbers."

Leaving Autumn to digest this, she gave her an apologetic touch on the cheek and bustled out.

There seemed nothing to do but join the others in the lounge.

The rain, though it was little more than a mist now, seemed to Autumn like prison bars. Standing at the window in the lounge, she wished desperately for sun. Conversation did not sparkle. When anyone spoke, it was around or over or under Helen Easterman. Perhaps it would have been better if they'd closeted themselves in their rooms, but human nature had them bound together.

Julia and Lucas sat on the sofa, speaking occasionally in undertones. Autumn found his eyes on her too often. Her defenses were too low to deal with what one of his probing looks could do to her, so she kept her back to him and watched the rain.

"I really think it's time we talked about this," Julia announced suddenly.

"Julia." Jacques's voice was both strained and weary.

"We can't go on like this," Julia stated practically. "We'll all go crazy. Steve's wearing out the floor, Robert's running out of wood to fetch and if you smoke another cigarette, you'll keel over." Contrarily, she lit another herself. "Unless we want to pretend that Helen stabbed herself, we've got to deal with the fact that one of us killed her."

Into the penetrating silence, Lucas's voice flowed, calm and detached. "I think we can rule out suicide." He watched as Autumn pressed her forehead to the glass. "And conveniently, we all had the opportunity to do it. Ruling out Autumn and her aunt, that leaves the six of us."

Autumn turned from the window and found every eye in the room on her. "Why should I be ruled out?"

She shuddered and lifted her arms to hug herself. "You said we all had the opportunity."

"Motive, Cat," he said simply. "You're the only one in the room without a motive."

"Motive?" It was becoming too much like one of his screenplays. She needed to cling to reality. "What possible motive could any of us have had?"

"Blackmail." Lucas lit a cigarette as she gaped at him. "Helen was a professional leech. She thought she had quite a little goldmine in the six of us." He glanced up and caught Autumn with one of his looks. "She miscalculated."

"Blackmail." Autumn could only mumble the word as she stared at him. "You're—you're making this up. This is just one of your scenarios."

He waited a beat, his eyes locked on hers. "No."

"How do you know so much?" Steve demanded. Slowly, Lucas's eyes swerved from Autumn. "If she were blackmailing you, it doesn't necessarily follow that she was blackmailing all of us."

"How clever of you, Lucas," Julia interjected, running a hand down his arm, then letting it rest on his. "I had no idea she was sticking her fangs in anyone other than the three of us." Glancing at Jacques, she gave him a careless shrug. "It seems we're in good company."

Autumn made a small sound, and Julia's attention drifted over to her. Her expression was both sympathetic and amused. "Don't look so shocked, darling. Most of us have things we don't particularly want made public. I might have paid her off if she'd threatened me with something more interesting." Leaning back, she pouted effectively. "An affair with a married senator…" She sent a lightning smile to Autumn. "I believe I mentioned him before. That hardly had me quaking in my shoes at the thought of exposure. I'm not squeamish about my indiscretions. I told her to go to hell. Of course," she added, smiling slowly, "there's only my word for that, isn't there?"

"Julia, don't make jokes." Jacques lifted a hand to rub his eyes.

"I'm sorry." Julia rose to perch on the arm of his chair. Her hand slipped to his shoulder.

"This is crazy." Unable to comprehend what was happening, Autumn searched the faces that surrounded her. They were strangers again, holding secrets. "What are you all doing here? Why did you come?"

"It's very simple." Lucas rose and crossed over to her, but unlike Julia, he didn't touch to comfort. "I made plans to come here for my own reasons. Helen found out. She was very good at finding things out—too good. She learned that Julia and Jacques were to join me." He turned, half blocking Autumn from the rest with his body. Was it protection, she wondered, or defense? "She must have contacted the rest of you, and made arrangements to have all her...clients here at once."

"You seem to know quite a bit," Robert muttered. He poked unnecessarily at the fire.

"It isn't difficult to figure out," Lucas returned. "I knew she was holding nasty little threats over three of us; we'd discussed it. When I noticed her attention to Anderson, and you and your wife, I knew she was sucking elsewhere, too."

Jane began to cry in dry, harsh sobs that racked her body. Instinctively, Autumn moved past Lucas to offer comfort. Before she was halfway across the room, Jane stopped her with a look that was like a fist to the jaw.

"You could have done it just as easily as anyone else. You've been spying on us, taking that camera everywhere." Jane's voice rose dramatically as Autumn froze. "You were working for her, you could have done it. You can't prove you didn't. I was with Robert." There was nothing bland or dull about her now. Her eyes were wild. "I was with Robert. He'll tell you."

Robert's arm came around her. His voice was quiet and soothing as she sobbed against his chest. Autumn didn't move. There seemed no place to go.

"She was going to tell you I was gambling again, tell you about all the money I'd lost." She clung to him, a sad sight in a dirt-brown dress. Robert continued to murmur and stroke her hair. "But I told you last night, I told you myself. I couldn't pay her anymore, and I told you. I didn't kill her, Robert. Tell them I didn't kill her."

"Of course you didn't, Jane. Everyone knows that. Come with me now, you're tired. We'll go upstairs."

He was leading her across the room as he spoke. His eyes met Autumn's half in apology, half in a plea for understanding. She saw, quite suddenly, that he loved his wife very much.

Autumn turned away, humiliated for Jane, sorry for Robert. The faint trembling in her hands indicated she'd been dealt one more shock. When Steve's arm came around her, she turned into it and drew the comfort offered.

"I think we could all use a drink," Julia announced. Moving to the bar, she poured a hefty glass of sherry, then took it to Autumn. "You first," she ordered, pressing the glass into her hand. "Autumn seems to be getting the worst of this. Hardly seems fair, does it, Lucas?" Her eyes lifted to his and held briefly before she turned back to the bar. He made no answer. "She's probably the only one of us here who's even remotely sorry that Helen's dead."

Autumn drank, wishing the liquor would soften the words.

"She was a vulture," Jacques murmured. Autumn saw the message pass between him and Julia. "But even a vulture doesn't deserve to be murdered." Leaning back, he accepted the glass Julia brought him. He clasped her hand as she once again sat on the arm of his chair.

"Perhaps my motive is the strongest," Jacques said and drank once, deeply. "When the police come, all will be opened and studied. Like something under a microscope." He looked at Autumn, as if to direct his explanation to her. "She threatened the happiness of the two things most important to me—the woman I love and my children." Autumn's eyes skipped quickly to Julia's. "The information she had on my relationship with this woman could have damaged my suit for custody. The beauty of that love meant nothing to Helen. She would turn it into something sordid and ugly."

Autumn cradled her drink in both hands. She wanted to tell Jacques to stop, that she didn't want to hear, didn't want to be involved. But it was too late. She was already involved.

"I was furious when she arrived here with her smug smile and evil eyes." He looked down into his glass. "There were times, many times, I wanted my hands around her throat, wanted to bruise her face as someone else had done."

"Yes, I wonder who." Julia caught her bottom lip between her teeth in thought. "Whoever did that was angry, perhaps angry enough to kill." Her eyes swept up, across Steve and Autumn and Lucas.

"You were at the inn that morning," Autumn stated. Her voice sounded odd, thready, and she swallowed.

"So I was." Julia smiled at her. "Or so I said. Being alone in bed is hardly an airtight alibi. No…" She leaned back on the wing of the chair. "I think the police will want to know who socked Helen. You came in with her, Autumn. Did you see anyone?"

"No." Her eyes flew instantly to Lucas. His were dark, already locked on her face. There were warning signals of anger and impatience she could read too easily. She dropped her gaze to her drink. "No, I…" How could she say it? How could she think it?

"Autumn's had enough for a while." Steve tightened his arm protectively around her. "Our problems don't concern her. She doesn't deserve to be in the middle."

"Poor child." Jacques studied her pale, strained face. "You've walked into a viper's nest, *oui?* Go sleep, forget us for a while."

"Come on, Autumn, I'll take you up." Steve slipped the glass from her hand and set it on the table. With one final glance at Lucas, Autumn went with him.

Chapter 8

They didn't speak as they mounted the steps. Autumn was too busy trying to force the numbness from her brain. She hadn't been able to fully absorb everything she'd been told. Steve hurried her by Helen's door before stopping at the one beside Lucas's.

"Is this the room your aunt meant?"

"Yes." She lifted both hands to her hair, pushing its weight away from her face. "Steve." She searched his face and found herself faltering. "Is all this true? Everything Lucas said? Was Helen really blackmailing all of you?" She noted the discomfort in his eyes and shook her head. "I don't mean to pry, but—"

"No," he cut her off, then let out a long breath. "No, it's hardly prying at this point. You're not involved, but you're caught, aren't you?"

The word was so apt, so close to her own thinking, that she nearly laughed. Caught. Yes, that was it exactly.

"It seems McLean is right on target. Helen had information concerning a deal I made for the company—perfectly within the circle of the law, but…" He gave a rueful smile and lifted his shoulders. "Maybe not quite as perfectly as it should have been. There was an ethical question, and it wouldn't look so good on paper. The technicalities are too complicated to explain, but the gist of it is I didn't want any shadows on my career. These days, when you're heading into politics, you have to cover all the angles."

"Angles," Autumn repeated and pressed her fingers to her temple. "Yes, I suppose you do."

"She threatened me, Autumn, and I didn't care for it—but it wasn't enough to provoke murder." He drew a quick breath and shook his head. "But that doesn't help much, does it? None of us are likely to admit it."

"I appreciate you telling me anyway," Autumn said. Steve's eyes were gentle on her face, but the lines and strain of tension still showed. "It can't be pleasant for you to have to explain."

"I'll have to explain to the police before long," he said grimly, then noted her expression. "I don't mind telling you, Autumn, if you feel better knowing. Julia's right." His fingers strayed absently to her hair. "It's much healthier to get it out in the open. But you've had enough for now." He smiled at her, then realized his hands were in her hair. "I suppose you're used to this. Your hair's not easy to resist. I've wanted to touch it since the first time I saw it. Do you mind?"

"No." She wasn't surprised to find herself in his

arms, his mouth on hers. It was an easy kiss, one that comforted rather than stirred. Autumn relaxed with it, and gave back what she could.

"You'll get some rest?" Steve murmured, holding her to his chest a moment.

"Yes. Yes, I will. Thank you." She pulled back to look up at him, but her eyes were drawn past him. Lucas stood at the doorway of his room, watching them both. Without speaking, he disappeared inside.

When she was alone, Autumn lay down on the white heirloom bedspread, but sleep wouldn't come. Her mind ached with fatigue. Her body was numb from it, but sleep, like a spiteful lover, stayed away. Time drifted as her thoughts ran over each member of the group.

She could feel nothing but sympathy for Jacques and the Spicers. She remembered the Frenchman's eyes when he spoke of his children and could still see Robert protecting his wife as she sobbed. Julia, on the other hand, needed no sympathy. Autumn felt certain the actress could take care of herself; she'd need no supporting arm or soothing words. Steve had also seemed more annoyed than upset by Helen's threats. He, too, could handle himself, she felt. There was a streak of street sense under the California gloss; he didn't need Autumn to worry for him.

Lucas was a different matter. Though he had nudged admissions from the rest of them, whatever threat Helen had held over him was still his secret. He had seemed very cool, very composed when he'd spoken of blackmail—but Autumn knew him. He was fully capable of concealing his emotions when there was a purpose to it. He was a hard man. Who knew better than she?

Cruel? Yes, she mused. Lucas could be cruel. She

still had the scars attesting to it. But murder? No. Autumn couldn't picture Lucas plunging something sharp into Helen Easterman. Scissors, she remembered, though she tried hard not to. The scissors that had lain on the floor beside Helen. No, she couldn't believe him capable of that. She wouldn't believe him capable of it.

Neither could she rationally believe it of any of the others. Could they all conceal such hate, such ugliness behind their shocked faces and shadowed eyes?

But, of course, one of them was the killer.

Autumn blanked it from her mind. She couldn't think of it anymore. Not just then. Steve's prescription was valid—she needed to rest. Yet she rose and walked to the window to stare out at the slow, hateful rain.

The knock at her door vibrated like an explosion. Whirling, she wrapped her arms protectively around her body. Her heart pounded while her throat dried up with fear. Stop it! she ordered herself. No one has any cause to hurt you.

"Yes, come in." The calmness of her own voice brought her relief. She was hanging on.

Robert entered. He looked so horribly weary and stricken, Autumn automatically reached out to him. She thought no more of fear. He clasped her hands and squeezed once, hard.

"You need food," he stated as he searched her face. "It shows in the face first."

"Yes, I know. My delicate hollows become craters very quickly." She made her own search. "You could use some yourself."

He sighed. "I believe you're one of those rare creatures who is inherently kind. I apologize for my wife."

"No, don't." His sigh had been long and broken. "She didn't mean it. We're all upset. This is a nightmare."

"She's been under a lot of strain. Before…" He broke off and shook his head. "She's sleeping now. Your head—" he brushed the hair from her forehead to examine the colorful bruise "—is it giving you any trouble?"

"No, none. I'm fine." The mishap seemed like some ridiculous comic relief in the midst of a melodrama now. "Can I help you, Robert?"

His eyes met hers, once, desperately, then moved away. "That woman put Jane through hell. If I'd just known, I would have put a stop to it long ago." Anger overpowered his weariness and he turned to prowl the room. "She tormented her, drained every drop of money Jane could raise. She played on a sickness, encouraging Jane to gamble to meet the payments. I knew nothing about it! I should have. Yesterday, Jane told me herself and I was going to enjoy dealing with the Easterman woman this morning." Autumn saw the soft, gentle hands clench into fists. "God help me, that's the only reason I'm sorry she's dead."

"Robert…" She wasn't certain what to say, how to deal with this side of his character. "Anyone would feel the same way," she said carefully. "She was an evil woman. She hurt someone you love." Autumn watched the fingers in his left hand relax, one at a time. "It isn't kind, but none of us will mourn her. Perhaps no one will. I think that's very sad."

He turned back and focused on her again. After a moment, he seemed to pull himself back under control. "I'm sorry you're caught up in this." With the anger gone from his eyes, they were vulnerable. "I'm going to go check on Jane. Will you be all right?"

"Yes."

She watched him go, then sank down into a chair. Each different crisis drained her. If possible, she was wearier now than before. When did the madness start? Only a few days ago she'd been safe in her apartment in Manhattan. She'd never met any of these people who were tugging at her now. Except one.

Even as she thought of him, Lucas strode in through the door. He stalked over to her, stared down and frowned.

"You need to eat," he said abruptly. Autumn thought of how tired she was of hearing that diagnosis. "I've been watching the pounds drop off you all day. You're already too thin."

"I adore flattery." His arrogant entrance and words boosted her flagging energy. She didn't have to take abuse from Lucas McLean anymore. "Don't you know how to knock?"

"I've always appreciated the understatedness of your body, Cat. You remember." He pulled her to her feet, then molded her against him. Her eyes flashed with quick temper. "Anderson seems to have discovered the charm as well. Did it occur to you that you might have been kissing a murderer?"

He spoke softly while his hand caressed her back. His eyes were mocking her. Her temper snapped at the strain of fighting her need for him.

"One might be holding me now."

He tightened his fingers on her hair so that she cried out in surprise. The mockery was replaced by a burning, terrifying rage. "You'd like to believe that, wouldn't you? You'd like to see me languishing in prison or, better yet, dangling from the end of a rope." She would have shaken her head, but his grip on her hair made movement impossible. "Would that be suitable punishment for my rejecting you, Cat? How deep is the hate? Deep enough to pull the lever yourself?"

"No, Lucas. Please, I didn't mean—"

"The hell you didn't." He cut off her protest. "The thought of me with blood on my hands comes easily to you. You can cast me in the role of murderer, can't you? Standing over Helen with the scissors in my hand."

"No!" In defense, she closed her eyes. "Stop it! Please stop it." He was hurting her now, but not with his hands. The words cut deeper.

He lowered his voice in a swift change of mood. Ice ran down Autumn's back. "I could have used my hands and been more tidy." A strong, lean-fingered hand closed around her throat. Her eyes flew open.

"Lucas—"

"Very simple and no mess," he went on, watching her eyes widen. "Quick enough, too, if you know what to do. More my style. More—as you put it—direct. Isn't that right?"

"You're only doing this to frighten me." Her breath was trembling in and out of her lungs. It was as if he were forcing her to think the worst of him, wanting her to think him capable of something monstrous. She'd never seen him like this. His eyes were black with fury while his voice was cold, so cold. She shivered. "I want you to leave, Lucas. Leave right now."

"Leave?" He slid his hand from her throat to the back of her neck. "I don't think so, Cat." His face inched closer. "If I'm going to hang for murder, I'd best take what consolation I can while I have the chance."

His mouth closed fast over hers. She struggled

against him, more frightened than she'd been when she'd turned on the light in Helen's room. She could only moan; movement was impossible when he held her this close. He slipped a hand under her sweater to claim her breast with the swift expertise of experience. Heart thudded madly against heart.

"How can anyone so skinny be so soft?" he murmured against her mouth. The words he'd spoken so often in the past brought more agony than she could bear. The hunger from him was thunderous; he was like a man who had finally broken free of his tether. "My God, how I want you." The words were torn from him as he ravaged her neck. "I'll be damned if I'll wait any longer."

They sank onto the bed. With all the strength that remained, she flailed out against him. Pinning her arms to her sides, Lucas stared down at her with a wild kind of fury. "Bite and scratch all you want, Cat. I've reached my limit."

"I'll scream, Lucas." The words shuddered out of her. "If you touch me again, I'll scream."

"No, you won't."

His mouth was on hers, proving him right and her wrong. His body molded to hers with bittersweet accuracy. She arched once in defense, in desperation, but his hands were roaming, finding all the secret places he'd discovered over three years before. There was no resisting him. The wild, reckless demand that had always flavored his lovemaking left her weak. He knew too much of her. Autumn knew, before his fingers reached the snap of her jeans, that she couldn't prevent her struggles from becoming demands. When his mouth left hers to roam her neck, she didn't scream, but moaned with the need he had always incited in her.

He was going to win again, and she would do nothing to stop him. Tears welled, then spilled from her eyes as she knew he'd soon discover her pitiful, abiding love. Even her pride, it seemed, again belonged to him.

Lucas stopped abruptly. All movement ceased when he drew back his head to stare down at her. She thought, through her blurred vision, that she saw some flash of pain cross his face before it became still and emotionless. Lifting a hand, he caught a teardrop on his fingertip. With a swift oath, he lifted his weight from her.

"No, I won't be responsible for this again." Turning, he stalked to the window and stared out.

Sitting up, Autumn lowered her face to her knees and fought against the tears. She'd promised herself he'd never see her cry again. Not over him. Never over him. The silence stretched on for what seemed an eternity.

"I won't touch you like this again," he said quietly. "You have my word, for what it's worth."

Autumn thought she heard him sigh, long and deep, before his footsteps crossed to her. She didn't look up, but only squeezed her eyes closed.

"Autumn, I...oh, sweet God." He touched her arm, but she only curled herself tighter into a ball in defense.

The room fell silent again. The dripping rain seemed to echo into it. When Lucas spoke again, his voice was harsh and strained. "When you've rested, get something to eat. I'll have your aunt send up a tray if you're not down for dinner. I'll see that no one disturbs you."

She heard him leave, heard the quiet click of her door. Alone, she kept curled in her ball as she lay down. Ultimately, the storm of tears induced sleep.

Chapter 9

It was dark when Autumn awoke, but she was not refreshed. The sleep had been only a temporary relief. Nothing had changed while she had slept. But no, she thought as she glanced around the room. She was wrong. Something had changed. It was quiet. Really quiet. Rising, she walked to the window. She could see the moon and a light scattering of stars. The rain had stopped.

In the dim light, she moved to the bathroom and washed her face. She wasn't certain she had the courage to look in the mirror. She let the cold cloth rest against her eyes for a long time, hoping the swelling wasn't as bad as it felt. She felt something else as well. Hunger. It was a healthy sign, she decided. A normal sign. The rain had stopped and the nightmare was going to end. And now she was going to eat.

Her bare feet didn't disturb the silence that hung over the inn. She was glad of it. She wanted food now, not company. But when she passed the lounge, she heard the murmur of voices. She wasn't alone after all. Julia and Jacques were silhouetted by the window. Their conversation was low and urgent. Before she could melt back into the shadows, Julia turned and spotted her. The conversation ceased abruptly.

"Oh, Autumn, you've surfaced. We thought we'd seen the last of you until morning." She glided to her, then slipped a friendly arm around her waist. "Lucas wanted to send up a tray, but Robert outranked him. Doctor's orders were to let you sleep until you woke up. You must be famished. Let's see what your Aunt Tabby left for you."

Julia was doing all the talking, and quite purposefully leading Autumn away. A glance showed her that Jacques was still standing by the window, unmoving. Autumn let it go, too hungry to object.

"Sit down, darling," Julia ordered as she steered Autumn into the kitchen. "I'm going to fix you a feast."

"Julia, you don't have to fix me anything. I appreciate it, but—"

"Now let me play mother," Julia interrupted, pressing down on Autumn's shoulder until she sat. "You're past the sticky-finger stage, so I really quite enjoy it."

Sitting back, Autumn managed a smile. "You're not going to tell me you can cook."

Julia aimed an arched glance. "I don't suppose you should eat anything too heavy at this time of night," she said mildly. "There's some marvelous soup left from dinner, and I'll fix you my specialty. A cheese omelette."

Autumn decided that watching Julia Bond bustle around a kitchen was worth the market price of an ounce of gold. She seemed competent enough and kept up a bouncy conversation that took no brainpower to follow. With a flourish, she plopped a glass of milk in front of Autumn.

"I'm not really very fond of milk," Autumn began and glanced toward the coffeepot.

"Now, drink up," Julia instructed. "You need roses in your cheeks. You look terrible."

"Thanks."

Steaming chicken soup joined the milk, and Autumn attacked it with singleminded intensity. Some of the weakness drained from her limbs.

"Good girl," Julia approved as she dished up the omelette. "You look nearly human again."

Glancing over, Autumn smiled. "Julia, you're marvelous."

"Yes, I know. I was born that way." She sipped coffee and watched Autumn start on the eggs. "I'm glad you were able to rest. This day has been a century."

For the first time, Autumn noticed the mauve shadows under the blue eyes and felt a tug of guilt. "I'm sorry. You should be in bed, not waiting on me."

"Lord, but you're sweet." Julia pulled out a cigarette. "I haven't any desire to go up to my room until exhaustion takes over. I'm quite selfishly prepared to keep you with me until it does. Actually, Autumn," she added, watching through a mist of smoke, "I wonder if it's very wise for you to be wandering about on your own."

"What?" Autumn looked up again and frowned. "What do you mean?"

"It was your room that was broken into," Julia pointed out.

"Yes, but…" She was surprised to realize she'd almost overlooked the ransacking of her room with everything else that had happened. "It must have been Helen," she ventured.

"Oh, I doubt that," Julia returned and continued to sip contemplatively. "I very much doubt that. If Helen had broken into your room, it would have been to look for something she could use on you. She'd have been tidy. We've given this some thought."

"We?"

"Well, I've given it some thought," Julia amended smoothly. "I think whoever tore up your things was looking for something, then covered the search with overdone destruction."

"Looking for what?" Autumn demanded. "I don't have anything anyone here could be interested in."

"Don't you?" Julia ran the tip of her tongue over her teeth. "I've been thinking about what happened in your darkroom."

"You mean when the power went off?" Autumn shook her head and touched the bruise on her forehead. "I walked into the door."

"Did you?" Julia sat back and studied the harsh ceiling light. "I wonder. Lucas told me that you said you heard someone rattling at the knob and walked over. What if…" She brought her eyes back to Autumn's. "What if someone swung the door open and hit you with it?"

"It was locked," Autumn insisted, then remembered that it had been open when Lucas found her.

"There are keys, darling." She watched Autumn's face closely. "What are you thinking?"

"The door was open when Lucas—" She cut herself off and shook her head. "No, Julia, it's ridiculous. Why would anyone want to do that to me?"

Julia lifted a brow. "Interesting question. What about your ruined film?"

"The film?" Autumn felt herself being pulled in deeper. "It must have been an accident."

"You didn't spoil it, Autumn, you're too competent." She waited while Autumn spread her hands on the table and looked down at them. "I've watched you. Your movements are very fluid, very assured. And you're a professional. You wouldn't botch up a roll of film without being aware of it."

"No," Autumn agreed and looked back up. Her eyes were steady again. "What are you trying to tell me?"

"What if someone's worried that you took a picture they don't want developed? The film in your room was ruined, too."

"I can follow your logic that far, Julia." Autumn pushed aside the remaining omelette. "But then it's a dead end. I haven't taken any pictures anyone could worry about. I was shooting scenery. Trees, animals, the lake."

"Maybe someone isn't certain about that." She crushed out her cigarette in a quick motion and leaned forward. "Whoever is worried enough about a picture to risk destroying your room and knocking you unconscious is dangerous. Dangerous enough to murder. Dangerous enough to hurt you again if necessary."

Staring back, Autumn controlled a tremor. "Jane? Jane accused me of spying, but she couldn't—"

"Oh yes, she could." Julia's voice was hard again, and definite. "Face it, Autumn, anyone pushed hard enough is capable of murder. Anyone."

Autumn's thoughts flicked back to Lucas and the look on his face when he had slipped his hand around her throat.

"Jane was desperate," Julia continued. "She claims to have made a full confession to Robert, but what proof is there? Or Robert, furious at what Helen had put his wife through, could have done it himself. He loves Jane quite a lot."

"Yes, I know." The sudden, sweeping anger in Robert's eyes flashed through her mind.

"Or there's Steve." Julia's finger began to tap on the table. "He tells me that Helen found out about some unwise deal he put through, something potentially damaging to his political career. He's very ambitious."

"But, Julia—"

"Then there's Lucas." Julia went on as if Autumn hadn't spoken. "There's a matter of a delicate divorce suit. Helen held information she claimed would interest a certain estranged husband." She lit another cigarette and let the smile float up and away. "Lucas is known for his temper. He's a very physical man."

Autumn met the look steadily. "Lucas is a lot of things, not all of them admirable, but he wouldn't kill."

Julia smiled and said nothing as she brought the cigarette to her lips. "Then there's me." The smile widened. "Of course, I claim I didn't care about Helen's threats, but I'm an actress. A good one. I've got an Oscar to prove it. Like Lucas, my temper is no secret. I could give you a list of directors who would tell you I'm capable of anything." Idly she tapped her cigarette in the ashtray. "But then, if I had killed her, I would have set the scene differently. I would have discovered the body myself, screamed, then fainted magnificently. As it was, you stole the show."

"That's not funny, Julia."

"No," she agreed and rubbed her temple. "It's not. But the fact remains that I could have killed Helen, and you're far too trusting."

"If you'd killed her," Autumn countered, "why would you warn me?"

"Bluff and double bluff," Julia answered with a new smile that made Autumn's skin crawl. "Don't trust anyone, not even me."

Autumn wasn't going to let Julia frighten her, though she seemed determined to do so. She kept her eyes level. "You haven't included Jacques."

To Autumn's surprise, Julia's eyes flickered, then dropped. The smooth, tapering fingers crushed out her cigarette with enough force to break the filter. "No, I haven't. I suppose he must be viewed through your eyes like the rest of us, but I know..." She looked up again, and Autumn saw the vulnerability. "I know he isn't capable of hurting anyone."

"You're in love with him."

Julia smiled, quite beautifully. "I love Jacques very much, but not the way you mean." She rose then and, getting another cup, poured them both coffee. "I've known Jacques for ten years. He's the only person in the world I care about more than myself. We're friends, real friends, probably because we've never been lovers."

Autumn drank the coffee black. She wanted the kick of it. *She'd protect him,* she thought. *She'd protect him any way she could.*

"I have a weakness for men," Julia continued, "and I indulge it. With Jacques, the time or place was never right. Ultimately, the friendship was too important to risk messing it up in the bedroom. He's a good, gentle man. The biggest mistake he ever made was in marrying Claudette."

Julia's voice hardened. Her nails began to tap on the table again, quicker than before. "She did her best to eat him alive. For a long time, he tried to keep the marriage together for the children. It simply wasn't possible. I won't go into details; they'd shock you." Tilting her head, Julia gave Autumn a smile that put her squarely into adolescence. "And, in any case, it's Jacques's miserable secret. He didn't divorce her, on the numerous grounds he could have, but allowed her to file."

"And Claudette got the children."

"That's right. It nearly killed him when she was awarded custody. He adores them. And, I must admit, they are rather sweet little monsters." The nails stopped tapping as she reached for her coffee. "Anyway, skipping over this and that, Jacques filed a custody suit about a year ago. He met someone shortly after. I can't tell you her name—you'd recognize it, and I have Jacques's confidence. But I can tell you she's perfect for him. Then Helen crawled her slimy way in."

Autumn shook her head. "Why don't they just get married?"

Julia leaned back with an amused sigh. "If life were only so simple. Jacques is free, but his lady won't be for another few months. They want nothing more than to marry, bring Jacques's little monsters to America and raise as many more as possible. They're crazy about each other."

Julia sipped her cooling coffee. "They can't live together openly until the custody thing is resolved so they rented this little place in the country. Helen found out. You can figure out the rest. Jacques paid her, for his children and because his lady's divorce isn't as cut-and-dried as it might be, but when Helen turned up here, he'd reached his limit. They argued about it one night in the lounge. He told her she wouldn't get another cent. I'm sure, no matter how much Jacques had already paid her, Helen would still have turned her information over to Claudette—for a price."

Autumn stared at her, unable to speak. She had never seen Julia look so cold. She saw the ruthlessness cover the exquisite face. Julia looked over, then laughed with genuine amusement.

"Oh, Autumn, you're like an open book!" The hard mask had melted away, leaving her warm and lovely again. "Now you're thinking I could have murdered Helen after all. Not for myself, but for Jacques."

Autumn fell into a fitful sleep sometime after dawn. This was no deep, empty sleep brought on by medication or exhaustion, but was confused and dream riddled.

At first, there were only vague shadows and murmured voices floating through her mind, taunting her to try to see and hear more clearly. She fought to focus on them. Shadows moved, shapes began to sharpen, then became fuzzy and disordered again. She pitted all her determination against them, wanting more than hints and whispers. Abruptly, the shadows evaporated. The voices grew to a roar in her ears.

Wild-eyed, Jane crushed Autumn's camera underfoot. She screamed, pointing a pair of scissors to keep

Autumn at bay. "Spy!" she shouted as the cracking of the camera's glass echoed like gunfire. "Spy!"

Wanting to escape the madness and accusations, Autumn turned. Colors whirled around her, then there was Robert.

"She tormented my wife." His arm held Autumn firmly, then slowly tightened, cutting off her breath. "You need some food," he said softly. "It shows in the face first." He was smiling, but the smile was a travesty. Breaking away, Autumn found herself in the corridor.

Jacques came toward her. There was blood on his hands. His eyes were sad and terrifying as he held them out to her. "My children." There was a tremor in his voice as he gestured to her. Turning, she fell into Steve.

"Politics," he said with a bright, boyish smile. "Nothing personal, just politics." Taking her hair, he wrapped it around her throat. "You got caught in the middle, Autumn." The smile turned into a leer as he tightened the noose. "Too bad."

Pushing away, she fell through a door. Julia's back was to her. She wore the lovely, white lace negligee. "Julia!" In the dream, the urgency in Autumn's voice came at a snail's pace. "Julia, help me."

When Julia turned, the slow, cat smile was on her face and the lace was splattered with scarlet. "Bluff and double bluff, darling." Throwing back her head, she laughed her smoky laugh. With the sound still spinning in her head, Autumn pressed her hands to her ears and ran.

"Come back to mother!" Julia called, still laughing as Autumn stumbled into the corridor.

There was a door blocking her path. Throwing it open, Autumn dashed inside. She knew only a desperate need for escape. But it was Helen's room. Terrified, Autumn turned, only to find the door closed behind her. She battered on it, but the sound was dull and flat. Fear was raw now, a primitive fear of the dead. She couldn't stay there. Wouldn't stay. She turned, thinking to escape through the window.

It wasn't Helen's room, but her own. There were bars at the windows, gray liquid bars of rain, but when she ran to them, they solidified, holding her in. She pulled and tugged, but they were cold and unyielding in her hands. Suddenly, Lucas was behind her, drawing her away. He laughed as he turned her into his arms.

"Bite and scratch all you want, Cat."

"Lucas, please!" There was hysteria in her voice that even the dream couldn't muffle. "I love you. I love you. Help me get out. Help me get away!"

"Too late, Cat." His eyes were dark and fierce and amused. "I warned you not to push me too far."

"No, Lucas, not you." She clung to him. He was kissing her hard, passionately. "I love you. I've always loved you." She surrendered to his arms, to his mouth. Here was her escape, her safety.

Then she saw the scissors in his hand.

Chapter 10

Autumn sat straight up in bed. The film of cold sweat had her shivering. During the nightmare, she had kicked off the sheets and blankets and lay now with only a damp nightgown for cover. Needing the warmth, she pulled the tangled blanket around her and huddled into it.

Only a dream, she told herself, waiting for the clarity of it to fade. It was only a dream. It was natural enough after the late-night conversation with Julia. Dreams couldn't hurt you. Autumn wanted to hang on to that.

It was morning. She trembled still as she watched the sunlight pour into her window. No bars. That was over now, just as the night was over. The phones would soon be repaired. The water in the ford would go down. The police would come. Autumn sat, cocooned by the blanket, and waited for her breathing to even.

By the end of the day, or tomorrow at the latest, everything would be organized and official. Questions would be answered, notes would be taken, the wheels of investigation would start to turn, settling everything into facts and reality. Slowly her muscles began to relax and she loosened her desperate grip on the blanket.

Julia's imagination had gotten out of hand, Autumn decided. She was so used to the drama of her profession that she had built up the scenario. Helen's death was a hard, cold fact. None of them could avoid that. But Autumn was certain her two misfortunes had been unconnected. If I'm going to stay sane until the police come, she amended, I *have* to believe it.

Calmer now, she allowed herself to think. Yes, there had been a murder. There was no glossing over that. Murder was a violent act, and in this case, it had been a personal one. She had no involvement in it. There wasn't any correlation. What had happened in the darkroom had been simple clumsiness. That was the cleanest and the most reasonable explanation. As for the invasion of her room… Autumn shrugged. It had been Helen. She'd been a vicious, evil woman. The destruction of Autumn's clothes and personal belongings had been a vicious, evil act. For some reason of her own, Helen had taken a dislike to her. There was no one else at the inn who would have any reason to feel hostility toward her.

Except Lucas. Autumn shook her head firmly, but the thought remained. Except Lucas. She huddled the blanket closer, cold again.

No, even that made no sense. Lucas had rejected her, not the other way around. She had loved him. And he, very simply, hadn't loved her. *Would that matter to him?* The voice in her brain argued with the voice from her heart. Ignoring the queaziness in her stomach, Autumn forced herself to consider, dispassionately, Lucas in the role of murderer.

It had been obvious from the beginning that he was under strain. He hadn't been sleeping well and he'd been tense. Autumn had known him to struggle over a stage of a book for a week on little sleep and coffee, but he'd never shown the effects. All that stored energy he had was just waiting to take over whenever he needed it. No, in all her memory, she had never seen Lucas McLean tired. Until now.

Helen's blackmail must have disturbed him deeply. Autumn couldn't imagine Lucas concerning himself over publicity, adverse or otherwise. The woman involved in divorce must mean a great deal to him. She shut her eyes on a flash of pain and forced herself to continue.

Why had he come to the Pine View Inn? Why would he choose a remote place nearly a continent away from his home? To work? Autumn shook her head. It just didn't follow. She knew Lucas never traveled when he was writing. He'd do his research first, extensively if necessary, before he began. Once he had a plot between his teeth, he'd dig into his beachside home for the duration. Come to Virginia to write in peace? No. Lucas McLean could write on the 5:15 subway if he chose to. She knew no one else with a greater ability to block people out.

So, his reason for coming to the inn was quite different. Autumn began to wonder if Helen had been a pawn as well as a manipulator. Had Lucas lured her to this remote spot and surrounded her with people with reasons to hate her? He was clever enough to have done it, and calculating enough. How difficult was it going to be to prove which one of the six had killed her? Motive and opportunity he'd said—six people had both. Why should one be examined any closer than the others?

The setting would appeal to him, she thought as she looked out at mountains and pines. Obvious, Lucas had called it. An obvious setting for murder. But then, as Jacques had pointed out, life was often obvious.

She wouldn't dwell on it. It brought the nightmare too close again. Pushing herself from the bed, Autumn began to dress in her very tired jeans and a sweater Julia had given her the night before. She wasn't going to spend another day picking at her doubts and fears. It would be better to hang on to the knowledge that the police would be there soon. It wasn't up to her to decide who had killed Helen.

When she started down the stairs, she felt better. She'd take a long, solitary walk after breakfast and clear the cobwebs from her mind. The thought of getting out of the inn lifted her spirits.

But her confidence dropped away when she saw Lucas at the foot of the stairs. He was watching her closely, silently. Their eyes met for one brief, devastating moment before he turned to walk away.

"Lucas." She heard herself call out before she could stop herself. Stopping, he turned to face her again. Autumn gathered all her courage and hurried down the rest of the stairs. She had questions, and she had to ask them. He still mattered much too much to her. She stood on the bottom step so that their eyes would be level. His told her nothing. They seemed to look through her, bored and impatient.

"Why did you come here?" Autumn asked him

quickly. "Here, to the Pine View Inn?" She wanted him to give her any reason. She wanted to accept it.

Lucas focused on her intensely for a moment. There was something in his face for her to read, but it was gone before she could decipher it. "Let's just say I came to write, Autumn. Any other reason has been eliminated."

There was no expression in his voice, but the words chilled her. *Eliminated.* Would he choose such a clean word for murder? Something of her horror showed in her face. She watched his brows draw together in a frown.

"Cat—"

"No." Before he could speak again, she darted away from him. He'd given her an answer, but it wasn't one she wanted to accept.

The others were already at the table. The sun had superficially lightened the mood, and by unspoken agreement, the conversation was general, with no mention of Helen. They all needed an island of normalcy before the police came.

Julia, looking fresh and lovely, chattered away. Her attitude was so easy, even cheerful, that Autumn wondered if their conversation in the kitchen was as insubstantial as her nightmare. She was flirting again, with every man at the table. Two days of horror hadn't dulled her style.

"Your aunt," Jacques told Autumn, "has an amazing cuisine." He speared a fluffy, light pancake. "It surprises me at times because she has such a charming, drifting way about her. Yet, she remembers small details. This morning, she tells me she has saved me a piece of her apple pie to enjoy with my lunch. She doesn't forget I have a fondness for it. Then when I kiss her hand because I find her so enchanting, she smiled and wandered away, and I heard her say something about towels and chocolate pudding."

The laughter that followed was so normal, Autumn wanted to hug it to her. "She has a better memory about the guests' appetites than her family's," Autumn countered, smiling at him. "She's decided that pot roast is my favorite and has promised to provide it weekly, but it's actually my brother Paul's favorite. I haven't figured out how to move her toward spaghetti."

She gripped her fork tightly at a sudden flash of pain. Very clearly, Autumn could see herself stirring spaghetti sauce in Lucas's kitchen while he did his best to distract her. Would she never pry herself loose from the memories? Quickly, she plunged into conversation again.

"Aunt Tabby sort of floats around the rest of the world," she continued. "I remember once, when we were kids, Paul smuggled some formaldehyde frog legs out of his biology class. He brought them with him when we came on vacation and gave them to Aunt Tabby, hoping for a few screams. She took them, smiled and told him she'd eat them later."

"Oh, God." Julia lifted her hand to her throat. "She didn't actually eat them, did she?"

"No." Autumn grinned. "I distracted her, which of course is the easiest thing in the world to do, and Paul disposed of his biology project. She never missed them."

"I must remember to thank my parents for making me an only child," Julia murmured.

"I can't imagine growing up without Paul and Will." Autumn shook her head as old memories ran through her mind. "The three of us were always very close, even when we tormented each other."

Jacques chuckled, obviously thinking of his own children. "Does your family spend much time here?"

"Not as much as we used to." Autumn lifted her shoulders. "When I was a girl, we'd all come for a month during the summer."

"To tramp through the woods?" Julia asked with a wicked gleam in her eyes.

"That," Autumn returned mildly, and imitated the actress's arched-brow look, "and some camping." She went on, amused by Julia's rolling eyes. "Boating and swimming in the lake."

"Boating," Robert spoke up, cutting off a small, nagging memory. Autumn looked over at him, unable to hang on to it. "That's my one true vice. Nothing I like better than sailing. Right, Jane?" He patted her hand. "Jane's quite a sailor herself. Best first mate I've ever had." He glanced over at Steve. "I suppose you've done your share of sailing."

Steve answered with a rueful shake of his head. "I'm afraid I'm a miserable sailor. I can't even swim."

"You're joking!" This came from Julia. She stared at him in disbelief. Her eyes skimmed approvingly over his shoulders. "You look like you could handle the English Channel."

"I can't even handle a wading pool," he confessed, more amused than embarrassed. He grinned and gestured with his fork. "I make up for it in land sports. If we had a tennis court here, I'd redeem myself."

"Ah well." Jacques gave his French shrug. "You'll have to content yourself with hiking. The mountains

here are beautiful. I hope to bring my children one day."
He frowned, then stared into his coffee.

"Nature lovers!" Julia's smiling taunt kept the room
from sliding into gloom. "Give me smog-filled L.A.
anytime. I'll look at your mountains and squirrels in
Autumn's photographs."

"You'll have to wait until I add to my supply." She
kept her voice light, trying not to be depressed over the
loss of her film. She couldn't yet bring herself to think
of the loss of her camera. "Losing that film is like losing a limb, but I'm trying to be brave about it." Taking
a bite of pancake, she shrugged. "And I could have lost
all four rolls instead of three. The shots I took of the
lake were the best, so I can comfort myself with that.
The light was perfect that morning, and the shadows…"

She trailed off as the memory seeped through. She
could see herself, standing on the ridge looking down
at the glistening water, the mirrored trees. And the two
figures that walked the far side. That was the morning
she had met Lucas in the woods, then Helen. Helen with
an angry bruise under her eye.

"Autumn?"

Hearing Jacques's voice, she snapped herself back.
"I'm sorry, what?"

"Is something wrong?"

"No, I…" She met his curious eyes. "No."

"I would think light and shadow are the very essence
of photography," Julia commented, flowing over the
awkward silence. "But I've always concerned myself
with looking into the lens rather than through. Remember that horrible little man, Jacques, who used to pop
up at the most extraordinary times and stick a camera

in my face. What was his name? I really became quite fond of him."

Julia had centered the attention on herself so smoothly that Autumn doubted anyone had noticed her own confusion. She stared down at the pancakes and syrup on her plate as if the solution to the mysteries of the universe were written there. But she could feel Lucas's eyes boring into her averted head. She could feel them, but she couldn't look at him.

She wanted to be alone, to think, to reason out what was whirling in her head. She forced down the rest of her breakfast and let the conversation buzz around her.

"I have to see Aunt Tabby," Autumn murmured, at last thinking she could leave without causing curiosity. "Excuse me." She had reached the kitchen door before Julia waylaid her.

"Autumn, I want to talk to you." The grip of the slender fingers was quite firm. "Come up to my room."

From the expression on the enviable face, Autumn could see arguing was useless. "All right, right after I see Aunt Tabby. She'll be worried because I didn't say good-night to her yesterday. I'll be up in a few minutes." She kept her voice reasonable and friendly, and managed a smile. Autumn decided she was becoming quite an actress herself.

For a small stretch of silence, Julia studied Autumn's face, then loosened her grip. "All right, come up as soon as you've finished."

"Yes, I will." Autumn slipped into the kitchen with the promise still on her lips. It wasn't difficult to go through the kitchen to the mud room without being noticed. Aunt Tabby and Nancy were deep in their morning argument. Taking down her jacket from the hook where she had placed it the morning of the storm, Autumn checked the pocket. Her fingers closed over the roll of film. For a moment, she simply held it in the palm of her hand.

Moving quickly, she changed from shoes to boots, transferred the film to the pocket of Julia's sweater, grabbed her jacket and went out the back door.

Chapter 11

The air was sharp. The rain had washed it clean. Budded leaves Autumn had photographed only days before were fuller, thicker, but still tenderly green. Her mind was no longer on the freedom she had longed for all the previous day. Now, Autumn was only intent on reaching the cover of the forest without being seen. She ran for the trees, not stopping until she was surrounded. Silence was deep and it cradled her.

The ground sucked and skidded under her feet, spongy with rain. There was some wind damage here and there that she noticed when she forced herself to move more carefully. Broken limbs littered the ground. The sun was warm, and she shed her jacket, tossing it over a branch. She made herself concentrate on the sights and sounds of the forest until her thoughts could calm.

The mountain laurel hinted at blooms. A bird circled overhead, then darted deeper into the trees with a sharp cry. A squirrel scurried up a tree trunk and peered down at her. Autumn reached in her pocket and closed her hand over the roll of film. The conversation in the kitchen with Julia now made horrible sense.

Helen must have been at the lake that morning. From the evidence of the bruise, she had argued violently with someone. And that someone had seen Autumn on the ridge. That someone wanted the pictures destroyed badly enough to risk breaking into both her darkroom and her bedroom. The film had to be potentially damaging for anyone to risk knocking her unconscious and ransacking her room. Who else but the killer would care enough to take such dangerous actions? Who else? At every turn, logic pointed its finger toward Lucas.

It had been his plans that brought the group together in the first place. Lucas was the person Autumn had met just before coming across Helen. Lucas had bent over her as she lay on the darkroom floor. Lucas had been up, fully dressed, the night of Helen's murder. Autumn shook her head, wanting to shatter the logic. But the film was solid in her hand.

He must have seen her as she stood on the ridge. She would have been in clear view. When he intercepted her, he had tried to rekindle their relationship. He would have known better than to have attempted to remove the film from her camera. She would have caused a commotion that would have been heard in two counties. Yes, he knew her well enough to use subtler means. But he wouldn't have known she had already switched to a fresh roll.

He had played on her old weakness for him. If she had submitted, he would have found ample time and opportunity to destroy the film. Autumn admitted, painfully, that she would have been too involved with him to have noticed the loss. But she hadn't submitted. This time, she had rejected him. He would have been forced to employ more extreme measures.

He only pretended to want me, she realized. That, more than anything else, hurt. He had held her, kissed her, while his mind had been busy calculating how best to protect himself. Autumn forced herself to face facts. Lucas had stopped wanting her a long time ago, and his needs had never been the same as hers. Two facts were very clear. She had never stopped loving him, and he had never begun to love her.

Still, she balked at the idea of Lucas as a cold-blooded killer. She could remember his sudden spurts of gentleness, his humor, the careless bouts of generosity. That was part of him, too—part of the reason she had been able to love him so easily. Part of the reason she had never stopped.

A hand gripped her shoulder. With a quick cry of alarm, she whirled and found herself face-to-face with Lucas. When she shrank from him, he dropped his hands and stuffed them into his pockets. His eyes were dark and his voice was icy.

"Where's the film, Autumn?"

Whatever color was left in her face drained. She hadn't wanted to believe it. Part of her had refused to believe it. Now, her heart shattered. He was leaving her no choice.

"Film?" She shook her head as she took another step back. "What film?"

"You know very well what film." Impatience pulled

at the words. He narrowed his eyes, watching her re-treat. "I want the fourth roll. Don't back away from me!"

Autumn stopped at the curt command. "Why?"

"Don't play stupid." His impatience was quickly be-coming fury. She recognized all the signs. "I want the film. What I do with it is my business."

She ran, thinking only to escape from his words. It had been easier to live with the doubt than the certainty. He caught her arm before she had dashed three yards. Spinning her around, he studied her face.

"You're terrified." He looked stunned, then angry. "You're terrified of me." With his hands gripping hard on her arms he brought her closer. "We've run the gamut, haven't we, Cat? Yesterday's gone." There was a finality in his voice that brought more pain than his hands or his temper.

"Lucas." Autumn was trembling, emotionally spent. "Please don't hurt me anymore." The pain she spoke of had nothing to do with the physical, but he released her with a violent jerk. The struggle for control was vis-ible on his face.

"I won't lay a hand on you now, or ever again. Just tell me where that film is. I'll get out of your life as quickly as possible."

She had to reach him. She had to try one last time. "Lucas, please, it's senseless. You must see that. Can't you—"

"Don't push me!" The words exploded at her, rock-ing her back on her heels. "You stupid fool, do you have any idea how dangerous that film is? Do you think for one minute I'm going to let you keep it?" He took a step toward her. "Tell me where it is. Tell me now, or by God, I'll throttle it out of you."

"In the darkroom." The lie came quickly and without calculation. Perhaps that was why he accepted it so readily.

"All right. Where?" She watched his features relax slightly. His voice was calmer.

"On the bottom shelf. On the wet side."

"That's hardly illuminating to a layman, Cat." There was a touch of his old mockery as he reached for her arm. "Let's go get it."

"No!" She jerked away wildly. "I won't go with you. There's only one roll; you'll find it. You found the others. Leave me alone, Lucas. For God's sake, leave me alone!"

She ran again, skidding on the mud. This time he didn't stop her.

Autumn had no idea how far she ran or even the direction she took. Ultimately, her feet slowed to a walk. She stopped to stare up at a sky that had no clouds. What was she going to do?

She could go back. She could go back and try to get to the darkroom first, lock herself in. She could develop the film, blow up the two figures beside the lake and see the truth for herself. Her hand reached for the hated film again. She didn't want to see the truth. With absolute certainty, she knew she could never hand the film over to the police. No matter what Lucas had done or would do, she couldn't betray him. He'd been wrong, she thought. She could never pull the lever.

Withdrawing the film from her pocket, she stared down at it. It looked so innocent. She had felt so innocent that day, up on the ridge with the sun coming up. But when she had done what she had to do, she would never feel innocent again. She would expose the film herself.

Lucas, she thought and nearly laughed. Lucas McLean was the only man on earth who could make her turn her back on her own conscience. And when it was done, only the two of them would know. She would be as guilty as he.

Do it quickly, she told herself. Do it fast and think about it later. Her palm was damp where the film was cradled in it. You're going to have a whole lifetime to think about it. Taking a deep breath, Autumn started to uncap the plastic capsule she used to protect her undeveloped film. A movement on the path behind her had her stuffing the roll back into her pocket and whirling around.

Could Lucas have searched the darkroom so quickly? What would he do now that he knew she had lied to him? Foolishly, Autumn wanted to run again. Instead, she straightened and waited. The final encounter would have to come sooner or later.

Autumn's relief when she saw Steve approaching quickly became irritation. She wanted to be alone, not to make small talk and useless conversation while the film burned in her pocket.

"Hi!" Steve's lightning smile did nothing to decrease her annoyance, but Autumn pasted on one of her own. If she were going to be playing a game for the rest of her life, she might as well start now.

"Hello. Taking Jacques up on the hiking?" God, how normal and shallow her voice sounded! Was she going to be able to live like this?

"Yeah. I see you needed to get away from the inn,

too." Taking a deep breath of the freshened air, he flexed his shoulders. "Lord, it feels good to be outside again."

"I know what you mean." Autumn eased the tension from her own shoulders. This was a reprieve, she told herself. Accept it. When it's over, nothing's ever going to be the same again.

"And Jacques is right," Steve went on, staring out through the thin leaves. "The mountains are beautiful. It reminds you that life goes on."

"I suppose we all need to remember that now." Unconsciously, Autumn dipped her hand in her pocket.

"Your hair glows in the sunlight." Steve caught at the ends and moved them between his fingertips. Autumn saw, with some alarm, that warmth had crept into his eyes. A romantic interlude was more than she could handle.

"People often seem to think more about my hair than me." She smiled and kept her voice light. "Sometimes I'm tempted to hack it off."

"Oh no." He took a more generous handful. "It's very special, very unique." His eyes lifted to hers. "And I've been thinking quite a lot about you the last few days. You're very special, too."

"Steve…" Autumn turned and would have walked on, but his hand was still in her hair.

"I want you, Autumn."

The words, so gentle, almost humble, nearly broke her heart. She turned back with apology in her eyes. "I'm sorry, Steve. I really am."

"Don't be sorry." He lowered his head to brush her lips. "If you let me, I could make you happy."

"Steve, please." Autumn lifted her hands to his chest. If only he were Lucas, she thought as she stared up at him. If only it were Lucas looking at me like this. "I can't."

He let out a long breath, but didn't release her. "McLean? Autumn, he only makes you unhappy. Why won't you let go?"

"I can't tell you how many times I've asked myself the same question." She sighed, and he watched the sun shoot into her eyes. "I don't have the answer—except that I love him."

"Yes, it shows." Frowning, he brushed a strand of hair from her cheek. "I'd hoped you'd be able to get over him, but I don't suppose you will."

"No, I don't suppose I will. I've given up trying."

"Now I'm sorry, Autumn. It makes things difficult."

Autumn dropped her eyes to stare at the ground. She didn't want pity. "Steve, I appreciate it, but I really need to be alone."

"I want the film, Autumn."

Astonished, she jerked her head up. Without consciously making the step, she aligned herself with Lucas. "Film? I don't know what you mean."

"Oh yes, I'm afraid you do." He was still speaking gently, one hand stroking her hair. "The pictures you took of the lake the morning Helen and I were down there. I have to have them."

"You?" For a moment, the implication eluded her. "You and Helen?" Confusion turned into shock. She could only stare at him.

"We were having quite a row that morning. You see, she had decided she wanted a lump-sum payment from me. Her other sources were drying up fast. Julia wouldn't give her a penny, just laughed at her. Helen was furious about that." His face changed with a grim smile. "Jacques had finished with her, too. She never had anything worthwhile on Lucas in the first place. She counted on intimidating him. Instead, he told her to go to hell and threatened to press charges. That threw her off balance for a while. She must have realized Jane was on the edge. So…she concentrated on me."

He had been staring off into the distance as he spoke. Now, his attention came back to Autumn. The first hint of anger swept into his eyes. "She wanted two hundred and fifty thousand dollars in two weeks. A quarter of a million, or she'd hand over the information she had on me to my father."

"But you said what she knew wasn't important." Autumn let her eyes dart past his for a moment. The path behind them was empty. She was alone.

"She knew a bit more than I told you." Steve gave her an apologetic smile. "I could hardly tell you everything then. I've covered my tracks well enough now so that I don't think the police will ever know. It was actually a matter of extortion."

"Extortion?" The hand on her hair was becoming more terrifying with each passing moment. Keep him talking, she told herself frantically. Keep him talking and someone will come.

"Borrowing, really. The money will be mine sooner or later." He shrugged it off. "I just took some a little early. Unfortunately, my father wouldn't see it that way. I told you, remember? He's a tough man. He wouldn't think twice about booting me out the door and cutting off my income. I can't have that, Autumn." He flashed her a smile. "I have very expensive tastes."

"So you killed her." Autumn said it flatly. She was finished with horror.

"I didn't have a choice. I couldn't possibly get my hands on that much cash in two weeks." He said it so calmly, Autumn could almost see the rationale behind it. "I nearly killed her that morning down by the lake. She just wouldn't listen to me. I lost my temper and hit her. Knocked her cold. When I saw her lying there on the ground, I realized how much I wanted her dead."

Autumn didn't interrupt. She could see he was far from finished. Let him talk it out, she ordered herself, controlling the urge to break from him and run. Someone's going to come.

"I bent over her," he continued. "My hands were almost around her throat when I saw you standing up on the ridge. I knew it was you because the sun was shining on your hair. I didn't think you could recognize me from that distance, but I had to be sure. Of course, I found out later that you weren't paying attention to us at all."

"No, I barely noticed." Her knees were starting to shake. He was telling her too much. Far too much.

"I left Helen and circled around, thinking to intercept you. Lucas got to you first. Quite a touching little scene."

"You watched us?" She felt a stir of anger edge through the fear.

"You were too involved in each other to notice." He smiled again. "In any case, that's when I learned you'd been taking pictures. I had to get rid of that film; it was too chancy. I hated to hurt you, Autumn. I found you very attractive right from the first."

A rabbit darted down the path, veering off and bounding into the woods. She heard the call of a quail, faint with distance. The simple, natural texture of her surroundings gave his words a sense of unreality. "The darkroom."

"Yes. I was glad the blow with the door knocked you out. I didn't want to have to hit you with the flashlight. I didn't see your camera, but found a roll of film. I was so certain I had things taken care of. You can imagine how I felt when you said you'd lost two rolls, and that they were shots of your trip down from New York. I didn't know how the other roll had been ruined."

"Lucas. Lucas turned on the lights when he found me." Suddenly, through the horror came a bright flash of realization. *It hadn't been Lucas.* He'd done nothing but simply be who he was. She felt overwhelming relief at his innocence, then guilt at ever having believed what she had of him. "Lucas," she said again, almost giddy with the onslaught of sensations.

"Well, it hardly matters now," Steve said practically. Autumn snapped back. She had to keep alert, had to keep a step ahead of him. "I knew if I just took the film from your camera, you'd begin to wonder. You might start thinking too closely about the pictures you'd taken. I hated doing that to your things, breaking your camera. I know it was important to you."

"I have another at home." It was a weak attempt to sound unconcerned. Steve only smiled.

"I went to Helen's room right after I'd finished with yours. I knew I was going to have to kill her. She stood there pointing to the bruise and telling me it was going to cost me another hundred thousand. I didn't know what I was going to do...I thought I was going to strangle her. Then I saw the scissors. That was better—anyone could have used scissors. Even little Jane. I stopped thinking when I picked them up until it was over."

He shuddered, and Autumn thought, *Run! Run now!* But his hand tightened on her hair. "I've never been through anything like that. It was terrible. I almost folded. I knew I had to think, had to be careful, or I'd lose everything. Staying in that room was the hardest thing I've ever done. I wiped the handles of the scissors clean and tore up my shirt. Her blood was on it. I flushed the pieces down the toilet. When I got back to my room, I showered and went to bed. I remember being surprised that the whole thing took less than twenty minutes. It seemed like years."

"It must have been dreadful for you," Autumn murmured, but he was oblivious to the edge in her voice.

"Yes, but it was all working out. No one could prove where they were when Helen was killed. The storm—the phones, the power—that was all a bonus. Every one of us had a reason to want Helen out of the way. I really think Julia and I will be the least likely suspects when the time comes. The police should look to Jacques because he had more cause, and Lucas because he has the temper."

"Lucas couldn't kill anyone," Autumn said evenly. "The police will know that."

"I wouldn't bank on it." He gave her a crooked smile. "You haven't been so sure of that yourself."

She could say nothing when struck with the truth. *Why wasn't someone coming?*

"This morning, you started talking about four rolls of film, and the pictures you took of the lake. I could tell the moment when you remembered."

So much for my talent at acting, she thought grimly. "I only remembered there'd been people down by the lake that morning."

"You were putting it all together quickly." He traced a finger down her cheek and Autumn forced herself not to jerk away. "I had hoped to distract you, gain your affection. It was obvious you were hurting over McLean. If I could have moved in, I might have gotten my hands on that film without having to hurt you."

Autumn kept her eyes and voice steady. He'd finished talking now; she could sense it. "What are you going to do?"

"Damn it, Autumn. I'm going to have to kill you."

He said it in much the same way her father had said, *"Damn it, Autumn, I'm going to have to spank you."* She nearly broke into hysterical giggles.

"They'll know this time, Steve." Her body was beginning to shake, but she spoke calmly. If she could reason with him...

"No, I don't think so." He spoke practically, as if he considered she might have a viable point. "I was careful to get out without being seen. Everyone's spread out again. I doubt anyone even knows you went outside. I wouldn't have known myself if I hadn't found your jacket and boots missing. Then again, if I hadn't found the jacket hanging on a branch and been able to follow your tracks from there, I wouldn't have found you so easily."

He shrugged, as if showing her why his reasoning was better than hers. "When you're found missing, I'll make certain I come this way when we look for you. I can do a lot of damage to the tracks and no one will know any better. Now, Autumn, I need the film. Tell me where you've put it."

"I'm not going to tell you." She tossed back her head.

As long as she had the film, he had to keep her alive. "They'll find it. When they do, they'll know it was you."

He made a quick sound of impatience. "You'll tell me Autumn, eventually. It would be easier for you if you told me now. I don't want to hurt you any more than I have to. I can make it quick, or I can make it painful."

His hand shot out so swiftly, Autumn had no time to dodge the blow. The force of it knocked her back into a tree. The pain welled inside her head and rolled through, leaving dizziness. She clutched at the rough bark to keep her balance as she saw him coming toward her.

Oh no, she wasn't going to stand and be hit again. He'd gotten away with it twice, and twice was enough. With as much force as she could muster, she kicked, aiming well below the waist. He went down on his knees like a shot. Autumn turned and fled.

Chapter 12

She ran blindly. *Escape!* It was the only coherent thought in her brain. It wasn't until the first wave of panic had ebbed that Autumn realized she had run not only away from Steve, but away from the inn. It was too late to double back. She could only concentrate as much effort as possible into putting distance between them. She veered off the path and into thicker undergrowth.

When she heard him coming after her, Autumn didn't look back, but increased her pace. His breathing was labored, but close. Too close. She swerved again and plunged on. The ground sucked and pulled at her boots, but she told herself she wouldn't slip. If she slipped, he would be on top of her in a moment. His hands would be at her throat. *She would not slip.*

Her heart was pounding and her lungs were screaming in agony for more air. A branch whipped back, stinging her cheek. But she told herself she wouldn't stop. She would run and run and run until she no longer heard him coming after her.

A tree had fallen and lay drunkenly in her path. Without breaking stride, Autumn vaulted it, sliding for a moment when her boots hit the mud, then pounding on. He slipped. She heard the slick sound of his boots as they lost traction, then his muffled curse. She kept up her wild pace, nearly giddy at the few seconds his fall had given her.

Time and direction ceased to exist. For her, the pursuit had no beginning, no end. It was only the race. Her thoughts were no longer rational. She knew only that she had to keep running though she'd almost forgotten why. Her breath was coming in harsh gasps, her legs were like rubber. She knew only the mindless flight of the hunted—the naked fear of the hunter.

Suddenly, she saw the lake. It glistened as the sun hit its surface. With some last vestige of lucidity, Autumn remembered Steve's admission that morning. He couldn't swim. The race had a goal now, and she dashed for it.

Her crazed approach through the woods had taken her away from the ridge where the incline graduated for easy descent. Instead, she came to the edge of a cliff that fell forty feet in a sheer drop. Without hesitation, Autumn plunged down at full speed. She scrambled and slid, her fingers clawing to keep herself from overbalancing. Like a lizard, she clung to the mountain. Her body scraped on jagged rocks and slid on mud. Julia's designer sweater shredded. Autumn realized, as the pain grew hot, that her skin suffered equally. Fear pushed her beyond the pain. The lake beckoned below. Safety. Victory.

Still, he came after her. She could hear his boots clatter on the rocks above her head, jarring pebbles that rained down on her. Autumn leaped the last ten feet. The force of the fall shot up her legs, folding them under her until she rolled into a heap. Then she was scrambling and streaking for the lake.

She heard him cry out for her. With a final mad impetus, she flung herself into the water, slicing through its surface. Its sharp frigidity shocked her system and gave her strength. Clawing through it, she headed for depth. She was going to win.

Like a light switched off, the momentum which had driven her so wildly, sapped. The weight of her boots pulled her down. The water closed over her head. Thrashing and choking, Autumn fought for the surface. Her lungs burned as she tried to pull in air. Her arms were heavy, and her feeble strokes had her bobbing up and down. Mists gathered in front of her eyes. Still, she resisted, fighting as the water sucked at her. It was now as deadly an enemy as the one she had sought to escape.

She heard someone sobbing, and realized dimly it was her own voice calling for help. But she knew there would be none. The fight was gone out of her. Was it music she heard? She thought it came from below her, deep, beckoning. Slowly, surrendering, she let the water take her like a lover.

Someone was hurting her. Autumn didn't protest. Darkness blanketed her mind and numbed the pain. The pushing and prodding were no more irritating to her than a faint itch. Air forced its way into her lungs, and she moaned gently in annoyance.

Lucas's voice touched the edges of her mind. He was calling her back in a strange, unnatural voice. Panic? Yes, even through the darkness she could detect a note of panic. What an odd thing to hear in Lucas's voice. Her eyelids were heavy, and the darkness was so tempting. The need to tell him was stronger. Autumn forced her eyes open. Blackness receded to a verge of mist.

His face loomed over her, water streaming from it and his hair. It splattered cold on her cheeks. Yet her mouth felt warm, as if his had just left it. Autumn stared at him, groping for the power of speech.

"Oh God, Autumn." Lucas brushed the water from her cheeks even as it fell on them again from his own hair. "Oh God. Listen to me. It's all right, you're going to be all right, do you hear? You're going to be all right. I'm going to take you back to the inn. Can you understand me?"

His voice was desperate, as were his eyes. She'd never heard that tone or seen that expression. Not from Lucas. Autumn wanted to say something that would comfort him, but lacked the strength. The mists were closing in again, and she welcomed them. For a moment, she held them off and dug deep for her voice.

"I thought you killed her, Lucas. I'm sorry."

"Oh, Cat." His voice was intolerably weary. She felt his mouth touch hers. Then she felt nothing.

Voices, vague and without texture, floated down a long tunnel. Autumn didn't welcome them. She wanted her peace. She tried to plunge deeper into the darkness again, but Lucas had no respect for what anyone else wanted. His voice broke into her solitude, suddenly clear and, as always, demanding.

"I'm staying with her until she wakes up. I'm not leaving her."

"Lucas, you're dead on your feet." Robert's voice was low and soothing, in direct contrast to Lucas's. "I'll stay with Autumn. It's part of my job. She's probably going to be floating in and out all night. You wouldn't know what to do for her."

"Then you'll tell me what to do. I'm staying with her."

"Of course you are, dear." Aunt Tabby's voice surprised Autumn even in the dim, drifting darkness. It was so firm and strong. "Lucas will stay, Dr. Spicer. You've already said it's mainly a matter of rest, and waiting until she wakes naturally. Lucas can take care of her."

"I'll sit with you, Lucas, if you'd like…all right, but you've only to call me." Julia's voice rolled over Autumn, as smoky as the mists.

Suddenly, she wanted to ask them what was happening. What they were doing in her own private world. She struggled for words and formed a moan. A cool hand fell on her brow.

"Is she in pain?" Was that Lucas's voice? Autumn thought. Trembling? "Damn it, give her something for the pain!"

The darkness was whirling again, jumbling the sounds. Autumn let it swallow her.

She dreamed. The deep black curtain took on a velvet, moonlight texture. Lucas stared down at her. His face seemed oddly vivid for a dream. His hand felt real and cool on her cheek. "Cat, can you hear me?"

Autumn stared at him, then drew together all her scraps and rags of concentration. "Yes." She closed her eyes and let the darkness swirl.

When her eyes reopened, he was still there. Autumn swallowed. Her throat was burning dry. "Am I dead?"

"No. No, Cat, you're not dead." Lucas poured something cool down her throat. Her eyes drooped again as she tried to patch together her memory. It was too hard, and she let it go.

Pain shot through her. Unexpected and sharp, it rocketed down her arms and legs. Autumn heard someone moan pitifully. Lucas loomed over her again, his face pale in a shaft of moonlight. "It hurts," she complained.

"I know." He sat beside her and brought a cup to her lips. "Try to drink."

Floating, like a bright red balloon, Autumn felt herself drift through space. The pain had eased as she stumbled back into consciousness. "Julia's sweater," she murmured as she opened her eyes again. "It's torn. I think I tore it. I'll have to buy her another."

"Don't worry about it, Cat. Rest." Lucas's hand was on her hair and she turned her face to it, seeking reassurance. She floated again.

"I'm sure it was valuable," she murmured, nearly an hour later. "But I don't really need that new tripod. Julia lent me that sweater. I should have been more careful."

"Julia has dozens of sweaters, Cat. Don't worry."

Autumn closed her eyes, comforted. But she knew her tripod would have to wait.

"Lucas." She pulled herself back, but now the moonlight was the gray light of dawn.

"Yes, I'm here."

"Why?"

"Why what, Cat?"

"Why are you here?"

But he moved out of focus again. She never heard his answer.

Chapter 13

The sunlight was strong. Used to darkness, Autumn blinked in protest.

"Ah, are you with us to stay this time, Autumn, or is this another quick visit?" Julia bent over her and patted her cheek. "There's a bit of color coming back, and you're cool. How do you feel?"

Autumn lay still for a moment and tried to find out. "Hollow," she decided, and Julia laughed.

"Trust you to think of your stomach."

"Hollow all over," Autumn countered. "Especially my head." She glanced confusedly around the room. "Have I been sick?"

"You gave us quite a scare." Julia eased down on the bed and studied her. "Don't you remember?"

"I was...dreaming?" Autumn's search for her memory found only bits and pieces. "Lucas was here. I was talking to him."

"Yes, he said you were drifting in and out through the night. Managed to say a word or two now and again. Did you really think I'd let you sacrifice your new tripod?" She kissed Autumn's cheek, then held her a moment. "God, when Lucas carried you in, we thought…" Shaking her head briskly, she sat up. Autumn saw that her eyes were damp.

"Julia." Autumn squeezed her eyes a moment, but nothing came clear. "I was supposed to come to your room, but I didn't."

"No, you didn't. I should have dragged you with me then and there. None of this would have happened." She stood up again. "It appears Lucas and I were both taken in by those big green eyes. I don't know how much time we wasted searching for that damn film before he went back to find you."

"I don't understand. Why…" As she reached up to brush at her hair, Autumn noticed the bandages on her hands. "What are these for? Did I hurt myself?"

"It's all right now." Julia brushed away the question. "I'd better let Lucas explain. He'll be furious that I chased him downstairs for some coffee, and you woke up."

"Julia—"

"No more questions now." She cut Autumn off as she plucked a robe from a chair. "Why don't you slip this on. You'll feel better." She eased the silk over Autumn's arms and covered more bandages. The sight of them brought added confusion, more juggled memories. "Just lie still and relax," Julia ordered. "Aunt Tabby already has some soup simmering, just waiting for you. I'll tell her to pour it into an enormous bowl."

She kissed Autumn again, then glided to the door.

"Listen, Autumn." Julia turned back with a slow, cat smile. "He's been through hell these past twenty-four hours, but don't make it too easy for him."

Autumn frowned at the door when Julia had gone and wondered what the devil she was talking about.

Deciding she wouldn't find any answers lying in bed, Autumn dragged herself out. Every joint, every muscle revolted. She nearly succumbed to the desire to crawl back in, but curiosity was stronger. Her legs wobbled as she went to the mirror.

"Good God!" She looked, Autumn decided, even worse than she felt. The bruise on her temple had company. There was a light discoloration along her cheekbone and a few odd scratches. There was a sudden, clear memory of rough bark scraping against her hands. Lifting them, Autumn stared at the bandages. "What have I done to myself?" she asked aloud, then belted the robe to disguise the worst of the damage.

The door opened, and in the reflection she watched Lucas enter the room. He looked as though he hadn't slept in days. The lines of strain were deeper now and his chin was shadowed and unshaven. Only his eyes were the same. Dark and intense.

"You look like hell," she told him without turning. "You need some sleep."

He laughed. In a gesture of weariness she had never seen in him, he lifted his hands to run them down his face. "I might have expected it," he murmured. He sighed, then gave her a smile from the past. "You shouldn't be out of bed, Cat. You're liable to topple over any minute."

"I'm all right. At least I was before I looked in the

mirror." Turning, she faced him directly. "I nearly fainted from shock."

"You are," he began in quiet, serious tones, "the most beautiful thing I've ever seen."

"Kindness to the invalid," she said, looking away. That had hurt, and she wasn't certain she could deal with any more pain. "I could use some explanations. My mind's a little fuddled."

"Robert said that was to be expected after..." He trailed off and jammed clenched fists into his pockets. "After everything that's happened."

Autumn looked again at her bandaged hands. "What did happen? I can't quite remember. I was running..." She lifted her eyes to his and searched. "In the woods, down the cliff. I..." She shook her head. There were only bits and pieces. "I tore Julia's sweater."

"God! You would latch on to a damn sweater!" His explosion had Autumn's eyes widening. "You almost drowned, and all you think about is Julia's sweater."

Her mouth trembled open. "The lake." Memory flooded back in a tidal wave. She leaned back against the dresser. "Steve. It was Steve. He killed Helen. He was chasing me. The film, I wouldn't give it to him." She swallowed, trying to keep calm. "I lied to you. I had it in my pocket. I kept running, but he was right behind me."

"Cat." She backed away, but he wrapped his arms around her. "Don't. Don't think about it. Damn it, I shouldn't have told you that way." He pressed his cheek against her hair. "I can't seem to do anything properly with you."

"No. No, let me think it through." Autumn pushed away. She wanted the details. Once she had them all, the fear would ease. "He found me in the woods after you'd gone in. He'd been with Helen down by the lake the morning I was taking pictures. He told me he had killed her. He told me everything."

"We know all of it," Lucas cut her off sharply. "He let out with everything once we got him back here. We got through to the police this morning." He whipped out a cigarette and lit it swiftly. "He's already in custody. They've got your film, too, for whatever it's worth. Jacques found it on the path."

"It must have fallen out of my pocket. Lucas, it was so strange." Her brow knitted as she remembered the timeless incident with Steve. "He apologized for having to kill me. Then when I told him I wouldn't give him the film, he slugged me so hard I saw stars."

Face thunderous, Lucas spun around and stalked to the window. He stared out without speaking.

"When he came at me again, I kicked him, hard, where I knew it would do the most damage."

She heard Lucas mutter something so uncharacteristically vulgar she thought she misunderstood. For a time she rambled about her flight through the woods, talking more to herself than to him.

"I saw you when you started your suicidal plunge down the cliff." His back was still to her, his voice still rough. "How in God's name you managed to get to the bottom without cracking your skull..." Lucas turned when Autumn remained silent. "I'd been tracking you through the woods. When I saw you were making for the lake, I veered off and started for the ridge. I hoped to cut Anderson off." He pulled on his cigarette, then took a long, shuddering breath. "I saw you flying down those rocks. You never should have made it down alive.

I called you, but you just kept tearing for the lake. I was on him before you hit the water."

"I heard someone call. I thought it was Steve." She pushed a bandaged hand against her temple. "All I could think about was getting into the water before he caught me. I remembered he couldn't swim. Then when I had trouble keeping myself up, I panicked and forgot all those nifty rules you learn in lifeguard class."

Very slowly, very deliberately, Lucas crushed out his cigarette. "By the time I finished kicking his head in, you were already floundering. How you got out so far after the run you'd had, and with boots that must weigh twenty pounds, I'll never know. I was a good ten yards from you when you went under the last time. You sank like a stone."

He turned away again to stare out the window. "I thought…" He shook his head a moment, then continued. "I thought you were dead when I dragged you out. You were dead white and you weren't breathing. At least not enough that I could tell." He took out another cigarette and this time had to fight with his lighter to get flame. He cursed and drew deeply.

"I remember you dripping on me," Autumn murmured into the silence. "Then I thought I died."

"You damn near did." The smoke came out of his lungs in a violent stream. "I must have pumped two gallons of water out of you. You came around just long enough to apologize for thinking I killed Helen."

"I'm sorry, Lucas."

"Don't!" His tone was curt as he swung around again.

"But I should never have—"

"No?" He cut her off with one angry word. "Why?

It's easy enough to see how you reached your conclusions, culminating with my last attack about the film."

After a moment, Autumn trusted herself to speak. "There were so many things you said that made me think…and you were so angry. When you asked me for the film, I wanted you to tell me anything."

"But instead of explanations, I bullied you. Typical of me, though, isn't it?" He drew a breath, but his body remained tense. "That's another apology I owe you. I seem to have chalked up quite a few. Would you like them in a group, Cat, or one at a time?"

Autumn turned away from that. It wasn't an apology she wanted, but an explanation. "Why did you want it, Lucas? How did you know?"

"It might be difficult for you to believe at this point, but I'm not completely inhuman. I wanted the film because I hoped, if I had it and made it known that I did, that you'd be safe. And…" She turned back as a shadow crossed his face. "I thought you knew, or had remembered what was on the film, and that you were protecting Anderson."

"Protecting him?" Astonishment reflected in her voice. "Why would I do that?"

He moved his shoulders in a shrug. "You seemed fond of him."

"I thought he was nice," Autumn said slowly. "I imagine we all did. But I hardly knew him. As it turns out, I didn't know him at all."

"I misinterpreted your natural friendliness for something else. Then compounded the mistake by overreacting. I was furious that you gave him what you wouldn't give me. Trust, companionship. Affection."

"Dog in the manger, Lucas?" The words shot out icily.

A muscle twitched at the corner of his mouth in contrast to another negligent shrug. "If you like."

"I'm sorry." With a sigh, Autumn pushed wearily at her hair. "That was uncalled for."

"Was it?" he countered and crushed out his cigarette. "I doubt that. You're entitled to launch a few shafts, Cat. You've taken enough of them from me."

"We're getting off the point." She moved away. Julia's silk robe whispered around her. "You thought I was protecting Steve. I'll accept that. But how did you know he needed protecting?"

"Julia and I had already pieced together a number of things. We were almost certain he was the one who had killed Helen."

"You and Julia." Now she turned to him, curious. Autumn gestured with her hands, then stopped as the pain throbbed in them. "You're going to have to clear things up, Lucas. I might still be a little dim."

"Julia and I had discussed Helen's blackmail thoroughly. Until her murder, we centered on Jacques's problem. Neither Julia nor I were concerned with the petty threats Helen held over us. After she was killed and your room broken into, we tossed around the idea that they were connected. Autumn, why don't you get back in bed. You're so pale."

"No." She shook her head, warding off the creeping warmth the concern in his voice brought her. "I'm fine. Please, don't stop now."

He seemed about to argue, then changed his mind. "I'd never believed you'd ruin your own film, or knock yourself senseless. So, Julia and I began a process of elimination. I hadn't killed Helen, and I knew that Julia hadn't. I'd been in her room that night receiving a heated lecture on my technique with women until I came down to see you. And I'd passed Helen in the hall right before I'd gone into Julia's room, so even if Julia'd had the inclination to kill Helen, it's doubtful that she would have had two identical white negligees. There'd have been blood." He shrugged again. "In any case, if Julia had killed her, she probably would have admitted it."

"Yes." Autumn gave a murmured agreement and wondered what Julia's lace-clad lecture had included.

"I've known Jacques for years," Lucas continued. "He's simply not capable of killing. Julia and I all but eliminated the Spicers. Robert is entirely too dedicated to life to take one, and Jane would dissolve into tears."

Lucas began to pace. "Anderson fit the bill. And, for reasons of my own, I wanted it to be him. Our intrepid Julia copped the spare key from Aunt Tabby and searched his room for the shirt he had worn the night of the murder. I nearly strangled her when she told me she'd done it. She's quite a woman."

"Yes." Jealousy warred with affection. Affection won. "She's wonderful."

"The shirt wasn't there. Julia claims to have an unerring eye for wardrobe, and I wanted to believe her. We decided you should be put on guard without going into specifics. I thought it best if you were wary of everyone. We decided that Julia would talk to you because you'd trust her more quickly than you'd trust me. I hadn't done anything to warrant your trust."

"She frightened me pretty successfully," Autumn recalled. "I had nightmares."

"I'm sorry. It seemed the best way at the time. We

thought the film had been destroyed, but we didn't want to take any chances."

"She was telling Jacques that night, wasn't she?"

"Yeah." Lucas noted the faint annoyance in her tone. "That way there would have been three of us to look out for you."

"I might have looked out for myself if I'd been told."

"No, I don't think so. Your face is a dead giveaway. That morning at breakfast when you started rambling about a fourth roll and remembered, everything showed in your eyes."

"If I'd been prepared—"

"If you hadn't been a damn fool and had gone with Julia, we could have kept you safe."

"I wanted to think," she began, angry at being kept in the dark.

"It was my fault." Lucas held up a hand to stop her. "The whole thing's been my doing. I should have handled things differently. You'd never have been hurt if I had."

"No, Lucas." Guilt swamped her when she remembered the look on his face after he had dragged her from the lake. "I'd be dead if it weren't for you."

"Good God, Cat, don't look at me like that. I can't cope with it." He turned away. "I'm doing my best to keep my word. I'll get Robert; he'll want to examine you."

"Lucas." She wasn't going to let him walk out that door until he told her everything. "Why did you come here? And don't tell me you came to Virginia to write. I know—I remember your habits."

Lucas turned, but kept his hand on the knob. "I told you before, the other reason no longer exists. Leave it."

He had retreated behind the cool, detached manner he used so well, but Autumn wasn't going to be shoved aside. "This is my aunt's inn, Lucas. Your coming here, however indirectly, started this chain of events. I have a right to know why you came."

For several seconds, he stared at her, then his hands sought his pockets again. "All right," he agreed. "I don't suppose I have any right to pride after this, and you deserve to get in a few licks after the way I've treated you." He came no closer, but his eyes locked hard on hers. "I came here because of you. Because I had to get you back or go crazy."

"Me?" The pain was so sharp, Autumn laughed. She would not cry again. "Oh Lucas, please, do better." She saw him flinch before he walked again to the window. "You tossed me out, remember? You didn't want me then. You don't want me now."

"Didn't want you!" He whirled, knocking over a vase and sending it crashing. The anger surrounding him was fierce and vivid. "You can't even comprehend how much I wanted you, have wanted you all these years. I thought I'd lose my mind from wanting you."

"No, I won't listen to this." Autumn turned away to lean against the bedpost. "I won't listen."

"You asked for it. Now you'll listen."

"You told me you didn't want me," she flung at him. "I never meant anything to you. You told me it was finished and shrugged your shoulders like it had been nothing all along. Nothing, *nothing's* ever hurt me like the way you brushed me aside."

"I know what I did." The anger was gone from his voice to be replaced by strain. "I know the things I said to you while you stood there staring at me. I hated myself. I wanted you to scream, to rage, to make it easy for me to push you out. But you just stood there with tears falling down your face. I've never forgotten how you looked."

Autumn pulled herself together and faced him again. "You said you didn't want me. Why would you have said it if it weren't true?"

"Because you terrified me."

He said it so simply, she slumped down on the bed to stare at him. "Terrified you? *I* terrified *you?*"

"You don't know what you did to me—all that sweetness, all that generosity. You never asked anything of me, and yet you asked everything." He began to pace again. Autumn watched him in bewilderment. "You were an obsession, that's what I told myself. If I sent you away, hurt you badly enough to make you go, I'd be cured. The more I had of you, the more I needed. I'd wake up in the middle of the night and curse you for not being there. Then I'd curse myself for needing you there. I had to get away from you. I couldn't admit, not even to myself, that I loved you."

"Loved me?" Autumn repeated the words dumbly. "You loved me?"

"Loved then, love now and for the rest of my life." Lucas drew in a deep breath as if the words had left him shaken. "I wasn't able to tell you. I wasn't able to believe it." He stopped pacing and looked at her. "I've kept close tabs on you these past three years. I found all sorts of excuses to do so. When I found out about the inn, and your connection with it, I began to fly out here off and on. Finally, I admitted to myself that I wasn't going to make it without you. I mapped out a plan. I had it all worked out." He gave her an ironic smile.

"Plan?" Autumn repeated. Her mind was still whirling.

"It was easy to plant the idea in Aunt Tabby's head to write you and ask you to visit. Knowing you, I was sure you'd come without question. That was all I needed. I was so sure of myself. I thought all I'd have to do would be to issue the invitation, and you'd fall right back into my arms. Just like old times. I'd have you back, marry you before you sorted things out and pat myself on the back for being so damn clever."

"Marry me?" Autumn's brows flew up in astonishment.

"Once we were married," Lucas went on as if she hadn't interrupted, "I'd never have to worry about losing you again. I'd simply never give you a divorce no matter how you struggled. I deserved a good kick in the teeth, Cat, and you gave it to me. Instead of falling into my arms, you turned up your nose and told me to get lost. But that didn't throw me off for long. No, you'd loved me once, and I'd make you love me again. I could deal with the anger, but the ice…

"I didn't know I could be hurt that way. It was quite a shock. Seeing you again…" He paused and seemed to struggle for words. "It was torture, pure and simple, to be so close and not be able to have you. I wanted to tell you what you meant to me, then every time I got near you I'd behave like a maniac. The way you cringed from me yesterday, telling me not to hurt you again, I can't tell you what that did to me."

"Lucas—"

"You'd better let me finish," he told her. "I'll never be

able to manage this again." He reached for a cigarette, changed his mind, then continued. "Julia roasted me, but I couldn't seem to stop myself. The more you resisted, the worse I treated you. Every time I approached you, I ended up doing the wrong thing. That day, up in your room…" He stopped and Autumn watched the struggle on his face. "I nearly raped you. I was crazy with jealousy after seeing you and Anderson. When I saw you cry—I swore I'd never be responsible for putting that look on your face again.

"I'd come up that day, ready to beg, crawl, plead, whatever it took. When I saw you kissing him, something snapped. I started thinking about the men you'd been with these past three years. The men who'd have you again when I couldn't."

"I've never been with any man but you," Autumn interrupted quietly.

Lucas's expression changed from barely suppressed fury to confusion before he studied her face with his familiar intensity. "Why?"

"Because every time I started to, I remembered he wasn't you."

As if in pain, Lucas shut his eyes, then turned from her. "Cat, I've never done anything in my life to deserve you."

"No, you probably haven't." She rose from the bed to stand behind him. "Lucas, if you want me, tell me so, and tell me why. Ask me, Lucas. I want it spelled out."

"All right." He moved his shoulders as he turned back, but his eyes weren't casual. "Cat…" He reached up to touch her cheek, then thrust the hand in his pocket. "I want you, desperately, because life isn't even tolerable without you. I need you because you are, and always were, the best part of my life. I love you for reasons it would take hours to tell you. Take me back, please. Marry me."

She wanted to throw herself into his arms, but held back. *Don't make it too easy on him.* Julia's words played back in her head. No, Lucas had had too much come too easily to him. Autumn smiled at him, but didn't reach out.

"All right," she said simply.

"All right?" He frowned, uncertain. "All right what?"

"I'll marry you. That's what you want, isn't it?"

"Yes, damn it, but—"

"The least you could do is kiss me, Lucas. It's traditional."

Lightly, he rested his hands on her shoulders. "Cat, I want you to be sure, because I'll never be able to let go. If it's gratitude, I'm desperate enough to take it. But I want you to think about what you're doing."

She tilted her head. "You did know I thought it was you with Helen on that film?"

"Cat, for God's sake—"

"I went into the woods," she continued mildly. "I was just about to expose that film when Steve found mc. Lucas." She inched closer. "Do you know how I feel about the sanctity of film?"

His breath came out in a small huff of relief as he lifted a hand to either side of her face. He grinned. "Yes. Yes, I do. Something about the eleventh commandment."

"Thou shalt not expose unprocessed film. Now—" she slid her arms up his back "—are you going to kiss me, or do I have to make you?"

* * * * *

REQUEST YOUR FREE BOOKS!

2 FREE NOVELS
FROM THE ROMANCE COLLECTION
PLUS 2 FREE GIFTS!

YES! Please send me 2 FREE novels from the Romance Collection and my 2 FREE gifts (gifts are worth about $10). After receiving them, if I don't wish to receive any more books, I can return the shipping statement marked "cancel." If I don't cancel, I will receive 4 brand-new novels every month and be billed just $6.24 per book in the U.S. or $6.74 per book in Canada. That's a savings of at least 22% off the cover price. It's quite a bargain! Shipping and handling is just 50¢ per book in the U.S. and 75¢ per book in Canada.* I understand that accepting the 2 free books and gifts places me under no obligation to buy anything. I can always return a shipment and cancel at any time. Even if I never buy another book, the two free books and gifts are mine to keep forever.

194/394 MDN F4XY

Name	(PLEASE PRINT)	
Address		Apt. #
City	State/Prov.	Zip/Postal Code

Signature (if under 18, a parent or guardian must sign)

Mail to the **Harlequin® Reader Service:**
IN U.S.A.: P.O. Box 1867, Buffalo, NY 14240-1867
IN CANADA: P.O. Box 609, Fort Erie, Ontario L2A 5X3

Want to try two free books from another line?
Call 1-800-873-8635 or visit www.ReaderService.com.

* Terms and prices subject to change without notice. Prices do not include applicable taxes. Sales tax applicable in N.Y. Canadian residents will be charged applicable taxes. Offer not valid in Quebec. This offer is limited to one order per household. Not valid for current subscribers to the Romance Collection or the Romance/Suspense Collection. All orders subject to credit approval. Credit or debit balances in a customer's account(s) may be offset by any other outstanding balance owed by or to the customer. Please allow 4 to 6 weeks for delivery. Offer available while quantities last.

Your Privacy—The Harlequin® Reader Service is committed to protecting your privacy. Our Privacy Policy is available online at www.ReaderService.com or upon request from the Harlequin Reader Service.

We make a portion of our mailing list available to reputable third parties that offer products we believe may interest you. If you prefer that we not exchange your name with third parties, or if you wish to clarify or modify your communication preferences, please visit us at www.ReaderService.com/consumerschoice or write to us at Harlequin Reader Service Preference Service, P.O. Box 9062, Buffalo, NY 14269. Include your complete name and address.

ROM13R

There's nowhere better to spend the holidays than with *New York Times* bestselling author

SUSAN MALLERY

in the town of Fool's Gold, where love is always waiting to be unwrapped...

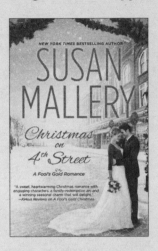

Available now wherever books are sold!

"Susan Mallery is one of my favorites."
—#1 *New York Times* bestselling author Debbie Macomber

www.SusanMallery.com

NORA ROBERTS

(limited quantities available)

TOTAL AMOUNT	$	_____
POSTAGE & HANDLING	$	_____
($1.00 FOR 1 BOOK, 50¢ for each additional)		
APPLICABLE TAXES*	$	_____
TOTAL PAYABLE	$	_____

(check or money order—please do not send cash)

To order, complete this form and send it, along with a check or money order for the total above, payable to Harlequin Books, to: **In the U.S.:** 3010 Walden Avenue, P.O. Box 9077, Buffalo, NY 14269-9077; **In Canada:** P.O. Box 636, Fort Erie, Ontario, L2A 5X3.

Name: _____

Address: _____ City: _____

State/Prov.: _____ Zip/Postal Code: _____

Account Number (if applicable): _____

075 CSAS

*New York residents remit applicable sales taxes.
*Canadian residents remit applicable GST and provincial taxes.

Silhouette®

Where love comes alive™

Visit Silhouette Books at www.Harlequin.com

SNR1013BL